TO SAVE **ONE**

TO SAVE ONE

KIMBERLY FIESE YULE

ISBN: 979-8-9990514-3-1

FOREWORD

For my children, Berkleigh, Britton, and Beckett, may you never feel the blackness that can drown you, never letting you see the light. For my dear person who shall remain nameless, my heart still aches to know the piercing pain you went through that day. When you couldn't take the pain anymore and almost surrendered to it, the Divine hand reached down from the heavens and lifted you up and held you so tight. You were given a lifeline, and for that day I am forever thankful.

> "I think the saddest people always try their hardest to
> make people happy. Because they know what it feels like to feel
> absolutely worthless, and they don't want
> anybody else to feel like that."
>
> — *Robin Williams*

PLAYLIST

To enhance your experience while hearing Evy's story, please refer to this playlist. The songs can be found on most music streaming platforms, i.e., Spotify, Apple Music, Pandora, etc. Thank you to the artists who make these songs that heal our hearts, make us smile, bring us to tears, make us dance, help us remember, and most importantly, enrich our lives.

Chapter 1: "I'm Not Okay" by Jelly Roll

Chapter 5: "You Said You'd Grow Old With Me" by Michael Schulte

Chapter 7: "Marchin On" by One Republic

Chapter 11: "Birthday" by Destiny's Child

Chapter 15: "Otherside" by Perfume Genius

Chapter 20: "Broken" by Joshua Radin

Chapter 21: "We Carry On" by Peter Groenwald

Chapter 31: "Rise Up" by Andra Day

Chapter 36: "Wherever I Go" by Noah Rinker

Chapter 41: "Butterflies" by Tom Odell, feat. AURORA

Chapter 43: "I Like It" by Enrique Iglesias, feat. Pitbull

PROLOGUE

HOW DO YOU MAKE SENSE OF SOMETHING SO SENSELESS?

'm trying to figure it out…I'm not sure I ever will. However, I found out the hard way that you will never fully know the ones you love.

In my deepest thoughts, it is usually music and film that will clear my mind or inspire me. Sometimes I think of my life being played out in these media. They serve as a roadmap to my life. Wouldn't life be easier if music were always playing? When words fail me, the art of music speaks for me. I see it as the melodic poetry of the soul. There are songs that can console or inspire you, build you up or tear you down. It is the bridge to get you to another place, and right now, so help me, I need to be in a different place.

So, if you're going to join me on this journey, you'll need some earphones to listen to the music that's going to get me through what's to come. I'll warn you, it's not going to be easy, as I have a lot to muster through from all the aftermath of the tragedy.

PART 1

CHAPTER 1

PRESENT – December 30, 2019

Playlist #1. "I'm Not Okay" by Jelly Roll

've been lying in bed for some time. I didn't really sleep well. My night was filled with awful dreams where I felt like I was helpless, and loss invaded my mind. Sometimes the quiet is more of an enemy than a friend.

The beep, beep, beep clanging in my ears, is urging me to get up. It is time, I know. This is not the way my day should start. I pull the covers over my head, hoping to fall back asleep, erase my mind, make this day not happen. My heart is heavy, like an anchor at the bottom of the sea, tethering me to a deep, dark place I don't want to go.

There's a knock on the door. It's my mother. "Time to get up, my sweet Evy! We need to be there by ten."

Be there, for what? To make my heart ache more? To feel more helpless than I already feel? Waves of nausea are surging in my body, bubbling up to my throat. My hands fumble, searching for my phone. Got it, alarm off. My fingers intuitively trace the screen.

Another day that I didn't receive my text message, my song verse of the day. Another knock. "Okay, I'm up."

Getting out of bed is hard, not just hard, but extremely hard. Step by heavy step, I reach the bathroom and look at myself. Eyes puffy, lips cracked, and sheet marks across my face—great, just beautiful. It wasn't a good night's sleep, nor had it been these past few days. My mind raced all night and wouldn't shut off. Could the outcome have been different if I had done something? Anything?

Another knock on my door. "We're going to be late, honey."

It's my mom again. Christ, where is the patience? She has been very patient with me and always is. It's me, I just can't seem to move.

A shower will do me good, I think, a*nd wash away all my pain, I wish*. I scrub my head and my body, trying to erase the inner pain, but it remains.

Twenty minutes pass, but I am finally ready. Staring at myself in the mirror, I drop my eyes quickly to examine what I'm wearing. *When was the last time I wore a dress?* At Fall Formal. That was a happy time. Dresses are for celebrating. No, I don't want to be dressed up for this. It all seems so contradictory. There's no celebration. I start down the stairs but remember that I forgot something. I quickly grab the soft velvet bag out of my pillowcase and put it in my pocket.

By now, Mom and I are in the car driving and I've tuned everything out. "Are you, okay?" she asks.

My mind is in another world. I pull out my phone and start videoing to get my mind off from what lies ahead. With all this heaviness I carry, can I capture the innocence that remains out there? I'm staring at the sky, the trees, trying to find solitude at a time when my head wants to explode with a powerful wave of pain. *Is that what it is? Pain?* Or is it the shame of helplessness that has endured since I received the news? Maybe both. A disbelief that shakes my core.

"Evy? Are you even listening to me? I'm worried about you. This will be tough today. Know that I love you." Mom grabs my hand.

And that is the moment I lose it. I let out a wail and begin to sob uncontrollably. Mom pulls over to the side of the road and stops. She wraps her arms around me bringing me to her chest. I am no longer that tough exterior shell of a teenager I like to think I am. I'm that little child enveloped in my mother's arms crying, wanting my mom to put a Band-Aid on it and make everything right. Please don't stop holding me, Mom.

The drive continues, and we both sit uncomfortably numb without further words. My mom continues holding my hand until we arrive. That is what I love about my mom, her unfailing support and love.

There are hundreds of people here, classmates, teachers, and so many others I don't know. All of us are gathering for the same purpose. Smiles, sad faces, hugs, endearing looks, all the while my head is spinning. From afar, I can see Henry and a few other friends. I catch that girl Chloe from my film class looking at me, and I try to put on a smile, she smiles back. I reach into my pocket and squeeze the bag hoping to feel some comfort.

CHAPTER 2

PAST – November 2018

"**W**owza! I'm speechless. You are sic! As in, you are truly beautiful," Briggs's mouth hung open with awe. He stood there dressed in a bright blue tux, with a yellow bow tie, and his Yeezys he had saved up for. Who can rock that kind of outfit? My goofy Briggs.

"Can't complain about you either, handsome," I said. "Uh, except for that smiley face pin you have on. What's up with that?"

"What? Seriously, are you saying you don't like it? It's my 'Be Happy' reminder," he said matter-of-factly.

"Do you need to be reminded?" I questioned.

"Not when I'm with you." He changed the subject and hugged me, picking me off my feet and spun me around effortlessly, laughing with that snorty laugh he has.

"No, seriously," I said to Briggs.

"That's a discussion for another time," he replied.

He held me close, kissed me longingly, then pulled me to his chest. I could hear the beating of his heart. In that instant, I felt so safe and perfectly where I needed to be. That's when I knew I loved him.

CHAPTER 3

PRESENT – December 30, 2019

My hand is gripped around the velvet bag in my pocket; it is giving me strength to stand here and endure all this. That, along with my mother who is here next to me, her arm laced inside mine. My knees slightly tremble. I am trying to overcome the waves of shattered breaths rising in my chest. We settle into the second row reserved for us. I see the casket on the altar. The music starts and I swear I'm about to lose it again.

The preacher begins. "We are here today to celebrate the life of Briggs Sullivan, a young man who brought joy to so many people."

I'm searching the room while I try listening to the preacher. I see eyes that are closed, eyes with despair, eyes that stare so blankly as if the world has stopped. But to me, it has stopped at this empty moment. I am numb, yet I feel the pounding of my heart in my chest, reminding me that I am here, still living. Mrs. Sullivan is sitting in front of me. She looks so fragile, barely hanging in there, with Mr. Sullivan's arm appearing to hold her up. Slumped, shoulders down, and dressed in a black dress, her body is trembling. This is what death does to those who loved them. It rips their soul. *Do you see your mother, Briggs? Do you see what you have done? Do you see what you've done to me? To all of us?* I can't stop looking at her. Her head turns and she catches me watching. Our eyes instantly lock. My breath is taken away as I see the pain in her eyes — the same pain she sees in mine. Her head nods and a slight parting of her mouth occurs, but she is unable to form a smile. Her hand stretches out toward me. I take her hand that feels so cold and yet so soft and hold hers in mine. Her son was ripped away from those loving hands. Tears start to form in her eyes.

"He loved you," she mouths and then releases my hand.

Tears sting my eyes. My mother wipes them away. I'm half hearing what the preacher is saying. My mother wraps her arm around my backside to hold me up too, for she knows that my soul is injured.

"I'll be honest," the preacher says. "It was with great difficulty that I prepared for today. How do you talk about losing someone so young? Briggs carried around so much pain that consumed him, despite his outward appearance. A pain that most people will never understand. A pain that has been put to rest now that he is with God."

There is a fog that weighs heavily in my head. I'm finding it hard to hear what the preacher is saying.

"There are times when we may not have words; for these times, there are prayers."

I've said so many prayers.

"Briggs took his own life to be with God. Our hearts are broken. We don't know the anguish Briggs carried with him, for no one does this without a great coercing pain that made him suffer to no end. We can only wish that he knew that we were here. So, God, I pray that you give us the strength to live with these feelings of guilt and anger and unanswerable questions. May we be a source to others that are suffering and be able to show them our love and support."

But I showed him those things. I feel a panic rise in my chest. *How did he not know I would love him forever?*

Mr. Sullivan gets up and goes to the podium. He is holding it together, carrying the strength that Mrs. Sullivan has lost. He clears his throat and swallows hard. His lips are pursed, and he stands there in a moment of silence.

"My heart was overjoyed from the minute I knew you were to be born, Briggs. My first child, my only child, my son. I held you when you were born on that fall day on October 9th. I continued to hold and guide you for eighteen years. But now my physical time with you is over. Had I known my time with you would only be brief," his voice begins to crack, "I would never have let go of you. I would still be holding you today."

He pauses, hangs his head low for a moment to recompose himself. He clears his throat again. "But now it is God's time to hold you until I can be by your side again. I will always remember our conversations, and your inquisitive nature, your love for others, and the energy you brought with your presence. You were the bright spot of my day, son. We were always so proud of the young man you were becoming. Briggs…your mother and I couldn't have loved you more, and we take comfort in knowing that you knew that. We wanted to share this video of Briggs with everyone. Please remember him for the person he was and the joy he brought. I want to thank Evylyn Peters for her help in the making of this."

I shudder as the video begins. It's the video I had been working on for Briggs by the request of his mother. She had asked me to make a surprise video for Briggs's graduation later this year. My love of filmmaking and being his girlfriend made it a no-brainer; I eagerly took on the job. I was pretty much caught up on the video and was planning to continue adding anything important that happened throughout the remainder of the year. That was…until Briggs changed the plan.

Mrs. Sullivan had called me a couple days ago, half in tears, and asked if I would mind finishing the video I had been working on so they could use it for the funeral. She didn't need my permission. I was still in shock and numb when she called, but out of respect, I somehow managed to say I'd do it. She asked me to add some music, brought me more pictures, and told me to finish it out anyway I felt appropriate. It wasn't too hard to select the music. Briggs had a "go to" playlist on Spotify. He dubbed it "Quieting the Buzz". Only now do I get the irony of the name.

The day she called, I sat in front of my computer screen and uploaded the remaining pictures. When you're in shock, it's God's way of protecting you and not allowing you to face reality. In my case, being in shock was the only way it allowed me to get through the making of this video.

What felt like only a few minutes that night, was hours of me staring at the screen watching the video over and over, unable to pull myself away. I got lost in the music and thoughts of my love. My mom had come to my room sometime that night to find me sitting there. She just hugged me, holding me tight. She put me into bed and laid down next to me. Otherwise, I may have never left that computer.

CHAPTER 4

PAST - August 2018

Briggs and his family had moved to Morro Bay in the late summer of 2018. He was the "new kid" our junior year. I had noticed him right away, but to be honest, it was hard not to notice him, with him being 6'5" tall. He was in my film class, and from what I saw, I found him to be kind, charming, and especially good-looking. I might have had a little crush on him, but I didn't really know him or think he even knew who I was, until one day in film class. Usually, he'd show up in film class completely oblivious to anything around him, but he would always be smiling and swaying his head to whatever beat was going on in his air pods. On the other hand, as much as I loved music, I knew better to take mine off before entering class. One day during our first week of class last Fall, our film teacher, Mr. Corbin, was trying to ask Briggs a question.

"Briggs? Can you tell me the year the first motion picture was created?" Briggs was in La-la Land and so caught up in his song, I had to tap his shoulder to get his attention.

Still clueless, he turned around and looked at me, took one of the pods out of his ear and put it close to my ear and said, "Oh, are you wanting to check out my tunes?" His blue eyes bore straight into mine.

I stumbled on my words, caught off guard by his piercing eyes and said, "Uh, yeah, maybe later, but Mr. Corbin is asking you a question." I pointed at Corbin.

Mr. Corbin squinted his eyes at Briggs, then turned to me and said, "Evelyn, I think you are going to need to help out this young man." The students started laughing.

I placed my hand on Briggs's shoulder giving it a slight squeeze and quietly said, "You owe me big time." Looking back at Mr. Corbin, I interjected, "1878." Briggs looked over his shoulder and smiled at me mouthing the words: "Thank you."

After class, Briggs waited for me outside the door. I felt this surprisingly instant giddy attraction to him when I saw him standing there. "I owe you a listen," he said, spinning around and finishing with a bow to me. "Madam Evelyn."

"Evy," I corrected him. "And well, I guess you do," I said, shaking his hand.

"Tonight at 6:00. Can you meet me at the docks?"

I about shit my pants. Trying to be cool, I checked my phone, looked at my calendar, and nonchalantly said, "I think I can swing it."

"6:00 it is," he smiled. "After you," he said, ushering me out the door.

I rushed home from school that day filled with excitement and finished my homework before getting ready. I started trying on a bunch of clothes thinking about what I should wear. After leaving a huge pile of reject clothes on the floor, I ended up in the same outfit I'd had on for the day. I was worried I would look too eager or overdressed. I touched up my makeup, brushed my teeth then sat on the edge of my bed with my phone. I wanted to make sure

I had my playlist uploaded, just in case.

The docks were a place that my bestie Henry and I liked to hang out at. Henry's parents have this amazing boat that he's allowed to take out. So, I found myself there often. He even gave me a key to the boat so I can enjoy when I want. Sometimes I just come here to think. I pulled into the parking area of the docks. When I got out of my car, I couldn't help but notice how perfect the evening was. The sky had the slightest hint of blue layered with a bit of haze. A gentle breeze stirred, giving just the right amount of chill in the air. I stood for a moment taking it all in, reached into my pocket and grabbed my phone. It was a moment I felt I needed to document; that's the filmmaker in me. I continued down the footpath until I reached the stairs. There he was, waiting on the docks for me with a little cooler by his side, moving his body and head rhythmically. Must be a good song. I snapped a picture of him without him knowing.

Once I got to the docks, I removed my flip flops and slid in next to him. It took him a second to realize I was there. I gave him a gentle shrug to his shoulder and said, "Nice evening; lost in music again?"

"Hey, hey, hey! Yeah, you caught me. You're here!" he said, pulling his headphones out of his ears, as if he was surprised that I showed up. He quickly wiped the wetness from his eyes. He put his arm around me and gave me the biggest squeeze.

We spent the rest of the night chatting nonstop about anything and everything. We laughed and talked about ourselves, friends, our families, etc.—all the usual get to know each other's topics. We bonded on our love of music and even compared our playlists.

He was talking about his music, and said, "Sometimes I can't put a finger on the way I'm feeling. But when I listen to music, I feel like my emotions and thoughts are being expressed in ways I don't know how to do myself. It's weird how music gets me like that. It's my therapy." Then he laughed. "I'm going to write songs one day, I think."

I knew exactly what he meant; he gets me. As long as I can remember, as a child, instead of a book, I would insist that my mom play music. As I got older, I couldn't fall asleep unless there was music playing. Life has always been sweeter with music by my side.

We were effortlessly becoming so comfortable with one another. It was getting late. As the sun was setting, he gently took my hand and placed it in his. Suddenly, I felt something powerful turn us toward one another. At that moment, we looked into each other's eyes. He took his other hand and brushed the hair out of my eyes. His hand rested gently behind my ear, slowly pulling me in to kiss me for the first time. This wasn't any ordinary kiss. It was a kiss that started a new beginning.

CHAPTER 5

PRESENT – December 30, 2019

PLAYLIST #2: "YOU SAID YOU'D GROW OLD WITH ME" BY MICHAEL SCHULTE

I snap back to the present when I see the picture of Briggs as a baby on the screen. Even as a baby, those big blue eyes shined. Briggs's eyes always pierced my soul.

The pictures continue. I almost can't stand to watch now. I can hear the sniffles and labored breathing of those crying around me. My eyes become flooded like an overflowing pool. No longer able to contain myself, the tears start to pour down my face. My heart feels like it's being twisted and stabbed. The unbearable pain of loss is engulfing me. *Is this the same torture Briggs constantly felt?* And these damn songs of his I put on the video, they are speaking to me, unveiling Briggs's pain. How did I not know?

The preacher has returned to the podium. "Let us all pray for the Sullivan family and for strength and comfort from God. Let us remember that life is a short journey, and we are all passing through. Tell your family and friends you love them. Smile at strangers, for a simple smile can make a difference. Celebrate each day and really live large, as life is a gift. The Sullivan Family thanks you for sharing this day of remembrance."

The seats are emptying, the mood is somber. I stay seated for a little longer with my mom. She patiently awaits my next move. Henry quietly slips in next to me. He doesn't try to talk to me, he just knows that being next to me is what I need.

Several people have come up to me to tell me what a great video I had made. All I can do is nod my head in agreement. It all seems so wrong. Am I supposed to say, *Hey, thanks, but I would have preferred it to be for his graduation instead?* I'm not able to face anymore of my friends at this moment, not even Henry. I just want to crawl in a hole.

My mother strokes my hair and says with a slight smile, "This is your time. Go take your moment with him." She straightens my dress and pushes the hair out of my eyes.

Instinctively, I put my hand in my pocket to reach for my velvet bag. I grip it intently for a moment, then slowly untie the strings. Reaching in, a sliver of a smile overcomes my face as I grasp Briggs's Happy Face Button. Trembling slightly, I pin the button on my dress over my heart. I turn to my mother. She nods her head and places a tissue in my hand. "I'll be here waiting for you," and she kisses my cheek. As I pass Henry, he gently smiles and nods his head.

The walk to the casket feels like I am walking down a dark tunnel with no light at the end. There are beautiful flowers draped over the casket. *Do people not know that the beauty of flowers will never replace the true emptiness of death?* I stand for a moment, hesitant to be near this bed in which my Briggs lay silent. *Deep breaths, you can do this.* My one hand touches the pin secured over my heart and I outstretch my other hand to place it upon the casket. I shudder as I feel no warmth, no life in this box. I'm shaking uncontrollably and tears begin to swell in my eyes. "Wake up, Briggs! Why? Why?!" Everything turns to black, and I can't stop crying.

—

In the back of the room sits Chloe. A small-framed, delicate young lady with frailties of a pixie, yet upright with a secure presence. Not wanting to be too close, as in too close to death, she keeps herself far from where Briggs's body lies. She had been way too close to death already. Tears start to roll down her cheeks as she watches Evy walk slowly up to the casket. She did not know Evy well, just on a social basis, but knew who she was and had a class with her. She thought about how hard it must be for this girl to lose someone she was in love with. A cold chill overcomes her delicate body as she sees Evy reach out to Brigg's lifeless shell. *How can someone want to leave this earth, when I'm trying so desperately to stay?* she says to herself.

CHAPTER 6

PAST – CHLOE – March 2019

The walls were stark white with a very sterile feel. The doctor's office was typical—nothing warm and inviting: no windows, just walls with diplomas hung on them. Chloe sat with her parents waiting for Dr. Sanders to come in. They had grown very familiar with this setting over the past year.

There was a knock on the door, and Dr. Sanders entered. He was a good-looking man in his late forties, impeccably manicured, hair perfectly parted on the left and combed over to the right. He had the iconic look of a doctor, wearing a white lab coat over a surgical green-colored set of scrubs.

"Hello, Chloe," he addressed her directly.

As petite as Chloe was, she sat tall with perfect posture, her nearly bald head covered with a medium length wig cut at the shoulders and braved the news she might be up against. She felt like she had already won the battle against cancer, ringing the bell commemorating her year-long battle just six weeks ago. She wanted to show her strength and determination in fighting this battle. She reached for both her parents' hands, her father on her right and her mother on her left. Chloe was prepared for any news Dr. Sanders gave her, good or bad.

"We've reviewed all the tests from your treatment. You've made very good progress and there is no sign of any tumors, but we are not out of the woods yet." He flips through her chart. "Bone sarcoma can re-occur, so we need to keep an eye on you. Sarcomas have a mind of their own and, as you know, they can return in the same place, or somewhere new, like in soft tissue or another bone structure. Your tests look great, and the numbers are where we expected them to be. Continue to be vigilant with your health. You will need careful observation and tests again in three months. I'll give you a referral for when you move. Any questions?"

Chloe felt relief and blew out a big breath.

CHAPTER 7

PRESENT – January 3, 2020

I had a horrible dream last night. I was hanging out with Briggs, and all of a sudden, he started grasping his chest and told me he couldn't breathe. I tried to help him, but I couldn't touch him. It was like there was an invisible wall between us that acted as an impermeable barrier. He kept saying *"Help me, help me!"* I was frozen and couldn't move. I was screaming, but my body wouldn't budge. *"Briggs!"* I shouted repeatedly. I could see tears in his beautiful blue eyes. Then I woke up, finding myself sitting straight up in bed. I was breathless and panting. It felt so real. I sobbed with guttural breaths. I felt so helpless in that dream. I wish I could have saved him.

My mom rushed into my room. She must have heard me. Without saying anything, she sat down on my bed and hugged me fiercely.

"It's okay. I'm here."

I was sobbing, "I couldn't help Briggs, Mom. I couldn't help him."

"It's not your fault, baby," she said, as she rocked me back and forth. She climbed into my bed and laid with me until I fell back asleep.

Mom must have left my bed early to get ready for the day. I find myself awake now and alone in bed. I feel horrible this morning. The dream left me with a pit in my stomach. It's back to the grind as school is back in session today. It seems too soon but, apparently, life goes on, even though it will be very different for me here on out.

I get a call from best friend Henry. I'm not sure what is possessing me to answer it, as I've been ignoring everyone who's been reaching out to me. Maybe it's time.

"Oh, sweet Evy?" Henry says with more pep than I was ready for.

Still half asleep, miraculously a slight smile creeps across my face, "Yes, my Queen?"

"I'm coming to get you."

"Uh, no, it's okay," I lie. I need him.

"Girl, you've been ignoring me. I've sent text after text and nothing. No judgment; I get it. But now it's my turn to take care of you. I'm coming no matter what. So, see you in forty-five minutes," Henry says and hangs up the phone.

I lay silent for a moment longer, then sit up in bed, looking at all the messages on my phone and realize that there is no text from Briggs. I'll never receive another one. There are over fifty texts and lots of snaps, especially from Henry, that I've neglected to answer since everything happened with Briggs. This past week has been a blur, and I don't even know how I got to today. I do know one thing for sure, I can always count on Henry to be there for me.

I've known Henry since kindergarten. Do you remember when you were younger and in class you had to line up in alphabetical order? You had to know who was in front of you and who was behind you. So, with me being a Peters and Henry being a Preston, without fail, he was always behind me. The first time we spoke was when we were lined up together on our first day of kindergarten. Mrs. Ching had told us to meet our line buddies. Henry was so excited when I turned around to say hi. I'll always remember him on that day. He had this amazing hair that swooped to the left, yellowish green eyes that sparkled, and dressed like he had just come from Sunday school, perfectly tucked and pressed.

"Hi, I'm Henry," he said, as he began hugging me, then slightly pushed me back to inspect me. I was in a light blue floral ruffled dress. "You look just like a princess, and I absolutely love your outfit. Maybe we can be friends and I'll be the prince?" Something told me we'd be best friends forever.

We managed throughout the years to be in each other's class except for fourth grade. I can recall how sad we both were. He looked at me and said, "Don't be sad. I promised you I'd always be there, so I'm going to come to your classroom every day and check on you." He never missed a day unless he was sick.

It's the start of a new semester today, my last semester of my senior year. It's hard to go back to school and see everyone, but I can't keep myself isolated much longer. Life continues to move on it seems, even without the ones you love. I'm no longer going to be able to hide from everyone. It's going to be hard going to film class, as there will be one empty seat where Briggs sat. It will be a terrible reminder of how much I miss him.

The doorbell rings, it's Henry. I can hear my mom as she opens the door, "Oh, Henry, I'm so glad you're here. I've missed you. Thank you for coming to get Evy. She really needs you." Waiting upstairs, my eyes roll, but I know it's true.

"Aw, missed you too. I wouldn't have it any other way. She's pretending to be strong, but I know better," he says. Chuckling, she gives him a hug and lets him in. More eye rolls from me.

Henry shouts toward the stairs, "Yoo-hoo, is my Princess ready?"

I'm gathering things for my backpack when Henry calls for me. "I'll be right there," I shout back. The velvet bag is on my desk. I reach in to grab Briggs's pin and place it over my right heart, pinning it to my shirt. Quickly I grab my camera off the desk and put it around my neck. Big sigh, time to put my real happy face on.

As I am coming down the stairs, I stop to take a pic of Henry. He immediately sticks his tongue out and squints his eyes. He never likes when I take his picture, unless it's for something he wants.

"Well, there she is, Ms. America, da da da," Henry sings. Henry is jumping up and down. "Girl, I am so happy to see you." He hugs me tight when I get to the bottom of the stairs. I hug back tighter, while tears start to well.

"Thank you, I've missed you too," *and I mean it.*

"You two have a great day. And Evylyn? Call me if you need me today; I'm here for you. Also, I hate to bug you about this, but when you get home, let's be sure to get the rest of your college applications in," she dutifully reminds me.

"Not a problem. I'm practically done. Love you, Mom!" Out the door we go.

Henry opens the car door for me. To my surprise, on the seat lays a small bouquet of sunflowers, my favorite, a small package of tissues, Visine, and a bag of sour gummy worms, another favorite. How did I get so lucky to have such a best friend?

He gets in from the other side and moves everything out of the way. "Flowers to bring you smiles, tissues because you're going to need them, Visine to hide the red eyes from crying, and the gummy worms just because you and I both love them." He then grabs my hand and says, "Let's take on this day." He turns on the car and turns the stereo on as I buckle up.

One Republic's song "Marchin On" comes on, all divinely orchestrated by my sweet Henry. We look at each other, I shake my head and muster a small smirk. I lean in close to Henry, laying my head on his shoulder. It feels good to smile. The windows roll down, the music is blasting, and we are on our way to school. We are marching on.

CHAPTER 8

PRESENT – CHLOE – January 3, 2020

At 6:30 a.m., Chloe's eyes open and she reaches over to grab her phone to turn off the alarm before it goes off. Like clockwork, she has a habit of always waking up before the alarm. Chloe has a routine she likes to stick with, especially with organization being her strong point. She shoots out of bed and jumps in the shower. When she is done, she dries off and puts on her robe. She takes the towel off her head, brushes her golden blonde hair, parting it down the middle making a perfect part. She is so happy that her hair has grown in and no longer needs to wear a wig. She blow dries her hair, which doesn't take long, as her hair has become quite thin over the past year having had prior chemo treatments. She must admit that she likes her new pixie hair style. Having short hair makes getting ready much easier and sure beats the bald head look that lasted longer than she cared for.

She looks in the mirror, noticing the black circles and hollowness under her eyes, thinking that maybe the fatigue she's had is catching up with her. She shakes her head and grabs for the concealer gently dabbing it under her eyes. "That should do it," she says as she applies it. Next comes the powder and blush, with just the right amount of mascara. "Not too scary now," she acknowledges out loud as she runs her fingers through her hair, a few strands coming out.

The prescription bottles are lined up at the back of her sink so she can see them all every morning. She makes a loud sigh, turns on the water and fills her glass. She unscrews every top, placing it carefully in front of its matching bottle. Then she pulls out a pill from each bottle, popping it into her mouth, and washes it down with water, one at a time from left to right. Afterward, each top is carefully placed back on top of its bottle and tightened.

After brushing her teeth, she spits and notices a small trace of blood in the sink. Standing at the mirror, she opens her mouth and inspects it carefully. A feeling of warmth flushes her cheeks. *What the heck? Where is this coming from?* She is puzzled and thinks maybe she is brushing her teeth too vigorously. Quickly, she turns on the water to clear the blood down the sink.

Next rule of order is making her bed. She straightens her sheets, pulls the comforter up, and fluffs her pillow. It is 7:30 a.m., perfect timing. With her backpack in hand, she heads out of her room and goes to the kitchen. Her mom has her usual breakfast ready for her: a cup of chai tea with coconut collagen creamer and two pieces of toast with butter. During her cancer treatments, bread became the only thing she could tolerate in the morning, and so it continues.

"Chloe?"

"Yes, Mom?"

She approaches Chloe with open arms and hugs her tightly. "You know, this is the first day of your last semester of your senior year. I have a feeling it's going to be your best one yet."

"Yeah, I'm feeling positive. I'm hoping this semester is much better than the last few. It should be."

CHAPTER 9

PAST – October 2019

Her junior year had been quite a struggle for Chloe, trying to keep up with school, when all the while dealing with endless visits to the "chair of terror" that spewed out her vial chemo treatments. To top it off, she and her family had just moved to Morro Bay for her senior year at the start of the Fall semester due to her father's job transfer. Not exactly the best way to start your senior year.

The year before moving to Morro Bay, Chloe noticed a lump in her leg and began having occasional pain in that same leg. She ignored it until about a month later, when she noticed that the lump had grown, so she went to the doctor expecting to hear that maybe she had an infection of some sort. Instead, she ended up being sent to more doctor visits, X-rays, CT scans, and blood draws—all to be told she had cancer: Osteosarcoma or cancer of the bone, stage 3, meaning it had started to spread. And so, the cancer treatments began. Despite the days of feeling nauseous or worn down from the side effects of chemo and radiation, Chloe still managed to be at the top of her class. She was valiant and determined to be Valedictorian, and even more determined not to let anyone know what was wrong with her. She felt had a lot to prove being the new kid. She managed to keep all of it her secret, well, except for one person.

It was last October, at the end of the day, and the bell at school had rung. Everyone rushed out of the film classroom, but Chloe. She had been feeling very uncomfortable and was experiencing a weird sensation in her leg which seemed to intensify throughout the day. She started to get up, but felt her left leg give a little, so she sat back down and decided to wait. She didn't want anyone to see her struggling. Once the pain subsided, she stood up, slung her backpack over her shoulder and started to walk toward the door, when her left leg intensified with a pain so terrible, it caused her leg to buckle under and fall. At that moment, Briggs had run back into the classroom to grab his air pods he had left. He saw her crash and rushed to her side. Too late though, she lay on the floor barely able to move.

"Hey, are you okay?" he shouted. No response. He leaned down to see if she was breathing and noticed tears rolling down her cheek. "Hey, I'm Briggs. Can you hear me?"

Chloe, embarrassed, swallowed hard, managed to open one eye, and in all the haze of what happened she mustered up a chuckle, "Just peachy. I was checking out the ground to see if it was comfy."

Briggs let out an unexpected hard giggle, then proceeded to lay down next to her. "Well, not sure what the appeal is down here on the floor, but figured I might try it as well." He crouched down and sprawled out right next to Chloe. A few seconds later he grunted, "Hmmm…I've definitely been more comfortable."

Chloe tried to inconspicuously wipe her tears, as she started to laugh. She turned to look at him, his face so engaging and reassuring. "Not sure what just happened there. I'm Chloe, by the way." Briggs said, "I already knew your name. You're the smart one; you make us all look bad. *Ha!* Well, this is nice and all, but I'm ready to get up if you are." He sat up and offered Chloe his hand. As he reached out to her, Chloe took his large palm in hers and allowed him to pull her up as her frail body offered minimal support.

"Here we go," and as he lifted her up, her once well-placed wig slid off her head and onto the floor.

"Oh God!" Chloe blurted out, and she hurriedly tried to grab it.

In an instant, chivalrous moment, Briggs reached down to grab the blonde bundle of hair on the floor at the same time and they came eye-to-eye. As he looked into her eyes, he saw her shame and knew that Chloe was horrified.

He took a step back and let her grab it. "Oh, whoa, you're such a chameleon. Who knew you were like Lady Gaga with all these cool hair changes?" Briggs declared. "You're one cool cat."

Chloe stood there; her short, patchy head of hair exposed. She was astonished, but pleasantly taken back by the ease in which he made her feel comfortable in this awkward situation. "Please don't tell anyone about this…uh, my wig. I'd be humiliated." She hurriedly placed the wig back on her head, then began smoothing down the hair.

"Oh gosh, never. So then, can I tell everyone about your graceful fall? Just kidding. Everything okay with you?"

"Yeah," she paused. "Yeah, I hope it will be," Chloe hung her head low to avoid letting him see the pain in her eyes. She adjusted the wig to make sure it was in place.

"You hope? I'm no expert, but that answer isn't convincing." He took a step back and squinted his eyes as he looked at her. "I know I don't know you well, and vice versa, but we just had a bonding moment on that floor. FYI, I'm actually a pretty good listener and the best secret keeper." His tone changed. He had his own secrets locked away. He pressed his pointer finger and thumb together on his right hand and demonstrated a zipper motion across his mouth. With a change in his demeanor and a seriousness in his voice he said, "These lips are sealed." He extended his hand to shake hers.

She hesitated for a moment, then outstretched her hand to meet his. Instead, he reached around her and gave her a warm friendly hug. "You know, there's something about you that actually makes me believe you," she said.

"So, what is it? You shaved your head because you're in a punk band? But don't want your parents to know?" he raised his right brow and cocked his head.

Chloe shook her head. "You got me." He had always been so nice to her and said "Hi!" when he passed her by in class. There was something about him that compelled her to trust him. *Perhaps with all that joking, could he be hiding his pain too?* She had seen him in class numerous times just seeming to be in his own distant world, and serious at other times. But then he'd light up around others. She didn't know what allowed her to let her guard down, but she decided to trust him with her burden.

"Actually, I have the Big C...cancer." That's it, it's too late, she had said it—cancer. She had come to hate that word, and rarely said it. She took a deep breath.

"I'm sorry. How did I not know?" he shook his head. "Am I that oblivious?"

"Geez, no, I'm just good at not letting anybody know my business. I should say I had cancer and am now in the recovery phase. Hence, the patchy short hair. No need to worry anyone, you know?"

Those words hit him hard. "I do know what you mean. Then I promise, it's our secret." And the newly found friends walked out of the classroom.

CHAPTER 10

PRESENT – January 3, 2020

The parking lot is filled with the chaos of cars and students, just what you would expect at the start of the semester. Henry drives us through the parking lot until he finally finds a spot to park. He turns off the car and turns to me. "We are still taking this day on together, right?"

"Yes, together, as always," I pause. "Henry?"

"Yes, my princess?" He leans in toward me and puts his head on my shoulder.

I run my fingers through his locks. "You're the best. And you have the best hair—damn you!"

Snobbily, he grabs my hand and inspects my fingers. "Yikes! Can't say the same about your fingernails. Eew! Please go get them manicured. Time for some self-care."

"Ha, you got me." I look at my fingernails and, admittedly, I'm a little grossed out. I look out the window, then smell the sunflowers to change the focus. The sun shines on the petals making them appear truly golden with tiny droplets of water sticking to the stems, glistening. I take a quick photo of them, then shove the sour gummy worms into my mouth with my wretched fingers. *It's going to be a long day.*

The halls are congested with everyone hanging out at their lockers. As we walk in, a quiet hush settles over the crowd of students, as people kind of stop what they are doing and look our way. Henry puts his arm around me. I knew this would be tough. My eyes immediately search all the faces, and I can see the pity in people's eyes. With the urging of Henry's hand on my lower back, I give a slight smile and a nod of my head to those that are watching me, and we continue our walk down the hall until I am stopped by the sight of Briggs's locker. It wasn't hard to spot. There are flowers, notes, and stuffed animals adorning his locker, in memoriam. He was loved; how did he not know that? I stop and look at all the adoration and support that is pouring in for him. Out of habit, I take my phone out and quickly snap some pictures, followed by a short video. People start gathering around Henry and me. An overwhelming sense of bewilderment engulfs me, and I am speechless. There are no words for how I feel. Henry to the rescue. He takes one look at me and knows he needs to be the one to say something.

He raises his hand, clears his throat and says, "Thanks, everyone, this is truly so cool. Here's to Briggs! May he forever be in our hearts."

"To Briggs!" everyone shouts.

With perfect timing, and nothing more than anyone needs to say, the bell rings and the crowded hall starts to clear.

I stand looking at Briggs's locker and remember how many times I had been here waiting for him. I'd wait forever if he could come back.

CHAPTER 11

PAST – OCTOBER 9, 2018

Playlist #4: "Birthday" by Destiny's Child

I had worried about what to get Briggs for his birthday. After all, it was a milestone birthday: 18! Although we had only been dating a couple months, we were practically glued at the hip. Every morning since the night after our first kiss, I would receive some sort of romantic lyric from a song in the form of Snapchat or a text message from him.

Briggs was caring, thoughtful, and plain genius, always coming up with something to wow me. So naturally, it was time for me to step up to the challenge. With the help of my mom, I worked all week long on his birthday surprise. I had planned a scavenger hunt via text messages and clues. I had called his mom to let her know what I was doing for him. She seemed thrilled and promised to take a picture of him going out to get his first clue. Then the night before his birthday, I went over and left the clue on the driver's-side windshield of his car. My plan was to get up early and send him a message before he could send me one.

When the morning arrived, I was up and ready to go. I sent my text to Briggs. I was so excited and proud of my clever scheme. I received a text from his mom that had a picture of Briggs in his car and the words "All went as planned." *Yes!*

Parts of the clues were verses from the "Birthday" song by Destiny's Child. I decorated his locker door with a big number "18" balloon tied to his locker and wrapped the door with bright blue birthday-themed wrapping paper with streamers taped to it. Inside his locker, I had placed the next clue. I waited at his locker with the biggest grin on my face and the camera in my hand. As soon as I saw him walking in, I started the video. He immediately spotted me and ran through the halls purposely acting like a goofball with his arms and legs flailing out to his sides. He was quite the sight to see. The funny thing about Briggs is he never cared what anyone thought of him, and he loved to goof off. He ran straight up to my lens and laughingly said, "Hey, hey!" and sang part of the song. *A-ha!* I knew he'd know the lines to my clues. He immediately gave me a kiss on my lips, then bear hugged me, lifting my feet off the ground.

"Happy Birthday, Briggs!"

"Look at you, being all slick! I love this little hunt you have me on," Briggs exclaimed.

"Yay! Well, it's not over. Time for your next clue," I pressed.

I watched him open his locker, and he kept peeking back at me over his shoulder, wanting me to urge him on. "Just open it!"

As he looked inside, I couldn't help but watch with excitement. My fingers were crossed in hopes he'd like what I had made him. He reached in the locker and grabbed my neatly wrapped gift. I had my favorite photo that my mom had taken of Briggs, and I made into a print and had it framed. He quickly unwrapped the present, then stretched out his arm admiring the picture.

"Whoa! Who is this good looking, amazing couple?" he asked. He paused for a moment looking at the picture, "Love this." He looked at me with eyes that made me melt and quietly said, "Thank you, Evy. This means a lot to me."

Briggs saw the clue attached to the inside frame, he grabbed it and began to dance and tap his feet as he sang the next clue. When he finished serenading me, he gave me the sly eye letting me know he was ready for the next move.

"Okay, let's go." He looked at me, raised his eyebrow, then looked back at the framed photo, stood there for a moment, and took everything in for another second. Closing his locker, he turned to me and grabbed my hand. On to class we went, giddy and excited. People stopped us in the hall to wish Briggs a happy birthday. Meanwhile, Briggs kept taking a few skips as we walked, just like a little kid. It melted my heart to see him so delighted.

I had arranged for Henry to bring Briggs his favorite snack to our film class: Ramune soda and Hot Cheetos. A strange combination in my opinion, but one Briggs had always liked to treat himself to. He loved the flavor of Hot Cheetos, but most of all savored licking his cheesy fingers after eating them. *So gross!*

He told me that every year at Christmas, he would find a Ramune drink in his stocking. He became obsessed with this drink not only for its taste, but especially because of the marble inside the bottle. His mission was to get the marble out. After many failed attempts of trying to remove it, he finally mastered it. He even posted, "How to remove the Ramune marble" to YouTube. Millions of people have seen his video. I'd never even heard of the drink, so I find it funny that millions have the same obsession. On top of that, he also managed to keep each marble from every drink of Ramune he ever consumed and saved them in a jar. Briggs found pleasure in the simplest of weird things.

When we walked into the room, Briggs let go of my hands and ran to his desk. I started filming. "Ramune? No way! And Hot Cheetos? *Shazam!* This day just keeps getting better." His excitement was contagious.

I looked over at Henry and mouthed, "Thank you."

Briggs grabbed the next clue and sang the words again in true Destiny Child fashion. When he realized he'd have to wait until lunch for the next clue he said, "What? I'm not sure I can wait that long, but for you I will!" He looked directly at me with a pouty face.

When lunch time came, Henry and I got to the cafeteria early with a few cupcakes and a candle. Not that we can light a candle at school, but what birthday celebration is complete without having a candle and making a wish? Briggs came strolling through the cafeteria high fiving a few of his friends, then came and sat down with us. Leaving the cupcakes on the lunch table, the three of us went through the line, grabbed our lunch, and sat down and ate.

"Pretty please, can I have my next clue?" Briggs asked with a pouty lip.

I pushed the clue and the cupcake close to him, candle on top. I snapped his picture. He cleared his voice and started singing again. He nodded his head, "Oh yeah, time to make that wish now."

I interrupted, "Birthday song comes first, and then you can blow out the pretend flame and make your wish." Once I started the song, Henry joined in and before you knew it, the students in the cafeteria caught wind and joined in too. Briggs blew out the pretend candle, everyone clapped. Briggs stood up and gracefully bowed several times.

When he sat back down, a serious look overcame him, as we waited for him to make his wish. His head hung low.

"Briggs?" No response. "Briggs? Everything okay?"

"Yes, yes, sorry. Just too many wishes to choose from." He looked away then planted his elbows on the table turning toward the cupcake. His mood suddenly lightened as he huffed and puffed and blew out that invisible flame.

The rest of the day went by quickly. Briggs was waiting at his locker for me at the end of the day.

"There's the birthday boy!" I smiled.

He did a little dance. "Just waiting for you."

"Well, you'll have to keep waiting until 6:00." I gave him a kiss on the lips.

We walked out to the parking lot and said our goodbyes after he walked me to my car. I needed to rush home to finish getting ready. My mom had just gotten home from work. She had stopped at the store to get the last-minute items I needed. She had also managed to wrap the gift I had gotten for Briggs and placed a bow on it. *Of course she did.*

"How'd everything go today? Was he surprised?" she asked with eagerness.

"Couldn't have turned out better. I think I really got him good. Thanks for getting everything." My mom was always making sure that my life was easier. She knew what I was thinking before I could say it.

"No problem," she said as she gave me a hug. "Now go get ready for the finale."

I ran up to my room and freshened up. Deodorant? *Check!* Brush my teeth and hair? *Check!* Makeup refreshed? *Check!* Grab my jacket? *Check!* Camera? *In the car.* I came back downstairs, and my mom was waiting for me. She had prepared two Bento boxes, bottles of water, and had baked her famous chocolate chip cookies, as she knew Briggs had requested her cookies several times before.

"I can tell you really like Briggs," she looked at me as she pursed her lips with a little smirk.

I shook my head yes, took a deep breath and said, "He's really something special."

"I can tell how happy he makes you. He really is such a fine young man. I couldn't be happier for you. You guys make a cute couple. Now go have fun and wish him happy birthday for me."

"Thanks, Mom, love you." I kissed her goodbye, grabbed the two bags she had packed, and ran out the door. As I was leaving, my mom called me back to grab a blanket. *What would I do without my mom?*

I arrived early at the docks and found our spot where we liked to hang. Laying out the blanket, I unpacked the meals and made everything nice and neat. I placed the last clue next to my gift, then set the mood with a little music from my playlist. I heard a car pull up and it was Briggs, perfect timing. I brought the camera up to my eyes and began snapping pictures capturing every essence of his soul as he approached me.

Just seeing all 6'5" of him walk down toward me with that shit-grin smile on his face, made my heart race. My mom was right—he was truly special. I stood up to greet him and he picked me up and swung me around.

"There's my amazing girl!" He planted a kiss on my lips.

I couldn't help but feel truly happy at that moment. "Hey, birthday boy! Ready for the rest of your birthday surprise?" I teased him as I held the last clue in my hand and gave it to him.

Briggs started to read out loud in his sing-song voice, and I joined in.

Coyly, he raised his left brow and tilted his head. "So...what's my surprise?"

I went to the blanket and grabbed the gift bag my mom had prepared for me to give him. I asked him to come join me. He opened the bag, slowly and carefully, taking each piece of tissue paper out, then folding it. He was teasing me.

"Oh my God, just open it!" I urged him.

He took the first gift out of the bag, held the handle, and carefully pulled out the record player turntable I got him. "No way! I've been wanting this. I'm pumped!"

I couldn't stop smiling. "There's one more present."

He reached in and pulled out the Billie Eilish album. "Yes! We love this record. I can't wait to play it." He held it to his chest. "Come here, I need to give you the biggest hug!"

Briggs reached around and held me close and long. It felt like time stood still. The sun had gone down, leaving the sky a magnificent pink, with a gentle wind blowing that caused the leaves of the tree to make a hush-like noise. In the background, the ocean waves delicately lapped at the marina docks. There was nowhere else I wanted to be but here in his arms in our favorite place. I wanted to capture this moment and took a mental picture that would be forever ingrained in my head and heart.

"Evy?" he whispered in my ear.

"Yes, Briggs?"

He continued to hold me but slightly released his hold so that we came face to face. "I can't thank you enough." His eyes bore into mine, and without any hesitation, he spoke the words, "I love you, like really love you."

In that moment as I looked into his eyes, I saw tears fill his eyes. He loves me. I felt the strangest sensation fill my body. It was as if this overwhelming calm of euphoria engulfed me, sending flutters throughout my body, yet filled me with a yearning ache in my heart that I had never experienced. It only took me a second to recognize that I was experiencing what being in love was. "I love you, Briggs." He gently leaned in to kiss me.

CHAPTER 12

PRESENT – January 3, 2020

Chloe is the first to arrive at Film class. She gives a hello to Mr. Corbin who is sitting at his desk. She picks out her seat in the front of the classroom, sits down, and unpacks the items from her backpack, arranging them systematically on her desk. She is ready to go. The students file in, including Evy and Henry.

Mr. Corbin makes his announcements to the class. He is my favorite teacher. He is like a hippie from the seventies. Long dark hair with a beautiful wave to it that goes past his shoulders. His face is angular, with sharp lines and a long, crooked nose that sits slightly off center. He is uniquely handsome, tall and thin, but muscular. His eyes are brown and almond-shaped, which soften his features. When he talks, his voice is mellifluous, which makes him sound like he is singing. "I hope everyone had a great break. I say that, but I want to acknowledge that I know this was a tough time for many of you with the loss of Briggs. His presence will be greatly missed in this class. I want to let you know that I am here for any of you that need to talk, and we also have counseling available." He pauses, turns his face and tries to discreetly wipe his tears. There was a hush across the room. He clears his voice.

"Excuse me," another pause. He walks to the middle of the room and stretches out his arms. "Okay, everyone, let's just do a big group hug. Come on! Get on up here." Slowly, one by one everyone joins Mr. Corbin gathering into a circle with arms locked around each other. I stand right next to Mr. Corbin, with Henry on the other side.

Mr. Corbin, or "Corbin" as we kids call him, continues, "It takes a village, and you know what? We are all on this journey together. I want each one of you to know that YOU are very important to me. I am here for you without judgment, got it? Got it?" He gently squeezes my side.

"So, on the count of three we are going to jump around and give a shout out to Briggs, with whatever you want to say. And yes, you heard me…jump! Ready?" as he raises his eyebrows. "One… two…two and a half…and three!"

And so, the words are being shouted out as we all jump and spin around.

"Coolest kid ever!"

"Tall mo fo!"

"We miss you, brother."

I grab my phone and start recording. I try, but something in me can't yell out loud. Pain has my words trapped inside me. Instead, I feel the need to capture all the love I am seeing for my Briggs. If I could only turn back time and show him how people admired him, but I can't. He is gone, and my heart sinks heavily in my chest. I look around and watch, taking it all in. These classmates of mine had loved Briggs too. People had cheered him on before, but sadly, this time it is a sendoff. I look into Henry's eyes and whisper, "I miss him so much. It hurts." He blows me back a kiss, then rests his hand upon his heart.

Once everyone begins to settle, Corbin says, "Okay, we're all good? Or as good as we can be right now? Awesome. Love you guys. Let's get down to business."

Yeah, Corbin was that cool. What I like most about him is that he treats the students with respect and instead of acting like he is the "boss" teacher, he is more like our peer. He asks kids about their day or their family. He wants to know what is going on in their lives. He doesn't treat students like most of the teachers do who just stand at their podiums and talk to them without compassion. He talks with you and listens. Corbin wants discussions, he wants your input. He has us all sit in a group and goes around asking for our thoughts. He has a style of teaching that inspires you to think and be inclusive of others. There are no rights and wrongs with him. He wants to hear how people think differently. "I totally understand now where you are coming from," he often says.

"First things first, let's get to the question of the day…" he begins.

This is how he always starts our class, with a random question out of nowhere. His mind must work in cryptic ways.

"What would you do with a thousand dollars, if I handed it to you today? Shay?"

Shay sits straight up in her chair. "I'd buy a VIP ticket to Coachella."

"Sweet, good choice. Chris?" he asks.

"Hmm? Well, I'd invest it in the stock market so I could make money on it," Chris boasts proudly.

"That's where the money is, Chris, investments!" Corbin nods.

There was never an explanation for his random questions.

"Okay, moving right along. Here's our semester assignment. I've put together three or four of you in a group. Yes, because as I've said, we are all in this together, and you guys are going to come up with your own film project. That's right, you're in charge. I'll give you some guidelines and a rough rubric to follow, but it's all flexible. I want your group to showcase something that interests you, means something, and/or maybe something you can use for your college applications for those of you going into film or whatever."

We gather into our assigned groups. Of course I had Henry in mine, as Corbin always knew he and I were inseparable. Henry is the ying to my yang. Henry even went up to Corbin the first time we had film class together and told him we were a package deal. Corbin said he'd take that note and jot it down. "Never separate Henry and Evelyn," he announced. That package deal got a little bit wider that year once Briggs and I became a couple. The three of us were glued together in class. We were a good team when we worked on projects. This time, it was back to just Henry and I. We watch as Chloe approached our table. I knew her, but not too well. She had been new to the school this past year and I'd talked to her several times. She was always so pleasant but reserved. Briggs had mentioned her several times to me and had told me they were friends and how cool she was. Any friend of his was a friend of mine. We had invited her out to meet us several times to parties and what not, but she never showed up. I think she was maybe just too serious about school or too shy to hang out with us.

"Hi, guys. I'm your third wheel," Chloe says smiling as she pulls out the chair.

"Hey, Chloe," both Henry and I chime in simultaneously.

She sits down and carefully places her notebook on the table. She reaches into her backpack and grabs her pen and places it to the right side of the notebook. As she is zipping up her backpack, she makes sure it is aligned perfectly on the back of her chair. She smooths out the sides of her hair as she turns to sit forward. I remember her having longer hair last semester. My guess is she opted for a new hairdo. Short hair looks cute on her.

"Oops, I need my water," and she turns again to grab her water jug situated on the side of her bag. She takes a big swig of her drink, wipes her mouth, tucks her hair behind her ears again and says, "Briggs was really an amazing person. He was so kind to me. I'll have to tell you the story of how I met him some day."

"Thanks, I'd like that very much," I smile. Henry squeezes my hand. He knows this is a tough day for me.

"It's good to have you in the group, Chloe. So, any thoughts on what you guys want to do?" Henry asks.

We watch as Chloe opens her notebook and looks over some of her notes that she has jotted down already. Both Henry and I peer down at our blank notebooks, then look at each other and laugh.

"Apparently, we don't!" Henry snickers.

"Sorry, I just like to get a head start. It was in the syllabus online," Chloe says as she makes a quizzical facial expression. "I tend to get ahead of myself at times."

"Yeah, because you're the smartest kid in the school I've heard. And that makes you a bonus for the team," I say as I pump my fist in the air.

The three of us sit and brainstorm some ideas for the remainder of the class. We throw out some suggestions and start to narrow down some topics when the bell rings.

Corbin speaks as we are packing up, "Let's have an idea by next class time. Sounds good? Have a great rest of your day guys!"

The students begin to leave the classroom. Henry, Chloe, and I stay back momentarily.

"Do you guys want to meet later tonight?" I ask.

Chloe is surprised by the question. "Oh, as in all of us?"

"Well, yeah, we are a group, right?" Henry says.

"I suppose you're right. Okay. Where should we meet? At the library?" Chloe wonders.

"No library for us. Too stuffy. Let's meet it at the docks at 5:30." I like my own idea. This is my safe place where I come to think. I know deep inside that selfishly it was also the place where Briggs and I always met, not to mention it's where Henry and I hang out: my haven. My suggestion gives me comfort, and I need some currently.

"Uh, sure. Where are the docks at? I've never been," Chloe says, sounding almost embarrassed.

"It's down at the boardwalk. We call it the docks. You're going to love it there. We can get some creative ideas going. I've got a boat there that we hang out on," Henry reveals as he gives her the address. We all exchange Snapchats, pack our stuff, then head out the door.

I spot Corbin watching us leave.

"Go ahead, guys, I'll catch up with you at the lockers, Henry."

Henry nods as he escorts Chloe out the door. "After you."

Once everyone is gone, I walk over to Corbin's desk. "Mr. Corbin?"

"Yes, Evy?" he says.

I pause for a moment, "Thanks for honoring Briggs today." I swallow hard. "It meant a lot to me." I bite my lip and hesitate with what I will say next. "Not many people will talk about the elephant in the room."

"No thanks needed. I knew this was a tough day for you kids and for you especially. He was a big part of this class." He continues, "I wanted to recognize that we are all suffering in our own way. We need to acknowledge our feelings. When you lose someone close to you, there's a pain that nobody will ever fix."

His words hit me hard. I'm standing here almost frozen and

lower my gaze to the floor and say nothing. I can see that Corbin is watching me and giving me a moment. I wonder if he's worn an armor of pain before. He acknowledges the moment of silence I need where perhaps words cannot or should not be said. Nobody but the person themselves, can truly understand what they are going through. He hangs on, waiting for me to talk. Somewhat embarrassed, I look up, wiping my tears. Corbin sees me and walks over to his desk, grabs some tissues and hands one to me. I straighten myself up, move my hair behind my ears and thank him. The silence continues for a few seconds longer. I touch Briggs's pin I am wearing on my chest. "Sorry…it's just been…a tough day."

Corbin has his hands behind his back fidgeting with something. When he brings his right hand back around, he holds a little rose made from tissue. He gives me a smile and hands it to me. It puts a smirk on my face. "Just a talent I have," he winks. "You might need this today. I'm here if you want to talk and there are counselors too," he says. "And hey, I like that Happy Face Pin you have on. I think I've seen it before," he says scratching his head.

Managing to muster a smile I peer down at the pin again, "Yeah, it belonged to Briggs." I feel the tears about to stream again, so I place the earbuds in my ears, hit play on my phone, and I walk out as I wave goodbye to Corbin avoiding any further eye contact.

CHAPTER 13

PRESENT

The end of the day has finally come. I am walking out to meet Henry by his car, when I see him being his silly self. He has my sunflowers in his hands waiting for me. Once he sees me, he starts waving the flowers coupled with a funny robotic dance until he gets my attention. I can't help but smile.

"Goofball. I'll take those flowers back, thank you."

"Ha, made you smile." Then he hugs me.

"So do you want to go home or hang out before we meet tonight?" he asks.

I don't really want to go home. My stomach is rumbling telling me I need to eat. I barely ate anything at lunch, as I just didn't have the appetite at the time. But now, I'm feeling like I need something.

"Let's grab something to eat and then go to the docks," I decide. I wanted to avoid doing the college applications that I had promised my mom I would do a little later. I sent my mom a text to tell her our plans and told her I'd see her after the docks. She was still at work.

"Deal," Henry said. "Blue Sky Bistro?"

"Yes." They have the best smoothies, and Henry knows I'm a

sucker for healthy food.

We arrive at Blue Sky, order our food and start talking about our day, when I receive a text from Briggs's mom. It catches me by surprise, making me catch my breath.

Hi Evy. I hope you are doing okay. Any chance you could stop by later this week?

Hi there. Sure. When is a good day?

How about Thursday?

Okay. I can come by after school. 6:00 work?

Yes. See you then. K.

Henry is in mid-sentence when he notices I'm not listening to him. "Uh, hello? You're a bit off. Who was that?"

"Um, Mrs. Sullivan. She wants me to stop by on Thursday."

"For what? Maybe they miss seeing you."

"She didn't say. I guess I'll find out Thursday."

Then both Henry and I get a Snap notification at the same time. It is our new highly organized friend, Chloe.

Hi guys. I'm leaving now and I will see you at the docks in 15 mins. She had drawn 5:30 on her Snap to remind us.

I look at my clock and realize it's time for us to wrap it up. So, off to the docks we go.

CHAPTER 14

PRESENT

We've learned to always keep a blanket in the back of our cars to have for the docks. It is an essential and today it comes in quite handy. We grab our stuff and start walking down toward the water. No surprise to either of us, Chloe has already arrived. She is standing there, leaning over and doing something to her left leg, like she is stretching it or something.

"Hey, Chloe! We're here," we shout together, which scares her a bit—oops! She loses her balance for a second and seems to wobble a bit on that leg she is messing with.

She collects herself, shakes her left leg, then replies, "Oh hi, guys. I made it. This place is beautiful. I see why you come here," she says, looking around.

"Yeah, it's chill here. Sorry, we sneaked up on you like that," Henry says as he reaches out to her and gives her a hug. He's a hugger. So, I follow suit. Chloe is so tiny and thin; she seems fragile almost like a China doll.

"Let's head over there," I say, as I wave them on to follow me.

The night is serene. This is my favorite time of day, when the sun is still in the sky, but the clouds start to settle in, dropping the temperature. I can feel the wind gently sweep at my hair. It sends shivers down my back. I catch my breath, completely expecting to see Briggs waiting for me at our spot. Then Henry calls out, "Here's our place," and I am snapped back to reality.

We roll out the blanket and sit down together. Well, Chloe and I sit, while Henry stretches out on his side like he is lounging at the pool. I take a group selfie. Chloe, sitting upright with perfect posture, places her legs so she can sit cross legged and starts arranging her notebook, pens, etc., in the space in front of her. I decide to play some music to help us get our creative juices flowing. "Do you mind? Any music you prefer?" I ask Chloe, as Henry knows it's protocol.

"I'm good with whatever. Not really. I like just about everything, except heavy metal. The noise and shouting in that genre makes me uncomfortable. I could never have been an 80s kid," Chloe scrunches her shoulders and shakes her head.

"Well, we wouldn't want that now, would we?" says Henry, imitating Chloe's head shake. "You're adorable, and just so you know, we don't like it either."

That put a smile on Chloe's face, and she lets out a chuckle. I can tell she is starting to warm up to us.

"How long have you guys known each other?" Chloe asks curiously.

Henry looks over at me and says, "I've known this princess since we were in kindergarten. She was my first girl crush, before I knew I was gay, of course, ha!"

Henry and I laugh while Chloe looks like she doesn't quite know what to say or if she should laugh.

Chloe lets out a little chuckle. "Oh, I didn't know. Uh, not that it matters of course," fumbling on her words.

"Evy, am I doing something wrong?" Henry asks.

I stick my tongue out at him. Chloe still looks confused.

"Maybe that's why I don't have a boyfriend? Am I not putting out enough gay vibes?" Henry questions jokingly.

"You are doing just fine, believe me," I laugh.

"Guess I'm out of the loop," Chloe grits her teeth. "You are my first official gay friend," she giggles.

"Baby, I was born this way," Henry says, which he loves to say proudly.

According to Henry, he was a beautiful baby, almost too pretty to be a boy. I don't doubt this, as to this day he remains incredibly beautiful. He said he never gravitated toward the typical male or female gender stereotypes. He likes to brag that he was the perfect gender-neutral child. He was fascinated with boats, sports, water, and hanging out with his dad. But he also enjoyed the finer things with his mom, learning about cooking, fashion, and the arts. His parents knew early on that he was gay and never thought twice about it. They adored him. "I never had to come out," he liked to boast. Henry was always Henry, no apologies needed. He was liked by all. Girls and boys had crushes on him. He tried to have a girlfriend a couple times. It never worked out, as he became more of a best friend than a boyfriend to them. He asked if I'd be his girlfriend once, and we both cracked up after he said it.

"Now that we have that out of the way, should we figure out what we're going to do for our project?" I ask.

We all start tossing out ideas: "Biography of a Senior" is Chloe's idea. "Your Life in a Movie" is mine. "Unapologetically Gay" is Henry's idea.

Chloe shakes her head. "I'll be honest, I'm not loving anything," and puts her pen down. She looks at her notebook, makes some notes, scratches out other things, then starts tapping her pencil.

Intently, she looks around, and then from what I can guess, she narrows her focus to the smiley face pin on my chest. "So Evy, what's the meaning of that Happy Face Pin?"

Instinctively, I grab my pin. "Um…," I was at a loss for words. This pin was my private link to Briggs. I look at Henry. He grabs my hand.

Henry butts in, "It was Briggs's."

"Gosh, I'm so sorry I asked. I noticed it earlier today, and it caught my attention."

"Don't apologize, it is what it is. Briggs used to wear it. He said it reminded him to be happy." Tears started to form, and the words come pouring out of my mouth. "I didn't know. I…I was his girlfriend, and I didn't know he wasn't happy. Why didn't he tell me how he was feeling?" I said it, the truth. I didn't know. *How did I not know that you were suffering so badly Briggs?* The immense guilt is suffocating me.

Chloe responds immediately, "It's not your fault. There are no words for your pain, except for to tell you that I'm here to listen to you if you need me. I know you don't know me well, but I'm here."

Henry leans in, and calls out, "Group hug!" He holds both of us around our waists, linking us all together. "It's all good. We all loved Briggs. Evy, I love you. And Chloe, I can already tell that I'm going to love you too."

Then suddenly it hits me, and I blurt out, "I've got it. I have an idea! Our project should be about suicide prevention. In memory of Briggs!"

I could see the light bulb go off in Henry's head. "Brilliant! Perfect way to honor our friend." Chloe was writing in her notebook.

I watch as I see her scribble some words down. When she finishes, she looks up at me and Henry and says, "That makes me happy. I agree. Let's do it!"

CHAPTER 15

PRESENT

Henry drops me off at home. I have made it through what has felt like a very long day. Mom is at home waiting for me. The minute she sees me, she runs over and hugs me.

"Hi, Mom. Love you."

"How was your day? Everything go okay?" she asks.

Everything was as good as it was going to be. "Yeah, I made it through. How was yours?"

I really admire my mom. She is truly the bomb. Everyone loves Charlotte. She works hard as a nurse in the OR. Mom raised my sister Julianna (Jules, she goes by) and me by herself. As beautiful as she is, she never goes on dates. She tells me her time will come one day. I think she's waiting for me to get out of the house and go to college before she starts to really date. When I ask her about why she doesn't, she dismisses me and says, "I only have enough love for you and your sister right now." She carries the weight of the world on her shoulders and wants to always be there for us.

Maybe it has something to do with my father dying when I was three years old, and my sister was eight. Sadly, I don't really have many memories of him, but my sister Jules does. Everything I know about my dad is from what others have told me. He was kind, athletic, handsome, artistic, and had a flair for movie making. He was a director / cinematographer/ producer. Brock Peters was well known in the industry. I get my innate creative side from him. My mother said my father insisted on naming me after his beloved grandmother Evylyn. I was his "little Evy." I keep a picture of him on my bedroom dresser. He was so handsome. If I ever have a son, I will name him after my dad.

One day he was out cycling early in the morning and was hit by a car. From what my mom was told, he died instantly. From that day forward, it has only been my mom, Jules, and I. Mom moved us up here to Morro Bay to get away from Los Angeles and felt it would be much easier to raise us here. I wonder what our life would have been like today if he were still alive.

I've never seen my mom have a bad day. She tells us that life is to be celebrated, and that's what she's done. If she does have a bad day, I'd never know. Positivity is her mantra, and that's why everyone loves her. When you get a hug from Charlotte, it feels warm, and meaningful. I can never get enough of her hugs.

Looking at the kitchen table, I can see that my mom has laid out the remaining college applications. I have already applied to a few colleges. Another thing about my mom is that when she puts her mind to something, she gets it done. There are no gentle reminders. College applications were on her mind starting first thing this morning. With all this Briggs stuff, I had pushed the applications to the side. Deadlines are next week, which means I don't have any flexibility left. I must get them done.

My dad graduated from USC, so it's been a dream of mine to go there too. That's my reach school. I'm also applying to UCLA, a few Cal State Schools, NYU, and Loyola Marymount. Los Angeles is where I need to be for the industry, but NYU in New York City is not a bad alternative. I want to major in Film just like my dad. I love everything about it: writing, producing, directing, and acting. I know my dad would be proud of me.

My mom said she knew I had the creative bug at age two. I was hooked on stories, and books completely fascinated me. She tells me how I loved to hear a story being read to me again and again, then I would retell the story in my own version. According to my mother, my versions were always so much better than the original. She may have been a little biased, but I must admit to this day, story-telling lights me up, whether it be through a book, a screenplay, or music. That's why I want to do film in college and especially for my career. I always have something to say.

My mom and I sit down. We go through each school's application to make sure we have all the requirements and forms filled out. We check my résumé, send off for transcripts, and make sure we have the correct emails for all my teacher recommendations. I upload the required film montage that represents my best creative work, and a small excerpt from a screenplay that I had won an award for from a young writer's screenplay contest. There is no room for making mistakes on these applications. My major is competitive, and I need to be able to stand out. We spend the rest of the evening getting the applications finished. We are finally done by 10:00 p.m.

"Stay right there," my mom insists. "It's celebration time."

She runs into her bedroom and comes out with a small present. "Open it."

"What's this for?" I ask curiously.

"Just because, so open it," she pushes it toward me. "I wanted to get you a little something to celebrate finishing the applications," she exclaims.

Right there is a perfect example of my mom wanting to celebrate the little things in life. Who gets a gift for finishing their college applications? I do! The box looks so pretty, I almost don't want to open it. I take a cute selfie with my present, then delicately pull the loose end of the yellow bow on top of the package to untie it. Inside the box is a small jewelry box. I pull it out and lift the top lid. To my surprise, there is a beautiful gold necklace with a heart pendant on it. I look at it, then look at my mom. "Aw, Mom! This is awesome. I love it. Thank you!" I embrace her with all my gratitude.

"I wanted to give you something to let you know you're loved and to tell you that I am so proud of you. Your Dad would be proud too," as she kisses me on the cheek and pulls me close. She takes the necklace out and places it around my neck. Then she turns me around to look at it. "The night your dad told me he loved me; he gave this to me as a gift." She reaches for the heart and turns it over. "On the back is the letter 'B', which your dad had inscribed on it for his name. He told me that when I wear it, that he would always be with me. I wore it for a very long time. But now it's yours. I know your dad means a lot to you, and so did Briggs." A heartfelt smile crosses her face with tears swelling in her eyes. "The 'B' will be there to remind you of both."

"It means that much more to me." I melt into her and hold her a little longer. I think to myself just how similar we are. We both lost our true loves way too early.

"Goodnight. I've got to get up early as usual." She gives me one last squeeze and a pinch on my butt, then off to her room she goes.

I look at my necklace and can't help but to try to picture my dad. One of the few memories I have of him is sitting on his lap and him showing me his camera. Vaguely, I can remember looking up at him and seeing his face. It's sad knowing that as times go on, our memories can fade.

I'm feeling tired too, so I turn off the lights, and walk upstairs to my bathroom to get ready for bed. I look in the mirror, take my pin off and place it carefully on my jewelry holder. My attention focuses on my necklace again. I grasp my necklace, turning it around to unclasp it. I hold it in my hand and flip the heart over to see the "B" inscribed on it. Grabbing my phone in one hand and the necklace dangling in the other. I lower the lighting, then hit video mode on my phone, and capture the necklace twirling and spinning. The necklace glistens and emits a golden ray around the room. At this moment, I feel hypnotized and try to divert my gaze into the mirror to snap out of it, and as I do, I feel a strange presence.

"Briggs?" I look around almost in a panic. I can't shake the feeling that someone was there. As I place my hand on the mirror, I feel warmth radiate deep inside me. "Briggs, are you here?" My heart starts racing. *Is my mind playing tricks on me?* "I feel you, Briggs. Are you here? Please, I miss you. Why did you leave?" I whisper. No answer.

As the silence settles in...the warmth leaves my body, and I suddenly feel chilled. I stand a moment longer, feeling completely out of sorts. Had I been transported somewhere for those brief seconds? I watch back my video several more times, hoping I had captured something, but I see nothing other than my beautiful necklace. I let out a big exhale, feeling defeated.

I brush my teeth then get into my pajamas and go to bed with Briggs on my mind. That was the weirdest sensation. It felt as if he had been there with me. My mind keeps racing with thoughts of Briggs, and it brings me to tears. I feel so lonely, and I miss him terribly. I grab my phone and pillow and go into my mom's room.

"Evy? Everything okay?" my mom says half asleep.

"Not really, I don't want to be alone."

She pulls back the covers on the empty side of the bed and invites me in.

"I'm here for you, sweets," she whispers.

No more words are needed to be said, I snuggle in with my mom and eventually fall asleep.

CHAPTER 16

PRESENT – January 6

It's Thursday and first thing this morning I receive a text from Mrs. Sullivan asking me if I'm still able to come over tonight. I reply, "Yes, see you at 6:00." It's going to be so strange to go to Briggs's house with him not there.

We are turning in our idea for the senior project for film class today. Henry and I meet up with Chloe at lunch before class. We had a Zoom chat yesterday and put everything together. With school getting back in session, we were all too busy to meet up in person.

When Henry and I arrive at the cafeteria, we see Chloe sitting at a far table. She has waters set out for us, and everything is set up like a business meeting. Don't get me wrong, I'm more than happy to have someone take charge, I can't complain. My mind has been spinning out of control ever since...that day.

"Yo, Clo!" Henry shouts out as he snaps his fingers in the air. He's never afraid to draw attention to himself.

He gets Chloe's attention fast, and she waves back with a big smile planted on her face. She stands up waiting for us. "Hi, guys." We all give a big group hug.

"How's it going?" I inquire.

"I'm glad we could all meet before class. I just wanted to show you what I put together after talking last night and wanted to make sure it looks good."

"You should really stop spoiling us. We are more than happy to do our part. But this guy is not going to complain," Henry replies.

"Well, we all have our own strengths. Pretty sure I'll fall behind on the creative side. So, I'll let you two handle that part," she says with a smirk.

"De-al-i-o!" Henry responds.

I nod; she has a good point.

Chloe has our proposal all typed up with a concise outline, placed neatly in a folder. We had all agreed on doing a documentary type film on suicide to educate our peers. With so many people being affected by Briggs's death, our thoughts are that perhaps it will help us all work through this and allow us to heal a little. It's going to be tough to do mentally, especially when I still can't grasp why he did what he did.

Film class starts. We are now all supposed to sit in our groups for the remainder of the year. I feel lucky about my group. Chloe is way cooler than I would have ever thought. Henry, well, he is always attached to my hip.

Corbin saunters in. "Hi, guys, good afternoon. I'm excited to see what kind of amazing ideas you've come up with. I'll be meeting with each of your groups in class today. So, take the time to iron out anything you need to do while waiting for me."

The students are all getting into their groups and the noise level of the rooms turns up a bit.

Corbin continues, "First, though, let's start out with the question of the day. What makes you happy?" he pauses. "Chloe?"

Chloe looks caught by surprise. "Waking up every day." I see her smile brightly,

Someone yells out, "Duh!"

"That is a wonderful thing. I agree, I'm thankful for each day myself. Kyle?" Corbin asks.

Kyle was that big kid who towered over everyone, husky and funny with a baby face, "Beer," he exclaims. "Uh, sorry, is that okay to say?" he chuckles as he looks around at everyone.

"If that's what makes you happy, you bet!" Corbin says, shaking his head.

The class laughs with him. He walks over to our table and sits down. Apparently, we are first on his list.

"So, what have you guys come up with?"

Henry speaks first. "It's a bit heavy, but we feel it's important."

"Sure, man, let's see what you got," Corbin says.

We all look at each other wondering who will be the first to speak up. Chloe, always so prim and proper, takes the reins. "Well, Mr. Corbin, we have decided to do a documentary on suicide and mental health to bring awareness to those topics. Considering the recent loss of Briggs, we feel it is important to address this."

I watch Corbin's response. He takes a deep breath, looks at us in the eyes one at a time, then hangs his head low. He is silent, a side of him I've never seen. I think to myself, *Oh, shit, he doesn't like it. Maybe too much? Maybe he's right.*

After a few seconds more of us doubting ourselves, Corbin finally breaks the silence and speaks.

He looks up and stares off into the distance as if he is looking somewhere far away.

"Brilliant...brilliant," he says softly. There is a pain in his voice I have not heard before.

"So, yes? All good?" I am feeling a little confused.

His demeanor changes. "Yes, absolutely. Kudos to you three!" He says victoriously. "I must ask though…are you sure you guys are ready to take this on? I mean, it's going to tug hard at your hearts with everything being so recent. And I mean hard, but I'm here to support you, one hundred percent." We look at each other and nod in unison.

"Most definitely," Henry says.

"All right, guys, run with it. Use your resources, and guidelines. I'm looking forward to this project."

Yep, we have the thumbs up. He smiles at us all. I could tell that the smiley face pin I am wearing has caught his attention again. I can see his eyes squint and a subtle thought-provoking grimace forms on his face. Self-consciously, I look down and grasp it. I respond with a nod of acknowledgment as I think of Briggs. *You are with me, Briggs.*

Class is over and we pack our stuff up and head out.

"I think he really likes our idea guys. What do you think?" Henry asks.

"For sure, but he had me going there for a second," I reply.

"Yeah, I thought, oh boy, back to square one," Chloe sighs. "He is right though; it is going to be a bit heavy. Suicide is a tough topic. But it will help us understand the whole mental health thing better." Chloe was never afraid to say what needed to be said. I like that about her. She's our little reality check.

CHAPTER 17

PRESENT

There is stillness in the air as I get into my car; so I roll down the windows to cool down. I blast my music as I head to Briggs's house. I love the feeling of air blowing through my hair and the coolness the wind creates as it softly touches my body. It's helping to free my mind from all my troubles, if only momentarily.

Before I know it, I've arrived at the Sullivan's home. My mind was so lost in thought during my drive, I'm not even sure how I got here. I'm a little apprehensive as I knock on the door, as I don't know what to expect tonight. Mrs. Sullivan opens the door, greeting me with a welcoming hug, calming my anxiety.

"Evy, so glad you're here," she holds on tight to me with her warm embrace. "It's so good to see you, thanks for coming over."

"Same. Thanks for having me," I say, happy my nerves have settled down.

She holds my hand as she guides me into the living room where Mr. Sullivan is standing. The home appears different from the last time I was here days ago for Christmas. Gone are the beautiful Christmas trees and decorations that gave nostalgia and warmth to their living room. I was hoping to still see "The Briggs Tree," which had ornaments hanging on it spanning his life. They had showed me Briggs's favorite ornament, the talking Darth Vader that they spent weeks looking for as Briggs had to have it. Once they got it home, they found out the light saber was broken. Briggs was convinced Darth Vader would lose his powers and cried for two nights worrying about it. We teased him, as the key chain he carried around had a light saber on it.

"Evy, how are you?" Mr. Sullivan asks pulling me in to hug me tight.

The Sullivans have always been so warm and welcoming. Every time I've been here, they made me feel like I was part of their family. Mrs. Sullivan would occasionally have little thoughtful gifts for me. "I love buying girl gifts," she would say.

We all sit down on the couch in their modern living room. They have a love for art, and it is well displayed with the vibrant paintings on the walls in almost every room. Each furniture piece is unique and carefully picked out. Walking around their house was like being at a gallery. It was the kind of home I wanted to have when I got older. The Sullivans attended art shows regularly. They would take Briggs and me to some of their events. We'd all get dressed up for date night, starting with dinner where they'd discuss the pairing of wines to meal selections, and finish at a gallery learning about emerging artists or art styles.

"You need to immerse yourself in all forms of art, whether it be culinary, music, or the visual arts," Mr. Sullivan preached.

With his advice and of course for the love of "art," Briggs and I would steal a moment away at the galleries on the weekends and find a secluded room to sit in and gaze at an art piece. We'd choose the same song, pop in our ear pods, hold hands and "immerse" ourselves. It was during moments like this that I'd catch him looking at me, and I'd smile back feeling connected, knowing we truly loved each other.

But here I was tonight without Briggs by my side, no one to hold my hand. I put on my best smile for the Sullivans, but inside my heart is aching for them.

Mr. Sullivan bites his lip and inhales deeply. He takes another second, "Evy, I'm sure this has all been difficult for you."

"Oh, um, I'm doing okay," I lie and regret saying that. "Well, I'm having a hard time. I miss Briggs. None of it sits right. I never expected Briggs to do something like this." I can feel the tears fill my eyes.

Mrs. Sullivan comes and sits next to me, immediately putting her arm around me. "It's so painful and impossible to understand. Briggs struggled with depression since he was in middle school. There was nothing specific to trigger it, which was the worst part. We tried everything to help him, and we thought he was finally in a good place once we moved here," she pauses. "Our hearts are breaking too, and we are lonely without...Briggs."

I cling to her, and we both hold on tight to one another. I can feel her warm tears sting my face. I feel an urgency to let them know that I didn't know to the extent that he suffered. "He would mention a history of depression, but he always tried to blow it off as if it was no big deal, like it was a thing of the past. He'd tell me he was okay, and I believed him."

Mrs. Sullivan pulls away slightly to look at me. "That's our Briggs. He didn't like to talk about it. He didn't want anyone to worry about him. He kept it deep inside."

Mr. Sullivan goes into the other room and comes back with a box of Kleenex. He has tears in his eyes too. "We all need these," and hands us each a tissue. "It's tough times for sure. We are here for you, Evy, please know that," he says.

"Yes, honey, we are both here for you anytime," Mrs. Sullivan chimes in. She looks me in the eyes to reassure me.

Mr. Sullivan continues, "We asked you here tonight to discuss a few things with you..."

My head swirls. The room quickly fills with a deafening silence. It wasn't an awkward silence, but a moment of reflection. I feel the warmth of Mrs. Sullivan's body pressed on mine and the eyes of Mr. Sullivan looking up toward the ceiling, searching, as if he was waiting for the roof to part and the sky to turn golden, only to deliver Briggs back to us.

The moment passes, and we are brought back to Mr. Sullivan's words. "Evy, Briggs was our only child. We had plans for him to go on to college and do wonderful things. We won't get to experience new milestones for him that parents get to take pride in. We won't get to celebrate his successes, his wedding or the family he could have had. No grandchildren, no...no more new memories with him," his voice is cracking.

I wipe the tears from my eyes.

"So, we wanted to do something for Briggs, something that I know he would want. He loved you and he was your biggest fan. We had never seen him so happy. He'd talk about you and light up. He'd brag to us about how smart and talented you are. Did you know that?"

I shake my head in amazement, "I felt the same about him. I truly did. He made me happy. There is no one like him." I feel so loved at this moment hearing that. I mean, I knew he loved me, and he would say complimentary things to me all the time like, "You're brilliant and you're going to big places, I can see it already." And I'd say back, "No, you're the brilliant one, you're the one going places." He'd dish out a compliment, and I'd give it right back to him. But did I truly know he told his parents the same things about me? No, but knowing this fills my heart.

Mr. Sullivan continues, "With Briggs being our only child, we had put away money for his college. But we know that's all changed. Evy, you are gifted, and we want to do everything we can to see you go on to do what you love. So, we have decided to set up a college fund for you."

"I, I…" I interrupt but I can't find the words to speak.

Mrs. Sullivan speaks up. "This is something Briggs would have wanted. By no means do we mean to insult you or your family, but it is truly the best gift from Briggs we can think of. He believed in you and so do we. Secondly, we plan to set up a scholarship and have a yearly recipient from here on out."

"I don't know what to say, this is so generous of you, but…" I stumble with my words again.

"No buts, the college account will be set up in your name. We need a little more information from you to finalize everything. Don't worry, we will talk to your mom, but we wanted to talk to you first."

"I don't know how she will take this," I say, contemplating carefully.

"We know your mother is very capable of sending you to college, and it's not about that," Mr. Sullivan bends closer, looking at me intently. "You're very special to Briggs and to us too, and selfishly, we want to see all the good things you will accomplish, it will bring us peace. You two shared so many similar interests. He loved you and so do we."

I am really taken aback and shocked by their gesture. They really want to do this for Briggs. For me? "Thank you is not enough,

I'm pretty sure I can't even come up with words that mean what's in my heart."

"No thanks needed, just go out there and make your place in the world," Mr. Sullivan says with his fist in the air as Mrs. Sullivan watches on with a look of satisfaction on her face.

"We have something else for you," Mrs. Sullivan whispers in my ear.

Something else, she says as if this wasn't enough already? I still don't know what to think about all this. My head is spinning.

Mrs. Sullivan squeezes my hand, then gets up and walks over to the bookshelf. She looks around and finds the item she is looking for. Carefully she lifts the sleek, blue, oval sculpture, and from beneath it, pulls out an envelope. She returns to the couch where I am sitting and sits back down next to me.

In her hands I can see the words on the envelope with my name written boldly in Briggs's handwriting. I feel a piercing pain in my chest, a wound that further digs into my already broken heart.

"Briggs left this sealed letter for you. We found it under his pillow addressed to you. It took us a couple days to find it...after finally going back into his room," she says in a tone that exposes her pain.

Mrs. Sullivan hands me the letter. I begin to tremble. I clutch the letter to my heart. For the past week, I realize what has bothered me to the core and has continued to pain me, is that I thought I would never get to hear from Briggs ever again. I'd never know why. *And now I get this letter.*

CHAPTER 18

PAST – December 25, 2019

I will never forget this day, as it was my last day with Briggs. Christmas morning, I woke up to my daily text message from Briggs: *Make my wish come true, All I want from Christmas is you, baby.* It put a smile on my face.

I sent one back: *I'm yours, can't wait to see you.*

We had plans to spend most of the day together. Briggs and I spent Christmas morning away from each other with our respective families for the usual Christmas exchange. My sister Jules was home for the weekend. She drove up from Los Angeles the night before.

Jules is the best big sister I could hope for. We're very close even though she's five years older. She's quite a free spirit, and more the upscale type. She is a makeup artist in Los Angeles and is really starting to make a name for herself. She likes to call me and tell me about her on set experiences.

She'd tease me, "You wouldn't believe who I got to do makeup on today!"

"Who?" I'd ask.

"Anne Hathaway. And her skin is just that beautiful."

Yeah, I'm proud of her, but also quite envious. She's such a cool chic. She and I look a lot alike. People can always tell we are sisters. We are both blonde and blue-eyed, but she came home this time with a platinum blonde color, and amazing curls. I have the more laid-back dirty blonde, natural curl look.

Christmas was my mom's favorite holiday, and it was my dad's too. She would put the tree up the day after Halloween. She said the nostalgia of Christmas brought her back to the days when she was a child. And when my dad died, she wanted to make sure that no matter what, we would always have a happy memorable Christmas. She'd spoil us with so many presents. She shopped all year long buying us stuff. We'd go to bed on Christmas Eve, and mom would wait until we were asleep to put the Santa presents out. In the morning, Mom would let us sleep in, but then would wake us up shouting, "Get up! Santa came!" Under the tree would be our Santa presents and always a present signed, "Love, Mom and Dad."

Christmas morning was awesome. The three of us woke up all in our matching pajamas, another tradition. Jules and I acted so surprised that Santa came and played along with mom. We made her breakfast while she got everything ready. She turned the music on, as we ate and laughed and talked about old memories.

Mom reached across the table grabbing and squeezing both our hands, and remarked as she did every year, "If only Dad could see you girls, he'd be so proud. He loved Christmas, we loved Christmas."

You could see the tears slowly filling the inner corner of her eyes refusing to let the tears stream, trying to be strong. Yet, her smile was so big, grinning ear to ear, beaming with pride, camouflaging the sentiment of sadness in her eyes.

"I miss Dad so much," Jules said.

"Me too," I added.

My mother said, "Well, that makes three of us." There was a long pause. "Okay now, leave the dishes on the table, let's head over to the tree to see what Santa brought."

To the tree we went to unwrap away. We opened all our presents, except the one labeled, "From: Mom and Dad." We always saved that for last. This year, "Mom and Dad" bought me a digital Nikon camera with a large lens. I was beyond thrilled, as my current camera was a little outdated.

"You're going to need this for film school," Mom said, giddy with excitement.

I got up and gave her a hug. "Thank you so much. I know Dad would have approved of this camera. And now I need to get into film school."

Jules received a lighting kit she had been wanting and a professional rolling makeup bag that she had been eyeing. More hugs and thanks. We watched Mom unwrap the purse we got her. I could tell she really liked it. Jules being the fashion forward kind of person picked it out.

"Please throw away that old one you have, Mom. This is way cooler!" exclaimed Jules.

Mom never bought much for herself; it was always about us.

Later that afternoon we were cleaning up the house when the doorbell rang. Finally, he arrived! I ran to the door to greet Briggs. When I opened the door, Briggs was standing there with a Santa cap on, a red thermal shirt, and suspenders with his jeans rolled up and flip flops on. He had a bag thrown over his shoulders.

"Ho! Ho! Ho! I come bearing gifts," he said in his best Santa voice.

I had the biggest smile on my face. "Merry Christmas!" I screamed, and I gave him a big hug and he hugged me back, holding me so tight. We lingered there for a moment longer.

He whispered in my ear, "Merry Christmas, my beautiful Evy."

"Thank you, I'm so happy you're here." I took his hand and rushed him inside.

"Smells good in here," Briggs said as he approached the kitchen.

Mom and Jules stopped what they were doing in the kitchen as we walked in.

"Merry Christmas, Briggs," they both chimed together.

"Hey, hey, Merry Christmas to you guys," he said with his arms stretched out wide ready to hug them.

"You are looking quite festive tonight," Mom said with her arm around him.

Briggs grinned and pulled on his suspenders.

"I hope you came with an appetite?" she inquired.

"Yes, Ma'am, and some presents!" You could see Briggs light up. "Hey, Jules, how's LA life?" He sat down, grinning with enthusiasm.

"It's busy, but a lot of fun. You two need to come down and visit me, I can show you guys the town," Jules replied with excitement in her voice.

She loves talking about the club scene, celebrity sightings, and the fabulous food in LA. And heck, we like to live vicariously through her. It's not like Morro Bay has much going on, it's just a sleepy little beach town known for its skateboard museum. She says I'll really start living once I go off to college, and that numerous opportunities for fun will come knocking. Amen!

We sat down to an early dinner. We laughed and listened to each other's stories. Briggs kept holding my hand under the table and squeezing it. When we finished stuffing our bellies, we got up from the table and helped clean up the kitchen. When we were done, we went to the family room.

"Everyone have a seat, it's time for presents," my mom excitedly burst out with a skip in her step as she headed toward the Christmas tree. This is her holiday, and I love seeing her in all her glory.

"I did warn you about my mom, right?" I whispered into Briggs's ear.

"Yes, and I love her spirit," he whispered back.

Meanwhile, Mom was searching under the tree gathering the gifts singing, *"Here comes Santa Claus…"*

She emerged from the tree. "Okay, Briggs, these are from all of us," mom smiled as she handed Briggs his stack of presents, then hugged him. She too whispered in his ear, "We so love you," and planted a little kiss on his cheek before sitting down.

"Thanks Mrs. P., love you too. You shouldn't have," Briggs said tenderly. He paused as if he was composing his thoughts then gave a trembling smile. "You guys are so good to me, and I want you to know how much I appreciate and love all of you."

I looked at Briggs, who appeared quite solemn. I placed my hand on his lap. He had slipped into one of his thinking moments. He collected himself, then turned to look at me. I smiled and locked eyes with him, waiting for his infectious smile. It took a minute, but there it was. He put his arm around me, giving me a big squeeze.

Jules planted herself down in front of us. "Go ahead and open them," she insisted.

Mom had picked out a rad sweatshirt from a local vintage shop that Briggs and I liked to go to. She also gave him some funny socks and a Dopp kit with his initials on it.

Briggs put his new sweatshirt on immediately, "Everything is so dope, thanks. My turn now."

He reached into his bag below the chair and pulled out a present for my mom and Jules.

"You did not need to do anything for us," Mom shook her head.

"I'm good with it," Jules laughed. "Let's open them!"

Mom pulled out a bottle of Caymus wine from the ornately decorated bag. Briggs knew my mom loved red wine. "It's my parents' favorite, and they insisted," he said. She came over and hugged him again.

"Wow, thank you. This is a really nice wine, and please thank your parents!" she said, thrilled.

It was Jules's turn now as she hurriedly unwrapped her present. "I love Capri Blue candles. They're my favorite smell. Thanks, B!" She too got up and hugged Briggs.

"I have another present here in the bag for you, Evy," as he turned to me to say.

I was filled with excitement. "Do you want to exchange gifts here or at your house?" I asked, wanting to make sure he had the option.

"Well, I'm here, aren't I? No time like the present! Get it?" he chuckled. I shook my head.

"Jules, I think it's time that we head to the kitchen and give them some time alone," she hinted as she touched Jules's shoulder and ushered her toward the kitchen.

"Yeah, right," Jules said.

I looked at Briggs and simultaneously we made the same raised eyebrow expression. "Thanks, Mom."

"Let's be silly and sit at the tree like we're kids," Briggs chuckled. He nestled his large manly frame next to me.

"Sweet, the tree looks pretty big from down here," I said as we both looked up together to the top of the tree and laughed. We held hands and Briggs turned to me to sneak in a little playful kiss.

"Who's first?" he asked.

"Me, please," I begged. "But I need another kiss first." I just couldn't get enough of him.

Briggs leaned over and placed his lips softly on mine. Then he placed his right hand under my chin and gently pulled me closer to him. His warm tongue slowly entered my mouth until my tongue joined his. I hungerly kissed him back. If his kiss was all I got for Christmas, it would be more than enough. I felt the presents between us getting crushed with our embrace.

"Oops, we're smashing the presents," I giggled. I examined the packages, and they looked pretty good despite the entanglement. "Here is your first present," I said with pride.

He unwrapped the gift slowly to tease me. "Come on, open it." I demanded.

He immediately tore off all the paper in a frenzy like an anxious little kid.

"A DJ music mixer!! Ev, this is awesome. Thanks," he said, giving me another kiss. He started reading the box and looking it over. "Very cool."

"Okay, here's your next one." I placed it in his lap carefully.

He picked it up and started to shake it. "Hmm, what could it be?" he jokingly asked.

I was mostly excited about this gift I was giving him. Briggs and I always took lots of selfies together. But there was one that became my favorite. We had been at the dock about a month ago, and out of the blue a big thunderstorm surprised us. We were instantly poured on, soaking us within seconds. Briggs started blasting his music from his phone and we both started running around in circles chasing each other like it was the most exciting thing we'd ever done.

He caught me and tackled me to the ground. We were muddy and laying on our backs laughing while the rain pummeled us. I took out my phone and snapped the most amazing picture, if I do say so myself. It captured the essence of our love. Briggs's protective arms were around me, with his mouth open wide catching the rain. My head was nuzzled into his neck and the smile on my face was that of a Cheshire cat. The picture exuded the love we had between us, the lightheartedness, the friendship, two souls entwined laughing at life and being best friends. I placed it in a frame and gave it to him as a gift. At the bottom corner of the frame, I had written the words: "You are my everything. Love, E."

When he finished unwrapping the gift, he held out the picture in front of him and his face got serious. He looked almost dumbfounded.

"This is the most resplendent picture, Evy. The rain day. I...I... I'm speechless."

I kissed his half open mouth. "It's my most revered picture of us."

"It means a lot to me. A lot." As I smiled back at him, I saw tears roll down his left cheek. "Wow, you got me. Best present ever."

I remember feeling a bit disconcerted when I saw him cry but told myself that surely these were happy tears. Briggs picked up his gift and presented it to me. "Your turn." Then he proceeded to wipe his eyes.

The small package was elegantly wrapped in an iridescent red paper with a perfectly tied gold bow around it. I was careful to undo the bow, then the paper. It was way too pretty to just rip it off. A beautiful little black box laid in my hands. I looked up at Briggs and he nodded as if to continue. I lifted the top of the box and inside was a dainty silver ring engraved with a musical note. Briggs reached over and took the ring from the box.

"May I?" he asked.

"Most definitely," I said breathlessly and extended my left hand to his.

"This is a pinky ring, because you are going to have to pinky promise me that you will love me forever."

I smiled with tears in my eyes and nodded my head yes. He had me crying too.

As he slipped the ring on my finger, we immediately locked pinkies. He cleared his voice and said, "The musical note symbolizes our first official date. I'll never forget that night. Music brought us together and continues to bind us. So, I found this ring quite fitting. And if you look inside, I have a little something inscribed."

I took the ring off and held it up to my eyes and read the inscription: "U R My Everything. B."

"Ha! We soooo think alike. That's why I love you."

"I love you more." A deep love that I couldn't describe.

We said our goodbyes to Mom and Jules as it was time to go to Briggs's home to see his parents. They walked us to the door, and everyone hugged goodbye.

"Thank you for spending a little Christmas time with us today. We loved our gifts but most of all we loved having you. Tell your parents Merry Christmas and thanks for the wine," Mom said, still full of the Christmas spirit.

"Will do. And thank you, Mrs. P. You are truly the best. And Jules, keep on killing it!'.

As we were walking out, Mom handed me my present for the Sullivans then waved goodbye. Briggs stopped and turned around to look again in my mother's direction. He paused as if taking everything in, smiled, and waved one last goodbye before turning back to head toward his car with me.

CHAPTER 19

PAST – December 25, 2019, continued

While he drove, I looked over at him and admired how handsome he was. He seemed rather stoic and quieter than usual. He caught me staring, grinned, and winked at me. His mood brightened as we laughed and sang all the way to his house.

Briggs's parents were home waiting for us in the living room. Mr. and Mrs. Sullivan were dressed formally, far different from my family's Christmas casual apparel. They always looked so nice and put together.

"Merry Christmas, Evy," they both exclaimed together as they stood up to greet us.

"Merry Christmas," I replied.

They came over to hug us.

"How was your Christmas celebration, you two?" Mrs. Sullivan inquired. She rubbed Briggs's shoulders.

"We had a good time, Mom. You like my new sweatshirt Evy's mom got me?" he twirled around as if he was in a fashion show.

"Very cool. And Evy, I see you have your ring on. Briggs couldn't wait to give that to you," Mrs. Sullivan said as she grasped my hand

and admired my ring.

"Lovely!" Mr. Sullivan chimed in.

We all sat down on the couch. Their Christmas trees were so beautiful. Another favorite was the Christopher Radko tree adorned with white lights. I looked around the room and noticed a piece of art that I hadn't seen before. "Is that a new art piece?"

Mr. Sullivan straightened up, "Good eye! It's the new Calder piece I got Anna for Christmas. Isn't it magnificent?"

"I love his use of primary colors," I said, trying to sound sophisticated and knowledgeable from all the education I learned at various art shows with them.

"Do you know he's mostly known for his kinetic sculptures?" Mrs. Sullivan divulged.

"I remember that fact," Briggs said.

We had a great night and sat around discussing memories of their Christmases with Briggs. I learned that Briggs was afraid of Santa until he was seven. He refused to sit on Santa's lap and wouldn't get near him unless his mom stood between him and Santa.

We exchanged gifts, then the Sullivans called it an early night. They were heading down to visit Anna's good friend Cari and her husband in Santa Barbara early in the morning.

Briggs asked me to wait one second. "I'm just going to thank them again, as I won't see them in the morning."

"Sure, go," I insisted. I sat down and waited on the couch.

—

Briggs went to his parents' door and knocked. "Mom? Dad?" He said trying to hold the tears in.

"Come in, honey," his mom said. "What's up, love?"

Briggs walked in, "I just wanted to tell you guys about how much I love you. Thank you for everything."

They did a group hug. "We love you so much son. We are proud of you," his dad said.

"Yes, we do," his mom added. The hugs continued.

Briggs stared into his parents' eyes, shifting his glance back and forth between them. He swallowed hard, "I couldn't have asked for better parents, and I appreciate everything you have done for me. Know that I love you both so much." Tears formed in his eyes as he hugged his parents once more. He quickly wiped away the tears before they could see them.

"You just made our night. Love you, Briggsy. We will be home late tomorrow. There are leftovers for you in the fridge. Be safe when you bring Evy home, okay?" his mom said as she rubbed his back. "I love you. Merry Christmas."

His dad followed, "Love you, buddy. Goodnight."

Briggs took a moment, "I love you guys more." Then he walked out the door.

He stopped outside their room placing his hand on the door and whispered to himself, *I hope you know how much I love you.* He sighed, took a moment then returned to Evy.

———

We waited a few minutes before going up to his room. We wanted to make sure his parents were asleep. Briggs grabbed his new music mixer and the picture I had given him, taking my hand as I followed him up. I plopped down on his bed. Briggs turned the lights on and found a place on his desk to set our picture on.

"Let's try out this mixer," he said eagerly and plugged the cord into the socket. He dropped his suspenders off his shoulders.

I watched his face light up as he was turning the knobs and making some killer melodies. "This is so cool, Ev!" I moved to the edge of the bed to watch him closer. I could literally watch him all day, he makes everything seem so exciting. Plus, it made me happy to know he loved his present.

About thirty minutes later, Briggs turned off the mixer and looked right at me, "Whoa, so cool. But now it's our time for a little Christmas snuggling." He went and turned off the light, then sat down next to me and placed his hand in mine. "I love you, Evy," he said in almost a whisper.

Our eyes met, and we held each other's gaze. "I love you too," I said breathlessly.

I was so drawn to him, and could feel my body tingling, filled with desire. He lifted his hands up to my cheeks, pulling me in. His kiss was slow and intentional, as I felt myself being lost in him. His kisses moved from my mouth to my neck. His fingers making their way to my shirt, gently brushing past my breasts to the bottom of my shirt. He lifted the shirt over my head, revealing my laced bra. I took my hands and slowly started to unbutton his shirt as he continued to kiss me. His hands found their way to the clasp on my bra, carefully unhooking it. His hands cusped and lifted my breasts as he leaned down to move his tongue over my flesh. My body was screaming with desire for him. He unbuttoned my jeans and helped me push them past my hips until they fell to the ground. I returned the favor and unbuttoned his jeans, carefully unzipping his zipper. I had to use a little force to remove his jeans and get his boxers down. I admired him as he stood there in all his glory, muscular and chiseled to perfection.

"You are so beautiful. You take my breath away," he sighed.

"And you are so amazingly handsome," I said.

Briggs led me to his bed and pulled the covers down. He quickly grabbed a condom out of his bedside table. He got in and subtly motioned for me to join him. We spent the next thirty minutes slowly exploring each other's bodies and making love. Briggs's eyes bore into mine, never leaving, searching deep into my inner soul, and I into his. Briggs continued thrusting tenderly inside me until sheer ecstasy riveted throughout our bodies simultaneously. We held onto each other so tightly, and then he collapsed upon my chest. Briggs burrowed his head into my neck, letting out a slight gasp, as I felt his body quiver. There was something so different about tonight. We didn't need words to tell one another how much we loved each other. We had allowed our bodies to give in to our souls, letting them escape and intertwine into one. I had never felt so loved and complete.

We stayed in each other's arms and held on tight. Briggs had showered me with so much attention tonight. I could have stayed like this forever. It was the best Christmas.

"Evy?"

"Yes?"

"I have one more Christmas present for you," he said in a more serious tone.

He rolled his body slightly, still holding on to me and reached into his bedside table pulling out a little velvet bag.

"For you…"

"Briggs," I pleaded. "You've already done enough."

"Oh, well, this is just a little something. Open it," he insisted.

I loosened the strings and tried peeking into the bag. Carefully

I shook the bag and out came a Happy Face Button onto my chest. "It's the Happy Face Button!" I smiled and looked at Briggs.

"I'm giving you mine."

"But you love that pin."

"Correct. But I love you, and I'm really in a good place now. You make me incredibly happy, and I want you to have that, so you know how much joy you have brought me. Promise me you will keep it and do something good with it?"

"Of course I will, I promise. But are you sure you want me to, have it?"

"I'm more than sure. From me to you. It's yours now. I'm passing the torch," he said, his warm hand clutching mine with the pin in between.

I carefully placed it back into the bag and held it to my heart.

"I guess I should probably get you home now before your mom comes looking for us," Briggs said almost regretfully.

We gave each other a long hug, then got out of bed and helped dress each other. Briggs drove me home, holding my hand, with Christmas music playing. We teased each other about all the stories our parents talked about us as kids. Briggs quietly pulled into my driveway. The porch and family room light were still on. I knew my mom would be waiting for me.

Briggs became quiet. I stared into his kind eyes and said, "Thank you, this was the best Christmas ever." I was elated.

Briggs cocked his head, looked at me and smiled. There was a slight tremble to his voice when he spoke. "I want you to know that I have never felt more loved than tonight. Nor have I ever loved someone so fiercely as I love you. Please know that."

"I feel the same. You know how much I love you too, right?" I wanted the same reassurance he was asking of me.

"I do. I do." Then he kissed me.

"Let me walk you to the door." He got out of the car and walked to my side to open the door. He held out his hand for me to hold as he guided me out of the car.

Briggs held my hand tightly. When we got to the door, he turned to look at me and held me by my shoulders at arm's length.

His brows knit together forming faint lines in his forehead. He looked at me with his eyes that shimmered with unshed tears as his lips slightly trembled. "I just want to look at you and remember everything about you and tonight for a second," he told me.

I stood there and smiled back at him, slowly melting. There was something different about him tonight.

He lingered a while longer. "Time for you to go in. I love you, Evelyn Peters. You're going to do great things."

"I love you too, Briggs Sullivan. Thank you for everything," I replied.

He kissed me longingly, held me tight, and watched me walk inside. I waved goodbye from the door and blew him a kiss. He caught it!

Then he said, "I'll love you forever." He stayed standing there until the door shut.

Mom was kind of waiting up for me, as she had fallen asleep in her robe on the couch. She woke just as I shut the door.

"Hi, sweets. How was your night?" she said sleepily and motioned me to come over next to her.

"It couldn't have been any better Mom. We had so much fun. And the Sullivans loved their book. Thanks for everything." I was still giddy with excitement from the day.

"Good to hear. I had a nice day with you guys too. Thanks for making my Christmas so special. Just having my girls home with me is the perfect gift." She hugged me and said, "Let's go to bed, I'm sleepy."

We both headed to our rooms. I turned on my light and got into my pajamas. Next stop was the bathroom to brush my teeth and wash my face. I finally got into bed, exhausted from the day. I looked at my new ring from Briggs, turning it around on my finger and caught myself smiling.

I took a selfie and sent Briggs a Snapchat: *Hope you made it home. Love, love, love my ring, but love you more.* I took the velvet pouch holding the pin he gave me and placed it under my pillow. I had a little piece of him with me and it made me bubble with joy.

Ding, he sent me a Snapchat back with his sweet smiling face: *I did! Glad you love it. Merry Christmas. I love you more. Sweet dreams.*

Heart emoji sent back. I screenshot his pic then closed my eyes and fell asleep.

CHAPTER 20

PAST – BRIGGS

Early Morning – December 26, 2019

PLAYLIST #6: "BROKEN" BY JOSHUA RADIN

Briggs arrived home, opened the garage and drove his car in. He was careful to be quiet, grabbed some water from the kitchen then headed upstairs to his room. It was going to be a long night ahead. He changed into his pajamas, brushed his teeth, then sat down at his desk and searched his drawers for pen and paper. The picture caught his attention. He could feel the heat rise in his body and the wet stingy tears scorched his face as he looked at the picture Evy had given him. "If only I could always feel that joy I see in the picture. I've tried," he said tearfully, as he hung his head low and began to softly weep. "Be strong, my love. I pray you can forgive me."

He put his headphones on then began to write. His face was intent and serious. Twenty minutes later his first letter was finished. He folded it up and slipped it into the envelope and sealed it. Carefully he wrote Mom and Dad across the envelope.

He got up from his desk and nervously paced around the room, bobbing his head to the music.

Briggs started arranging his room, making it tidy and neat. Everything needed to be in order. Walking over to his window, he opened the blinds, opened his window and looked outside. The stars were bright and twinkled brilliantly. His eyes scanned the sky, feeling more than content. For Briggs, the beauty of the night gave him confirmation to the end of the most perfect chapter of his life. The day was everything he imagined it would be. The beauty would soon be overshadowed by what was to come.

Briggs plugged in his record player and opened it up. He removed his earbuds and placed them on the desk. Looking at the album Evy had given him for his birthday, he took the record out of its cover and placed it on the base of the player. He manipulated the dials, adjusted the volume, then lifted the arm to place the needle on the record. He marveled at this old-but-new-again technology and watched the record spin around and around while the eloquent haunting music of Billy Eilish played.

He sat back down and sighed. Briggs grabbed the pen and started writing the most important and hardest letter he had ever had to write. When he was done, he looked at his phone to check the time. It was 2:37 a.m. and time for bed. The sickening feel of pain and turmoil had crept back into his mind and body, instantly knocking out all the joy he had felt that day. Briggs set his alarm as tomorrow would be an early start. He laid in bed trying to conjure up the memories from today, he wanted to wash the unending pain away. A tear rolled down his cheek as he thought of his beloved Evy. He managed a smile, and before long he drifted into sleep.

At 6:00 a.m., Mr. and Mrs. Sullivan crept upstairs to say a silent goodbye to Briggs before leaving on their day trip. They never liked to leave without some sort of goodbye. That was their tradition. His mom quietly opened the door with his dad right behind her. They both peaked their heads into Brigg's room and saw Briggs sleeping. His beautiful face and crazy head of hair, on the pillow peeking out from under the covers.

"I love you, sweet boy," his mother quietly whispered. She smiled at her husband. Mr. Sullivan shut the door behind them. They went back downstairs and off they headed to Santa Barbara for the day.

The alarm rang at 7:00 a.m. Briggs lingered in bed for a moment, remembering the warmth and love he shared with Evy right there only hours ago. He could smell her sweet citrusy scent on his sheets. Ten minutes passed, and he knew it was time to move forward. After turning his music on, he jumped in the shower.

He let the steam from the shower fill up the bathroom. His hair was washed, and his body cleaned. Next came flossing and brushing of his teeth and shaving of his face. He wanted everything including himself to look perfect. Briggs got dressed in his favorite pair of jeans, and the white Rolling Stones T-shirt emblazoned with the famous mouth and tongue that Evy had loved. *Who doesn't love the Stones?* he thought to himself. He made his bed then grabbed the two letters, carefully placing them under his pillow. He knew his mom would find them there. From under his bed, he pulled out a strategically hidden box. The carefully crafted box contained everything he needed. He grabbed his phone, car keys, the picture Evy had given him, and his headphones and headed out of the bedroom. He took a good look around, wanting to make sure that everything was in place. "Bye, room," he said with his voice slightly quivering, and shut the door.

Briggs wasn't hungry this morning, and his stomach was already uneasy, so no need for food, it was pointless. He walked around the house looking at everything one last time. As he walked into his parents' bedroom, he stopped and stood for a moment. Under his breath he whispered, "I'm sorry, Mom and Dad. Thank you for loving me." He got choked up. He could feel the pain settling itself in again like a poison to his body. *It's time,* he said to himself. Nodding his head, and straightening his shoulders back, he put on a brave smile and walked toward the garage.

Briggs opened his car door, reached over and placed everything on the driver's side. Picking up the box, he went to the back of the car. Opening the box, he took out the narrow, metal cylindrical cup, scissors, socks and duct tape. He stuffed the tail pipe with the socks, placed the cup over the end of the pipe and began taping the duct tape around the base of the cup to secure it to the tailpipe. "Okay, that's done," he mumbled to himself.

He sat in his car, shut the door and grabbed the keys to put them in the ignition, but didn't turn the car on just yet. He placed his earphones on, then cued up his "Quieting the Buzz" playlist on his phone. As he looked over at the passenger seat, he carefully grabbed the picture frame from Evy. He stared intently at "their picture", then held it to his heart for a long moment before placing it on his dashboard where he could see it. The final thing left was to send Evy her morning message. Briggs started typing rapidly.

I love you eternally. You are my everything. Please love me forever.

These were the words to let her know she will be forever with him. His fingers trembled as he hit send. Evy would be sound asleep and wouldn't wake up for a while. He turned his phone to airplane mode and hit play. His hand grasped the keys and without hesitation he turned the car on. "Please forgive me God," he said out loud. "I can no longer take the pain." The music played in his ears, Briggs looked at the picture of him and Evy on the dashboard and smiled. As minutes passed by, he could feel his eyes get heavy. His mind slipped into a dream-like state, his body felt so light as if he were flying. Thoughts of Evy flooded his mind. He had never felt so at peace within himself, all the pain had left his body, as he took his last breath.

CHAPTER 21

PRESENT – January 6, 2020

I leave the Sullivan's house clutching the letter in my hand still in disbelief. My mind is spinning, but somehow, I manage to get in my car and start it. I don't want to let go of the letter, for I know, Briggs too, had held it in his hands. It's been almost two weeks since he wrote it and left it for me. Those same hands that had lovingly held my face just a short time ago. There were so many emotions bottled up inside of me. Grabbing my phone out of my back pocket I quickly call my mom. "Answer, answer, answer, please."

"Mom?" I say with such angst and desperation.

"I'm here, Evy, I've been waiting for your call. Are you okay?" she says sounding worried.

I can't speak, instead I let out a whimper.

"I'm here. Take a moment," she urges.

All that I can get out is a cry. I use my shirt to wipe my tears. Silence.

"Mom, they gave me a letter from Briggs." My mouth quivers saying these words.

"Why have you only got it now? Do you need me to be there

with you? I can leave work."

I shake my head. "The Sullivans just found it in his room. And no. It…it's just going to be sooo hard to read Mom."

"Yes, it will be," she pauses before talking again. "Yes, it will."

"Maybe I'll go to the docks. I'm still sitting here in front of the Sullivan's house," as my eyes stare at the garage.

"Are you okay to drive?"

"Yes, I think so. I'll give myself a few minutes," I reassured her. I continue to focus in on the garage. A sick feeling clenches my gut as I realize that is where Briggs was found.

"That's a great idea. Will you text me when you get there?" she asks.

"Of course. Mom?"

"Yes?"

"Thanks, I love you." My voice is still trembling.

"Love you more," and she makes a kiss sound for me to hear.

A few minutes go by, and my anxiety recedes enough for me to drive. I hope the Sullivans hadn't noticed me just sitting in my car outside their home. Carefully, I fold the envelope and place it underneath my shirt and tuck it into my bra. I go on autopilot and drive to the docks.

CHAPTER 22

PRESENT – January 6, 2020

The sun had set early, so the darkness of the night has brought its own calmness as I arrive at the docks. I grab my phone, keys, and the blanket from the back of my car and walk down to my/our spot. It's a horrible feeling knowing that Briggs and I won't be here together ever again. I lay the blanket out on the ground, leaving some room to pull it around me. There is a chill in the air, and I can feel the wind blowing in my hair as I look out at the water. I reach into my shirt and pull out the letter. With my finger, I carefully trace my name Briggs had written out. "Evy."

There were many nights like tonight that I had sat right here with Briggs. One of the times, right as winter break let out, we came here to celebrate two weeks of no school. "Are you getting excited about college?" I asked him that night.

"Uh…not really," he replied.

"Seriously? It's going to be so fun. Being on our own and stuff."

"Yeah, that's what they say," then he sighed.

"Come on!" I playfully jabbed him in his ribs as I noticed he had his Happy Face Pin on. "You know you'll have a blast. How are your applications going?" *I sounded like my mom.*

"Slow. I'll get them out there, I'm sure. How are yours coming along?"

"Not doing too bad. I've been working on them. We're still applying to the same places, right?" I asked.

"Yeah, but I don't know about college. Feels pointless, I don't know," he said, sounding defeated.

"That's silly. You're so smart, of course you'll go. We're all going to do this college thing together: The Three Musketeers," I say, referring to Henry, Briggs, and me.

"Cheerio! You're the brilliant one. You're beautiful, smart, bold, amazing, and all these qualities are going to get you noticed. Henry is going to do his interactive media stuff and invent all sorts of shit. And me? I have no clue."

"What happened to music producer/writer extraordinaire? I'm still waiting for my song."

He started twiddling his thumbs as a distraction. "It's hard to make money in that. Just a pipe dream. I'm just not sure. Okay, change of subject. Let's make plans for having fun over the break. Donuts tomorrow morning?" He gave me a squirrely smile.

"Deal!" I said as I kissed him.

My mind wandered back to that day. I don't think he had plans to go to college, as he knew he wasn't going to be around. He was trying to tell me, and I missed the clues again. *Goddam it, Briggs.*

I am anxious to open the letter, but also afraid to at the same time. My heart wants to hear from Briggs, but my mind wants to be my guardian and protect me from the pain of his unspoken words. My velvet bag is with me in my pocket, as it has been by my side since Briggs gave it to me the night before he left this world. He knew I would need that Happy Face Pin. He knew it, and I didn't. *How could I have not known?* I loosened the strings of the pouch and let the pin fall into my hand. Staring at the pin, I shook my head. "It reminds me to be happy," he had told me. He had struggled and I didn't know the extent of his pain. I secure it to my shirt, and right then, I promise that I will continue to always show that smiley face to the world. My mind drifts back to the envelope. Slowly, I open it, careful to keep it as preserved as possible, as I need to keep every ounce of "something Briggs" to have forever, knowing I will no longer have him. My hands tremble as I pull the letter out of the envelope. My phone provides the light to help me read the letter. And so it begins:

My Beautiful Evy-

I sit here knowing that the most beautiful thought is that I was lucky enough to have loved you completely and that I was loved just as completely and unconditionally by you. I found solace in my heart, knowing that we had a love like this. Unbeknownst to you, you found me as a broken soul, only to pulse life and hope into me. But Evy, I could never be whole. The love you poured in, seeped through my cracks when I was alone. And although your love kept coming, the demons inside me pushed everything out. I don't suppose that you will ever understand that, but there was a pain burning inside me every day. A pain so strong, it engulfed me and would take over every ounce of my being. I had to fight with myself daily, putting on smiles, telling myself I could win. But I couldn't win, Evy. You saw the best side of me, in ways no others could see, but the worst side of me is what I had to deal with. It was not a battle I cared to share with others, not you, not my parents. I tried so many things—medicines, counseling—but things only worked temporarily.

You need to know that you did no wrong, in fact you were the best part of me. You were always the highlight of my day, saving me from the monsters within. I envied you and your outlook on everything. I never had the pleasure of being that comfortable in my own skin. Promise me that you will never blame yourself? You need to know that both you and my parents could not have showed me more love or support if you had tried. I could not have been more grateful for two of the most caring and nurturing parents, or a love like yours. I asked God for his forgiveness, as I've lost the fight and I'm ready to be in a place where there is no pain, no struggle, and where I am whole. Please forgive me. Evy, I so deeply love you. I will forever be by your side watching you from above. I believe in you. You are the brightest light and will do amazing things. Stay happy and smile.

I love you,

Briggs

Tears continue streaming down my cheeks as I fold the letter and place it back inside the envelope, holding it tight to my heart. I put my earbuds back in and turn on Briggs's "Quieting the Buzz" playlist. I need to take in his words and channel him. I curl up with the blanket around me. My insides feel empty, as if somebody has tied a cord around them, pulled hard, and yanked my soul out. A thunderous shiver runs through my body, feeling like an explosion is about to happen. My body surrenders to the pain, and I let out a guttural cry from deep within my empty shell. My heart aches for Briggs. *If this is how I was feeling, how bad was the pain that Briggs had gone through every day?* My feelings of being so mad at Briggs for leaving us take a back seat. I sit and cry, not so much for my feeling of sorrow, but for the realization of the constant affliction that Briggs was suffering.

Not knowing how long I've been sitting here; I see a light approach me and turn down my music. I am startled when I hear my name called out in a very familiar voice.

"Evy! Evy?"

The light blinds me as I look toward the light.

"Hey, love," Henry calls out to me. I can see the shadow of a tiny figure along his side: Chloe. My sadness turns to relief. My friends have come.

"Henry? Chloe?" I ask.

Simultaneously they both respond "Yes!" as they run toward me. Henry's running and Chloe is doing more of a gallop with a limp.

I stand up only to almost be tackled by them.

"Thank you, guys, for coming. I needed some love right about now. How did you know I'd be here?" I ask curiously and squeeze them tight for what seems like forever.

"Your awesome mom said you might need us. She couldn't leave work, but wanted us to be there for you," Henry replies.

"So, here we are," Chloe interjects.

We continue our group hug, as tears stream down my face. That was so sweet of my mom.

"I love you both," Chloe says.

"Girl, we love you!" Henry shoots back.

"Me too. And thank you both for being here for me."

We sit back down on the blanket, with me in the middle and Henry and Chloe on either side, wrapping their arms around me. No words are needed as we sit and listen to the crash of the water against the docks. Henry lets go of our hold and reaches into his backpack. He pulls out three Ramune sodas and three bags of Hot Cheetos and passes them to us.

I can't help but smile at his thoughtful gesture. Hopefully Henry has filled in Chloe on the Ramune/Cheetos obsession.

"I want to give a shoutout to Briggs. Pop the tops and push the ball down!" Henry demands.

We all do as instructed and watch the ball drop and the bubbly fizz surface to the top of the bottle. How sweet was that of Henry to have Briggs's favorite things for us?

Henry reaches his bottle to the sky, with me and Chloe following suit. "We're thinking of you, buddy. We miss you; you shit-grinning, handsome guy up there!" Henry toasts.

"May you rest in peace and watch over us all. I'm not happy about this, you know? Until the next time we meet," Chloe laments.

My turn. "I'll love you forever. And Briggs?" I pause, "I'm going to make you proud." I place my hand over the Happy Face pin and hold it close to my heart where Briggs will always be."

We continue staring into the twinkling sky. I wonder how many souls are up there looking down at us. *Please take care of my Briggs,* I pray silently to the abyss of the sky above. I hope someone is listening.

PART 2
PRESENT

CHAPTER 23

Henry, Chloe, and I arrive together to film class the following week. Mr. Corbin greets us right before class starts.

"Hey, guys, can we chat for a second?"

We all look at each other and shrug our shoulders.

"No problem, what's up?" Henry asks.

"Mrs. Wall, the counselor, would like to meet with your group and me to discuss the logistics and give some guidance on your project, being that it is a trigger-type subject. Would today or tomorrow after school work?" Mr. Corbin asks.

Chloe, forever the organized one, gets on her phone to check her calendar. "Unfortunately, I am leaving school early tomorrow, but today will work for me."

"Works for me," I say.

Henry chimes in, "Me too. What do you have going on tomorrow, Chloe?"

She takes a minute, fumbling with her words, "Oh just an appointment. No big deal."

"Great! Let's just all meet here at the classroom today at 4:00. I'll let Mrs. Wall know," Mr. Corbin says.

———

The "end of the day" bell rings, and it's time to get together for our meeting. I arrive first, wanting to get my thoughts organized before they get here. I think Chloe has been rubbing off on me lately.

Corbin is already in the room waiting.

"Hi, Evy, come on in," he instructs me.

"Hey, Corbin," I say, feeling drained from the day.

I drop my backpack down on the table and start taking my things out.

"How are you dealing with everything?" Corbin asks.

I stare back at him blankly, a little caught off guard, not really knowing what to say.

"Can I ask you about your pin? I feel like I've seen it somewhere before."

I hesitate, instinctively grabbing my pin situated above my heart from Briggs, "That's two loaded questions." I avert my gaze and hang my head.

"Sorry, you don't have to say anything. I know it's got to be a difficult time. I want you to know I'm here. I've been there," he reveals.

"What?" I ask hesitantly, raising my eyes to his. *He's been in my shoes?*

Corbin inhales a deep shaky breath while rubbing his hands together. He scrunches his eyes tightly, bringing his hand between them pinching at his nose. He shakes his head then opens his eyes. "You see, I lost my older brother to suicide. Wills was only sixteen. I was twelve. My family didn't ever speak about it," he bites his lip as he pauses briefly. "They packed up all his things immediately, sold our house and moved out of town. It was as if Wills never existed. It tore us apart. Nobody ever asked if I was okay. I had to go through a lot of therapy as an adult to work out the guilt and sadness I felt. I don't want anybody to ever feel the way I felt. It nearly destroyed me."

Ouch. "I'm so sorry, Corbin," I say, the sorrow pouring back in.

"It's all good now. I'm telling you this as I care about how all you kids are doing and want you to know you are not alone and that your feelings are validated," he says reassuringly.

Taking a deep breath, I respond, "Thank you. I'm having a hard time, but I'm hanging in there. My mom and friends have been amazing. But I really miss Briggs…" Corbin holds my stare and nods his head to go on.

"This pin," my voice is quivering, "is from Briggs. He used to wear it. He said it reminded him to be happy. He gave it to me the night before…before he died." I can't hold back and start to cry.

Corbin takes my hand and gives it a squeeze. "That pin must be very special to you. I think we all need to be reminded to be happy. You wear it nicely."

I wipe the tears from my eyes and manage to say, "Most definitely."

I stop feeling sad for myself and reflect on what Corbin has said to me. I had no idea Corbin had gone through the same thing. We were now connected through a club neither of us wanted to really be in. It all started to make sense about our quirky Mr. Corbin: his happy carefree spirit, the random questions he asks. There was nothing that random about him after all. He was genuine, and he wanted you to know he really cared about you. He grew up without anyone caring about his feelings, and he changed that cycle. *He is my new hero.*

Our conversation is interrupted when Chloe arrives with Henry.

He escorts her in, followed closely behind by Mrs. Wall. Now there's a character. She is not your typical counselor. She was known for her frequent hair color changes. Today's hue is light blue.

"Hello, everyone," Mrs. Wall announces as she makes her way in, causing Chloe to turn around to see who was talking.

There is a myriad of "hellos" being spoken before she takes a seat next to Mr. Corbin and me.

"Thanks for meeting with me, guys and gals. Good to see everyone here," Mrs. Wall says in her charismatic voice. It's kind of hard to take her seriously with that blue Disney *Frozen* hair.

She continues, "First of all, how are you guys doing with the loss of your classmate?"

"As expected," Henry speaks up.

Chloe and I both nod our heads in agreement.

"Honestly, it's tough," I confide.

"Thanks for sharing. It's a hard time for all of us. Please know that I'm available for counseling. My door is open any time," she pauses, then turns her gaze toward Corbin. "Mr. Corbin, here, brought your project idea to me for approval and a little guidance. The topic of suicide can be extremely touchy. I've reviewed your submission and think you guys are on to something and I want to be here to help guide you."

Chloe speaks up, "We are extremely passionate about this. We were all friends with Briggs, and we don't want to see this happen again. We want to do something to help those with mental health issues."

They keep talking about the project as I tune out to my own thoughts. My mind is racing in regard to my talk with Corbin. There was and still is a stigma about suicide. I had so many questions. Would his brother still be here if he had better resources for help?

Would Briggs still be here? How many kids are dealing with feelings of hopelessness and isolation? Are we not paying close enough attention to the signs? Where is the support when you need it? Even Corbin didn't have the support until he was older. We have counselors at school, but that's not enough. How can we help? I look down at my happy face pin. *That's it!*

"Do you think you can expand upon the idea to make a bigger impact?" Mrs. Wall says as she thumbs through the project outline.

I blurt out, "I do! I have an idea." I'm not sure what possesses me to speak out, but something inside me is telling me to do so.

"See this Happy Face Pin I have? Briggs used to wear it to remind him to be happy. He gave it to me, as most of you guys know. He wore it, but nobody knew his struggle. Why can't we start something with these pins? Pass them out to someone when they are having a bad day? If they're sad, they can take one. We don't have to keep the feelings of sadness, anxiety, and loneliness inside us. The pin will let others know we may need help. It would encourage us to seek those out with struggles and show them a smile, or ask how they are doing? I've learned the hard way, that we don't know what others are going through. We can make a difference." I have rattled on, barely taking a breath.

Corbin smiles at me. "That, my friend, is an incredible idea."

All five of us spent the better part of the next hour designing an outline and talking about how we can accomplish this new project I proudly named: "The Happy Face Project."

"Well, this was a great session. I'm proud of you guys. I'm all in. But now, I need to get on the road. Somebody must feed my kids," Mrs. Wall says as she gathers her things and stands up. Her blue hair still has me cracking up.

"Thanks for your time, Mrs. Wall," Corbin says.

We all say thank you, too.

"Okay, guys, I can't wait to see this idea launch. We kind of got off track about the film project, but no doubt, you three will do great. Let's tie 'The Happy Face Project' into the film and that will be a fantastic way to launch the program," Corbin says with an exuberant look on his face.

"We are on it!" Henry exclaims in syllables.

We pack up our things and walk out of the classroom with Corbin after he locks the door behind us.

In the parking lot, we make plans to meet on Thursday at the docks at 5:00 p.m. After hugging us, Henry gets into his car and says his goodbyes. He's off to sail with his dad. Chloe and I walk together as we are parked next to each other. I can tell she still has that limp.

"Evy?" Chloe says.

"Yeah?"

Chloe continues, "I really like your idea, the pin is brilliant. I can't imagine not wanting to live. It breaks my heart to know that people suffer. Nothing could make me happier than to be able to help someone."

"Thanks, Chloe, I agree. We are going to do something good. I can't bear to lose anyone else."

Chloe nods her head and hugs me goodbye. "Me neither. See you at school."

CHAPTER 24

The next day, Chloe leaves school early to go to her doctor's appointment. Yesterday, she got concerned after feeling a sharp pain on the way home. She meets her mom and dad outside the office. They all go in together and sit in the waiting room, talking and catching up with one another. Her mother wants to distract Chloe from the real reason why they are there: to see if the cancer is back. Within twenty minutes of waiting, they are called back to Dr. Lucy Neeves's office.

The office is filled with light coming in from a wall of windows. The furniture is modern, and not the most comfortable, but the aesthetics of the office give it a clean look. It is unquestionably an improvement from Dr. Sanders's office. They had been here once before when Chloe first moved to Morro Bay to establish transfer of care. She had liked Dr. Neeves, as she had given her the impression of being a warm and caring doctor. Chloe had been due for her routine follow-up, and it just so happened that these nagging symptoms that had been creeping back in had come with perfect timing. They sit and wait again.

There is a knock on the door, and in comes Dr. Neeves. Today she is in a navy blue dress with her white doctor coat over it and her hair pulled back at the nape of her neck. Her appearance matches that of the office, neat and clean, with no nonsense.

She walks in giving Chloe's shoulder a squeeze and says, "Well, hello, Chloe and family," acknowledging her mother and father also.

She sits down and looks right at Chloe. "How are things going for you young lady? This is your senior year, right?"

"Yes, Ma'am," Chloe replies.

"Have you been feeling, okay? Anything you are concerned about?" Dr. Neeves asks as her eyes scan back and forth from Chloe to her parents.

Chloe reaches into her purse and pulls out a small notebook. "I've been keeping track of some symptoms I've been having," and she opens the cover to the page where she has written down a calendar. She looks at her parents, knowing that she is about to reveal symptoms she has not shared with them.

"Symptoms? I thought you said only your leg had been giving you some trouble. Why didn't you tell us?" her mom frets and reaches out to hold her hand.

"Sorry, Mom and Dad, I just didn't want to worry anyone," she says apologetically.

"Oh, Chloe, honey," her mom shakes her head with worry. Her dad reaches out and holds Chloe's other hand to provide a united front.

Chloe releases the grip of her parent's hands, and straightens upright, reviewing her notes before speaking. With much poise and courage, she tells Dr. Neeves of her symptoms. "I've been having stomach pains, and I thought nothing of it until the other day when the pain got pretty bad."

She looks at her parents, who were looking at her with eyes wide open, somewhat dumbfounded by this revelation.

"Go on," Dr. Neeves instructs.

"My left leg is still feeling a little weird. It's been that way since I was diagnosed. But sometimes it gives out on me. But good news, my hair has finally grown back." She wants to end on a high note and smiles brightly to erase her parents' fears.

"How long has this been going on?" Dr. Neeves is typing away on her computer.

"About three to four months," Chloe says looking at her notebook, although she knows exactly how long she's been aware of some changes. "And I did notice a little blood from my mouth the other day when I was brushing my teeth. I was probably brushing too hard."

"All right, let's do a quick exam. I'll meet you in the room across from us. Chloe, just have a seat on the table after you change into the gown," she says.

Chloe nods. The three of them get up and walk over to the room as instructed. Her parents wait outside while Chloe quickly changes. She opens the door to let her parents in when she is done. Once inside, Chloe gets up on the table and is gobbled up by the gown, with her petite legs dangling. Her mom sits, and her dad comes over and stands by her side. He looks at Chloe admiring the young, sophisticated lady she has become.

He gave her a hug. "We are here for you, Chloe, you know that? Right?" He takes a seat as Dr. Neeves knocks on the door and announces she is coming in.

She washes her hands before beginning her exam. While Chloe is sitting up, she instructs Chloe to open her mouth while she shines a bright light to the back of her throat, then in her eyes to check her pupils, before putting it back into her jacket pocket. Using her fingers, she traces under Chloe's chin, neck, and subclavian area. Next, she uses her stethoscope to listen to her heart, as her parents watch her every move.

"Lift both arms up, please," as the doctor's hands make their way to the axillary area then down her arms.

"Great, let's lay down now."

Chloe does as she is instructed. Dr. Neeves covers her legs with a paper sheet, then carefully lifts her gown to expose her stomach. The exam continues with her hands examining her abdomen.

"Take a deep breath now," Dr. Neeves's hands linger there a little longer.

"And again," she says as she has one hand pressed under her rib cage while two fingers from the other hand tap on the hand pressed against her stomach. Chloe tries to watch as Dr. Neeves continues pressing on her right side under the rib cage.

"Any pain or tenderness here?"

"Not currently," Chloe says with relief.

"Bend your left leg for me," her instructions continue. "Now fully extend it out straight." Chloe did everything she asked but had trouble fully extending her left leg.

Dr. Neeves uses both of her hands to examine the left leg more carefully. Her hands start at the upper thigh, kind of squeezing and massaging the leg all the way down to her foot.

The same routine was done much quicker to the right leg.

"All right, you can sit up now," she says as she holds Chloe's dainty hand and helps her upright. "Let's get some lab work today, and I'm going to have my nurse schedule a CT scan this week."

"Is everything okay?" Chloe's dad asks nervously.

Dr. Neeves acknowledges Chloe's rights as a patient. "Chloe, do I have permission to discuss everything with you and your parents?"

"Of course, please."

Dr. Neeves has sat down again and is fervently charting on her computer, but she pauses and looks up. "We need to get your abdomen and left leg checked out. Do I have a little concern? I'll give it to you straight…yes. I'm a doctor that treats cancer. I will always be concerned when a patient walks into my room. I take all your symptoms seriously. I must put all the pieces together, and I can do that once I get the CT scan and the blood work back. Let's circle back next week on Wednesday and go over everything."

"Most definitely," Chloe replies, trying not to sound worried. Dr. Neeves didn't really have an affirmative answer, which could be either good or bad. Very democratic of her, she thinks. Chloe likes accomplishing and excelling at things, having perfect order, organizing, doing tasks, and checking things off her list. The waiting game always makes her nervous and feel out of control. She knows she is at the mercy of the art of medicine now.

CHAPTER 25

I wake up in a panic, dripping sweat from the same bad dream I had of Briggs drowning and me not being able to save him. My heart is racing so fast, and I can't stop crying. It felt so real. I hate it. I instinctively reach for my phone, expecting to see my usual morning text from Briggs. *What is going on with me? I feel like I'm losing it.* One minute I'm fine, and the next minute the reality of it all chokes me. I get up and get ready for school, and before leaving, I place the pin on my shirt.

Mom has already left for work. She left me a little note saying, "Hang in there." How does she always know what to say to me when I need it the most?

I want to get out of the house a little earlier than usual today, as I don't want to be alone with my thoughts. I send Henry a message letting him know that I will meet him at school.

When I arrive at the parking lot, I am one of the first ones there. Geez, I really did leave early. I need to sit for a minute and take a deep breath. I pull down the driver's side mirror to look at myself and I can see how bad my eyes appear. Still puffy, oh yay.

I decide to take a walk around campus and do a little filming to get some shots for our film project and take my mind off everything. Somehow, I find myself in the hallway of Mrs. Wall's office. As I'm filming, I zoom into her office window and see her sitting there. Oh, crap, she sees me, and now she's waving at me. I look around and see if I can escape, but now she's walking to the door. Too late to get away now, so I turn my camera off and politely smile at her.

"Evylyn, good to see you. Were you stopping by to talk? I was hoping to see you sooner than later." She waves me in.

Lucky me, there's no turning back now. *Maybe it was no accident that I came to her office*, I begin to think.

"Well, kind of," I try to convince myself.

"Kind of, shmind of? You're here. Have a seat. Your eyes are a little puffy this morning. Are you okay?"

I put my fingers to my eyes. "Thanks for noticing." Or making me feel more self-conscious.

"Just keeping it real. You just lost your boyfriend. I know you are hurting." She is pulling me in.

I bite my lip trying to keep myself from crying. "Yeah, right now is not the best time in my life."

"Tell me about it." She is direct and intentional. "Sit right there in the green chair."

I do as I'm told. I hesitate before speaking. "Besides the terrible fact that Briggs is no longer here, I keep having this dream that Briggs is drowning, and I can't save him. I woke up freaked out." My heart is breaking just saying this out loud.

"Evylyn, listen carefully. What Briggs did was not your fault."

"But I missed so many signs. Why would someone do this? I could have done something." I felt myself sinking in the green tweed chair, as if I was sinking in a jungle pit of vines. I need Tarzan to swoop in and rescue me.

"Evelyn, it is not your fault. Nobody can ever really know what another person is feeling no matter how well you know them. What you are experiencing is grief. All these crazy emotions, they are valid. Your mind is trying to work things through. Acknowledge that they are normal feelings. Allow yourself to feel these emotions, good or bad." She waits for my eyes to meet hers.

"Unless I'm wrong, from what I've seen, you've got a pretty good support system, right?"

"Yes," I nod, trying to sit back up in the chair.

"Don't be afraid to talk to your people about how you're feeling. Share memories of Briggs with others. Speaking of, would you mind sharing something about him with me?"

My mind starts to race. There were so many good things about Briggs. I pause for a long moment. "Briggs was obsessed with tennis shoes. He had this bright yellow pair of Yeezys. Oh man, he absolutely loved them, but I did not. They were so loud, but he could pull them off." A chuckle came out of me unexpectedly.

"There you go. I see a smile on that pretty face of yours," Mrs. Wall, with her blue hair, exclaims.

She was right. A smile did cross my face, and it felt good to remember the happy side of Briggs.

"You see, Briggs would want you to remember him for the good things. Smile with those sweet memories, girl. Spread joy."

The morning bell rings, giving me an excuse to get out of there. I stand up to leave and look at her, seeing her in a new light. "Thanks, Mrs. Wall. I appreciate your time."

"No thanks needed. That's what I'm here for. My door is always open," she grins.

My hand grips the doorknob, and I pause to look back, "You rock the blue hair well." Mrs. Wall grins, shakes her hair back and forth, then fluffs the ends. *There you go, I'm spreading some joy.*

CHAPTER 26

The day drags on, but lunchtime is here, and I get to spend time with Henry and Chloe. I seem to cheer up at the sight of them. What I love about my friends is that Henry always has some drama going on even though nothing is too pressing or a real issue. Just a Henry issue. And then you have Chloe, whom I've just started to get to know but love already. There is something entertaining about her, even though she is just being herself. She really has a sweet soul and could never harm a fly. The two are like polar opposites, and I balance them off in the middle. Today Henry is worried about his Supreme backpack collab with Vans not being delivered in time for an outfit he wanted to wear later this week. Chloe is neatly pressed, manicured, and tightly wound. I know I keep saying it, but it's weird how things get back to normal and life goes on despite death. Henry looks at me quizzically and points to my eyes. He's about to say something, which I'm sure it's about how I look. So, before he does, I blurt out, "Don't even think about it."

The day continues to move slowly, but on a positive note, my eyes are finally getting back to normal, and the puffiness is gone. Amen and a double amen as it's time for film class. Mr. Corbin is in another one of his excited moods. He starts out by asking his question of the day. "If you had to live your life based on a movie, which movie would you want it to be?"

"Michael?"

Michael is one of the quieter guys in the class. He has a nerdy appearance. You know, the kid with thick rimmed glasses, a button-down short-sleeve shirt, and carries his pens and pencils in his front pocket? That's him to a T. "Give me a sec." He grits his teeth and pushes his glasses up. "It would be *The Godfather* and I'd be Vito Corleone."

We all kind of giggle. Michael as *The Godfather*? Here's this tiny guy ready to be unleashed as the ultimate Mob Father.

"You mean to tell me you've been hiding your fierceness all this time? I love it," Corbin says with his power fist in the air.

He then turns to look at this girl named Amber in our class who is always standoffish. Rumor has it she's quite strange. "Amber?" He calls out.

Amber appears to be put off by him calling her name. "Today's not a good day," she clamors back pouting.

"Haven't heard of that movie," Corbin replies. I can hear some giggles. "Let's talk after class, okay?"

Amber gives Corbin the eye roll.

I wasn't asked the question, but I could tell you that I'd choose *The Notebook*. Briggs as Noah, and I as Allie. Briggs departing the world would be compared to Allie and Noah's seven-year separation, but Briggs would come back by a twist of fate, just like Noah. He would love me forever, and I him. We would write the story of our love together and die together of old age. Could you come back to me, Briggs? I want to grow old with you. *If you're a bird, I'm a bird.*

We get started on our group work. We are making a lot of progress, in fact, I think we are way ahead of most of the other groups. Today is our day to look up tons of information on suicide. We write down the hotline numbers, statistics, support groups, organizations, anything that deals with the topic. Who knew this was all out there? There are even non-profits created in memory of those who've ended their life by suicide. I guess I have been living in a bubble, sheltered from the reality of mental health issues. Nobody talks about it, and that's why people slip through the cracks. Just the thought of it burdens my heart with a heavy feeling again. *Ugh!*

Chloe thumbs through her organizer. "We are still meeting tonight, correct?"

"Yep, 6:00 o'clock. The usual," I say.

"Want me to pick you girls up and all go together?" Henry asks.

"If you can pry yourself away from the mailbox waiting for the all-important backpack!" Chloe giggles.

"Oooooh, burn," I laugh. "Good one, Chloe. Didn't know you had it in you!"

"Oh yeah, I've got fire all right," she roars like a fierce lioness.

Henry and I laugh at Chloe. She is really starting to come out of her shell.

"Good plan, Henry. See you guys around 5:45ish?" I ask.

CHAPTER 27

I make it home after school. Mom is in the kitchen cooking and waiting for me. She is dressed in skinny jeans, heels, and a pink ruffled top of some sort.

"Whoa! Mom, what are you up to tonight?" I hug her tight. "You look great." I forget she has a life too sometimes.

"Thanks, Ev. Just going to dinner with some friends," she says, trying to downplay it.

"Friends?" I'm wondering if there is more to it than that.

"Just a group from work going out for dinner. But not to worry, I made you some veggie spiral pasta."

I'm going to miss her like crazy when I go off to college. All these great meals she spoils me with won't be delivered to my dorm room. I dread to think of cafeteria food. *Blah!* "Yum! You know I can feed myself Mom, but thanks for dinner. So, Chloe, Henry, and I are all meeting tonight for our film project at the docks."

She pulls out two chairs from the kitchen bar to sit at. "I'd love for you to fill me in on it."

I spend the next fifteen minutes telling her about "The Happy Face Project." "So that's what we have planned. It's a little more than just a senior film assignment. We are hoping to turn it into a program at school to help kids deal with mental health."

When I finally finish talking, my mom looks at me in a loving way. "Evelyn Peters—that's brilliant! I'm so proud of you. I think that's exactly what the school needs—heck, all schools." She embraces me tightly.

She glances at her watch. "Oh, crap, I'm running late. Love everything about your guys' ideas. See you later tonight?"

"Of course. Have fun, Mom." *Who is the mom now?*

I eat my meal and clean up the dishes. Perfect timing, because as I am finishing up, I hear a knock on the door. It's Henry. He'd never just sit in his car and honk for me. He's formal, and always a gentleman. His mom raised him right.

"Come in," I yell to him. He enters. "I'm ready, I'm ready, I'm ready," I say in my best SpongeBob SquarePants voice.

He rolls his eyes at me with his hands on his hips. "Still no backpack," Henry whines.

"You're still cool, don't sweat it."

"Yeah, you're right," he says as he puckers his lips in a sexy way and raises an eyebrow.

"Like yourself much?" I say laughing.

We head out the door arm in arm. He opens my car door and away we go to Chloe's house. When we arrive, she is sitting outside her door ready with her bag. She stands up when she sees us and walks to the car with a little hobble.

Henry rolls down his window and calls out, "I guess I'm a little late?"

Chloe is checking her phone. "Five minutes to be exact. Not bad. I can forgive you," she shoots back.

"Get in, Queen," Henry motions with his thumb pointing to

the back seat.

"Hi, Clo!" I high five her delicate tiny hand.

We drive to the docks with the windows rolled down, the music blasting and all of us singing out loud.

Once we arrive, Henry gets out and walks to the back of the car and pulls the blanket out from the trunk. I get the job of carrying the water, and we head out to our spot. The grass has turned a patchy brown color from the effects of the occasional winter weather. Henry lays the blanket out for us all to sit on. We sit down and Chloe spreads out all the outlines and charts we have been working on.

We agree to just about everything: how we'll start the film, how we'll approach the topic of suicide, how we will flash the Suicide Hotline number and website across the screen, what we plan to do about making a difference, introduce "The Happy Face Project" launch, and most importantly, place the dedication to Briggs at the end. We also decide to make T-shirts. Henry will oversee designing them, and we'll sell them to raise money to buy Happy Face Pins to give out. We're all pumped about this project. What delights me the most is that Briggs would be proud of us.

I'm so happy that we are making such good progress. We've been working hard trying to make this project evolve into something truly meaningful. Feeling a bit emotional, I look at both Henry and Chloe and smile. In a time when my heart is hurting, these two people of mine are helping me mend.

"What are you smiling about?" Henry asks me.

"Just you two. Thank you both for helping make this project so special." I'm trying not to cry and purse my lips awkwardly.

"It's very important to me too," Chloe says, speaking up.

"Ditto, no thanks needed. We're all in this together—for Briggs," Henry replies.

It is getting dark, and the cool air has started to settle in. The moon above is gleaming in an otherwise dark sky above us. Chloe looks up and notices it first.

"Do you ever wonder what's really in the sky? Other planets? Other people? Afterlife?" she says inquisitively.

"You're going to get a neck ache cranking your head back like that," Henry says. "You need to lay down to look up at the moon and sky."

Henry lays back first, and I am the next to follow. The sky is spectacular. "Come on, Chloe," I instruct her. "Lay back!"

Chloe seems to be in another world. "Oh, right, sorry." She arranges her things neatly, repositions herself and lays back with us.

We're all laying down now looking up at the dark, twinkling sky. Three friends, brought together by different circumstances, all comfortable in the stillness of the night. I'm listening to the waves crash against the docks and can feel the calming of my soul. I look at both of them, then back up to the endless landscape of the sky. I am amazed that you can find some of the most peaceful tunes in nature's music. My mind starts to wander, and thoughts of Briggs begin to populate my mind.

"I miss Briggs. Terribly," I say, breaking the silence, somewhat choked up and feeling vulnerable.

Henry and Chloe both reach over and grab my hand.

"I know you do, Evy. My heart hurts for you," Henry says quietly.

Chloe speaks up. "Did I ever tell you how I met Briggs?"

"No, as a matter of fact, you haven't. I'd like to hear," my heart is beating fast, wanting to know more.

Chloe takes a deep breath. "I need to preface the story with a little information before telling it."

"Go on," Henry encourages.

"Just to be upfront with you guys, I'm okay and everything is okay right now."

"Go on," Henry encourages again.

Chloe hesitates for a moment keeping us in suspense. "Before moving here, I…I…had cancer!" Chloe announces courageously.

"What?" I turn to look at her and my attention peaks even more.

"Girl, what?" Henry adds.

Chloe takes a deep breath. "Like I said, I'm okay. But yes, I was diagnosed with osteosarcoma or bone cancer. By the time I had moved here, I had finished my chemo, radiation and all that cancer stuff. My hair hadn't grown back yet, and I wore a wig until just recently." She went on about how Briggs had helped her when she fell that day. "I asked him to keep it our secret, and he promised me. Noticing from the shocked faces both of you have, I guess he did."

"He didn't even tell me and I'm…I was his girlfriend." *Wow!* I thought. That's my sweet Briggs, and what a secret keeper he was.

"Number one: You could always trust that guy. He always had your back," Henry lamented. "And number two, which should really be number one: Chloe? You just threw me for a loop. What the heck?" Henry sits right up looking dumbfounded.

Chloe responds, still laying down seemingly relaxed. "Yeah, I had just moved here and didn't need to draw more attention to myself or be pitied. I didn't want to be 'That New Girl with Cancer'."

I am sitting up by now, "Whoa, it means all the world to us that you're confiding in us. I mean, man, that's a heavy thing to keep to yourself. And all is good now?" I stare down at her tiny little frame.

"As far as I know. I have routine follow-up tests tomorrow." Chloe says trying to convince herself everything will be fine. She wanted to cut the subject off as she didn't want too many questions. "So, I hate to end such a lovely night, but I probably need to get back."

"You just dropped a bomb on us and now you're like, 'Sorry, I've got to go?'" Henry's eyes pierce Chloe's. He throws his hands in the air. "It's a big deal to us, Chloe."

"Agreed," I interject.

Henry is standing now, somewhat in a tizzy. "You are going to keep us posted on everything. Got it?"

"If that's what you want, I will." Chloe straightens her clothes then starts to get up. Henry reaches his hand out to her. "Oh no, you don't. Allow me to help you up, Madame Chloe."

"So now I get the royal treatment. Had I known, I would have played the cancer card and told you two earlier," she chuckles. Like a true Royal Queen, she positions herself back on the ground, purses her lips with a tilt of the head and outstretches her hand toward Henry. "Thank you, kind Sir."

Henry, ever the gentleman, lends his hand out to hers and helps her up. I put my hand out and he pretends like he is going to help me, then says, "Psyche," as he pulls his hand back. I fall back to the ground. So much for thinking he is a gentleman, *geez*.

"Just kidding, come on, Princess, we've got to go," and he helps me up.

I nudged him in his ribs. "Bad Henry. Bad."

CHAPTER 28

Chloe, along with her mom and dad check into the radiology center. Chloe is uneasy and is feeling as nervous as she was the first time she was told she had cancer. "It's just the necessary steps I have to do," she tells herself as she looks around the waiting room, trying to remain positive. There are several seating areas, and they take the back corner. Mrs. Wirrick fills out the paperwork, turns it in, and the wait begins.

About twenty minutes later the door to the waiting room opens, "Chloe Wirrick?"

Her Dad speaks up, "We will be right here waiting for you."

Chloe is led back by a nurse named Nicole down the long, narrow white hall to room number two. She instructs Chloe to take off any jewelry and to please take everything off except her underpants. Chloe does as she's told, then opens the door to let the nurse know she is ready.

Nurse Nicole takes Chloe to the next room. "Any allergies? And when was your last food intake?"

"No, Ma'am," Chloe responds. "Last night around 8:00 p.m." She could feel her tummy rumbling.

Nicole starts her rehearsed mechanical spiel, "Your doctor has ordered a CT scan with contrast. So, I'll be putting an IV in your hand to allow us to push the radiotracer and contrast through. The radiotracer is pushed first, then we wait for a little bit. Once we get the first set of pictures, we'll stop, and I'll come back in and push more contrast fluid in your IV. You'll feel a warm flush or even a sensation that you've wet yourself, but it will go away. Also, you may get a temporary metallic taste in your mouth. The most important thing is that you stay as still as possible once the machine starts. We will be talking to you and letting you know what we are doing, okay? Any questions?"

"No, Ma'am, I've done this before. Thank you." Although Chloe wonders why she would thank someone for doing this to her.

The nurse instructs Chloe to hop up on the gray faux leather table and to lay down. Chloe does exactly that. She looks straight up at the barren ceiling awaiting her next instructions. "Nothing like the docks," she thinks to herself, wishing she could be there with Henry and Evy.

"I'm going to get the IV started now, okay?" Nicole the nurse says as she ties a stretchy blue band around Chloe's wrist. "Now make a fist for me. You're going to feel a little sting from the Lidocaine."

Chloe feels the quick prick of her hand followed by the stinging of the Lidocaine that lasts for a few seconds. She watches as the nurse inserts the catheter into her vein, success. Tape is placed to secure the IV, and the trickle of blood on her hand is wiped clean.

"All done," Nicole says beaming with pride of her expertise in IV placements. "Now I'm going to flush the radiotracer in through your IV so that the radiologist can see your internal organs better. Once I do, you'll wait here for about thirty minutes. Then I'll take you to the X-ray room. Pushing the medicine now."

Chloe takes slow breaths, trying to keep herself calm, she wants to be a good patient. Memories of this procedure pop back in her mind.

"I'll see you in thirty minutes," nurse Nicole says as she leaves the room.

Time to clear my mind and meditate, she thinks. Meditation is what got her through all her cancer treatments.

Her favorite thing while meditating was to picture herself flying. Her body would lift with ease and soar into the sky, flying like a bird. It felt exhilarating being able to swoop over trees and bodies of water and look below. She could flap her arms, lifting herself off the ground. Within seconds she was airborne, ascending into the sky above. Soaring high she feels limitless, free from any pain, or ailments. She lets her mind relax and take her on a journey.

The nurse comes back to get Chloe and leads her to yet another room. The room is cold and makes Chloe shiver a bit. She pulls her blue and white hospital gown tighter around her. Placed in the middle of the room is a large, round machine in the shape of an upturned donut with a narrow table going through the middle; the CT scan. Chloe knows it well.

Nurse Nicole taps her hand on the table portion. "Here we go. Go ahead and get up on the table with your feet toward the middle of the scanner."

Being the perfect patient, Chloe makes her way onto the table and adjusts her position to do as the nurse asks.

"I'll come get you when you're done. The tech in the room over there will be instructing you on what to do. The most important thing is for you to be as still as possible. Any questions?"

"No, Ma'am," Chloe says, sounding confident more for the nurse's sake than hers.

When nurse Nicole leaves the room, Chloe is left lying on the sterile, uncomfortable table ready to be swallowed up by the X-ray machine.

"Hi, Chloe," the tech's voice comes across the speaker. "We are ready to start the procedure. I'll be giving you instructions. Are you ready?"

"I am," she replies. The table starts to move like a conveyor belt, bringing her body slowly toward the donut machine. *Fly,* she tells herself. *Fly high.* And away she soars.

CHAPTER 29

The weekend came and went quickly. Chloe, Henry, and I went to see a movie on Friday night.

We'd been dying to see *A Long Day's Journey Into Night*, for its fifty-five-minute 3D long take. Critics had raved about its cinematic brilliance, and being filmmakers, it was a must see for us. It didn't disappoint.

I spent Saturday at home in my room writing a paper for my English class. At least I enjoy writing. Give me math or science and I'm lost. But writing of any sort comes easy for me. I've been writing stories since as early as I learned to write. My mom has saved everything I've ever written. She tells me one day I'll be a famous writer, and I'll want to see where I got my start.

Around 6:00 p.m., my mom knocks on my door. She is dressed in black jeans and an electric blue colored sweater with short boots on. "Mom and daughter date night?" she asks.

"Yes! Great idea and good timing. I just finished my paper. Give me thirty minutes to get dressed?" I notice my mom has started taking a new interest in her looks. There has been something different about her lately. She'd been going to Spin class on her days off. In place of her usual style of pulled back hair with a knot at the nape of her neck, she is wearing her hair down and curled. Weird to say this, but my mom is looking hot.

"See you downstairs in thirty," she says with such delight in her tone.

I change my clothes, then go to the bathroom and splash water on my face to wake up. I take a good look at myself in the mirror. Maybe I need to take better care of myself? I can't let my mom look better than me. I take out my makeup and put a dab of concealer under my eyes and powder to finish. Add a little blush and mascara, and presto! What a difference it makes in my appearance. As I am brushing my hair out of my eyes, the pinky ring Briggs had given me catches my attention. I twist it around so I can see the musical note. I let out a large sigh. "Oh, Briggs." I head downstairs.

Mom and I go to eat at our favorite Italian restaurant on the Bay. To start, we order bruschetta to share, and Mom gets a glass of her new favorite cabernet: Caymus. For dinner I order the daily gnocchi special, and mom goes with the spaghetti Bolognese. We are having a great time catching up. We are both so busy during the week, so nights like this are cherished. Despite feeling stuffed, we manage to split a Tiramisu for dessert. As we are walking out the door, we bump into Mr. Corbin. He is with a guy friend who seems to be about the same age. It's kind of weird to see your teacher in a non-school setting. I have to remind myself he's a normal person with a life.

"Hey there, Evylyn," he says grinning.

"Oh, hi, Mr. Corbin!"

He is still smiling. "Fancy running into you here."

"Right?" I turn to my mom who is right behind me. "Um, Mom, this is Mr. Corbin, my film teacher."

"We've met," my mom confides with a smirk on her face.

Corbin's grin gets even bigger, "Hi, Charlotte, good to see you. You look so nice tonight."

He already knew her. He'd never mentioned that to me. *Something is weird here.* Was he flirting with my mom? Did I see him wink at her? I can't help noticing their eye contact. I keep glancing back and forth watching them. They are obviously not strangers. "That's interesting. You guys know each other?" I am feeling puzzled.

My Mom immediately answers. "We've met through mutual friends before."

Corbin introduces his friend "Monte" to us. "Monte, this is my student Evylyn, and you've met Charlotte."

"Hi, ladies," Monte chimes in.

Then as if he is trying to change the subject, Corbin puts out his hand to shake mine then my mother's. "Good to see you ladies. Have a great rest of your night."

My mom is unbelievably giddy. "You two enjoy your dinner."

We get outside and I turn to look at my mom with my nose scrunched up in wonderment,

"Mom? You know my teacher?"

"Yes, I told you, we have some mutual friends."

"And that's all?" I am quite skeptical.

"Yes, Evy," she replies, although her face may have said something different. "I do get out of my cage sometimes."

"Interesting," I hiss back.

CHAPTER 30

Monday has come too fast. It's getting harder to be motivated about school. My Mom says I have "senioritis." I must agree. I wish school were, only four days long, actually three, with Mondays and Fridays off. When I go to college, I'm going to try to get Fridays off. I've heard a lot of kids say that they never have Friday class. I'll keep my fingers crossed.

I wake up this morning feeling the need to see the blue-haired Mrs. Wall today. I don't have an appointment, but figure I can walk by and see if she is in. I knock on her door as I look inside her office searching for her and must take a double look. She is now pink-haired Mrs. Wall. She waves me in. I feel a sense of relief that she is here.

"Happy Monday, Evylyn," she greets me. "Are you here to talk?"

"Yeah, do you have time? And you can call me Evy by the way." I enter her office and sit in the green chair again, although I don't feel as uncomfortable in it this time.

"Okay, Evy. What's up?" she asks.

"How long does grief last?" I need to know.

She ponders for a moment. "That's a good question. We all work our way through grief at our own pace. There's no right answer to your question. Everybody is different. Each day that passes will get easier for the most part, and you may have setbacks along the way. But it's okay to feel a wide range of emotions."

"But it's hard…to make sense of what Briggs did. I just don't understand it."

Mrs. Wall moves her chair closer toward the desk. "Have you ever considered that perhaps it's not ours to understand?"

"I was afraid of that. Do you think that's why I keep having a horrible nightmare about Briggs? In my dream he can't breathe and no matter how hard I try; I can't help him." The thought of the dream sends shivers up my body.

"I sense and feel your pain." Mrs. Wall reaches across the desk and offers her hand.

I place my hand in hers and she holds it tight. "Can I share a story about Briggs with you?"

"Yes, please." I need to hear about him. She has my undivided attention.

"One day this past November, Briggs came to my office unannounced, carrying a bag. He placed it on my desk and asked me if I would do him a favor. When I asked him what kind of favor, he replied, 'I need you to give this bag of stuff to a kid in our class.'

"I asked him what was in the bag. He told me had brought some new clothing, a few gift cards, and an envelope with money in it. He wanted me to anonymously give it to the young man, as he had noticed that he was wearing the same thing every day.

"'He said to me, "The kids make fun of me." I can't bear to see them do that to him. I want him to feel special. He deserves it.'"

My heart starts warming so intensely, it takes my breath away.

"That's the kind of person Briggs was…caring and considerate. He had such a good heart. I've never in all my years had someone do something so special like that. I'll always remember him for it," Mrs. Wall with the now pink hair says.

I wipe at the tears forming in the corner of my eyes. I sit with that memory for a second.

"Thank you for that story," my mouth starts twitching, trying not to tremble. I nod my head again and again, "Yeah, I needed that." I manage to break a smile.

CHAPTER 31

PLAYLIST #8: "RISE UP" BY ANDRA DAY

Chloe is getting ready to leave for school. She is just about ready to walk out the door to her car when her cell phone rings. She can see the name "Dr. Neeves" come across her phone.

"Hello? This is Chloe," she answers.

"Hi, Chloe, this is Liz from Dr. Neeve's office. She'd like you to come in tomorrow at 4:00 p.m. to go over the results. Does that work for you?"

"Can we make it 4:15 so I don't miss school?" Chloe asks.

"Um, let me look here at the schedule."

There is a long silence. Chloe takes a deep inhale.

"Uh, yes, that works. We will see you at 4:15 tomorrow," Liz from the office says.

Chloe hangs up the phone. Her mom is close by listening.

"Was that the doctor's office?" her mom asks.

Chloe, a little startled, answers, "Yes, Dr. Neeves wants to see me at 4:15 tomorrow. I guess." She feels a sinking in her stomach.

"I'll let your father know. Let me drive you to school tomorrow, then we'll pick you up and take you to your appointment so we can all go together. I'll arrange for your brother to stay with a friend after school."

Chloe composes herself, "That sounds like a great plan, Mom. Thanks." She put on a brave face and smiles at her mom. She gathers her backpack and water bottle.

Her Mom walks toward her and places her arms around her. "Are you okay?"

"I will be. I've got you and Dad by my side," she says as she grins trying to reassure her mom.

They walk out the door each heading to their own car. Chloe feels thankful her mom has offered to drive her tomorrow. She feels unsettled and must admit to herself that she really is scared this time. She can't shake the feeling something is wrong.

Chloe gets into her car, and sits for a moment. *Music. I need music,* she thinks to herself. Evy and Henry have been rubbing off on her. She reaches for her phone and scrolls through Spotify. "That's it!" The music starts to blare as she musters a smile.

CHAPTER 32

The next thirty hours waiting for her appointment goes by at a snail's pace. It's uneventful, minus the anxiety Chloe is trying to ward off. The waiting game is gnawing at her deep within. She is feeling so many mixed emotions. 3:45 p.m. is finally here. "Amen," she says under her breath to herself. She hurries to meet up with Evy and Henry at the lockers.

"Just wanted to say bye to you guys. I'm heading to my doctor appointment," Chloe says as she comes up to Henry and Evy.

"I'm keeping my fingers crossed for you," Evy says to her.

"Thanks."

"You'll let us know afterward, right?" Henry asks.

"Yes, of course," Chloe nods then hugs them both. "Talk later." She heads down through the hall and out the front door.

Chloe's parents are outside at the curb waiting for her. They have just pulled up in their black Tesla. She spots her mom and dad and waves at them. She is happy to see them even though she knows where they are going. Chloe gets in the car, and they are off to her appointment.

"How was your day?" her dad asks.

"Pretty good. I aced my English test."

"I have no doubt you did, smarty pants," her mom chimes in.

There is quite a bit of traffic for some reason today. Chloe, being a stickler for time, keeps checking her watch worried that she will be late. She looks out the window to try to calm herself, all the while her mind is racing. She thinks of what she wants to say—no—*needs* to say to her parents.

"Mom? Dad?"

"Yes," they both reply in unison.

"Whatever the results are, I'm okay with it. I've made peace with it."

Her mom turns around to look at her, and her dad looks back at her through the rearview mirror.

"We are all in this together, you know that, right?" Her mom's hand reaches toward Chloe.

Chloe takes her mom's hand and replies, "That, I can count on."

Twenty minutes later they arrive at Dr. Neeves's office, with five minutes to spare. Chloe checks in and joins her parents who have already taken their seats. A Snapchat arrives on her phone from Evy. It's a picture of Evy and Henry morphed into monkeys from the Snapchat filter. Across the picture Evy has scribbled *"You've got this!"* Chloe's face lights up. She looks at the picture and thinks to herself how thankful she is for those two. She replies with a returned monkey Snapchat filter of herself and the words *"MUA-Love your little monkey." I don't think I'd make a good monkey,* she thinks as she looks at her own picture, and hits send.

"Chloe?" the nurse calls out.

"Yes?" Startled, Chloe stands up with her parents and follows the nurse back down the hall.

The nurse has her stop at a station to get her weight and blood pressure. As she jots it down, she notes that Chloe has lost two pounds from the last visit. When she's done charting, she brings them to the consult room to wait for the doctor.

About five minutes later, Dr. Neeves knocks on the door and comes into the room. She takes a seat at her desk in front of the three of them. Chloe can't help but wonder what a difficult job Dr. Neeves must have. She must sit in front of people every day telling them news they may or may not want to hear.

Dr. Neeves begins, "Chloe, I'm going to give it to you straight." She pauses. Chloe can see a more serious look come across the doctor's face. Her body flushes and endures a sickening feeling that is flooding her body. She instinctively grabs for both of her parents' hands.

"I had hoped for better news, but I am sorry to say that your cancer is back." Another long pause.

Chloe's mom gasps, and Chloe turns to look at her. "It's okay, Mom."

"Please tell us the findings," her dad urges.

"Yes, please," Chloe encourages more answers.

"All right, the leg that you are having trouble with, where the original tumor was, has only a small tumor, but it's between the patella and tibia junction probably causing the pain and problems you've been having."

"That's not too bad," Chloe's mom says.

"There's more," Dr. Neeves interrupts. "The scan shows multiple new tumors dispersed all throughout the abdomen and encompassing the pancreas. We are now dealing with soft tumor sarcoma."

"How many new tumors? And at what stage?" Chloe asks without flinching, trying to be brave. She wants to cut to the chase.

Dr. Neeves looks at Chloe, then to her mom and dad, "Chloe, I am sorry, but you have significant metastasis. The cancer has progressed to possibly Stage 3 or 4 this time. Your tumor markers are also quite high. It's not what I was expecting."

"So, what can we do? Is Chloe going to be okay?" her dad asks in a panicked voice.

"This type of cancer at this stage is very difficult to treat, but it can be done."

Her Dad stands up, "Difficult? What are you saying?"

Chloe starts to feel ringing in her ears and perceives a wave of nausea overcoming her.

"Mr. and Mrs. Wirrick, Chloe, what I'm saying is that it appears that the cancer has spread rapidly in a short amount of time, and it concerns me."

"What is the cure rate?" her mom asks while Mr. Wirrick starts pacing the room.

"I don't have all the answers now, but in my experience, this is a very aggressive cancer. Cancer is very person dependent, so I'll need more information and tests."

"You've got to be kidding me, right?" Her dad's voice is growing louder.

"Dad, it's okay. Dr. Neeves? What are my options?" Chloe tries to get back in control.

"Chloe, we need to get more scans to see the extent of the metastasis past the abdomen. I suspect there may be further involvement in this type of circumstance."

Mr. Wirrick is still pacing. "For Christ's sake, is there any treatment? I need answers!" He shouts in a voice much louder than either Chloe, or her mother has ever heard.

Chloe turns and looks at her dad feeling bewildered, "Please, Dad."

Her mom extends her hand out to Chloe's dad and mouths, "Sit!"

Mr. Wirrick paces momentarily, then sits back in his chair, resting his head in his hands, not wanting to look up. "I'm sorry. I'm sorry."

"Continue please," Mrs. Wirrick says to Dr. Neeves.

"I know it's not what any of us expected. I want to get more scans as soon as possible. I want to do some research and consult with some colleagues, but the likelihood is that we will need to implement a very intensive chemotherapy regimen."

Chloe can't stop her head from spinning. She is numb. She had the feeling earlier that things might not be okay, but she didn't want to believe it.

"I'll have my nurse schedule the PET scan as quickly as possible, along with a follow up appointment. We will have more answers at that appointment. Any questions for me Chloe? Chloe?"

Her mom nudges her, "Um, I'm sorry. What did you say?"

"Do you have any questions for me?" Dr. Neeves repeats.

Drowning in disbelief, Chloe realizes that she is slumped over, so she straightens herself up. "No, Ma'am, not currently. I guess we will know more after the next round of tests?" she says, trying to put on a positive front.

"Correct. But please feel free to call my office if you have any questions."

"Thank you." Chloe nods her head in response. *And I'm thanking her for bad news?* she says to herself. She gets up from her seat followed by her mom and dad and walks out of the room leaving Dr. Neeves at her desk. Her Dad stops and turns to look back at Dr. Neeves.

Chloe hears him say, "She's my baby," as he chokes on his words. "My baby." He looks directly into Dr. Neeves's eyes to plead with her. A few seconds pass, he turns to leave and catches up with his girls.

The ride home seems to take longer than usual. There is light chit chat between the Wirricks, but regardless, there is an overwhelming silence in the air that hangs heavily, weighing everyone's hearts down. The devastating news has left them all feeling severely wounded.

Chloe inhales deeply, cutting the silence. "I don't want my friends to know. They already have so much going on…Please let's just keep this within our family."

Chloe, trying to get her mind in a better place, begins to stare out the window and take in her surroundings. To shake off the pit in her stomach she is feeling, she decides to look around try to feel an appreciation for things she has never noticed. She senses the need to start to see things in a new light now. She is distracted by the ding from a text message. It's Evy.

How did things go at the doctor?

Chloe stares at the message hesitating before responding. *Everything is good.*

Great news monkey. I'll let H know.

Yeah, great news, she says to herself. She presses her forehead against the window staring out at the road trying to find something to be happy about.

CHAPTER 33

There is a strange pull on my soul this morning. Do you ever have that feeling that there's something you need to do, but can't figure out exactly what it is? That's how my morning starts. My mind is distracted and all I can think of is Briggs. Intuitively, I keep pulling up my phone and looking at our old text messages, almost expecting to receive one any minute from him. My thoughts distract me so much that I can't get out the door on time. I almost forget my backpack and must turn around to get it. I feel like I am running in circles endlessly, and I don't know why. As I'm walking out the door, I see my mom in the kitchen. I run quickly to give her a hug.

"Good morning, Mom," I say, kissing her cheek. Her skin feels so soft and warm.

"Morning, love. Have a good day. Do you have plans later?" she asks as she sips on her morning tea.

"Group project stuff again," I reply as I head toward the front door in a hurry. "Bye, Mom, got to go."

"Evy? Keys?" she says smiling as she dangles my keys in the air.

I look back hurriedly, "Oh, right. Might need those." I run back into the kitchen and grasp them from her hand.

"I'm losing it today. Thanks, Mom." I'm out the door in a hurry.

I call up Henry when I get into my car. "Henry?"

He answers on the second ring. "What's up, gorgeous? Are you on your way to school?"

"Barely. Just got in the car. Can I come get you?"

"Of course. I'm ready when you are, sunshine."

In less than ten minutes, I arrive at Henry's house. He is sitting on his porch staring intently at his phone.

As I'm pulling up, I hit the button to roll down the window and shout, "Need a ride?" My music is blaring with my Citizen Cope playlist.

"Only from you, but hold on!" Henry rushes into the house and comes back out in a couple minutes.

He seems frazzled as he gets into my car. But once he's settled, he gently takes my hand and squeezes it while giving me an odd look. I steer the car back onto the road and head toward school.

"I'm glad you called me today."

"Everything okay with you?" I can feel that strange pull again. Something is up.

Henry takes out his phone, tapping his finger on the screen. He clears his voice before speaking. "Do you know what popped up on my phone?"

"No, tell me," I insist.

"Well, I completely forgot about this, so don't be mad, okay? And for the record, I'm only following the instructions."

Not knowing what he is about to say makes my stomach turn somersaults. Surprises are not my favorite thing lately. *Please don't be anything bad,* I think to myself. "Hmm, do I have to promise?" I ask him.

"Yes, although I know you will still love me regardless." His eyes plead with me like a hurt puppy dog needing to be picked up as he says it.

"Enough already, let it out, Henry. What is it?"

"Keep your eyes on the road. Okay, so Briggs," he pauses, leaving his mouth open and teeth showing in an *uh-oh* kind of way.

He has my immediate attention. Does he really think I can just drive and not be bothered by the mention of Briggs's name? I stare with blazing eyes at him, then look in the rearview mirror so I can pull over.

"I'm pulling over." I move lanes, and the car comes to a stop. I raise my voice. "What is it, Henry? What about Briggs?" I can feel the heat rise from my chest to my head.

Henry takes a big sigh. "Truth is, I completely forgot about this until I got a reminder on my phone this morning when I was waiting for you. I swear. That's why I ran back into the house."

I can tell that Henry is feeling uncomfortable, which is an unusual emotion for him. As he continues talking, he starts squirming in his seat and pulls something from his pocket, "Right before Christmas, Briggs gave me this envelope." He sheepishly holds it in the air for me to see.

My eyes pop open larger than they have ever been. A sense of disbelief gets the better of me. My heart is beating out of my chest.

"What the hell, Henry? And you forgot to tell me?" My bottom lip trembles.

"In all fairness, he said he wanted to do something special for you and to keep it a secret until today. Maybe a little treasure hunt for you, kind of like you had done for him on his birthday last year, is how he phrased it to me. So, I didn't think twice about it. I completely forgot. So much has happened recently. That's all I know," he pauses, and puts on a forced smile cocking his head, "But

I remembered today thanks to my phone alarm."

He reaches his hand out with the envelope and offers it to me. "Sorry, Ev, and you know I love you and would never keep anything from you intentionally." He hugs me.

"I know…I know," I say, accepting his apology. I give the envelope in his hands a once over before taking it. Trying to lighten up, I remark, "And you didn't even try to open it? Such restraint, Henry."

"As if!" he banters back.

I stare at the envelope, shaking my head in perplexity. I glance at the screen on my phone. "Shit, Henry. Look what time it is. I can't read this now; we're going to be late, and I don't want to be all emotional before school starts. You need to hold this for me. I'll wait until after school." Henry delicately takes the envelope back from me and places it inside his backpack "Got it. I will keep it safe. Hang in there, Ev. I didn't mean to drop this bomb on you, just following orders."

"That's why I love you, Henry." With my mind a little boggled, I somehow manage to drive us to school.

CHAPTER 34

Chloe's morning was to start with her follow up visit to Dr. Neeves's office. She rode with her parents and sat in the backseat with her ten-year-old brother Ben. They had to drop him off at school before the appointment. Ben was a good kid and looked up to Chloe. She couldn't help but admire the sweet innocence he possessed. She reflected to herself at that age when she was free of worries and most importantly free of cancer. Scooting closer to Ben, she puts her arm around him. He looks up and smiles brightly at her. She's sensible to the need to hold on to every minute now and holds him tighter. The car slowly pulls into the school driveway.

"We're at my school!" Ben says with so much excitement in his voice. He grabs his backpack and opens the door.

"Bye, Mom and Dad. Bye, Chloe. I love you!"

"I love you too, buddy," Chloe says with as much cheer as she can muster.

"Have a good day, Ben," her parents say in unison.

As Ben shuts the door, from out of nowhere, a pain inundates Chloe's abdomen. Her smile turns to fear, as she catches her breath and clutches her side, trying not to mutter a sound. *Dammit,* she thinks. *Dammit.*

The Wirricks arrive at the parking lot of Dr. Neeves's office. Mr. Wirrick gets out first and opens Mrs. Wirrick's door, then goes to Chloe's door and opens hers. He holds his daughter's hand as she emerges from the car. His grasp lingers longer than normal, as he wraps his fingers around her delicate hand tightly. Her mom joins them, and they form a circle and hold each other.

"We've got this, right?" Mr. Wirrick says, trying to hide the faltering of his voice.

"Team Chloe," her mom says with a forced enthusiasm.

Trying to hide her own fear, Chloe responds after taking in the sight of both of her parents, "I love you guys."

They hold hands and walk toward the office as a force to be reckoned with.

Within fifteen minutes of arriving, they are called into the room to wait. This time, upon sitting, they immediately hear a knock.

Dr. Neeves arrives with a chart in her hands and takes a seat facing the Wirrick family. The air in the room becomes heavy and silent. Chloe looks at Dr. Neeves and sees a solemnness in her face that she has not seen before. Chloe begins to experience a warm, stingy, flushing sensation and her heart starts pounding in her chest. She knew before she heard the words. "I'm sorry to let you know Chloe, but the cancer has metastasized to other areas in the body. It's stage 4 cancer."

Her mom cries out in a shriek like a wounded animal and covers her mouth. Her dad stares ahead blankly. The world stops for Chloe. Her ears start to ring and momentarily, she has a lapse of unconsciousness. From the dark she emerges, flying high over mountains, into the clouds, soaring across the sky seeking comfort and peace. But somewhere in the distance she can hear something that startles her. "To the brain." Suddenly Chloe feels the loss of her arms, her momentum declining and her body becoming heavy, diving down, falling quickly from the clouds until she is saved by someone's arms. She snaps back into the present, finding herself in her mother's arms, wrapped tightly around her. Words start to formulate in her ears in slow motion fashion, "Ulti…mately…it's…terminal…but…we can…prolong the…cancer…with high doses…of chemo, which may…give you up to…six months longer…I'm sorry, Chloe."

Chloe, now conscious, sits with those words for a minute, and collects her thoughts. "I'm not going through chemo again. It's not worth it. I want to do it my way."

CHAPTER 35

My day passes slowly making it difficult to concentrate on schoolwork. I text my mom to ask if we can meet for dinner tonight. "Going to have a tough day today," I tell her. The contents of the envelope have made my mind spin. All day long my thoughts have drifted to why? *What could it be? Why did Briggs plan this?* He absolutely knew he wasn't going to be here to give it to me. That fact alone felt like a dagger cutting into my heart and wounding me again and again. The raw pain of grief and helplessness are the worst pain to experience, and I was in the throes of it. My sweet Henry can see that I'm sinking and has even suggested that we skip out for lunch and read it then. My heart wants to, but my rational side reminds me to wait, and so I have. Despite realizing that I alone am putting that excruciating pressure on myself by not opening the envelope now, I still can't bring myself to do it. Some things are better in a different setting, and school is not the place to have a mental breakdown. I needed to be at "our" place—the docks.

Speaking of prevention, I decide to stop by Mrs. Wall's office, hoping to catch her. What I have started to realize is that there is true value to being able to talk freely or being heard by someone who doesn't really know you. They can be much more objective without judgment or feeling like you're burdening them, so to my quirky school counselor I go. Mrs. Wall, now lavender-haired Mrs. Wall, greets me with a big, "Howdy!" It must be Texan day.

"Giddy up," I reply with a smirk as I imagine Mrs. Wall riding on a horse in a cowboy hat, lavender hair flowing in the wind as she rides off to the sunset. I'm happy I can find a little humor today. I walk myself to the green chair and sit. Maybe I'm getting used to this routine.

"Good one. Must be my southern roots coming out," she says giggling.

"Are you from Texas?" I inquire as I drop my backpack next to the chair.

"Yes Ma'am! I grew up in Austin, Texas. They say you can take a girl out of Texas, but not the Texas out of the girl," she giggles a bit more and slaps her hand on the desk for added emphasis.

"I didn't know that," I say, giving a wink and cocking my head to the side giving my best Texas impersonation. With my phone still in my hand, I can't resist the scene I clearly see coming, and snap a quick picture of Mrs. Wall, mostly to humor myself.

"Fun fact, it's illegal to milk someone else's cow in Texas. Max fine is ten dollars. Heck, I'd do it just to do it. Ten dollars is nothing."

I'm sitting here in the jungle green chair getting a kick out of her. "You don't say?"

"It's theft of personal property. Anyhoo, what do you have for me today?" she says as she slicks her hair back out of her eyes.

"Well, here's a doozy. Henry gave me an envelope from Briggs today. He said that Briggs had asked him to give it to me today." I emphasize, "Specifically today. And to top it off, when I woke up this morning, I had a weird feeling like I had forgotten something."

"How are you feeling about that?" She stares straight at me, but with gentle eyes.

How was I feeling? Like shit. I want to throw up. Feelings of despair start bubbling up inside me. I want to hold back my truth, but I let it out. "Mad! I'm mad. I'm sad, I'm hurting. I'm…I'm just overwhelmed." Tears stream down my face. My hands are drawn to my eyes pressing on them, hoping I can stop the tears.

Mrs. Wall gives me a much-needed moment.

Barely catching my breath, I manage to spew out more words, "I'm so mad! It means he knew he was going to be gone. He planned his death. He knew…I didn't." Defeat had set in.

There is a long steady silence, as I wipe my tears and try to conjure up a smile. "That's what's going on."

Mrs. Wall draws in a deep breath, "It seems he did know, Evy. The pain he was carrying around must have been so unbearable for him. That breaks my heart." She went on, "Know that I see you. I see your pain. And you know what? I'm here for you. You're going to hurt before you heal. And more than anything, I wish I could take your pain away."

"Thank you," I reply, knowing she really means it.

"Briggs must have had a good reason to have Henry give you that envelope. Did you open it yet?"

"What?… No." My mind is foggy and I'm not really listening to her. "Wait, wait! That's it. It would have been our one-and-a-half-year anniversary. I've felt off all morning, like there was something I was missing. Oh, shit, it's our anniversary." The daggers start back chipping away at my heart. Suddenly, I'm mad at myself. *How could I have forgotten?* Typical of Briggs, to remember. He was so thoughtful, always thinking of others and especially me.

Mrs. Wall gets up from her desk and comes to my side and

hugs me from behind. "I'm sorry, Evy," she says as she rests her head on mine.

Her hug feels not only surprising, but much appreciated. Because at this moment, what I really need is my Briggs.

My thoughts turn to him as he had the best hugs. I recalled the day after our "first date" at the docks. I had arrived at school by myself and had just gotten out of my car, when I noticed Briggs had parked a spot over. Excited to see him, I took a chance and went over and knocked on his window. No surprise, he didn't hear me, as he had his earbuds in, and his head and shoulders were swaying with the music. His fingers were tapping on the steering wheel like a drum. He amused me, so I knocked again while pressing my face to the glass. He must've finally noticed something in the corner of his eye. Because as he turned to look, he about jumped out of his seat when he saw me. I couldn't help but laugh seeing this extremely tall guy hit his head on the roof of the car. He leaped right out of his car, as quick as he could, all the while cracking up with a contagious laugh and literally grabbed me, bringing me close to his body, arms wrapped around me, and swung me around. He didn't let go of me, nor did I want him to. There was comfort and belonging in his embrace making me feel safe. If only I could be in his arms right now.

My thoughts return to the present, almost forgetting that Mrs. lavender-haired-Wall is right next to me. Reeling my mind back in, I respond, "I appreciate you listening to me. Thank you."

"That's my job, no thanks needed. And, Evy?"

I look back at her, raising my chin up, and wiping my eyes again.

"Take comfort in knowing that someone as special as Briggs will not be forgotten. You're making that happen."

Her words make me smile. "True, thanks for the reminder." Before walking out the door, I quietly whisper, "I appreciate you."

I continue walking in a daze down the hall until I hear "Princess!" being called by Henry.

"What's up, H?"

"Sorry I sprung that on you. You look a bit desolate still."

"Caught me. I just left Mrs. Wall's office. I'm just having such a hard time with all this."

"I know, and I'm right there with you. This all sucks. It's hard to keep a happy face on some days. And, because I know how much you are hurting. You hurt, I hurt." His lips start twitching, doing his best not to break down.

"You hurt, I hurt," I echo his sentiments. Then we give each other a hug, mine more of a long clinging hug in honor of Briggs. "I love you. I'm wallowing in my own grief and forget that you might be hurting too. You know, Mrs. Wall has been very helpful to me with everything. Maybe you should go see her. But I'll warn you, she is now lavender-haired." I try to lighten the mood before I get swallowed up again in grief.

A smirk immediately pops up on my face as I remember snapping her picture. "Check this out." I take out my phone and show Henry her picture. It's a fantastic shot of her; her mouth wide open mid-laugh and her eyes are twinkling.

"Good one," Henry laughs. "It's an epic pic. Maybe I should go see her. At least just to see the hair. *Ha.*"

We compose ourselves and continue walking to our next class when Henry remarks how he hasn't seen Chloe at school this morning yet. Come to think of it, neither have I. I wonder what she is up to, so I send her a Snapchat of Henry and I making a funny kissy face, and I caption it: "*Where's our monkey?*" We make it to English class just in time, but I still haven't received a Snap back.

It isn't until we arrive at our film class that we finally catch up with her. Henry and I are at our seats already when she walks briskly into the classroom. She arrives a bit winded right as the bell rings, which is unusual for our Ms. Organization. She looks discombobulated or something. I can't put my finger on it.

Henry rises out of his seat and sings out to her, as I wave, "There she is, Ms. America!"

Chloe fumbles awkwardly with her backpack trying to free her arms and wave back with her best pageant wave and a smirk. Her face is flushed and from what I can tell, her eyes seem a bit puffy.

"Hi guys!" She gives an exasperated semi-type of smile and takes her seat. Her phone dings, and she starts searching for it. Once she finds her phone, she looks at the screen with a grimace. She looks up and turns to us to say, "Sorry, just seeing your Snap."

"All good? We didn't see or hear from you all day." I speak.

Henry adds, "We missed you. Where were you?"

I see Chloe elongating her neck and straightening herself up. Her face starts to flush.

"I... I…"

She was interrupted by Corbin before she could tell us. "Hello, class. Happy end of the day. Let's start the class off with this question today: All right, all right, all right," he is wringing his hands moving swiftly around the room. "What is the one film you secretly love but don't like to admit?" He looks around the room, spins in a circle, stops and points his finger at his first prey.

"Randy, you're on deck."

Randy, dressed in all black with his dark long locks and brown eyes looks up from his desk, "Aw, Dude. I need to think."

"Dude? Think away, but I'm coming back to you," Corbin says. "Let's see, Susie?"

Susie perks up when she hears her name. She's a bit of a drama queen, always talking in exclamations and questions, "Oh wow? I knew you'd call me!" She pauses, rolls her eyes way too many times, "I'm going with…*Sharknado*? Fan girl of Tara Reid! Don't hate me!"

Corbin says, "Well, I'll admit, I've seen all six movies. Good one. Now back to you Randy."

"Okay, I've got it. You may not know this, but aliens are my jam. I'm going to say *Close Encounters of the Third Kind*. I get so stoked about UFOs and all that stuff," Randy is geeking out as he says it.

Corbin continues walking around the room, squinting his eyes one minute, then raising his brows the next as he speaks, "Nice retro throwback to my generation. And I'm sure you're wondering what your favorite teacher would say, so I will let you know…and the winner is: *The Room*!"

"Boo," a couple people yell out along with a few laughs.

"Hey, now, *The Room* is absolutely a cult classic. This movie kills me. Take *The Room* as a comedy, and you can't help but laugh. True narcissism at its best. Plus, there are so many classic lines! Spotlight please. Chloe, can you come up here?" Chloe looks around, "Me?"

"Yes, have a seat on my desk."

She does as he asks and approaches the desk and pops up on it to sit.

"Thank you, Chloe, let's set the scene. You are Lisa, Johnny's girlfriend who has just accused him of abusing her. You are apathetic to my response. And you will have two lines," then he whispers quietly in her ears. "Got it?" he says out loud.

Chloe positions herself on the desk ready for the scene. "Got it!"

Corbin magically transforms himself into Johnny Wiseau's character, letting his hair out of the ponytail, shaking his head back and forth to loosen up his hair. I decide to stand up and pretend to be the director.

"Okay, ready on set? Scene One, take one, and…action!" I clap my hands. My video starts, I'm not going to miss the chance to get this on film.

In his best impersonating impression, Corbin's voice changes and the scene begins. He walks up to Chloe in anguish taking the scene very seriously.

The scene peaks with Corbin giving every ounce of his acting ability. Both hands are made into fists, positioned on either side of his face. He drags them down slowly as he delivers his scene stealing moment.

Chloe walks away from Corbin and delivers the last line unemotionally as directed.

The scene is over, as Corbin and Chloe take a bow. The whole classroom gets to their feet, with a standing ovation and clap endlessly. Henry lets out a two-finger whistle.

"Thank you, thank you," Corbin and Chloe reply together. Chloe seems to be in a much better place now from when she walked into the classroom earlier, her heart a little lighter it seems.

"All right, that was my Oscar performance of the year. Thank you, Chloe. Now enough of my self-indulgent silliness, let's get to work on our projects," Corbin says exhilarated.

Henry, Chloe, and I join at our usual table.

"Performance of a lifetime, Chloe!" Henry says with enthusiasm. "That was pretty funny!"

"Right? Totally wasn't expecting to be put on the spot like that, but I should know better with Corbin," Chloe says.

"Loved it, Chloe." I looked around at the two of them. "What have we got guys?"

Henry jumps in first. "Everything is falling into place. My design for the T-shirt is finished. Want to see?" He reaches into his backpack and pulls out a folded piece of paper that has the design on it. He unfolds it and places it in the middle of the table ever so proudly.

My eyes scan the design with joy. The front of the T-shirt is very simple with the words "HAPPY FACE" in all caps. The back design has the same smiley face emoji as my button with the website address at the bottom www.happyfaceproject/Briggs.com. It is simple, and to the point, just as we had discussed. I had secured the domain name a week ago and Chloe had been working on the website. Everything was coming together, and I couldn't be more pleased.

"Nailed it, Henry!" Chloe shouts out.

"You guys like it?"

"As if? Hell, yeah. So what color are we going to do the shirts?" I ask with curiosity.

"Yellow or white shirt, with black lettering. What do you think?" Henry asks.

"Why don't we do both? Two styles. Is that okay?" Chloe wonders.

"We can do whatever we want. Both it is! I'll get it sent out. The guys say they can get these printed as soon as we give him the okay."

"Debbie downer here, but how are we going to pay for this? I've got some money saved up, but definitely not enough," Chloe says with a hint of sadness as she starts to calculate the costs in her head.

"My Mom and Dad are floating me on this. We will pay them with the profits until they recoup their money, and the rest is our profits that we will use to buy the pins and pay for whatever else is needed. So, are we good to send to press?"

"Yes! Do you think we can start selling them next week?" I want to know. I'm so ready to get this project off the ground. I'm ready to launch this, for Briggs.

"For sure, I'll let you guys know," Henry says beaming with pride.

We open the website and add some footage and pictures we had taken over the past few weeks. Most of the footage was already in our iMovie clip I'd been editing for the class presentation, so it was easy to transfer the digital footage. Henry had been working on the music, adding songs we had found that would add impact to our presentation and to the website. Besides working on the website, Chloe has been gathering the statistics and resources associated with suicide. Lucky for us, both projects have fallen easily in sync with one another and didn't add that much extra work.

The best part about this, is that it doesn't feel like work or boring old school. What the three of us are doing is a labor of love. I've heard that term many times, but I've never been able to say I've ever done anything that gives me this much pleasure. I thought I had, with films I've created, and music mixes I've put together. Most of those things were for me to enjoy. And yes, I've shared my stuff with others, but more for the entertainment of it.

What we are doing now I realize, is making a difference and doing something for others. We are bringing a long-overdue awareness to mental health. Tragically, it was not done in time to have saved Briggs or anyone else who has lost their life due to mental health issues. That fact makes me terribly sad. If only I could have done something, Briggs would be at this table sitting here with us. I miss him.

I look up and smile as I watch my friends continue to work. Henry is helping Chloe on the computer, and they are laughing. "You are my people," I couldn't help but say. They both stop and look at me.

Chloe blows me a kiss and Henry, being the cheeky guy that he is, says, "And don't you forget that."

CHAPTER 36

PLAYLIST #9: "WHEREVER I GO" BY NOAH RINKER

Early evening is my favorite time of day. The hours before sunset, when the sun has cooled, but the darkness has not set in, bring me peace. It's like the world slows down for just a short time, calm settles in and everything is just right. It's my time for thinking and solving life's problems. So, I like to come to the docks right after school and channel my thoughts. Henry gave me the envelope from Briggs at the end of class. He knew I wanted to be at the docks when I open it. "Do you need me there?" he had asked in his sweetest voice.

"I'll be okay," I had insisted. "Just give me a little time, then swoop in and take care of me."

I hurry to my/our spot with my trusty blanket to lay on the ground. The envelope is in my hand, my body is on pins and needles, feeling more like pins, but I'm anxious to read it. First, I need to take a picture of it and capture whatever essence of Briggs I can. Then, I slowly edge my finger along the seam to gently open the sealed envelope, careful to preserve it. My fingers start to tremble as I pull the letter from it. Only it isn't a letter. Across the top of the lined paper are the words: "MY SONG FOR EVY." I take another picture, getting every square inch of the written words. *Holy shit, it's a song. Briggs had written me a song.* Another piece of my heart feels like it is being ripped from my chest. I catch my breath, and it hurts to swallow. He promised he'd write me a song one day, and he did. Tears stream uncontrollably down my cheeks. I wrap my arms around my legs, pulling them to my chest and hold myself tight, rocking in a hypnotic sway, song in my hand, and sobbing.

A few minutes later the tears have ceased, because truly I think I've cried every tear I have. There is a surge of confidence that begins to radiate within me. *I can get through this,* I say to myself. Before I can read the words, I collect myself, wiping my face with my shirt, and taking a deep inhale, followed by an even bigger exhale. My fingers and body are numb. "You can do it," I tell myself again. And so, I begin to read the words painstakingly crafted by Briggs for me.

THE BEST OF ME

Days were dark until you came along
Too heavy to bare all alone
Eyes that dug into my soul
Lifting me out of my despair

If I lose my way, you hold me tight
Your heart beats in synch with mine
In your arms, the place I know
Where your love frees my mind

(Chorus)
Will you be the best of me,

Strong when I'm weak,
Let me breathe you in deep
So you will be the best of me
Best of me

I was broken but you saw me whole
Gave me your heart and eased the pain
Hold me in the love you made
Warm, and soft and oh so sweet

Stay close my love, for I may fall
Only strong because you're near
My quiet certainty, my safest place
Seal my wounds with your soul

(Chorus)
Will you be the best of me,
Strong when I'm weak,
Let me breathe you in deep
So you will be the best of me
Best of me

Only you can see what I can't see
You're the love I need to rid the dark
You make me known when I hide
Elevate me to a place of peace

You are who I need to be,
I want to climb into your soul as one
Show me your way my love
For without you I'm not whole

You will be the best of me,
Strong when I was weak,
You breathed me in deep
You will always be the best of me
The best of me
Please, my love, be the best of me

My hands hold this everlasting gift that will forever be with me. On one hand, my heart leaps with abundant joy, touched by the most amazing words, but on the other hand, the wound in my heart opens wider, allowing for more pain to seep into my soul. Two juxtaposed emotions suspending me in a black hole, not knowing how to feel or where to land. But what I do know is that these bewitching words from Briggs are meant for me. He wanted me to feel him, feel his presence, feel his love, even though he isn't here with me.

Then suddenly, a strange warmth engulfs my body sending chills throughout, my skin flushes, and I am gasping as my breath is taken away. "Briggs?" I whisper, looking around. I swear I felt him. I close my eyes and stay still for a moment inviting him back. "Are you here, Briggs?"

"Briggs?"

Nothing. My eyes wander searching for him. Sadly, only the sounds from the crashing waves respond to me. *Swish! Swash! Crash!*

Holding the paper, I open it again to re-read the words of my song hoping to feel Briggs again. In my heart, I knew at that moment he had been with me and hopelessly, I need him to come back. Minutes pass and sadly, he doesn't.

Meticulously, I place my song back into the envelope and slide it into my backpack. Uncrossing my legs, I get up and walk toward the water, where the lapping of the waves continue calling for me. I watch the water ebbing in the most harmonious way. The waves are gurgling and splashing, kindling their own glorious sympathy. At times like this when the day is settling, and the boats have come in, the ocean gets its turn to create unparalleled music. Hypnotically, I watch my reflection in the water, expecting Briggs to come from behind me, hugging me, lifting me off the ground.

This was our place, the place where we got to know each other's deepest thoughts, and know each other in many ways, as friends, and as lovers. We fell in love over and over here. Had we been able to, we would have stayed here together forever. I have so many wonderful memories here, but one in particular happened about two months after we started dating.

It was a Friday night, and Henry had invited us to go out on his family's boat. He took the three of us out and we cruised the ocean, staying close to shore. We listened to music, laughed and watched the sunset together. About two hours in, Henry heads back to the marina. Once we got there, he handed over the keys to me and said he had to get back home as he had dinner plans with his family, but he told us to stay and enjoy the boat at the docks and to lock up when we left. He winked at me as he left. "Say goodbye to the third wheel," he said. We stayed of course. I think Henry had planned all along to give us some alone time. Briggs and I sat at the bow of the boat in the still of the night. It was as if we were the only two people in the world. We were deep in conversation, but I can remember his deep blue eyes that matched the ocean turning to me, staring into mine, cutting deep into my soul. I knew at that moment; I would be forever lost in him. He gently kissed me, our tongues entwined, searching, each giving each other permission to explore. I took Briggs' hand and walked him to the lower cabin. It was this night that Briggs and I made love for the first time. I wanted to stay there all night wrapped in his arms and never leave his side.

CHAPTER 37

I must have been walking around the docks for a while before Henry and Chloe arrived. Startled by their voices, I turn to see them as they are coming in my direction. Henry is waving fervently at me. "We are here!" I can hear him say. I glance back at the water one more time looking out into the distance before turning to meet them. "Coming!" I shout back.

I start walking back up hoping I don't look like a disaster, but I realize they won't care. Henry turns to wait on Chloe before joining me. She walks with her usual grace, perfect posture, and that wonky leg. He holds her hand, walking alongside her as if he's escorting someone famous. He is dressed in pressed white shorts and a pink linen button down. Henry is destined for the good life, impeccable manners, good looks, and all the wow. Chloe is in the same outfit she wore to school: an A-line dress with a belt cinched at the waist making her already petite frame look even more petite. And here I am in my high waist jeans, a cropped tank and a swollen face from crying. *I've got to up my game,* I decide.

"Just taking care of Ms. Daisy here," he says as they approach.

"Daisy? Don't you mean Miss Chloe?" Chloe retorts.

"Clo, please tell me you've seen the movie *Driving Miss Daisy?*"

"Noooo, never." She scrunches her nose. "I guess that means I need to?"

"Uh, yezzzzzz. You've been missing out. My mom and I have watched it several times. It's an oldie, but a classic. You'll get a kick out of it."

He turns to look at me, then gets closer and starts examining me closely, shaking his head back and forth. "Oh no, my Princess, I knew I should have been here earlier." He gives me a big hug with Chloe looking on with worry in her eyes.

"It's all good. I needed some 'alone' therapy. It's really been a day."

Chloe speaks up, looking surprised by what she says, "I know what you mean! Dammit." She made an oops gesture with her mouth. "Crap, I mean, are you okay?"

"Yeah, as good as I can be, just sad." I exhale deeply. "Did Henry tell you?"

She nods her head. "Yes, he did. What was inside? I mean...if you're okay with telling me?"

"Of course. Here, let me get it so I can show you guys." The burdensome pain of heartache returns to my body.

"Was it another letter?" Henry asks as he scoots closer to me.

"No, he wrote me a song. Can you believe that?"

Henry draws in his breath, as I hold the envelope close to my heart. "Here, one of you read it out loud. I just can't," I say in all seriousness.

Henry made the short arms gesture, putting his hands next to his shoulders like a T-Rex, showing he can't grab the letter. "Holy shit, I don't think I can. I'm just too emotional. Chloe, you do it."

"Me? Well, I'd be honored to." Chloe delicately extends her hand out to take the paper and begins to read the hauntingly beautiful words out loud, without any hesitation, or pause.

I close my eyes as Henry holds my hand and listens to the words written just for me. I can concentrate on the words better this time, taking in every single syllable, running a melody in my head to Briggs's words. Henry is tapping away at his knee to the words; he too, is creating his own melody.

Chloe manages emotionally to keep it together, speaking in her eloquent voice, enunciating every word perfectly, creating a masterpiece for our ears. When she finishes the last verse, she hangs her head low. I see the look on her face, eyes squinting, emanating a low breath followed by a deep inspiration. We all sit silent for the next few moments.

I break the quiet. "He knew he wasn't going to be here. It's killing me knowing that."

Chloe is the first to respond, "Yes, that's got to be hard. Those words though, they're a true gift…he was troubled, but it is so evident that he loved you, Evy." Chloe wipes at her eyes. "Sorry, I'm just a little emotional."

She touches Henry's leg for reassurance, which causes him to burst out in an ugly cry, "God, me too!"

Well, shit! Their crying starts a chain reaction in me, and I begin to cry. Then suddenly, Henry snorts, not just snorts but snotty snorts. He looks embarrassed. I lose it and for some reason I start cracking up, trying to cover my mouth. Chloe looks at me, then busts out in a voracious laugh, followed by Henry. We can't stop laughing hysterically. My belly hurts from laughing so hard. It's exactly what we needed to lighten the mood.

The giggles finally end, well almost. Once I contain my laugh, I thank them both for being here. Henry asks to look at the song again.

"May I take a pic of the song? These are epic words," Henry says.

Henry, like me, likes to document moments. He arranges the song on the blanket, snaps a couple pictures, and hands it back to me. "Just beautiful," he says under his breath, putting his hand to his heart. He sends me the shots via text.

Carefully, I put the letter away again in my backpack, when the thought comes to me that I haven't asked Chloe about her day. "Chloe, what about you? Where were you today, you never said?" I question her.

Chloe goes from sitting up, perfectly poised, to looking like a deer caught in the headlights. "Oh," she pauses, smoothing out her dress. "Yeah, I was at a doctor's appointment. Anyhoo, are you guys ready to get started?"

"Back it up, I thought everything was, okay?" says Henry.

"Yes, I'm good. They just wanted to do some standard follow-up tests; you know. Routine stuff. Update me on my meds."

"You'd tell us if something was wrong, right?" I want to know. She seems a little off today.

"For sure, standard follow up. Cancer never really ends for cancer patients. They test you month after month, year after year to make sure nothing has returned. It's a waiting game. Has it returned or not? I told you guys, the doctor said I'm good. Yay me."

"Thank the universe, as we love our Chloe!" Henry announces.

The thought of cancer terrifies me. Knowing something could be growing in you, lurking in the shadows and waiting to be found. It would be like living in a constant nightmare scene. Poor Chloe, so tiny, yet brave facing this monster we call cancer. "It has to be scary for you, right?" I say with concern, not so sure everything is so hunky-dory.

"Yes, it just becomes a new normal. So, I'm learning to appreciate every day, like noticing the little things…like you two goofballs,"

Chloe lets out a little giggle. She was changing the subject.

We stay for another hour or so working on our project. We film some needed scenery and each other. The sun starts to set signaling the time to wrap things up. It has been a long simmering day, with my emotions being on a rollercoaster. I think my dinner with Mom will do me some good.

CHAPTER 38

Mom is waiting for me at The Boat restaurant. I walk in to find her in a back booth looking out the window. I stop for a moment before walking back, I can't help but to just watch her. It strikes me how beautiful she is. The sun gleams on her face, making her complexion glow and her light brown, sun-kissed hair with loose waves frame her face. She looks radiant. When you're a kid, you just think of your mom as "your mom." But lately, I have found myself appreciating my mom for who she is and what she is. She is so much more than my mom, she has quickly become my friend, my confidant, and someone I really like. My heart hurts for a moment realizing that our time together is slowly narrowing with me heading off to college. Mom sees me, grinning with a big smile and immediately starts waving. I smile back, holding back my unexpected tears and approach the table. *Geez, could I be any more emotional today?* I slip into the booth.

"Hi, sweets," she says as she hugs me.

I hug back tight, holding on a little tighter and a little longer. She holds me and kisses the top of my head. The smell of my mom comforts me, everything beachy and fresh mixed together. I start tearing up, this time the flow can't be stopped. My Mom continues to hold me, cradling me in her arms until I settle down.

"Tell me about your day?" she says as she grabs her napkin from her lap and wipes my tears.

I need a second to collect myself before speaking. I use my sleeve to wipe the snot running down my nose from crying—nice manners, I know. Reaching into my backpack, I grab the song from Briggs and carefully place it on the table.

"It's from Briggs. He gave it to Henry before everything happened. He wanted Henry to give it to me specifically today, which is," I take a deep breath, "would have been…our one-and-a-half-year anniversary."

My Mom's eyes grow big, and a look of sorrow crosses her face as she looks into my eyes. "Oh, Evy."

"He wrote me a song. I want you to read it," I say meekly.

The server comes to the table introducing herself and asks what we'd like to drink. She is wise enough to see that she is interrupting a moment and takes the cue. "I'll get you guys some water and be back shortly," she says.

"That would be wonderful, can you give us ten?" Mom says with a wink.

"Not a problem," the server says and hurries away.

Mom takes hold of the envelope, brushing her thumb over my name written on the front and carefully removes the letter. She unfolds the paper and smoothing it out flat, then wraps her arm around my shoulder. I can't help but lean in and place my head on her chest as she begins to read. I can hear her heartbeat, and I let the rhythm of her lifeline lull me. There are moments her hand squeezes me tighter and pulls me in. Gently I feel a drop of wetness on the side of my face and realize it's a tear coming from my mom.

My tears start to stream again.

Mom inhales deeply, then exhales before speaking, "My words are failing me." She holds me tight and leans her head against mine with a small kiss on my head.

We sit in a comfortable silence for a couple moments before she speaks again and turns to look into my eyes. "It was his way to make sure you knew how much he loved you. You meant so much to him. I know that doesn't make it easier for you but take it in for what it is…an extension of his love. He wanted you to know that in some way he will always be with you."

I need to blow my nose before speaking as my sinuses are all clogged up from crying. "Yeah, that's what Henry, Chloe, and Mrs. Wall tried to tell me today. It's just…it's hard knowing that he had this all planned and I didn't know he wouldn't be here."

"You couldn't have known. The truth is that the only person we can ever really know is ourselves. I'm proud of you that you are talking with me, your friends, and especially your counselor at school. When your father died, I struggled. I needed to be strong for you and Jules. Oh boy, did I struggle with so many things. I didn't get to say the things I wanted to say to him before he left this earth. I didn't get to hold his hand or stare into his beautiful eyes one last time. I never got to hear from him again. Our lives all blew up and all my dreams of a future with your father and our family were shattered. There was a lot of pain to struggle with. I fought so hard to keep that pain away until one day my therapist told me it's time to surrender. Sometimes," she pauses, "You too will need to learn to surrender to deal with what you're grappling with."

I chew on that thought for a moment, literally almost biting my tongue off. The server comes back to the table with glasses full of water and places them on our table.

"You girls ready to order?" she asks.

"Um, sure. I'll get the Buddha bowl." Mom looks at me.

"I'll get the same, no onions, please. Thanks," I respond. I don't have much of an appetite, but fuck it, I'm surrendering.

CHAPTER 39

The shirts we designed for The Happy Face Project finally came in. Henry promised to bring them to school today. I spot him as I am hanging signs in the hall. He is wearing the yellow version of the shirt with white jeans making quite a striking impression as he wheels in a couple big boxes on a dolly. I had to whistle at him. "Looking good, hot stuff!"

"You know it!" he shouts back. "Get over here."

I run up beside him and follow him to the table. We were allowed to set up a table in the hall outside the cafeteria to sell them. Chloe is already there at the table decorating and setting up the posters. We had hung up posters about our project earlier in the week promoting our website and the sale of the shirts to create some buzz.

"Hi, guys," she beams as she sees us. "Today's the day!"

We all high-five when we arrive at the table.

"Let's do this," Henry says. He opens one of the boxes to reveal the shirts and pulls one out. He admires it, then proudly announces, "Ladies, our official Happy Face Project shirts." He turns the shirt around for us to see. It's awesome.

"You girls need to put your shirts on. Which color do you want?"

I choose the white version as does Chloe. The two of us go into the bathroom and change into our T-shirts. The bell rings to remind us that classes are starting, so we leave the boxes there and head to our classrooms. Walking around school in our shirt feels like an honor. I'm getting a lot of thumbs up. We have a successful sale at lunch time. Then at film class we present Corbin with a shirt. He insists on buying it and immediately puts it on over his current shirt. Our film classmates all want to purchase them too. Corbin allows Henry to run to grab more shirts.

"Time for a class picture. Everyone put your shirts on. Evy, will you do us the honor?" Corbin asks.

"I insist." I take my camera out of my backpack, while everyone is lined up in the front of the classroom. I snap several pictures and do a little bit of video mode too. I give Susie, one of our classmates, my camera, and have her take one of Chloe, Henry, and me, and another one of the three of us with Corbin. We are let out of Corbin's class early so that we can get to our table before everyone starts getting dismissed for the day.

Henry is looking through the boxes. "Well, we are doing pretty good with sales. We've sold at least about half of our stock. Not bad for the first day."

"Not bad at all," Chloe repeats.

I smile nodding my head in agreement. *We are doing this for you, Briggs,* I say to myself as I look up hoping the roof will part and I can investigate the heavens and see Briggs smiling down at us, at me.

"Looky here," I hear coming from close by, snapping me out of my stupor.

"Mrs. Wall! Thanks for stopping by," I say. *In your now lavender with pink-tipped hair,* I say to myself. That lady has some spunk.

"Hi, guys. Great job. Love the shirts. I'm here to buy some," she says with a plethora of perkiness and dangling a hundred-dollar bill. "I need four for my family."

"Wonderful," Chloe says.

"You remember Chloe and Henry, right?" I say as I step back to line up with both of them.

"Memory of an encyclopedia," she boasts. "I'm proud of what you guys are doing. Everyone feeling okay?" She looks around at each of us.

"Yes, Ma'am," we all say in unison.

"The pink tips are the bomb, Mrs. Wall. Go, girl," Henry smiles and nudges me in the ribs.

"Flattery will get you everywhere," she snorts with a cackling laugh and does a little dance. "I need two X-large yellow for me and Mr. Wall and two white smalls for my kids, please."

Chloe takes her money as Henry starts rifling through the boxes to find her requested sizes.

My eyes get big, and I let out a laugh as I watch this interesting lady do her thing. Surely her quirkiness needs to be bottled up and sold.

"Can we meet again next week? Say Wednesday after school? I want to see your progress on the project and touch base."

Looking around with raised eyebrows at Chloe and Henry, I shrug and say, "That works for me."

"Me too," Henry says.

Chloe starts scrolling through her phone, takes a minute without looking up and says, "Yes that works. Let me write it down."

"Can you take our picture, Mrs. Wall?" I ask.

"Great idea," she says as I hand my phone to her.

The three of us gather behind the table. We all pose to show off our shirts. Henry has a big mischievous grin on his face as he squeezes my butt unexpectedly in good fun, causing me to awkwardly jump. He must have done the same to Chloe, as she lets out a squeal.

"Quite the ornery one, Henry," Mrs. Wall says, pointing her finger at him. "We are set then. See you rockstar seniors next week or sooner if you need me," Mrs. Wall says as she winks at me, then at Henry and Chloe.

I give a long-exaggerated wink back, my mouth is open in a gotcha, "Thanks for your support, Mrs. Wall."

"Toodles," she yodels as she prances away.

I almost expect her to jump in the air and click her heels together. I look at the pictures she took. She got some great shots, and in one of them she caught Chloe and I candidly in funny positions as Henry was pinching us. We stay about thirty minutes longer, staying busy selling more shirts. As I glance at my phone, the time stamp on my phone gets my attention. "Shoot!" I say out loud. "I've got to get going in a few minutes."

"Where are you off to?" Chloe asks as she starts putting things away.

"Meeting Mom for dinner."

"Tell her I said hello," Henry says. "What has she been up to?"

"Busy working. But I think she has been out with friends lately. Guess she's finally enjoying herself," I say.

"Good for her. She's too 'hot' to be staying home," Henry remarks.

"Eew, Henry? Is that appropriate?" Chloe gags, squinching up her nose.

"Uh, I'm calling it as it is. No shame. Beauty is beauty," Henry snaps back. "And girl, you're pretty hot yourself," he smiles as he gives Chloe a squeeze, causing both Chloe and I to start laughing.

We get everything packed up and bring out the boxes to Henry's car. We surprisingly sold a lot of shirts and will have plenty of money to pay for the Happy Face buttons and the project now. We decide to also post the shirts on our Instagram stories in hopes to sell them. It's amazing how much support we have received from our classmates and teachers already. We are on our way to doing something good.

CHAPTER 40

It turns out we made a couple thousand dollars on the shirts, selling every single one of them and received some donations. We exceeded our goal. Next step is to order the Happy Face Pins. To celebrate, we collectively decided last week to be rebels and go off campus to meet for lunch at Blue Sky Bistro today and to skip the first class after lunch. Senioritis is kicking in.

As I am parking, I swear I see my mom's car pulling out of the parking lot, but I think maybe I'm wrong. Maybe I'm going crazy. There are a thousand cars just like hers. She's working today anyway, so it couldn't be her, I tell myself.

I walk into Blue Sky wearing my ever-present pin over my heart. We wanted an exact duplicate of the one Briggs wore, so I have it for comparison. To no surprise of my own, I arrive to find Chloe at the booth waiting for us. I don't know how she is always so early. I need to take a few pointers from her. Suddenly out of nowhere, these two arms wrap around me and lift me off the ground. I scream and the whole restaurant looks at me. Embarrassed, I can see Chloe laughing at how startled I am.

"Henry! You scared the shit out of me. I almost peed my pants."

"Eew! Remind me to buy you Depends next time I'm at the store," he says snarkily and kisses my cheek.

"As if, WTF!" I chuckle as I catch my breath relieved to know I wasn't being abducted by some crazy person. "Don't do that again!" I pinch him in the stomach.

A man hurriedly approaches our table. And what? It's Corbin.

"Everything okay here?" He takes a double look. "Aw, it's you guys," Corbin says as he acknowledges each of us. "Up to no good I see?" he adds.

"Correct, sir. You did not see us!" Henry says straight faced staring at Corbin. "Top secret mission."

"Oh, right. Not like it's a school day today or anything," he says mischievously.

"You do not see us," Chloe speaks up. "We are doing schoolwork, but we were transported to this restaurant. It was out of our control."

Corbin looks around the restaurant and avoids eye contact with us. "Is someone talking to me? I hear voices but I don't see anyone, hmm, so strange."

We all cover our faces pretending to hide, only fooling ourselves of course. Mr. Corbin walks away from the table acting bewildered and looking around the room like he's searching for the voices. "Didn't see anything," he says loudly as he walks out the front door of the restaurant.

"So much for our clandestine meeting," I say.

"Corbin's cool, we're good," Henry says, taking his fork and banging it on the table. "All good."

Chloe looks at both Henry and I, shaking her head. "I swear you guys are a bad influence on me," she says sternly. "But honestly, I love it. I'm breaking the rules, and it feels damn right good. Jesus, now I'm cursing, and I mean *geez,* not Jesus. See what you guys are doing to me? Bad influences!"

Henry puts his arm around Chloe. "You're a rebel without a cause, and it looks good on you, Chlo! Now I just need to get you a black leather jacket and a cigarette to complete the look."

There's never a dull moment with Henry. And I do think Chloe is really enjoying coming out of her comfort zone and making some big social strides. Something has changed with her. She's no longer that wallflower. I see her newfound boldness. It's like she's reinvented herself or maybe she's finally just letting loose. Whatever it is, I like it.

On the way back to school, I feel the need to call my sister. I haven't talked to her in a while, and just need to hear her voice. I give her a ring.

CHAPTER 41

PLAYLIST #10: "BUTTERFLIES"
BY TOM ODELL, FEAT. AURORA

I pull into the parking lot at school just as I'm ending my call with Jules. I'm about to get out, when my attention is drawn to a monarch butterfly that just landed on my car's windshield. Gasping from the site of this beautiful creature, my breath is taken away and the memories begin to unfold.

Briggs had picked me up around 11:00 a.m. on a Saturday morning back in November for a surprise date destination. When I awoke that morning I checked my phone, and as always there was my text from Briggs. *"When you touch me, I feel butterflies."* It sent chills up my spine wondering what he had in store for me. All he told me the night before was that I needed to bring my camera and be ready for something spectacular. We listened and sang to music as he drove and within thirty-five minutes, we were pulling off the highway into an exit heading toward Pismo Beach.

"Pismo Beach, huh?" I asked.

"Well, not just Pismo Beach, we are going to somewhere special like I promised," he teased me, still not letting me know where we were going. He drove a little farther carefully watching the road signs for the next turn.

"Close your eyes now, my princess," he instructed. "I'll come open the door for you so, wait right here, and no peeking."

I did as he instructed. The car door opened, and I felt his hand grab mine. He lifted my hand up to escort me out of the car, then placed the camera around my neck. Once I was standing, he circled me around and I could feel his presence in front of me. The surroundings were quiet and peaceful, and I could feel the sun shining on my face and the distant sounds of waves crashing on the shores.

"Okay now, open your eyes."

When I did, I still didn't know where I was. All I could see was Briggs's handsome face and his steely blue eyes sparkling at me, his 6'5" body was blocking my view.

"Well, you make a better door than a window," I joked. "Where are we?" I couldn't wait to know.

"The Monarch Butterfly Grove. One of my favorite places," he gushed.

"I've heard of it, but have never been," I had to admit.

"It will be a great surprise then." He took my hand and led me down the path to the entrance of the grove.

"Here it is."

Still unsure of where he had taken me, I looked ahead to see a small grove of eucalyptus trees with vibrant orange beautiful flowers.

He continued, "Thousands of Monarch butterflies migrate here to find warmer climates and stay until late February. If you look up in the trees, all the pops of color you see on the trees are Monarch Butterflies." I took my camera out and started snapping some pictures. We headed inside the grove watching our steps on the gravel

186

path, our heads pointed up into the trees.

"Let's get closer, I can't wait to see," I said, smiling with excitement. We walked hand in hand into the grove which was not that large. Butterflies were floating all around us. I caught Briggs grinning with delight as he peered into the sky, then at me for confirmation. We continued until he brought us to a bench to sit on.

As soon as we looked up, we saw a flurry of butterflies fluttering all around us. "This is amazing," I said as I brought my camera up to my eyes to start snapping more pictures.

He wrapped his arm around me and said, "See? Surprise! Isn't this incredible? I knew you'd love it."

I turned to look at him, and a butterfly landed on his shoulder. I managed to capture this moment on my phone. "Look! There's one on your shoulder."

"Ha, don't move, Evy. There's one on the top of your head," he said as he carefully reached for his phone to take a picture of me.

"I'm in love with this place. How awesome is this?" I said in wonderment. "Is it still there?"

"Yes, stay still," his smile widened. "Do you know that if a butterfly lands on you, it can be a spiritual symbol for life after death. Like an angel sent from heaven," he squinted his eyes and nodded. "These little guys must have something to say."

I thought about what he said for a moment, then whispered, "Maybe it's my dad checking in on us." At the thought of this, my heart yearned for my father.

"Maybe it is," he replied and kissed me with his warm honeyed lips.

We sat in silence for a minute, continuing to look up at the sky in wonderment, watching these delicate creatures fly dizzily above us. I looked at my text from him this morning and recited it out loud to him. They were words from the song.

Then he whispered in my ear more verses. He took his phone and turned on his playlist and started playing the song "Butterflies." It was magical sitting there with him as we watched these mystical creatures fly above us.

Carefully I get out of the car, ever so aware to make sure I shut the door without making a sound or jolt. My finger gently slides over the windshield positioned next to the Monarch. Then, without much hesitation, its tiny little legs stretch out and clasp a hold on to my finger, perching itself ever so delicately. The orange and black wings gently open and close. I'm mesmerized watching this elegant flower of the sky allowing me to rejoice in its presence. I can't help but wonder if it's a sign from Briggs. He had told me that day that butterflies were supposed to bring you hope and peace. I stand frozen, making no sudden movements, and I am lost in thought wondering if Briggs's spirit is here looking up at me through the eyes of this butterfly. A few more seconds pass and sadly the Monarch begins to flap its wings at a faster pace and tenderly takes off. I watch the butterfly lift itself into the sky and fly away. Perhaps I, too, need to fly away from the grief everyone says I'm experiencing. *Grief!* Yeah, well, whatever the hell it is, I don't like it. I don't like it at all.

I stand for a moment feeling bewildered and wipe at the corners of my eyes, drying the tiny tears. I think of the transformation my life is going through and remember the words from the song he played that day. I hold hope that one day I am going to be okay.

CHAPTER 42

Over the past month, Chloe found herself bouncing from appointment to appointment. She could physically feel herself getting weaker, and strange pains were rearing their ugly heads here and there, catching her off guard most of the time. Regardless of anything she was facing, she told herself that every day she woke up would be an amazing day. She made a list of things she wanted to experience and do. She took great pride in writing down a motivational thought on a sticky note every morning and placing it on her mirror in the bathroom. Her mirror was starting to look like it had a new frame made from the yellow papers.

Today's thought was: *What we do for others will be remembered.* She was proud of herself for thinking of that one. She got out her marker and carefully wrote down this thought. She read it three times out loud, then gave the paper a quick kiss, slapped it on the mirror like she was giving it a high five, looked in the mirror, smiled and said to herself, *You are going to make a difference for somebody.* She cocked her head, then looked in the mirror again inspecting herself a little closer. Her eyes seemed to look a little hollower and she shrugged it off by reminding herself that she was in fact happy to be alive and how her blue eyes still had a magnificent sparkle to them. *Think positive!* she tells herself.

School had seemed to be a lot less time consuming as a graduating senior. She allowed herself to study less and have for more free time. Her grades were amazing despite less effort. Why she hadn't had more of a balance of life and school before, she wasn't sure. Over the years Chloe had worked so hard at school, studied many long hours, chose school over social activities, all for what? *Darn!* she thought to herself. *I could have had a little more diversion.*

Mrs. Wall had told her this week that she had Valedictorian in the bag by a long shot if she didn't go crazy and fail all her classes. As if! One thing for sure, is that Chloe would never let her grades slide, as she has always prided herself in being smart. It was who she was, and she loved to learn, but she did reflect on how having a balance of fun and studies would have been a little more memorable. "Bygones, I have the here and now to make those changes," she reminded herself.

She felt cool skipping lunch and going off campus with Henry and Evy a couple weeks ago. Maybe she was becoming a rebel like Henry had said. Meeting them in class had been the start of her evolution. She was quite thankful for the comradery they had brought to her life. The unfortunate loss of Briggs had, in a sense, brought them together. It amazed her how something so tragic turned into something that had helped them all heal in a time of need.

Her mantra of the day correlated well with who Briggs was as a person. He had made Chloe feel so safe and welcomed every time she saw him, especially as a new student. His smile alone was contagious, but his acts of kindness would never be forgotten by her, like the time he secretly stopped by her locker shortly after the fall incident and slipped a card inside for her. She recalled finding it in her locker, completely surprised. She read the words, "You are stronger than you know, and braver than you think. Stay golden. – Briggs" She had kept that card for inspiration. He was like the big brother she never had.

Chloe couldn't bear to think of another kid losing their life because they couldn't see that life could be better. She had been working so hard on the project with the other two. All their meetings and time spent together collecting data, researching suicide, making the video—it was all coming together beautifully. For all of them, it was an act of love for Briggs. Chloe felt the thorns of cancer daily, but when she was working on this cause, she felt energized and renewed. It helped her forget what she was dealing with. She knew she had a purpose now and a legacy to leave, and time was running out. And for this, she wanted to give it her all until she couldn't.

Today is Chloe's third appointment with her psychiatrist, Dr. Ronald Earl. He is an older gentleman, tall with kind eyes, square jaw, and a receding hairline of dark brown hair with a military-like buzz cut. She can remember walking into his office for the first time and seeing boxing memorabilia in the shelves, and pictures of, what she had guessed were him boxing. One of the plaques adorned on the walls was an honor he had earned as Heavyweight Boxing Champion in 1969. How he went from boxer to psychiatrist she had no idea, but she wanted to know. When he walked into the room, you couldn't help but immediately feel his presence. He was broad shouldered, and muscular, reminding her of John Cena, the wrestler. Initially, she was a bit intimidated, but once he started talking to her, he had put her at ease. He was kind of fun and playful, even with a serious situation such as Chloe's. He was easy to talk to, and she liked that.

"Chloe, we've gone through all the testing, and after reviewing the results, it's apparent that you know what you are up against. I'm going to commend you, as you are a strong, brave young woman. So, do you have any questions for me?" he asks with a sincerity in his tone.

Chloe sits fittingly in the chair, legs crossed in a comfortable position and replies, "Always a loaded question." She pauses for a moment, twitching her mouth and thinking, then replies, "Actually, yes." Wanting to turn the tables on him and take the focus off her for once, she asks, "What made you go from being a champion boxer to a psychiatrist?"

He chortled. "That's what you want to know? Well, instead of killing all my brain cells, I decided to use them. To be honest though, I still have a love for the sport, and I like to box in my down time. I do it more for exercise now. The days of aches and pains from getting beat up are over for this old man. Thanks for asking. But seriously, feel free to reach out to me if you need anything, otherwise we will continue our conversation in the next few weeks."

Chloe was proud of herself for coming out of her shell, so to speak, and being bolder with her conversations. She had nothing to lose, but so much to gain. *No regrets,* she told herself. She walked out of the office feeling pleased with their session today.

CHAPTER 43

I've been sitting on my bed finishing homework and had just texted Briggs's parents about our project. They had told me they were more than impressed to know we were bringing awareness to suicide and mental health and asked if we needed anything. I sent a message back and asked them to come to the presentation. They replied they'd love to come, "Wouldn't miss it." I have truly missed them and missed being at their house with Briggs.

Then I hear a ding and see that I get a Snapchat from Henry: *Get on Zoom now, I'll send link.*

Curious, I pull up my email and press the Zoom link from Henry. I log on and Henry's handsome face is waiting for me.

"What's up, bud?" I ask.

Right after asking, Chloe pops up on screen. "Hi, guys. What's going on?"

"Girls, it's time for an impromptu dance party, be ready to shake your asses!" Henry yells out in a wild voice that I'm sure makes both of us wonder what the heck is going on with our gracious Zoom host Henry.

"What the F, Henry?" I say with a growling laugh.

"What are we supposed to do?" Chloe chimes in.

"I've been working on some songs and I'm in a dance mood. Stop what you are doing now. Let's dance!" Henry grabs his phone and starts to blast "I Like It" featuring Pitbull from it.

"You want us to dance? Seriously?" Chloe questions.

"Hell, yeah!" Henry shouts.

I watch Henry jump around his room and sure enough, I start to do the same. Chloe starts to move around, straightens up her bed, and clears everything off. She pushes her hair behind her ears then places her hands on her hips.

Henry shouts out, "Dance queen!"

Chloe looks around, moving her eyes side to side then puts her hands in the air. "Okay, okay!" She starts to shake her hips and awkwardly starts to dance.

Wow, she's letting her guard down. The three of us are all cracking up, dancing and letting loose at our online disco. I can see that Chloe is mostly watching us. I can't stop smiling. I love Henry for his spontaneity. It always drawn me in.

Henry takes his shirt off and starts dirty dancing, one of his party moves. I watch as Chloe's mouth opens wide with embarrassment, but I can see she is having fun with it, despite her blushing.

Several minutes must have passed with us all crazy dancing. Then suddenly, I see the door to Henry's room open. He clearly doesn't hear anything as he continues with his dirty dance moves while his mom comes in. I stop dancing immediately, as does Chloe. We are both watching as his mom sneaks up behind him and starts dancing behind him. Next thing you know, he turns around in a spin and sees his mom dancing and comes to a quick halt. The look on his face is priceless. Both he and his mom are roaring with laughter.

He looks back at the screen at us and says, "Why not?"

He grabs his mom and swings her around, then dips her backward. It's so cute to see the two of them. Surprisingly Mrs. Preston has some amazing moves. I know where Henry gets it from.

Chloe starts clapping when the song is finished, and so do I. Both Henry and his mom take a bow.

His Mom looks into the computer camera and says, "Glad I could give you girls a good laugh."

Chloe adds, "Hello, Mrs. Preston."

I confide, "Girl, you got the moves."

"Well, good to entertain you girls. I just wanted to let you know dinner is ready, Henry. See you girls soon, I hope," Mrs. Peters says, as she waves goodbye and shakes her hips as she leaves the room, slapping herself on the ass on her way out.

"I'll be down in a minute," he shouts back. "Well, that was an interesting dance party with our surprise guest," Henry laughs.

"Now back to serious business," he continues. "Are we all ready for our presentation on Friday?" Chloe nods her head yes.

I respond, "Yes, I just want to pass some ideas by you guys before talking with Corbin. I need your input on this slight expansion of the senior project with the Happy Face Pins that Mrs. Wall and I came up with during our sessions. Here goes—"

"Like what?" Henry says.

I continue, "So we have plans for the pins to be distributed in boxes that will be hung on the walls in school. Those that need a little cheering up can grab a pin and wear it. Our project focuses on reaching out to those we see wearing the pin and asking them how they are doing and letting them know we care. The suicide hotline number will be on the back of each pin as well as Mrs. Wall's direct line, as discussed. That way, those in need will have a few more options for help. I also want to make sure that teachers recognize that if someone has a pin, to address that person and make a referral to the counselor. Mrs. Wall told me that she has started training at the local suicide prevention center and will be geared up soon to receive students. Secondly, she has scheduled an in-person training for our teachers and wants us to be there too. Are you cool with that?"

"That's brilliant, most definitely," Chloe says with enthusiasm. She thinks for a second, then as if a light goes on in her brain, she adds, "Why don't we make a little addition to our film project and add the concept of the pins to our presentation?"

"Perfect, I'm basically finished with my part. Got all the music, etc., finished. Evy, can you get the extra footage, then send it over to Chloe to edit?" Henry adds.

"No need to ask. It's a done deal. And Chloe, I'll help with the edit. I have some ideas," I say. "Okay then, Henry, once you get our footage, you can wrap it up. I know we are going to have to hustle, but we have a few days before the presentation. Thanks guys, I'm so excited."

"Let's meet Wednesday night to go over everything, okay?" Chloe says as she gets out her notebook and jots down the date.

"Afterschool at my house?" I ask.

We all agree.

CHAPTER 44

The week went by pretty fast. I spent some time in Mrs. Wall's office going over our presentation and having her help me with some fact checks. She's really pumped up about our new program. In celebration of it, she let me know that she planned to color her hair yellow, as yellow symbolizes happiness, hope, and spontaneity. *Isn't she just the spitting image of a sunflower?* I'm laughing, thinking about that image of her I have in my head.

Today is my day to see Corbin. Our group finished almost everything up except a few things I need Corbin to help me with. As I walk into the classroom, I see Corbin standing at the window looking outside deep in thought.

"Hi, Corbin!" I shout out.

"Hey, hey, just watching the birds on the tree. Springtime is nest-making time. Do you ever watch birds?" he asks.

"Oh, uh, no, never really. Isn't that for old people?" I say jokingly.

"Hey, I guess that means I'm getting old, or I am that old person. Damn. Anyway, good to see you."

"Yeah, you too. I'm excited about this project, and we've just about wrapped everything up," I say.

"Cool, have a seat," he says as he pulls a chair out for me. "I have a couple of surprises for you guys. Hopefully I didn't overstep."

Corbin goes to his desk, opens the drawer and pulls out a stack of pamphlets or something and smacks them on the desk for me to see. "First surprise. Here you go."

Curious, I pick up one of the pamphlets and read over it. "Whoa, are these for us?" I ask.

"Yes, I ordered them from the Suicide Hotline. Thought they might be helpful. Hopefully I didn't overstep," he says to me with his eyebrows raised.

"Actually, brilliant. Thank you. Great idea, somehow, I over-looked this detail. We have pamphlets with our project for the school, but having something official from the Suicide Hotline is a perfect addition to our presentation," I say, truly thanking him. I'm curious. "So, what's the second surprise?"

"That will have to wait. And no problem, I am more than hap-py to help with anything, just let me know," he says. "I only wish that this kind of support and awareness for mental health was in place back when my brother needed it. I know it could have made a difference," he goes on to say.

My heart felt a horrible piercing hearing him say that. It must be so hard for him.

I looked at him intensely. "Do you ever really heal?" I ask him, knowing that my heart still feels split wide open.

He sits silent for a second with his eyes staring away from me. He swallows hard, and I watch the pain rise in his chest and face before he can let the words out, I can see the answer is "no".

"Not really, Evy, I'm sorry to say that in my experience, you don't ever truly heal. You manage, you remember, life goes on, but you don't forget that pain of knowing what they did and that they're gone. Sometimes the rawness of it all still boils up and startles me at times. You know, I spent so much time trying to solve 'why' Wills, that's my brother's name, decided to take his life. Oh, I'd ache to the point of having to curl up in a ball and cry. But after a while, I realized I had to give him ownership of his decision." Corbin pauses and wrings his hands together with his head hung low.

I watch as his head starts to rise back up, and when his head is fully lifted, he has an enlightened smirk on his face. I let him continue.

"Now, I refuse to allow the stigma of suicide to define him. I celebrate the good things about him like how kind he was, his funny sense of humor, and how he'd crack up reading the *Peanuts* comics, which were never really that funny, his athleticism, and so many other things. Whenever I go to, let's say a concert, I think about how much he would have liked being here with me. Sometimes I even jot down thoughts about him in a journal. So, Evy, if I can tell you anything, talk about Briggs, it helps. Celebrate Briggs, as he is so much more than how he ended his life. So much more." Corbin inhales deeply then blows out his breath with a heavy sigh and shakes his head, running his fingers through his hair.

"Wow, sorry about that. I just unloaded a lot on you, Evy. Thanks for listening whether you wanted to or not. It helps me, but unfortunately, you just got way more than you bargained for." His mood turns, and he lets out a little giggle then jumps up and begins to pace the room.

"Not a problem. Unfortunately, we're kind of in the same club now," I say, fidgeting my thumbs. "And...I'm glad you were able to share about Wills. In a weird way, it helps me to feel better about everything with Briggs."

Corbin continues pacing around the room. He looks out the

window again, then looks over his shoulder at me to ask, "And speaking of Briggs, how is your mental health?"

"Well, besides feeling bipolar with my daily emotions, I'm hanging in there. Can't say I'm okay, but I'm finding that this project is really helping me. Most of all, I hope it will help others too." I truly do.

"Believe me, it will. You guys are doing something much needed here at the school. Heck, I should have thought about doing it. Anyhow, show me what you wanted me to look over." Corbin comes back to the desk and sits across from me.

"Yeah, I wanted to show you the rough video and make sure it all looks good. We are going to go over the presentation one last time tonight to finalize everything, so I need your input." I take out my computer and pull up my Vimeo account and within a minute I have the video on the screen. I fast forward to the last portion where I was worried about the transition from the stories to the facts portion.

I stare at Corbin scrutinizing his reaction as he watches what we've created. He seems interested and is raising his eyebrows. Then he gives a quick pound with his fist on the desk once it's over. My fingers are crossed that he likes it.

"You guys amaze me. Great job. I think you transitioned that scene well. I'm looking forward to your presentation tomorrow. And word has it that our principal Mrs. Arndt and Mrs. Wall will both be there. You guys now have celebrity status, so you better knock it out of the park."

"*Ha!* Thanks for the added pressure," I cock my head sideways as if to say *Really?* I pack up my laptop, then a perfect idea pops into my head.

"Corbin? Could you email me a picture of Wills? I'd like to

include him, if that's okay?"

"Cool, very cool. Yes, I will. Thank you." He wipes a surprise tear from the corner of his left eye.

"See you tomorrow then," I say smiling and start to head out the door. God knows, I don't want to make a grown man cry, or me. I squeeze my/Briggs's pin that is on my shirt and hold it close to my heart as I exit the room. I text Mr. and Mrs. Sullivan and remind them about the presentations tomorrow. I immediately get a response: *We wouldn't miss it.* I smile with delight.

CHAPTER 45

Talking about Briggs with Corbin, stirred me up in a way that consumed my every thought. I couldn't get Briggs out of my mind and needed to talk with him. It kills me to know that I can't physically talk with him, but something is pulling me to go visit his grave. I stop by the grocery store and pick up a Ramune drink and Hot Cheetos, get back in my car, and turn the music up. I select my song and drive to Briggs's gravesite with the windows down and music blaring.

The parking lot at the cemetery is bare. It makes me feel better, as I have my music on full volume, and it would have been awkward pulling up with someone there trying to have some peaceful moments with their loved one. It's not like I'm all cheery—I'm actually quite sad—but the music helps to calm my anxiety. The sun is shining, and a few clouds are making for a very tranquil environment. I grab my backpack, my blanket, and bag of goodies and head toward the cemetery.

My head feels like it's spinning, but somehow, I make it to

Briggs's grave. *Grave? How awful does that sound?* Seriously awful. It makes me cringe. *Resting place? Maybe that sounds better.* This is hard for me. I want him here with me now, laughing and holding me. Instead, I find myself here all alone, empty and heartbroken. The grass has grown over where he rests. Another sign that life continues. I place the blanket down and try to get comfortable. My eyes search my surroundings and lock in on his headstone. It reads: "Our beloved son Briggs Oliver Sullivan, may you always keep dancing to the music." I catch my breath. I take my phone out and take a picture of those words.

Oh boy, did Briggs love to dance. And he didn't just dance a little. He was a hard-core, all-out dancer. He told me he had begged his parents to let him take breakdancing lessons when he was little. He'd surprise me sometimes by breaking out a move or two randomly, especially when he had his air pods on listening to his music. He always made me laugh watching a tall guy with real rhythm dancing. Who says, "White men can't dance"? Turns out my Briggs could beat anyone on the dancefloor doing all the spins, pops, and moves.

I can remember when I first started dating Briggs, and Henry and I went with him to this house party at our friend Chase's house as his parents were out of town. Tons of people from school were there. Henry had brought his synthesizer and was playing DJ and spinning the tunes. He then announced he had a dedication to Briggs, something he loves to do, and told everyone to clear the dance floor as it was time to get down. Everyone scrambled to move the furniture out of the way, then Briggs made his way to the center of the floor. People gathered around while Henry changed the beat from house party to breakdancing music of the 80s. "Bust A Move" came on and so did Briggs. He pulled out a neon yellow bandana from his back pocket and tied it around his head like the Karate Kid. He was in full force, getting his groove on, doing the caterpillar, then flipped over on his back spinning, on to top rocks, power moves, and freezes. I clearly recall the smirk on his face and twinkling in his eyes, fully alive, laughing all the while he was dancing. We all cheered him on. At the end of his "performance" he grabbed me from the crowd and lifted me up, swirling me around and fervently kissed me on the lips feeling the electricity he was giving off. I loved that night. He was happy, I know he was.

My thoughts return to today. A long sigh leaves my body. I look back at the headstone. It's time we had a talk. "Hi, Briggs. I'm here. I really miss you. No, like it hurts so bad at how much I miss you. I wanted to come see you and tell you about what's been going on. Henry and I have become good friends with your buddy Chloe whom you had told me about. She's so cool and Henry and I just love her. You always had a way of connecting with good people." I'm sitting on the blanket while plucking the overgrown grass out. I adjust my position, trying to get comfortable, and turn to face his headstone again.

"So, I want to tell you about a project the three of us are doing in Corbin's class for our Senior project, but first..." I pause, and open the Ramune, then push the white ball down just like Briggs had taught me and watch as all the fizz starts to quietly explode in the bottle. I take a big sip, then open the bag of Cheetos. I munch on a few, then take another sip. I feel so many emotions build up in me fizzing like the Ramune bottle, ready to explode, and then literally I do. "I know this sounds weird, and a day late and a dollar short, but this project is being done in honor of you Briggs. That's right, we are doing this project for you. Yep, we are making a fuss out of you whether you like it or not. We don't want this to happen to anyone else. And you know what, I'm just so mad at you for leaving us, Briggs. I would have helped you, we all would have. You left us all to pick up the pieces of our shattered hearts. I don't know why you couldn't let us help you. You know we would have. Your parents, Henry, Chloe, me, and everyone else who knew you, are in pain. We can't let this happen to anyone else. I know you were in pain, but we are in pain now too." Tears are indisputably pouring out of every orifice of my face; complete water works are turned on.

I know I'm about to hyperventilate, and so I try to slow my breathing by pulling my knees to my chest and squeezing my arms tightly around them. I need to let out my anger; it's been building and building and now I'm exploding. I stand up and shout out loud, "Damn you, Briggs! How could you not tell me what was going on with you? I would have done anything for you. I loved you. I love you; I will always love you. I need you. Do you hear me? How could you leave me?" I'm sure I look like a crazed person, but I don't give a shit.

I collapse back down to sit, and bawl my eyes out, shaking, and taking in a much-needed pity party, complete with Ramune and Cheetos. Maybe ten minutes pass before I quit crying and suddenly, I feel a silencing calm overcome me. I think I cried out every stored-up fluid I have in my body, something I'm getting too good at. I take a deep breath to make sure I'm still breathing…and grab a hold of my Happy Pin on my chest to give me strength.

"Well, see what being gone does to me, Briggs? Did you ever think of that? I came here to tell you what we are doing, and I end up imploding on you instead. Honestly, I think I needed that, needed to tell you. And somehow, I feel better," I say and sigh deeply. I can feel some sort of quietude inside me now.

I continue in a rapid stream of consciousness telling him all about The Happy Face Project. "By the way, Mrs. Wall is excited too. She's even changing her hair color to yellow in celebration. And did you know that Corbin lost a brother to suicide? He's so proud of us for doing this and says he wishes they would have had something like this to have helped his brother. I'm going to make you proud, Briggs—we all are. We are going to make a difference, and this isn't the end of it. On a different note, Henry is doing great, and Chloe told us she had cancer, which you knew about and never told me. But I'll forgive you for that one. She says she's doing great. I don't know though, I worry about her, as she's been going to the doctor a lot, but says it's just typical maintenance follow-up stuff."

I catch my breath before continuing, "And, Briggs, sometimes I swear you are with me. I feel your presence. Am I crazy? I hope you really are near me, watching me and guiding me. If so, please, please keep visiting me. I miss your daily texts and music lyrics. I miss those blue eyes of yours, your smile, your hugs. I just...miss you." And with that, I say my peace.

I finish my Ramune, which has now lost its fizz, and shove down the rest of the Cheetos and look at my cheesy orange-covered fingers. I lick off the Cheeto residue, despite knowing my mom would be grossed out by the germs. "Never put dirty fingers in your mouth," she always tells me. "But for you Briggs, I'll do anything. Well, I've got to go now. I'll see you soon." But before I leave, I turn on my phone. "Almost forgot, this one's for you, Briggs, I love you." I turn up the song "Talk to You" and find myself doing a little swaying to the music, Briggs style, as tears roll down my cheeks and my heart aching for Briggs.

CHAPTER 46

Henry picks me up this morning and we make our way over to Chloe's house to grab her. We joke that we've become the three misfit "chums" since we all have issues. *Boy, do we.* Chloe was outside waiting for us. As she approaches the car, I notice that she seems thinner than she usually is and that leg of hers seems to be giving her more trouble. She smiles big as she gets in, hugging me and high-fiving Henry, beaming with happiness. I don't know, maybe she is okay.

"Good morning, chum! Are you ready for our monumental presentation?" Henry calls out to Chloe as he starts to drive away.

"You betcha. I've been counting down to this day. Did you guys remember to grab everything?" Chloe says curiously. She is not one to forget things.

"Oh no, was I supposed to bring something?" I jokingly add, wanting to frazzle her a bit.

"Very funny. Ha-ha. I'm just checking. You know me, a bit

OCD," Chloe replies.

"You don't say? A bit, or perhaps over the top?" Henry says. "And once again, that is why we love you. You are the syrup to my pancake, the X to my O, the ying to my yang. And that goes for you too, Evy. Need I go on?"

"Do please," I insist.

Henry continues, "The wax to my ear, the snot to my nose..."

"Eew, gross. Enough, Henry. Got it, thanks," Chloe responds.

We make it to campus early, as we have permission to go to Corbin's class before school starts to get everything set up. Corbin greets us at the door all smiles.

He shakes our hands as we walk in. "Good morning, guys. It's your big day."

"Indeed, it is," I say. "Thanks for letting us come in early."

"No problem. The room is all yours. Make yourselves comfortable. Don't mind me, I'll just be here if you need me," Corbin says as he heads to his desk and takes a seat.

The AV equipment was in the room waiting for us as Corbin had promised. Henry heads over there and starts setting up the computer and connecting it to the screen. We had to get everything ready now so it could be brought into the gymnasium for the presentation. Chloe had her flash cards out going over them and making notes. I was getting out the brochures and the pins to set up. I look at the basket full of pins and can't help but see all the smiley faces staring back at me. How many times did I see that pin on Briggs and not even recognize the importance of what a smiley face meant to him? Suddenly I feel a hug around my waist. It's Chloe, she must have seen me staring at the pins, and knew I needed a hug. I squeeze her hand wrapped at my side.

Henry decides to join us in our hug. We stay like this for a minute longer not wanting to let go. Three chums in a web weaved together by fate and tragedy but lifted at the same time with a common goal to be there for each other.

Henry calls over to Corbin, "Hey, Corbin, get over here and join us."

I see Corbin's face light up, his eyes bright as he looks at us. He immediately gets out of his chair and joins us. Our arms open to make the circle wider for him to join. Henry pulls out his phone and the music starts playing "Best Day of My Life." I grab my phone from my back pocket and snap photos of us. We all start to jump around in a clockwise fashion, singing the words out loud. And that is how we start our morning, celebrating life.

My day has been a whirlwind, and suddenly, it's about time to give our presentation. Henry, Chloe, and I had planned our outfits and changed in the bathrooms before we got to the classroom. We all wore white jeans with our yellow highlighter Happy Face shirts. Chloe decides to dress it up a bit with a rhinestone belt. She kills me, where is she getting this bold new outlook? Good for her. I make sure to compliment her on it. Henry is super metro with his Gucci driver shoes. *And me?* Well, of course, I keep it typical old me wearing white Converse. I keep forgetting that I need to glam things up—oh, well. All the students are in their seats waiting for class to start. There are a couple other presentations today besides ours. The bell rings and Corbin starts the class with his daily question.

"Question of the day," Corbin cocks his hand to the corner of his mouth as if it's on the down low, and says, "Which I may say is quite appropriate to the start of our presentations," he pauses, then continues, "What part of your brain causes stage fright?"

"Seriously?" yells out Susie. "Are you trying to freak us out?" Everyone laughs.

"Hypothalamus," Chloe speaks up with her hand in the air.

"You are correct, Chloe. The hypothalamus secretes adrenaline, which is your flight or fright hormone. And you can use that to your advantage by psyching yourself up. Touché, Susie. Bygones." He does a little 180-degree spin, then asks, "Does anyone have stage fright here in the class?"

Several people raise their hands. But once again, Ms. Bold, the newly feisty Chloe starts to talk again.

"I do, or did, but have gotten so much better over the years," she says matter-of-factly.

"And what have you done to help with your stage fright?" asks Corbin.

"Well, I'd like to say that you are correct in saying that you can use it to your advantage. Did you know that Margaret Thatcher had stage fright? She was quoted as saying, 'The energy you derive from it gives you more courage to press onward with what you have to say.' Furthermore, she liked to say: 'Come on, old gal, you can do it,' before each time she talked publicly. And TBH, I do the same, except I say, 'Come on, gal,' instead of 'old gal'. It works, I'm here to prove it."

Several chuckles are heard throughout the classroom. "Bravo," Corbin claps. Then the rest of the class claps. Chloe stands up from her desk, looks around, and takes a bow. Look at her go. She is fierce, and I love it.

It's time to head down to the gym now. Corbin wants the entire student body at the high school to see the senior presentations.

CHAPTER 47

As I'm watching the gym door open, I see Mrs. Arndt and Mrs. Wall, or, shall I say, Mrs. Yellow Sunflower with her new bright yellow hair? She's wearing black, hence the sunflower reference. They are followed by a…news crew? *What?* The camera on one of the guy's shoulders shows some news affiliate I can't quite make out. *Oh wow!* Are they here to film our presentations or what?

Corbin is grinning ear to ear, shouting, "Come on in, everyone. I have a little surprise for all of you. I invited KSBY of NBC news to come see what you guys have been up to this last semester of your senior year."

So that was his second surprise he was telling me about? Smooth move, Corbin. I'm impressed and giddy with excitement. Way to get the word out about what we are doing for mental health, so this is truly a fantastic move on his behalf.

The camera crew wave their hands at us as does Mrs. Arndt and Mrs. Wall. There's a lot of commotion and the news crew begins filming. Mrs. Wall tells us all to just act normal, they are going to get some footage. Then my mom walks in, *another total surprise*. I had told her about the presentation, but had no idea she would show up what with work commitments and all. I run and give her a hug. She looks beautiful and is in the cutest sundress. Mr. and Mrs. Sullivan walk in, as do Henry's Mom and Dad and Chloe's parents. I hug them all, as does Henry and Chloe, and lead them like a herd of goats to the bleachers to sit together. Several other parents are walking through the doors, then the students all start pouring into the bleachers filling up the gym.

Game time! The first group of students do their presentation on teen pregnancy prevention. They do a great job and receive lots of applause. I'm impressed with their delivery. I don't really get nervous about talking, I get super pumped up and love the feel of adrenaline surging through my veins. We had pulled the paper out of the hat that had designated us as the second presentation. We were already up behind the curtains waiting and making sure we had everything ready. It's our turn now. The three of us look at each other knowing we need to deliver our message loud and clear.

Henry takes our hands, squeezes them and starts to sing, "Best Day of My Life." Then he plants a kiss on each of our cheeks.

"It's go time!" I speak.

We all nod and head toward the stage to take our place. I accidentally bump into that Amber girl from film class. She is not happy about it and scoffs at me. I apologize, but she still gives me the stink eye. *Geez*, it's not like I meant to do it. I can't let this frazzle me, so onward I go.

The lights go dark as per our instruction. We wanted to create a darkness and set the tone for the seriousness of our topic. I turn on the music, and the presentation starts. We selected the song "Be Still" by the Fray as our introduction to set the tone. It's about being present for someone when they are hurting or feeling helpless.

The video starts simultaneously with the music which consists of pictures of various young adults that look sad, isolated, happy, normal and then Wills's face, Corbin's brother, is highlighted in the montage. As the song ends, Briggs's beautiful face transitions in, illuminated and radiant. The screen then fades to black. As a hushed silence fills the room, I can sense the eerie presence of mourning, and stillness throughout the crowd.

Chloe stands in the center of the stage with the lights still dark, a single light shines upon her face as she begins the presentation. "Suicide is the fourth leading cause of death among fifteen- to twenty-nine-year-olds." She continues to talk about the statistics.

I look around the room and examine the faces of the people in the crowd. I can see the impact the presentation is having upon them. As Chloe is ending her speech, the lights turn on. I try taking a few pictures and get some video footage. I capture Chloe beaming with pride before she exits the stage. *Well done, girl, well done.*

Henry is up next and replaces Chloe, shaking her hand with a quick kiss on the cheek as they pass each other. Henry begins: "In a society that seems more connected than ever before, why do we still struggle to open up to one another about mental health and depression? It's essential to create awareness and remove the stigma from these serious issues." He continues addressing the crowd, engaging them, holding their attention. *He's killing it.*

The next video starts with a montage of candid interviews we did with students and their thoughts about mental health. Most of the students' faces are shielded to protect their identity. Stories are told by the students of problems and feelings they have or have en- countered. There is a cameo from Mrs. Wall, filmed in her lavender hair phase. She was excited to be included in the video.

My turn has finally come. I've been ready for this presentation since we came up with the idea. There has been a fire burning inside me wanting to let others know that there is help, there is support, there is hope. I've felt swallowed by the grief of not being able to recognize that Briggs was hurting. Suicide didn't exist in my world. I was immune to it. I didn't know anyone who had done this, so in a sad sense, it wasn't my problem or something I worried about. If I was oblivious, how many other people are too? Too many, I'm afraid. I know now that we must talk about it and remove the stigma. Let's make this a normal conversation among our peers with no judgment. We can be vigilant about bringing awareness to mental health and recognizing that our outward appearances and social media posts aren't representative of what's truly going on inside our hearts and minds.

Henry introduces me, as I walk out to the stage. He bows as I take my place. "All yours, make him proud," he says in a gentle tone.

"Love you, Henry," I whisper back.

My part is to present our solution. I stand in front of everyone. I see my mom proudly watching me. She nods to let me know that she's here for me, here for Briggs. Mrs. Wall, the sunflower, catches my eye and she waves at me then gives a thumbs up. I take a deep breath and grab hold of my Happy Face Pin placed above my heart. I look at the ceiling hoping Briggs is looking down at me.

For the next five minutes, I stand before them with confidence and pride, baring my soul as I talk about The Happy Face Project. I allow myself to be vulnerable and share my story about Briggs and how I came to know the Happy Face Pin. I am wearing it proudly on my shirt over my heart to show everyone. I also discuss the implementation of our new project with the help of Mrs. Wall and the faculty, pointing to the table we set up with the brochures and pins. "If someone looks sad or down, offer them the Happy Face Pin. It's a small gesture that can make a difference." I elaborate further, "And when asking someone how they are doing today, try to ask if they are happy, as everyone will tell you they are good. But are they happy?"

I end my speech with sorrowful words: "Briggs Sullivan, I'm sorry we didn't have this program while you were with us, but we are going to do our best to make sure this doesn't happen again." When I finish, the clapping starts and everyone starts to stand one by one like a wave rolling through the crowd, leaving a sea of people cheering us on: a standing ovation. Henry and Chloe gather next to me, and we join hands and take a bow. Corbin and Mrs. Wall come up on stage and congratulate us. I am almost suffocated by Mrs. Wall, the Sunflower, but I embrace her support. It feels so good to finally get this program out there. I take a deep breath. *We did it.*

Corbin quiets the crowd down as we walk off the stage. The news crew is waiting for us as we head down the stairs. They are bombarding us with questions and want interviews. I hear our names being called, and we gladly acquiesce to their requests. The more press, the more people will hear about this.

After a whirlwind of questions, the interviews are finally over. Our parents have been waiting in the wings for us. Once we are free, they gather with us to celebrate. Mr. and Mrs. Sullivan hug me and Mrs. Sullivan whispers in my ear, "I love you, Evy. Thank you from the bottom of our hearts." I hug her back tighter. Then my mom embraces me with her quiet strength and says, "You were all fantastic and brave. Love you." It was a myriad of thank you's and hugs. It's great seeing Henry and Briggs's parents who are like my own, and we finally get to meet Chloe's parents.

Time for all of them to leave and say their goodbyes, as the three of us hurry back to our seats to listen to the rest of the presentations. I sit and look up quietly whispering under my breath, "So what do you think, Briggs?"

CHAPTER 48

We became local celebrities overnight. The news stations had aired our presentation and talked about the implementation of The Happy Face Project. It turns out our project went viral. Mrs. Wall got her five mins of fame too and was beaming with joy when she discussed how the school will be making a "safe place" for mental health. She was sure to mention how it was the three of us students that wanted to bring change to the school. It's been a good week since our presentation, but the buzz is still going on.

Mrs. Wall calls Chloe, Henry, and me into her office during the third period today. We all arrive around the same time.

"Hi, hi, hi! Sit down you superstars," she instructs us.

We all look at each other like "What's going on?" I find my green chair and take a seat. I'm getting used to this chair now, and it feels comforting, or maybe it's my imagination.

She continues, "I have such exciting news to share with you guys! The school got a call from *The Today Show* in New York and… they want to interview all of us for their show and do a segment on your project. Can you believe it?"

"Whoa, that's amazing news," Chloe says looking astonished.

"Hot damn!" Henry yells out loud.

I can't find the words to say anything, I'm flabbergasted. We are making change, putting the word out there, and bringing awareness. We are doing it.

"Evy? Did you hear me?" Mrs. Wall asks.

"Uh, yes. Yes, I did. I'm just…taking it all in." I bite my lip hoping to keep the tears in. But in my heart, I can feel something firing up, repairing the brokenness. I beckon a smile, "We're in, right, guys?"

"You bet," Henry says as Chloe responds, "Most definitely. The three chums."

Mrs. Wall is full of excitement, "Hot diggity then, it's a deal. I'll pass on the info to Mr. Corbin. They mentioned possibly doing it next week."

Henry is giddy with excitement. "Works for us, right, guys?"

Chloe and I simultaneously reply "Yes!" She starts to clap with much enthusiasm.

"Such wonderful news for our students, our school and most importantly your project. I'll keep you guys in the loop. This is going to be so fun!" Mrs. Wall says, clapping her hands in a repeat performance of Chloe's.

We scuffle out the door feeling pretty damn cool. I stop for a minute and look back at Mrs. Wall. "Uh, Mrs. Wall? Are you staying with the yellow or mixing it up for next week?"

Bewildered, she raises her hands to touch her hair, "Oh, the hair. Good question. Well, what do you think, Evy? Something new and wild or more subdued?"

"Surprise me!" I say and wink at her as I leave her office.

CHAPTER 49

I get home, feeling just plain exhilarated. Happiness feels like it's oozing out of me. It's been a while, but it's been one of those days where things seem to be just right. Once I'm inside, I kick off my shoes, grab a drink, and sit down on the couch with my computer, cross-legged. I start scrolling through my emails and see something from USC. *Holy shit, this could be important.* I'm a bit freaked out. I take another look and sure enough, it is from USC. I hesitate for a moment. This could be a deal killer for my good day or on a positive note, it can make it even better. I'm so nervous, but I decide to get it over with. Shakily, my finger hits the cursor to open the email. A letter pops up on the screen. I squeeze my eyes shut for a minute and then I begin to read.

"Congratulations! I am pleased to offer you admission to the University of Southern California as part of the entering class of fall 2020. This offer is being extended to you because of your outstanding achievements…"

Holy shit! I've been accepted! I don't even bother to finish reading the rest of the letter. I'm exploding with excitement and jumping around. My dad, oh my God, he would be so proud. I did it Daddy!

My face burns with happiness. This has been my dream, my dad's dream and my mom's. I snap a picture of my screen with my phone. Okay, I'm calling my mom first. I can't press the buttons on my phone quick enough. She answers and I switch to speaker mode.

"Mom! Oh my God, oh my God, oh my God!" I scream into the phone.

"Evy, slow down, is everything okay?" my mom says with concern, freaking out a bit.

"Yes! Mom! I got accepted to USC!"

"What? USC? Oh, Evylyn Peters, of course you did. Congrats, honey. I bet your dad is smiling down at you right now, probably filming this moment!" Her excitement resonates through the phone.

"I had that exact thought. I need to call Jules and let her know. We're going to be in Los Angeles together. I'm flipping excited!" I say, unable to contain myself.

"Me too," my mom says.

"That will make it easy for me to visit both of you now. Job well done, Evy. I'm so proud of you. It's a big day in the Peters's house. Well, you call Jules and share the news. I'll be home shortly. Love you."

"Love you too, Mom." I say as I get off the phone feeling pumped up. I pick up the phone again and realize that I'm about to call Briggs and I stop myself. "God dammit, Briggs, you're supposed to be here to celebrate with me." I scroll through my pictures and find one of Briggs and just look at him. My exuberance turns to melancholy in a matter of one second as I stare at his piercing eyes. "I'm going to USC, Briggs. I wish you were coming with me." My breath is shallow and heavy. I remind myself what Corbin told me.

Celebrate Briggs! I tell myself to turn it around, as this is an exciting day for me. I continue to talk to his picture. *Actually, you'd have looked quite handsome in cardinal and gold with me.* That thought alone makes me laugh, as Briggs did not like that cardinal color at all—"too boring." He had said he would have only worn the magnificent gold color if he "had" to go to USC. He liked his bold colors for sure.

I purposely change my focus and send a Snap of my acceptance letter to Henry and Chloe.

Immediately I get responses from both. Henry sends back a pic of me as a Princess and writes: *"Whoa, superstar! Well, deserved."* Chloe snaps back a picture of her face with her eyes and mouth wide open: *"Congratulations! Such wonderful news. You rock."*

I quickly call Jules, and she too is over the top excited for me. "My little sis is going to be in LA with her big sis. We are going to have so much fun together," she tells me.

"I can't wait. And Jules, can you come in for my Prom and do my makeup?" I ask her.

"I'd love to. Just tell me when. I've got some great new makeup I want to try out on you."

"Sweet, it's next month. And could you do Chloe's makeup too? I know she'd be thrilled. Henry may even want a touch up knowing him."

"It's a date. I'll be there. Can't wait to see you. Congrats again, Ev. Good things are headed your way," Jules says lovingly.

CHAPTER 50

Chloe couldn't help but notice how exhausted she had been feeling these past few weeks. Her pain had been more noticeable daily. Nausea had set in from some of her medicines, but she had been doing her best to hold it all together. Until now, when she is walking up the stairs and feels her body give away, collapsing with a sickening thud. Everything goes black.

"What was that?" her dad yells out with no response. He looks around then rushes to the stairs. He sees Chloe laying at the bottom. "Chloe? Chloe? Are you okay?" There was no response. He yells out to his wife "Wendi, call 9-1-1!" He checks her pulse, and he feels a steady beat. "Thank God," he says.

"What's wrong, Jon?" she says in terror. She picks up her phone and dials 911 as she runs to Jon's side. "What happened, Jon? Oh, Chloe!" She kneels by her side, tears are streaming down her face. She sees the panic in Jon's eyes.

"911, what is your emergency?' she hears from the speaker of her phone.

"My daughter fell down the stairs."

"What happened, Ma'am?"

"I don't know, I just heard a terrible noise and found her here. I think she fell," she shouts out.

"Ma'am, is your daughter breathing?" the operator asks.

Jon kneels and listens to Chloe's mouth as he shakes his head yes.

"Yes, she is," Wendi replies to the voice on the line.

The operator continues, "Do not move her. We have dispatched an ambulance to your house. I will stay on the phone with you until they get there."

"Hurry, please," she begs. "Hurry."

"They will be there as fast as they can. Just stay on the phone with me."

Jon is gently stroking Chloe's hair. "Hang in there, baby girl. Your Mom and I are here with you."

Wendi sits next to Chloe and Jon holding Chloe's hand.

"The ambulance will be there in five minutes." They both hear the words coming from the phone's speaker.

After a few minutes Chloe starts to stir, her eyes slowly start to open. She looks up to see her parents staring at her. "What happened?" she asks.

"Oh, Chloe, thank God," Jon leans down and kisses her forehead.

"Don't move, honey. Stay still. The ambulance is on its way. Are you okay?" Wendi asks, looking into Chloe's eyes.

"I think so, my leg hurts," she says as she tries to move.

"Stay still," her dad instructs her. "Do you remember what happened?

"I, I was going up the stairs and started to feel really weird, like tired or something. And now here I am," she cocks a smile, "laying on the ground."

The sound of the ambulance is heard by all three of them. Ben, her younger brother, walks down the stairs, and is surprised by what he sees, "Chloe, what happened?" he shouts out, his voice trembling.

"Just laying around and wanted to have a party here at the bottom of the steps. All good," Chloe tells him.

"What? That's weird," he says, scratching his head. "That ambulance noise sounds so loud."

"The ambulance is at the house to check out Chloe, but she's going to be okay, Ben." Wendi says for everyone to hear. She prays over Chloe for everything to be okay.

A knock on the door is heard. Wendi gets up to answer the door. "Come in, come in. She's awake now," she says to the ambulance crew. "Right this way."

"Hi, guys," Chloe says as she hears them come into the room. "I'm okay, but my parents aren't."

"Very funny," her dad blurts out.

The paramedics spend the next ten minutes doing neuro tests and various exams on Chloe. She can move her eyes, arms, fingers and toes. But her left leg, the bad one, is causing her excruciating pain, more so than previously. Once they determine she is not a spinal risk, they help her sit up. "We can take you to the hospital for further evaluation."

"No, no. I'm okay guys. I have cancer and I just got weak and must have passed out. Other than my leg, I think I'm fine," Chloe tells the paramedics.

"Parents? Shouldn't we take her?"

Jon and Wendi both look at Chloe. Her dad speaks up, "We'd prefer for you to go; probably a smart idea."

"It's not going to change anything Dad. I'm okay, really," she says, not so sure herself.

"This is against my better judgment," the lady paramedic says as she slowly helps her up with help from the other paramedic.

They slowly lead Chloe to the living room as her parents watch with concern. Chloe can feel the pain in her left leg and walks with an exaggerated limp. They sit her down on the couch and ask her how she is feeling.

"My leg is a bit gimpy, but that's nothing new. I'll be okay," she says feeling a bit exhausted. The female paramedic bends down and checks out Chloe's leg, examining it for breaks, cuts, bruises and range of motion and certifies that her leg is physically okay. They give her and her parents concussion precautions and reasons to go to the hospital. "Thanks for your help, guys, I truly appreciate it." Chloe smiles and waves at them as they head toward the front door.

Her dad sees the paramedics out then heads back toward the living room. Her mom sits next to Chloe on the sofa and wraps her arms around her. "You gave us quite the scare. I'm worried about you, honey. We can still take you to the hospital."

Ben hugs on Chloe too, as she kisses his forehead. "Thanks, guys, I'm okay. But honestly, I do need to go to the restroom. Excuse me for a minute if you guys don't mind," Chloe says as she stands up, but finds that putting pressure on her leg hurts quite a bit as she tries to take a step. "Actually, Mom, I might need a little help, my bad leg seems to be a bit sore." Her dad comes to her side.

"It's the old annoying cancer leg," Chloe explains. "It seems like it got worse all of a sudden."

"Well, that can't be good. Let me help you," her dad says as he and Wendi help Chloe to the bathroom.

"Definitely not working well," Chloe says as she hops on her other foot and keeps as much pressure off the bad one.

"Do you think it's worse from the fall?" her mom questions.

"Yeah, but it's been giving me a lot of trouble lately," Chloe says as she gets to the bathroom. "I've got it from here," she says as she holds on to the sink and hops toward it. She shuts the door, unzips her pants and sits on the toilet. She examines her leg. It looks okay, just like the paramedics had said. She closes her eyes and takes a deep breath. Under her breath, careful not to let her parents hear her she whispers, "It's happening."

Her dad stands against the wall "I'm going to go buy you crutches. I don't like this, and you can't be hopping around the house and getting hurt again."

She has no intention of fighting him on this one. She's going to need them. "Okay, Dad. Good idea," she shouts out from the bathroom.

CHAPTER 51

Henry insists on driving me to school. He said he called Chloe earlier to see if he could pick her up too, but she said she would meet us there. Henry and I are standing at our locker when something catches my eye. "Shit, is that Chloe?" I ask Henry.

"Uh, where?" Henry says as his eyes search around.

"Oh my God, it is. Look!" I point to Chloe coming down the hall with crutches.

"Girl, what?" Henry is taken off guard as he sees Chloe and hustles down the hall to help her.

I watch as the two come near the locker. "What happened? Are you okay?"

Chloe musters a smile pushing past any pain she must be feeling and says, "Just needed a little drama in my life."

"No, seriously, what did you do?" Henry pleads for the answer.

"All this fuss about nothing, I'm fine," Chloe says trying to convince us and maybe herself.

"Spill it," I insist she tells us.

Chloe pauses for a moment, "Okay, okay, I felt a little dizzy last night when I was going up the stairs and fell. Don't worry, I didn't fall far. Just managed to hurt my bum leg and my dad insisted I get crutches. I'm just making him happy."

Henry is puzzled, "Everything is okay, right? You promise?"

Chloe puts on her best smile, "Of course guys, my medicine makes me a little dizzy and hence, I lost my footing with my bad leg and fell." She pushes the crutches toward Henry and says, "See? I'm good," and makes a little cautious spin, stumbling a little.

Henry immediately catches her. "Whoa, take it easy, tiny dancer. You better keep these crutches under your arms all day long. Got it?"

I stand looking at Chloe, her tiny body seems to be getting thinner, and frailer since earlier in the year. I know she's telling us she's okay, but geez, something is different. *How am I just noticing this now?* Maybe it really is her medicine. Henry's voice distracts me.

"Guys, I mean Princesses, I wanted to wait, but damn it, I'm so excited. I just…can't even…" Henry blurts out in excitement. He reaches into the back of pants and pulls out two envelopes. "Beautiful ladies, these are for you," he says as he gets on one knee and hands an envelope to each of us. He continues, "And Chloe, if you're not feeling up to it, no worries, we can push it out to another date. No pressure, I mean it."

I let Chloe take the lead so I can get it on film. Chloe opens her envelope, while I'm snatching a picture of her with Henry down on one knee. She begins to read, as I catch up and tardily open my beautifully crafted invitation. He always adds the special details.

I smile remembering when Briggs had gotten down on his knee a few weeks after we had started hanging out. We'd spent every day together and the more I got to be with him, the more I liked him and didn't want to be without him. He had brought me to the Morro Sand Trail near Morro Rock. He made me listen to his "Quiet the Buzz" playlist, with one earbud in mine and the other in his as we walked hand in hand. Briggs loved nature and wanted to share his love of it with me. He found peace in the little things, even in a rock. In fact, he collected lots of rocks on our way to the beach that day.

"I see why you love this place," I told him as I took in the peacefulness.

"I've been coming here lately to…well, escape sometimes," he said in a way that made it sound like he was choosing his words carefully.

"Escape from what?" I asked somewhat dumbfounded.

"Honestly? Myself."

"What do you mean by that?"

Briggs reached for my hand and held it tight, squeezing it. "You know, I just get in my head sometimes and get mental, I guess. When I get into one of those moods, nothing seems to help quiet my brain and I need to escape." He kept looking ahead avoiding my gaze.

I stopped walking, which kind of yanked Briggs back a little. "Can you tell me about it?"

He stood with quiet reflection for a second, as though unsure if he wanted to open Pandora's box. "I've told you about my depression. There's something inside me that I just can't explain. It eats at me. It's hard for me to even understand. Counseling has never worked. It's pointless. So, sometimes the best therapy is to be somewhere like here to quiet the thoughts in my head. It turns my frown upside down."

I studied his face, "But I want to understand. Are you doing okay right now?"

"Yes of course. All good," he said, trying to reassure me with a smile.

I could also see a hint of sparkle in his eye, which made me believe him.

"When I'm with you I'm always okay. And this place makes me happy, so I wanted to bring you here and share it with you." His hands glided out to his sides as if he was saying welcome to all this grandeur.

I wasn't buying it at first, but he did seem enthusiastic about us being here. I still had to ask, "You'd tell me if things were otherwise, right?"

Briggs looked around and saw a wildflower patch adjacent to the path we were on. He leaned down and picked a group of purple hued flowers and handed them to me. "Of course I would," he said delicately kissing my forehead. "Flowers for my lady." Then out of the blue, I felt his warm tongue lick my forehead like a cat and heard him let out a giggle.

It made me squeal. "*Eeeewwww.* Thanks for the lick."

He laughed back. "Isn't this place incredible?" He grabbed my hand and continued leading me down the path as I placed the flowers behind my ear.

We walked until we couldn't walk any further, arriving at the beach with the famous Morro Rock making an impressive imprint in the horizon. The sun was beginning to set. Billowy layers of orange and red populated the sky with bursts of golden rays streaming from the sun. There were thousands of rock piles creating their own art form. Briggs removed his air pods and asked me to put my hands out and cusp them as he started taking the rocks he collected along our walk and placed them in my hand. He reached into his pockets and grabbed the remaining few rocks and kept them in his hands. He asked me to sit and so I did. He took the rocks and started placing them around me. Then he reached for my hands and carefully removed the rocks from my hands and sat down. We sat cross-legged looking at one another as he placed the remaining rocks around us completing a full circle. The surf crashed in the distance, and the birds were taking flight, hovering over us in a protective way. The moment was magical.

"Now that I have you in my circle, you are all mine," his eyes dazzled as he stared deep into mine. My previous worries from moments ago slipped away with ease like the water receding into the ocean.

My heart fluttered as Briggs turned to me to kiss me longingly. I took a pause, with my forehead pressed to his and whispered under my breath for only him to hear me, "And you are all mine…forever." The most amazing sensation of deep longing and love for Briggs took over my body, and I felt it to a depth I never had experienced. This moment showed me how lucky I was to have him in my life. I showered him with more kisses and pulled him in, wanting his body pressed into mine. We sat and watched the waves in silence yet joined together in our souls. He was mine.

I hear Henry talk and my thoughts return to the present. "Yes, I will be there tonight, Henry. I wouldn't miss it," Chloe says. She is smiling with a new sense of energy.

"That makes two of us, thank you, kind sir," I say, curtseying to Henry. "And Chloe, let me pick you up tonight."

"Oh right, good idea," Chloe spouts back, looking down at her leg.

The bell rings and we are off to class.

CHAPTER 52

I know Henry has probably gone all out and is asking us to Prom. We had already talked about going, I mean it was a given that the three of us would go together, but he insists on being formal about it, which I will admit that I love. I can't help but wonder if Briggs were still here, would we have had Chloe in our group going to Prom? I'd like to think we would have. Afterall, she and Briggs were friends, and maybe by now we would have all been friends.

Mom told me she was going out with her friends tonight and would see me later, so I really have a free evening ahead of me. I decide to curl my hair tonight and put on makeup. I've been wanting to get dressed up, a promise I've been telling myself to up my game, so I might as well.

I find a cute jean mini-skirt and pair it with a light blue tank sort of top. My instinct is to go for tennis shoes, but instead I opt for a low nude heel. I top my look off with a little touch of pink lipstick. I look at myself in the mirror and I like what I see. I grab my backpack and check to make sure my camera is there. Then I go to my desk and reach for my Happy Face Pin and place it on my shirt. It is time to go get Chloe.

Chloe is outside waiting, with the crutches nowhere in sight, but is now holding a cane. Well, that's new. I pull up with my windows down and music blaring as Chloe limps her way toward my car using the cane. And I'll be darned, she's wearing a leather jacket over a flowy sundress. Our little "rebel" has gone bad girl. I see her laughing and shaking her hips, dancing to the music coming from my car.

Chloe yells over the music, "I've upgraded to a fancy cane, much more my style and easier to dance with," she says entering the car.

"Look at you rocking the cane and leather. Aren't you a cool chic?" I say, laughing back with her as she takes a seat. "How's the leg doing?"

"It's fantastic, just needing a little security per my parent's orders. No worries. All good. Nothing is going to stop me tonight," she says convincingly.

There's a new girl in town and it's our Chloe Wirrick. I smile and keep the tunes coming as we head to the docks. "Rebel Yell" is first on the list. We arrive and walk over toward the boats when I spot my mom and what appears to be Chloe's parents, the Sullivans and the Prestons. Nice move, Henry; he pulled that one off without us knowing. My eyes become misty. *Damn, I'm so emotional lately, but I must feel what I'm feeling, right?* On the ground leading to the boat, there is a red carpet, yes, a red carpet rolled out with the parents on either side ready to take our pictures. I stop and start snapping pictures myself. I see Henry positioned at the end of the carpet dressed up looking dapper as ever. I start to run toward everyone, when I remember Chloe is next to me and realize running is not the best idea. I link my arm around hers and stroll up together.

We are covered in hugs by everyone. It's so cool to have them here. I couldn't be happier and I'm especially thrilled that Briggs's parents are included. We get various pictures with the whole group, each family, etc. Then Henry announces for everyone to follow him. We all head toward the boat dock and there, proudly displayed on the Preston's boat is Henry's sign with a huge purple bow with lights dangling off the bow. The sign reads: "Chloe and Evylyn, will you sail away with me to Prom?"

"Well, what do you think girls? Shall we go to Prom?" Henry asks in a formal tone.

Chloe and I say "Yes!" at the same time. The parents all clap. It's one big happy fest.

"Then away we shall go," Henry instructs us all.

We all file in line and head to the boat. Henry and his father are the first to step up on the boat to help everyone on. They insist that Chloe gets on first, with her father following closely behind her to make sure she is safe, then we all get on one after another. The boat is decked out with balloons, and ribbons and there is a beautiful arrangement of food on the outdoor table and a bottle of champagne with glasses. My camera is out, and I am making sure I get all this on film. It's quite beautiful what he's done.

While we are all talking and grazing on the food, Henry heads to the table and picks up a bottle of champagne. He pops the cork, and the bubbles spill ever so delicately over the mouth of the bottle. He fills all the glasses with just the right amount of champagne, then picks up one of the glasses along with a fork and makes a clinking noise to get our attention. "Everyone come on over, as I'm about to make a toast," he says.

We gather around him, and each of us grab a glass and raise it as we give Henry our attention. I have Mom on my right, and the

Sullivans on my left. Mrs. Sullivan squeezes my hand, and I squeeze back. I turn and smile at her. She has tears welling up in her eyes. I know her pain; I know it well.

I catch Chloe clutching her stomach and wincing in pain, I think. She stands still for a moment. Her Mom notices it too. She walks over to Chloe and immediately grasps her arm. Chloe closes her eyes and takes deep breaths. I'm not sure what that's all about. She seems to be better now as she just gave her mom a nod indicating that she is okay.

"Here's to my gorgeous dates, Evy and Chloe. Thank you for saying yes, as now I have the honor to take you both to Prom and I am certain it will make Briggs proud to know that I am taking care of his girls. Love you, bro. I also want to thank all of you ah-mazing parents for coming and for being our support system through all this. You guys rock! Cheers!" Henry says as he lifts his glass higher.

I look around and I'm humbled by the presence of everyone. "Cheers!" we all say simultaneously and toast our glasses with smiles on our faces. My mom kisses me on the cheek. My thoughts drift to Briggs.

"You look beautiful," she whispers in my ear, bringing me back to here and now.

"Thank you, Mom. Looking fantastic yourself," I say, as I look her over. "You've got a glow up going on, Mom!"

"A what?" she says laughing.

"Transformation, Mom, and in a good way," I wink at her. "A glow up."

According to Chloe, she has never had alcohol before, and tonight she decides it's time to check it off her list. She takes her glass and shotguns the champagne and looks quite proud of herself. She wipes her mouth exasperated and says, *Wow!* out loud.

Not bad for a rookie. "Nice slam there, Chloe."

Chloe looks like a deer caught in the headlights and giggles, "Guess, I've been missing out. That went down smoothly. *Yum.*"

Mr. Preston speaks up, "Thank you guys for coming out tonight. I know it means so much to Henry and all of us. Now that's all the champagne you kids get, as we want a safe night, got it? We will leave you guys to continue your celebration. We've left the bottles of sparkling apple juice for you. Don't get too crazy, now. And Henry? Epic Promposal. Well done, son, well done. Love you kids. Let's get a few pics before everyone leaves if you don't mind."

And with that, we take more group pictures, and we say our thank you's and goodbyes. I help Henry with the ropes and buoys. Chloe tries to help but I tell her to sit down and take it easy. Henry gets his phone and Bluetooths the music for our enjoyment. Within ten minutes we are off boating. The sun is setting, and the sky is illuminated with the sun's yellow and orange rays. The breeze in the air is gentle and gives just the right amount of cooling effect. With dark nearing, we never go far, but we like to anchor just a little way away from the docks.

When I'm on the boat, I feel at peace, succumbing to the gentle rocking of the waves. Just as music is my saving grace, so is the ocean. We all sit quietly, taking in the music and the beauty of our surroundings, until we find a place to anchor. I have so much to be grateful for, and moments like this help me reflect on my blessings. Although I am painfully missing Briggs, I am grateful for my chums Chloe and Henry. Henry catches me looking at him and he smiles back at me, then blows me a kiss. Chloe is sitting with her knees to her chest and looking up at the sky.

Henry feels satisfied with our location, so I go to the bow to help him anchor the boat. I inhale the chilled air filling my lungs and look out to the horizon where the ocean and sky gently join one another. I will miss the ocean when I head off to school. I'll be about a good thirty minutes from Manhattan Beach, and I can handle that. But I won't be able to just drive to the docks and hop on Henry's boat anytime I want. That will be a bummer.

The music is blaring, and we are now hanging out on the stern of the boat. We are talking, when I notice Chloe reaching into her leather jacket. She pulls something out and has it in her hand. I look again, and my eyes get huge. What the what? She has taken a joint out and placed it in her lips. She takes a lighter out from her other pocket. I'm thinking, *She's taken this "rebel" thing a bit too literally.*

"Does anyone mind if I light up?" Chloe says nonchalantly.

Henry's eyes get as large as mine. "Whoa, my sweet innocent Chloe, are you smoking weed?" he says in disbelief.

Chloe straightens up and replies, "Bingo. My meds give me nausea and I figure I might as well try it out." She told us that her doctor had prescribed her medical marijuana in both a gummy and smoking form earlier this week and hadn't had a chance to try it. "Never a better time than now," she says. She shrugs her shoulders then takes the joint and presses her lips around it, takes the lighter up to the joint, and takes a long drag that is cut short as she starts to cough violently.

I'm in complete disbelief, or maybe shock. *What happened to the old Chloe?*

Henry nestles up to Chloe and says, "Dear God, let me show you how." He takes the joint out of her mouth and shows her how to inhale. "This is how you do it." Meanwhile, Chloe is still coughing up a lung.

"Maybe I should stick with the gummies," she says finally able to breathe. "It looks so easy when I watch others smoke," she shakes her head.

"For you, gummies are probably the way to go. But try one more time," Henry encourages Chloe, his eyes starting to look a little glossy. He mimics smoking a joint.

Chloe gives it a second try, this time just taking a gentle inhale. "Like that?" she asks surprised she didn't gag this time.

"Perfect!" Henry smiles, almost laughing.

Chloe looks at me directly, "Evy? Do you want a drag?"

"Nooo, I'm good. Designated driver. But you have at it. I've got you covered." I'm just going to sit here and watch this comical scene unravel.

"That's it for me, just something to take the edge off," Chloe says as she extinguishes her joint on one of the nearby plates.

"Chloe, I'm sorry you haven't been feeling okay, is everything all right? I mean you are doing okay, right?" I ask Chloe, needing to know she's not keeping anything from us.

"You'd tell us?" Henry joins in.

"Guys, seriously, the meds are a standard preventative therapy. I'm as good as I'm going to get. And right this minute, I'm feeling quite amazing," she giggles and presses her hands into her eye sockets trying to stop herself from laughing so hard. "This is good stuff, guys." We all start to laugh with her.

"Chloe's stoned," Henry shouts out.

My bad habit of snort laughing kicks in. It is quite a silly moment and although I'm as sober as can be, I have a case of the uncontrollable giggles, which makes my stomach start to hurt. The music is playing, and I can't help but get up and dance. Henry decides to join me. He starts spinning me around while Chloe looks on. She is still laughing but starts clapping and hooting as she watches us.

Henry dips me back and brings me back up and holds me close, continuing to swirl me around. The song ends with us both being exhausted, so we take a seat back next to Chloe. The next song comes on and it's a remixed version of Abba's "Dancing Queen." I hear Chloe speak up.

"Hey, this is my song!" she says in a high-pitched voice.

She grabs her cane and carefully pulls herself up. Henry jumps up to make sure she is steady on her feet. She lifts her hand in the air as if to say, "I got this."

The sky is midnight black and there are more stars in the sky shining brighter than I have seen in a long time. Chloe has moved herself to the back of the boat and she begins to sway like the waves of the ocean, feeling the song and taking it in with her eyes closed. Her cane is nowhere in sight. She starts to sing out loud.

I kid you not, I'm sitting here mesmerized as right before my eyes I see something in Chloe change. She starts to spin around, arms wide open, twirling like a graceful ballroom dancer. There is no sign of weakness in her leg, it's as if she has elevated herself out of her body. There is magic in the air, and I feel it so deeply. Henry starts to sing and cheer her on. He puts his arm around my waist and holds me tight as we all join in together singing.

A shadow of light, from where it came, I do not know, casts itself upon the deck almost spotlighting Chloe as she is floating like an ethereal angel spinning in the air. The moment takes my breath away. I have never seen her like this: free spirited with not a care in the world. She is in a matrix we can't enter. I nudge Henry in disbelief, as we continue to gaze at Chloe having her moment, having her dream, and dancing all her pain away, as if her life depends on it. I smile as the tears stream down my eyes from what I can only guess is the indescribable utter awe I am feeling watching my sweet Chloe, the dancing queen.

CHAPTER 53

Our *Today Show* appearance is in an hour. Chloe, Henry, and I arrive in our Happy Face shirts and white jeans to Mrs. Wall's office, only to be greeted by a platinum-haired Mrs. Wall and a camera crew. Mrs. Wall has her shirt on too, as we had planned. I will say, she is all dolled up and ready for her fifteen minutes of fame. Her hair is smoothed straight, and she has a new makeup assortment on her face. Corbin shows up right after us, dressed similarly.

I go to give Mrs. Wall a hug, and as I do, she says, "Thumbs up or down on the platinum? I wanted to tone it down a little for the interview. What do you think?"

I really like her new look, so I can honestly say, "Spin around for me," which she does, then I say, "Perfect choice, very Hollywood. Makes you very Marilyn Monroe."

She gets giddy and claps her hands, "You don't say? I was trying to channel that Marilyn vibe, you know?" She smooths out her hair then places her hands on her hips twisting them, and knees slightly bent making a pose.

"Nailed it, Wall! Full on Marilyn. Hollywood won't know what hit them," I tell her.

She squishes her nose and purses her lips with excitement and skips off to talk to the director. I think I made her day. Anyhow, we all get mic'd and told to sit in the seats that are already lined up with our names on them. There is a big TV monitor already playing the *Today Show* for us to see. We are told that Jenna Bush Hager and Hoda Kotb will be interviewing us. I'm thrilled because my mom will be excited as she loves to watch them and I've caught them a few times in the morning when I have a few minutes while getting ready for school. They are quirky and fun and seem down to earth. Just the kind of chicks I can relate to. If anyone had asked, they would have been my choice for the interview, so I'm excited. Chloe says she doesn't know anything about them. The director tells us that they will film the interview, edit it down to the allotted time and it will air on next Monday's show. He then hands us some of the questions they will be asking us so that we are familiar with them.

"Two minutes to go," the director shouts out. "Now remember not to look directly in the camera. If you mess up your words, no worry, that's why we have the beauty of editing. Be natural, and pretend like we aren't here, just like you guys are having a normal everyday conversation. All good?"

Henry is on one side of me and Chloe is on the other. Jenna and Hoda pop up on the television. "Hi, guys, are you ready?" Jenna asks. We all look at each other excitedly and say, "Yes!"

Hoda speaks next, "Evylyn?"

I raise my hand and say "Hi, you can call me Evy." I'm feeling my adrenaline firing up. She acknowledges the others, "Noted. So that leaves Henry," he nods. "And Chloe."

"Yes, Ma'am. It's a pleasure to meet you ladies," Chloe says, back in her proper Chloe mode. Jenna and Hoda smile back. "We are so excited to meet you and hear about what you guys did. Here we go," Jenna says.

I hold both of their hands, and as we hear the director do the countdown, "Five, four, three, two, one, and action," my heart starts to beat faster. I'm in my element. This is exactly what I want to be doing in my near future.

The interview lasts a good fifteen minutes. They made us feel comfortable and we even joked around a little at the end. We each had a minute or two to be highlighted and my voice broke a little (as did my heart) when they asked me about Briggs and how he had inspired our project. I think Hoda may have even shed a tear, I saw her pause and swallow hard. She's very empathetic in her interviews—actually, that's what my mom says, and I think she's right.

When the interview is over, we all high five and give hugs. I excuse myself and head over to the director and tell her about my passion for directing. She lets me see the clips of what she's caught on film. I'm pleased and can't wait to see the finished project. She gets my email and says she will send me the segment when they are done. *How cool is that?*

The camera crew follows us around the school after the interview to get more footage for the show. They film a small segment with Mrs. Wall, Corbin, and Principal Arndt before leaving. Principal Arndt tells us that she is going to have a surprise assembly Monday morning so the entire school can see the interview. The Happy Face Project is going to launch on a bigger scale, I just know it.

CHAPTER 54

Last week, both Henry and Chloe received their college acceptance letters. Henry got into the University of California Los Angeles's Herb Alpert's School of Music to pursue his dream of being a music producer. I'm so happy, as we will not be far from each other. He begged me to go to UCLA with him, as I found out I did get accepted also, but he knows how important USC is to my dad and me. And no surprise, Chloe was accepted by both Harvard and Yale to study Biology as she plans to be a scientist and one day cure cancer. Knowing her, she will do just that. I thought I was smart, but I'm wired right-brained smart, and she is left-brained smart. Henry's a mix of both brain sides.

It's a big day today and I'm so stoked! We get to see how our *Today Show* interview turned out. Henry insisted that he pick up both Chloe and me this morning so that we could arrive together.

We are talking about the interview on the way to school, when Chloe asks, "Would you guys mind filming me giving my Valedictorian speech?" Chloe asks.

"As in, on graduation day?" I ask clarifying her question.

"No, before. I'd like to give it a practice run; you know. Make sure I come across as intelligent and calm."

"Chloe, you're the most confident person I know," Henry adds. "You'll be amazing."

Chloe cocks her head to acknowledge his faith in her, "Why thank you, but you know how I am. I like things perfect."

"That's the Chloe I know," I respond. "Just let me know when you are ready."

Chloe looks back at her phone looking at her calendar once again, "Probably in the next couple weeks, thanks."

We make it to school and the three of us are now sitting together in the gymnasium with everyone in the school waiting to watch our segment. They reserved the first row for us, *how cool is that?* We are VIPs today. It appears that there are a few other reserved seats that I assume are for Mrs. Wall and Corbin. As I look around, I see the Happy Face Pin on many students' shirts. I place my hand over Brigg's pin and squeeze it, as I swell with pride seeing our idea come to fruition.

Principal Arndt walks to the middle of the gym where a podium is placed in the middle of several large movie screens. Corbin and platinum Mrs. Wall come and sit down in the seats next to us just as I had figured. We all acknowledge each other, as Mrs. Arndt starts to speak. I quickly text my mom to make sure she is watching.

Are you ready to watch?

Mom: *Wouldn't miss it. We are all gathered around at the nurse's station ready to watch it. It's going to be so cool getting to see my brilliant daughter on TV.*

Yay, promise to be honest and let me know if we did a good job or messed up! Got to go. Love you.

Mom: *Don't you worry, you got this. Love you more. *kissy face emoji**

I hear my name, it's Mrs. Arndt asking me, Henry, and Chloe to stand up. Henry has to help Chloe. As we stand, clapping erupts. We turn and wave at the crowd. I am filled with gratitude watching everyone. They have helped us make this project a success, so cheers right back to them.

Mrs. Arndt speaks again. "Students take your seats. The show is about to start."

And with that, the audio video team gets the monitors turned on, lights dimmed and before our eyes in large scale, the *Today Show* appears on the screen. Al Roker is discussing the weather and when he finishes the camera cuts to Hoda, Savannah, and Craig sitting at their half-circle desk. Hoda speaks up and says, "Coming up after the commercial break we'll be talking about some amazing kids from Morro Bay, California, who are making a difference at their school for mental health and suicide awareness. You're not going to want to miss this."

Mrs. Wall and Corbin lean forward to acknowledge us. Mrs. Wall's smile is enormous, and she appears to be panting with enthusiasm. Corbin gives us a thumbs up, which I return right back to him. Henry is all giddy, wiggling in his seat then pokes both Chloe and me in the ribs, causing Chloe to let out a squeal. "Are you guys ready for our fifteen minutes of fame?" Henry asks.

"I'm stretching it out to at least fifteen days," Chloe smirks back as she adjusts herself so that she is sitting tall and smooths out her skirt.

"You know it, Henry," I respond.

The commercials are over, and a hush falls silent in the gym. Hoda appears on the screen. She begins, "Our next segment is about what a small group of students in Morro Bay, California, did for a school project to bring awareness to suicide prevention after losing one of their closest friends." The segment begins with Chloe, Henry, and me walking down the locker hallways at school. Jenna's voiceover begins to talk about suicide statistics while pictures of teens with depressed looking faces are splashed against the screen. Then the segment turns to the three of us sitting in Mrs. Wall's office.

The first one they show answering a question is me, when I was asked about the impact "my boyfriend's" death has had on me. I see myself visibly deflate on television, as if my life was being sucked out of me. It hurt then when they asked the question, and now this deep wound inside me is ripped open again. Next, Corbin is spotlighted on how his assignment sparked our project. He talks about how proud he is of us and how it was truly our idea, and he immediately knew it would be a special project of love. Chloe is very stoic in the interview and commands attention as she talks about how we came together on the idea. Henry talks about how we fundraised with the shirts and help from Mrs. Wall and Mr. Corbin.

Jenna asks me about the pin and how it became the center of our project. I proudly tell them why Briggs would wear a pin and how significant it became to me. Next Mrs. Wall is seen talking about the training of the teachers and some students to help recognize those that may need help. She goes on to say that more students are seeking counseling and have opened up to her about how they are feeling mentally.

The segment ends with Hoda saying, "I hope we are going to see more schools implementing The Happy Face Project. So, if you're having a bad day, put on your Happy Face Pin to let others know you may need that extra smile or hug today." Then the suicide hotline number scrolls at the end.

Everyone at the assembly stands up and claps. I hear lots of hoots and hollers. I hug Henry and Chloe tightly and I feel a sense of peace overcome me. Corbin comes over and tells us, "Well done." We open our circle to let him in and join in on the hugs. Principal Arndt has made her way to the podium again. She announces that the assembly is over, and we can all return to our regularly scheduled classes.

Chloe looks at Henry and me with a mischievous face and says, "Let's blow this joint."

Shocked, mostly because those words are coming from Chloe, I ask, "Like…skip?"

"I've never done it officially before, like most of the day, so why not?" She says matter-of-factly. "To the docks?"

Henry responds looking pleased, "To the docks we go!"

CHAPTER 55

Chloe was awakened in the middle of the night with the worst stomach pain she had experienced so far. The remainder of the night she spent awake as the pain had kept her up. She didn't want to bother her mom and dad. Writhing in pain, she musters enough energy to sit herself up on the edge of her bed and takes a deep breath hoping to get through it. "You've got this, Chloe, you are stronger than the pain," she says to herself. She begins to quietly sing.

She pauses and grabs at her stomach and begins to shake a little. She uses the sleeve of her nightgown to wipe the tears from her eyes, then starts up again gently rocking herself.

Chloe straightens up, adjusts her nightgown then reaches for her cane. She lifts herself out of bed carefully with the aid of the cane. She takes a moment to get steady on her feet, and in the dark, makes her way to the bathroom carefully taking each step. As she walks, she continues to sing the words out loud hoping to soothe her pain.

She braces herself against the bathroom counter to give her better balance, then releases the cane resting it against the counter. She flips on the vanity light and shuts her eyes so as not to be blinded by the light initially. With her eyelids squinted, she begins to take in the light. Sleepily, she turns on the faucet and grabs her glass, placing it under the spit to fill it. She turns off the water and examines the counter trying to find her pain medicine. "There it is," she says as her shaky hand reaches for her medicine. She uses the little bit of strength she has to twist off the cap. She places two pills in her mouth and washes them down with water, almost choking. Once she stops coughing, she manages to snatch the hand towel and wipes the water off her face and the front of her gown. The pain rears itself up again, causing Chloe to take hold of the countertop.

"Ugh, please let this stop," she whispers, her head hanging low trying to endure the pain. A minute passes, as does the intensity of the pain. Steadily she lifts her head back up and catches her reflection in the mirror. Her appearance is changing, and she can tell. Her cheeks seem a bit more sunken, and her skin is pallid. Her hand springs to her mouth, almost gasping when she sees herself. *Great, I look like I feel...Hell!* and shakes her head.

She takes a hold of her cane and situates herself. With her bad leg leading and outstretched, she gauges her balance. She knows she doesn't need a fall on top of the pain she is already having. Chloe takes several deep breaths, then without any hurry, she trudges across the floor until she reaches her bed, the pain in her abdomen is still slightly present but more manageable. Quietly she gets back into her bed pulling the covers around her and lays her head down on the pillow. After a minute, and not feeling too much better, she reaches for her phone and opens it to her meditation app and taps on the screen. With her eyes closed, she concentrates on the track playing, taking deep breaths in through her nose and back out. Tears start to roll down the sides of her delicate face. "Fly high and far," she whispers. "You've got this."

—

"Briggs?" I yell out. I'm in a total panic and my heart is beating out of my chest, I'm breathing fast, I need to find him. My first reaction is to grab my phone and look for his text. When I do, it takes me a minute to realize that I'm sitting up in bed and it's the middle of the night. "What the hell?" It was a dream, a lousy dream that tricked me. I thought I had a chance to save him. He needed me and wanted me to find him. It felt so damn real. My mind fills with images from my dream: Briggs calling me telling me he needs me right now. I beg him to tell me where he is, and he can't tell me. I hear the panic in his voice. He's struggling to get the words out. I hear him crying. I keep begging him to hang in there and tell him I need to know where he is. But I have no idea where he is and so I begin to run, but it's dark and I can't seem to see or move. That's when I wake up from that shitty dream; right in the middle of me trying to find him so I could save him. Once again, I am reminded that I couldn't save him. My body begins to tremble, and I close my eyes. It's like I'm in a nightmare of a nightmare. I grab my comforter and pull it toward me tightly. There is a quiet knock on the door which causes me to sit up, startled.

I can hear my name being called by Jules. "Evy? Everything okay? I heard a scream."

It's Jules, thank God. She came in last night to help Chloe and me with our makeup for Prom later today. "Come in," I say with a tremor in my voice. I can see her shadow approaching, so I scoot over in my bed to make room for her.

Jules comes to my side, sits, and wraps her arms around me. She is holding me closely and gently rocking me. "A bad dream?" she asks gently, stroking my hair. She smells of notes of sugared citrus and tropical fruits reminding me of the Capri No. 6 candle we always love to burn in the house.

Never have I had bad dreams, until this whole thing with Briggs. Even though my dad was killed, I've never had a bad dream about him. I've had amazing dreams where I see my dad and we talk, and everything is peaceful. Those are the kind of dreams I need to have about Briggs. I inhale deeply, "Yeah, another Briggs dream. And not a good one."

She squeezes me tighter. "I'm here if you want to tell me about it."

Despite feeling thankful that Jules is here, I yawn, feeling extremely tired and wanting to go back to bed. The last thing I need is bags under my eyes for Prom, but I need to express my fears and get them out or I may not be able to get back to sleep. I take another big breath, "I dreamed that Briggs was calling out to me to save him. I physically couldn't get to him or find him. I wanted to save him, and I couldn't. This same dream haunts me all the time."

"Oh gosh, Ev," Jules says as she embraces me with a mama bear hug.

Tears start to well up in my eyes as my mind races with the uncomfortable thoughts I'm having. "What if he…" I nuzzle my head into her neck holding on for dear life. "What if he called out to me or called my name when he took his life? What if he was wishing he didn't do it and wanted to live and needed me…and it was too late? This weighs on my heart heavily. Like maybe I could have saved him." I can physically feel my heart hurt saying the words.

Through the light peering into the room, I see Jules has tears rolling down her own face. "Listen, my sweet, sweet sis. You loved him and gave him everything you could, and he knew that. Briggs made a choice independent of you. We will never really know the whys. Tell me that you will give yourself grace."

"I am trying, it's just so tough. And I was supposed to do Prom with him today."

"I hear you, Evy. But I know you, you will carry Briggs in your heart and make it an amazing day, especially with Henry and Chloe being by your side. And I can't wait to make you up so beautiful."

Her words flow into my heart and make me grin, "I'm glad you are here with me, Jules. Thank you."

Jules releases her embrace of me and whispers in my ear, "What do you say we get some beauty sleep?"

And just like old times, she grabs a pillow, scoots me over and lays down next to me. "I love you, Evy. Sweet dreams," she says gently scratching the top of my head.

My lids are heavy, begging for sleep. "I love you more, Jules. Good night." With that, I close my eyes and hope to drift off back to sleep.

CHAPTER 56

woke up this morning feeling better than I thought I would. My excitement for Prom must be outweighing my night of terror. When I awoke, I had to look through my photos of Briggs to remember the happy times. I needed to see his smile, to reassure me that he's in a better place. That, and reading his texts he had sent to me, remind me of the love he had for me. I do this quite often when I miss him, which is daily if I'm being honest. As I've been told by many, I'm grieving. My Mom told me, grief is love. It makes sense as my love for him is so strong, and that's why I'm grieving him so deeply. So, I make a promise to myself that I will celebrate Briggs especially today and carry him and my love for him in my heart and on my sleeve for everyone to see.

I am surprised to see that Jules has already set up the lighting, the chairs are placed, and her makeup stand is ready to make us look like superstars for Prom. My excitement is beginning to percolate!

Mom and Jules are in the kitchen sitting at the table talking as I walk in. The sun is beaming in through the windows casting a beautiful light that somehow illuminates both in such a gorgeous way. I feel so lucky that these two ladies are my family, my support, and very much a part of who I am.

Mom's arms are outstretched toward me, "Good morning, sleepyhead."

I walk directly into her arms and go in for a much-needed hug. She feels so warm and cozy, always filled with unconditional love. I love her hugs, even at this age. She's my safe place.

"Ugh, another bad dream last night," I admit.

"Aw, Jules told me. So sorry, Evy," she says as she sways me. I pull back after a few seconds,

"Okay now, enough fuss about me. The good news is I woke up and have decided I am going to have an amazing day. It's Prom! Plus, Briggs would want me to enjoy every minute, right?" I'm proud of my "stay positive" attitude.

They both respond, "That's right!"

"Well, to start everyone's day off even better, I've made your guys' favorite breakfast this morning: French toast with lots of powdered sugar!" Mom says proudly. "Have a seat, girls." She grabs an oven mitt and goes over to the oven and pulls out the tray of piled high French toast that she has been keeping warm and sets it down on the breakfast table. She then heads to the refrigerator and pulls out a bowl of freshly sliced strawberries and a can of Reddi-Whip cream and sets them down at the table, before taking a seat herself.

The smell is incredible and it's making my mouth start to drool. "*Wowza,* looks delish. Thanks, Mom."

"*Ooh yum*, yes, thanks," Jules adds.

I take the Reddi-Whip can and spray whipped cream all over my French toast and some into my mouth. Yes, it's my favorite thing to do. We all dig in and eat, chatting, and catch up some more from where we left off from last night.

"You know we have a picture of you at twelve months old holding a can of Reddi-Whip trying to put the whipped cream in your mouth. It's one of Dad's and my favorite pictures of you."

"Yes, I've seen that adorable picture, and some things just don't change, do they?" I grab the canister out of my mom's hands and spray another fluffy pile of whipped cream in my mouth, savoring one of my favorite tastes, then pass it on to Jules so she can spray it in her mouth before making it back to Mom.

Once we stop laughing, I tell Jules, "In all seriousness, Chloe is coming at 2:30 and Henry will come around 4:00 to give us enough time to finish hair and makeup. You know he's very vain and wants a little makeup himself."

"Of course he does, not a problem. I figured he'd want some glam," Jules says.

Mom grins, "Henry kills me. FYI, I have the photographer and parents coming at 5:00, so you guys will have a good hour for pictures. The limo comes at 6:00 p.m."

"Perfect, yay! And dinner reservations at 6:30, and Prom at 9:00," I say as I start clearing the dishes off the table. My turn to wash them before heading upstairs to shower.

I'm realizing how much my shower is needed. I have the music blasting from Brigg's playlist. The hot water is running over my body, pounding on my shoulders, and calming me. It's helping to wash away the heaviness of last night. The shower cap is covering my hair to keep it dry because Jules told me not to wash it as dirty hair styles better. I have a picture of the updo I want. It's partially up and partially down. Briggs would tell me how much he loved my long hair, but he loved it most when my hair was out of my face so he could see my eyes.

The steam in the shower is starting to build up as my eyes close and my mind starts to drift to a day not too long after we started going out. Briggs had picked me up in the late afternoon so we could go kayaking. The day couldn't have been more beautiful, the temperature was in the mid 70s, the sky was blue, and there had been a light wind. Another typical California day. We each rented a one-person canoe. With our life jackets on, we brought our canoes down to the shoreline to enter the water. The wind had picked up a little by then, causing my hair to blow in my face, making it difficult to see. Briggs had been watching me and chuckling as I struggled, trying to move the hair out of my eyes. I keep a spare ponytail holder on my wrist for instances like this, so I took it off my wrist and pulled back only my bangs and twisted them into a knot high on top of my head while I was bent over. When I stood back up, Briggs had stopped laughing mid-laugh and just stared at me. I looked around wondering if I had missed something or my hair looked funny when I heard him say, "You're incredibly beautiful. When your hair is pulled back like that, it makes your eyes stand out to the point they hypnotize me. I am at your command."

His words made me blush, as I had felt some sort of electricity pulse through me. "Well then, I command you to come give me a kiss." I puckered my lips and waited for his warm lips to join mine.

As he approached me with a hip-hop, dance-like move, he began to sing, "In the similar words of Notorious B.I.G., 'Evy, Evy, Evy, can't you see?'" Then he planted a lingering kiss on my lips and held me tight.

When I caught my breath, I laughed as I said, "Those sound more like the words of Notorious Briggsie." I pulled him back in for another kiss.

When I open my eyes, I am brought back to the hot steam in the bathroom. My hands reach out into the fog fumbling to find the faucet dials. Upon turning off the shower I realize how steamy it is. "Well, shit, now I need to air out my bathroom."

Immediately I open the door to get out all that humidity. I dry off, grab my robe and place it around my body. I brush out my hair, then put some face cream on to moisturize. Next follows the body lotion, cleaning of the ears with Q-tips, another quick brush of my teeth, and then I put my ring on from Briggs, and I'm ready.

CHAPTER 57

2:30 p.m. came quickly. Jules had already finished my hair, and boy did it turn out amazing. *I love, love, love it.* It gives me a sophisticated Boho look. She even placed some baby's breath flowers within the side braids. My makeup is on point: my cheeks are popping, lips are a pinkish, red hue, and thick false top lashes are giving me a dramatic eye. I feel like a movie star ready to walk the red carpet, which I have promised myself that I'm going to do one day. I give Jules a big hug and as I'm thanking her, I hear a knock on the door. It's Chloe, and she has arrived wearing a white button-down top and black leggings with ballet flats. She's carrying her bag on her shoulder and using her cane.

Chloe looks filled with excitement as if nothing is going to ruin her day. This will be her day to shine, as I have never seen her get all dolled up. And nowadays, nothing is holding her back anymore.

Mom is headed to the door as Chloe comes in. "Good afternoon, Mrs. Peters," Chloe says with a wide bubbly smile. I'm wondering if her giddiness is from gummies or that she is truly excited, *or maybe both?*

Mom hugs Chloe and welcomes her in. "Hi, Chloe, let me take

your stuff. I'll bring it over to the 'makeup' area."

"Hi, chum! Are you ready to get all glammed up?"

"Oh wow, you already are. You look like a golden Goddess. Your hair and makeup are incredible," she starts to fan herself like she's getting flustered. "I am ready, but I still need to grab my dress out of the car."

I can see she is struggling a little bit with her walk. "Thank you, it's Jules's magic. Let me go get it for you."

I go to her car and walk back into the house carrying Chloe's dress. She chose a floor-length, strapless, emerald-green empire waist dress that I'm dying over. It's quite a bold color choice for Chloe who tends to wear more muted soft colors. Jules has Chloe already sitting on a chair and is brushing her hair out. Chloe is holding a hand mirror looking at herself. "So, we're going with more of a sleek look, Chloe?"

"Yes, being that my hair is not so long, as you can see, I'm thinking old Hollywood glam meets current day sophisticated glam. Maybe a mashup between Grace Kelly and Charlize Theron. Is that possible?"

"Yes, gotcha. I'll do my best," Jules says. She scrolls through her phone and comes up with her hair album. "What do you think of this?" She shows Chloe a picture of a model's hair from one of her most recent photo shoots.

"That is gorgeous. Do you think I can pull it off?" Chloe asks.

"With that beautiful face of yours, you can pull off whatever you want," Jules responds and I nod in agreement.

"You're going to make my head pop with all these compliments. Let's do it," Chloe says, clapping her hands in excitement.

Jules is with Chloe finishing her hair and makeup while I help Mom in the kitchen get ready for our guests. I hear Jules call my name, so Mom and I go out to see what she wants. Standing before us is the most elegant and beautiful version of Chloe. She looks stunning and royal in her emerald-green gown, with her hair slightly poofed and slicked back, eyes sparkling.

Chloe picks up the sides of her gown, lifting her dress off the floor and slowly spins around. "What do you think of Chloe?" Jules asks, looking proud of the transformation.

"Whoa, Chloe, you are dazzling, meow!" I say. I grab my phone and snap some photos of her.

Mom has her hands over her mouth in surprise and adds, "Wow, you have always been a beautiful girl, but whatever magic sprinkle dust Jules put on you, just made you even more beautiful. Both of you girls are going to cause a stir tonight. Jules, I need some of that magic."

The doorbell rings and I yell out: "Come in," knowing it's Henry. The handle turns and Henry saunters in with a suave sway, dressed in a royal blue tux, wearing a yellow bow tie, green flowers on his lapel, and carrying two flower corsages in his hands, topped off with a smirk on his face.

Henry stomps his foot, then stands to attention. "Lovely ladies, your prince has arrived." He takes a bow. "Now let me see my girls," he says as he approaches us. He gives Mom a hug first. "Good to see you, Mrs. Peters." Then he hugs Jules, then Chloe, and me together. He steps back to admire us. "Jules, you are the schizzle. I'm drooling over these two beauties. Dang, I'm going to have the hottest girls at Prom."

"Flattery gets you anything you want," Jules says.

"Love how your bow tie and handkerchief match our dresses. Good move." I also admire his Happy Face Pin on his lapel. *That's my boy.*

"As if you'd doubt me, I knew your dress colors, so Mom had the bow tie specially made. I have to say it's quite snazzy." He looks at himself with approval.

We all giggle as Jules asks Henry to have a seat in her chair. She drapes a towel over his shoulders so she can get busy on him.

"I'm going to bring out some water for you kids," Mom says as she heads toward the kitchen.

"Chloe, come help me with my dress if you don't mind?" I say, eager to get into it. The parents will be coming soon, and I want as much photo time as possible.

—

The parents all arrive at the same time. It's cool that everyone gets along with one another. I'm especially happy to have the Sullivans here and for them to be a part of everything. They had insisted on paying for our limo tonight in honor of Briggs.

Jules is taking our pictures in front of the backdrop Mom ordered for us. We take single photos of ourselves, then a group photo of Henry, Chloe, and me. Then each family with each kid. Mom, Jules, and I take pictures together as Henry takes the lead as the photographer. The Sullivans and I take a picture together, which I will be sure to frame and give to them. The last shot is of the entire group on a self-timer. We do a serious picture followed by a goofy one. After the frenzy of pictures, it is time to leave. I thank and hug the Sullivans for coming. The parents all wave us goodbye, as Henry, Chloe, and I step into our limo ready to be whisked off to dinner.

CHAPTER 58

We are having such a great time at Prom. The cheesy theme is: "A Starry Night" but it works. I do love Van Gogh. I especially admire his "Sunflowers" painting, as it is my favorite flower, thanks to Briggs. We've been dancing and talking with so many people. I look around knowing that all my classmates will soon be moving on to bigger and better things. These times together are fewer and fewer. I want to really take it all in. The music is pumping and I'm scoping the room watching others. I take my phone out and start snapping pictures here and there. I can see happy couples, guys in groups, and girls in groups, people dancing. I realize somehow, I'm by myself.

My eye catches Chloe across the room talking to this guy named Owen. He's a senior too, about 5'10" and so he towers over little Chloe. I'm intrigued with what I'm seeing. There seems to be some kind of flirting going on, and... what? It appears that Chloe seems to be doing all the touching. He's reciprocating and seems to be into whatever she is dishing out. *You go, girl.* I must tell Henry this, but where is he? I'm searching the room, when I hear an announcement coming from the stage and I'll be damned, it's Henry. No surprise, as he is no stranger to being the center of attention. *What is he doing?* The music is turned down and all eyes are on Henry. *This ought to be good,* I think to myself. He has everyone's attention. I mean, that tux alone is an attention grabber.

"Hey, hey, hey," he says in his best sexy Henry voice. "I hope you guys are all having the best Prom ever," the crowd claps and hoots in response. "I wanted to take a moment here to give a shoutout to our dear friend Briggs who's up there having his own Prom. I can bet you he's dancing around like a maniac."

I can hear people around me in a whispered voice say, "Aw." And some chuckles are heard too.

"I have an early graduation gift for his and my favorite girl, Evy," he says pointing at me.

I am taken aback for a minute, *like what?* People are turning to find me and look at me. *Tell me this isn't uncomfortable.* I did not expect this whatsoever. I make an awkward smile and start fidgeting with my fingers. *What can this be all about?*

He continues, "Our guy Briggs was not only a masterful dancer, and lover of music, but he was also eloquent with his words. So Evy, from Briggs and me to you. If I may, may I have this dance in his honor? This song is for you, my princess. If you know, you know."

My face is flushing, and I can feel heat rise from my chest to my ears, slowly burning as the music begins. Henry walks off the stage, down the stairs and heads toward me as the crowd clears making a pathway for him to find me. I can feel the magic in the air as the song starts and perks my ears.

Henry approaches me with the confidence of a prince coming to get his princess and extends his hand out to me. I grab a hold of his hand as he pulls me in. He drops his arms to my waist, and my arms encircle his neck. My eyes blaze into his.

"Henry, what in the world is going on?"

His lips part into an enormous grin, as he says nothing, and I'm confused until I hear the first three words of the song that is blaring around us: "*Days were dark...*"

I know these words, as they are the words I have ingrained in my mind from the song Briggs wrote to me. My promised song from Briggs. His last written words and here they are speaking to me in one of the most beautiful melodies I have ever heard. My eyes begin to brim with tears as I try to hold back a burst of raw emotion that has taken me over like a tidal wave. Feeling weak, I succumb to the wave, the tears spill, and I gasp, searching for air. But it is in these crashing waters of words that I quickly find my peace in a safe harbor letting the music swallow me up.

I look up to Henry's kind eyes telling me that he has me. I can see the tears swelling in his eyes too. I realize at this moment that it is Henry who created this song.

I find my breath and search his eyes. "You made this song for me didn't you, Henry?" I could hear his voice singing Briggs's words in a folksy paired back ballad that soothed my ears.

"Well, yes. I hope I did his song justice. Do you like it?"

"Are you kidding me? It's magical, it's from the heart of my two favorite boys. I...I...,"

Henry puts his finger to my lips to let me know no more words are needed. He begins to gracefully lead me around the dance floor as we move to the perfectly eloquent mix of Briggs's now-spoken words and the delicately haunting musical notes mixed with Henry's unique voice. My head rests against his broad shoulders, nuzzling in. I hold him tighter as my body feels like it's floating and transporting me into an alternative reality where Briggs has put a spotlight on me, watching from the heavens above. I feel each word pierce into my heart, but instead of wounding me, they are filling my heart, causing it to grow and find an exhilarating abundance of love and acceptance.

The song is ending, as I whisper into Henry's ear, "I love you. This truly means more to me than you will ever know. Thank you, thank you." I gently kiss his cheek.

"Anything for you, Evy. I'm glad you like it," he says then holds me close and lifts me up, swirling me with a final spin.

"Like it? I fucking love it. Your melody captured his words and painted a vision for me. My heart is leaping out of my chest. Briggs would more than approve." I close my eyes and inhale deeply taking in the last few moments.

My body is brought back down to the dance floor. I almost forget where we are, until I see the people dancing around us. My eye catches Chloe and I watch her as I take a second look.

"Oh my gosh," I gasp, breaking up our moment.

"What is it?" Henry asks.

"I think the music moved Chloe also. She just grabbed Owen and started kissing him. Look!" I point in her direction.

In a split second, we stop dancing and watch as Chloe begins to snog down with Owen Baker.

Henry shrieks, "I'd say we just witnessed our wild child being unleashed."

Chloe sees the two of us standing here in shock looking at her. Without any shame, she raises an eyebrow and gives us a thumbs up. She turns back to Owen and plops another kiss on his lips. I'm going to go out on a limb and say that Prom night is an evening none of us will ever forget.

CHAPTER 59

I'm staring at the time on my phone, counting down the minutes. School is about done for the day, so I start to pack up my backpack. I'm so ready to get out of here. As I zip up my bag, the bell rings. *Sayonara,* it's been a long day. I had two tests today and stayed up late last night studying. My caffeine buzz ended hours ago, so I'm basically brain dead now. I'm halfway down the hall and reach for my earphones when I realize I must have left them in the class. *Shit!* I turn around and head back to the room in a fast jog as I don't want it to be locked. Yay, the door is unlocked, so I walk in. To my surprise there is someone still there. It's a girl in my class named Amber, and apparently, I have surprised her also. She looks up suddenly and I see black stuff all over her face. Oh *geez,* I think she's crying. She turns her back to me and starts to occupy herself by acting like she's packing her stuff up. For a split second I feel awkward, until I realize my training with the Happy Face Project is kicking-in in full gear.

I step toward her with caution, wanting to get closer to assess the situation. I can hear her sniffle and see her bring her hands to her face most likely wiping away the smudges on her skin. I spot my headphones and reach down to get them as I say "*A-ha!* There they are."

"What?" she asks me.

"Oh, hi there, Amber. Sorry, didn't mean to startle you. My headphones, I accidentally left them. But I found them. Yay for me."

In a monotone manner she responds, "Yeah, yay. I guess things could be worse."

The way in which she is talking and the smudges on her face that she has failed to remove when she wiped her eyes, clue me in to the fact she's not okay. I remind myself to ask a question that is open ended and one that keeps the conversation going.

Her body language is not inviting, but I won't let that deter me, so I take a seat at the desk next to her and begin to talk. "Amber, it looks to me like you had a rough day." She keeps her back to me.

"You could say that. My life fucking sucks."

"I'm here for you if you want to talk to me about it."

Slowly she begins to turn toward me. "I don't really know you."

I'm trying to keep her engaged. "You're right, but that doesn't mean I don't care or want to help. I know what it's like to be upset and be in pain."

She's staring at me, giving me the once over and I watch as her eyes land on my chest, presumably on my pin from Briggs. She points at my pin. "I guess you do. You're the one who lost your boyfriend, right?"

"Briggs, yes, that's why I wear this pin. For him, when he wore it, it was a reminder to him to be happy, as he wasn't always happy, and I didn't know. It's also a reminder that he needed help, and he didn't feel safe enough to talk to someone."

"What's the point of talking to someone? It's not like talking to someone can make your life magically better," she says as she shrugs her shoulders. She starts to fidget with her fingernails and avoids eye contact again.

I need to pull her back into our conversation. "I can tell you; it helps having someone hear you and validate you. Amber, I promise you that you are not alone. I'll let you in on a little secret. After Briggs died, I struggled terribly. And to be honest I'm still struggling every day. But I went and met with Mrs. Wall, and after the very first meeting with her I felt a little better. And the next time I met with her I felt even better. I've learned talking to someone helps you unload your feelings, and helps you understand what's going on with you. And when I wear my pin, I know I have someone who cares about me. People do care about you. And I care about you, so I'm going to give you something." I pull my backpack to my lap and open it. I search the bottom of my bag where I keep the pins in a Ziplock bag, find it, and pull it out.

"Here, I want to give you one of our Happy Face Pins." I keep my hand stretched out; palm open with the pin in the center of my hand. "I want you to have this."

She hesitates to move, "This is from that project you did? I saw you guys at school and on the news."

As I'm about to give her the pin, I notice multiple red shiny cuts across her forearm and wrist. It's no rumor, she is a cutter. I try not to stare. "Yes, I'd like to give you one. Put it on your shirt or anywhere you'd like. There's a number on the back to call if you need to talk to someone." I flip the pin over to show her, then offer it to her again. "The counselors and teachers at school are trained to be on the outlook for the pins. They are here to help and want to make a safe space for anyone to talk."

Amber takes the pin and squeezes it in her hand, then stretches her leg out, and places it in her pocket. "Thanks, Evy."

"No thanks needed. I know that we don't know each other well, but if you ever need to talk, I'm here and so are our counselors. There is help available."

Amber stands up and puts her hand in her pocket where she placed the pin. She takes a deep inhale, "I'll keep that in mind."

The cuts on her arm catch my attention again. I avert my eyes, even though I know she saw that I saw them. "Please do, and one more question. I just need to ask you…do you have any plans to harm yourself?"

Self-consciously, she looks down at her wrists and turns them inward to hide her scars before answering. "You see my scars, huh? Doesn't mean I'm trying to kill myself; I'm going to be fine."

"I want you better than fine, got it? I'll walk out with you if that's okay?"

She looks at me, and says "Thanks, but no thanks. I'm cool." She begins to rummage through her backpack trying to look distracted.

I stall for a second as I'm having a moment. That was tense. I run the scenario through my mind, hoping I said the right things. I feel compelled to try one more time. "Help is available if you need it," I say. But she continues to ignore me. I turn and walk out the door.

CHAPTER 60

Chloe is sitting on the examining table, and her mom is in the chair next to the table as they wait for Dr. Neeves to come in. Chloe is having a hard time sitting up straight as her abdomen has been getting larger and making her uncomfortable to the point that she is only wearing stretchy clothing or dresses that don't bother her waist. Her mom watches with concern as she sees Chloe fidget and can tell she's not comfortable. The pain in her abdomen has been present almost daily now. She has had to take pain medication which then causes her constant nausea. Then there's the anti-nausea meds or sometimes the gummies which help. But despite whatever cocktail of medications she is taking, she has not been able to shake the pain and the fatigue. She has noticeably lost a lot of weight, and she was already quite petite to begin with.

Chloe had thoroughly researched the symptoms she would be experiencing over the course of her disease. She knew her body would start to deteriorate, but didn't realize how rapidly things would happen. There was no win-win situation here for Chloe. She could have gone through chemo and lost her hair, felt like shit, and not be able to be at school or be with her friends and be miserable, or take things into her own hands, which she did. The truth is that her illness is terminal, and nothing will change that, but she can control how the remaining days of her life will be spent. She is in control of her cancer, doing it her way. She knows she still needs to see Dr. Neeves, but she doesn't mind, as she has become comfortable with Dr. Neeves after these past couple months.

Dr. Neeves reviewed Chloe's scans again before entering the room. This part of being a doctor she has never liked: delivering bad news. She too can see the drastic changes that have happened to Chloe and keeps her reaction in check. She has learned to not let her patients see any sort of concern. But the one thing she always notices is the sparkle in Chloe's eyes that says, "I'm still happy to be here." As she acknowledges Chloe, she sees that the sparkle is there, but it appears dimmed today. She inhales deeply, in awe of this brave girl who sits before her.

"Good afternoon, Chloe," she says.

Chloe is sitting on the table with her legs dangling and swirling in nervous anticipation but manages to sit still and grin broadly upon Dr. Neeves' entrance. "Good to see you, Dr. Neeves."

She acknowledges Chloe's Mom seated with a nod, then directs her attention to Chloe. "How have you been doing symptom-wise, Chloe?" Dr. Neeves asks as she comes to the table.

"Well, I could be better and not have cancer, but other than that, mentally, I'm happy to be here and taking in each day as it comes."

"I have always loved your positive attitude, Chloe; that's important," Dr. Neeves replies. "But let's also talk about how you're doing physically. I want you to be comfortable."

Poignantly Chloe says, "My outlook may not be quite as optimistic on that matter. I can tell you that my little tumor friends are not quite so little anymore." She presses her hand to her dress to expose the outline of her belly.

Dr. Neeves knew from her experience that there would be a drastic physical change in Chloe. "I reviewed your scans and saw the tumors. It's not what I want to see, but it is typical with the progression of sarcomas as you know."

"Yes, I'm aware of the prognosis, as I have been doing my research. I have all the symptoms: enlarging stomach, fatigue, nausea, pain, etc. I've always been a rule follower for most of my life, and I'm proud to say that I'm pretty much textbook if I do say so myself."

Dr. Neeves admires her bravery. "And you still haven't changed your mind with treatment? We can go over your options again?"

"Thank you, but I'm good with my decision. I don't think I have much time left and I'm going to continue my path," Chloe says with confirmation as she looks at her mom.

Her mother places her hand on her leg and looks back at Chloe holding back her tears.

"How's your pain management?"

Without hesitating, Chloe speaks up, "To be quite honest, my pain is getting worse, sometimes it's unbearable. Perhaps I could use something a little stronger for nighttime." She watches as she sees her mom's eyes close, and her head shake side to side ever so slightly. It's difficult for her to see her mom upset. She puts her hand on her mom's shoulder.

"Not a problem, we will get you taken care of on the pain management side. I will write you a script for a substantial amount of morphine to take as per the protocol we discussed," she says as she is writing in her electronic medical records. "Oh, and Chloe, have you been in touch with Dr. Earl or have another appointment scheduled with him?"

"Yes, Ma'am. All good on that end."

Dr. Neeves asks Chloe to lie down, then performs Chloe's physical with careful attention to her heart, lungs, and abdomen. "Deep breath again," she instructs. She jots down her findings. "Is this tender?" she asks Chloe as she presses on her abdomen.

"Yes, Ma'am, it is," Chloe says wincing.

She helps Chloe sit up.

"Mrs. Wirrick? Any questions from your end?" Dr. Neeves asks.

Chloe's Mom pauses, then takes a deep swallow, "How will we know?"

Dr. Neeves looks somberly at Chloe, "Chloe will know. And Chloe? You have my number if you need anything. Do you have any more questions for me?"

"No, but I wanted to thank you for taking care of me. I'm thankful for you and I appreciate your knowledge and the care you have provided for me. May I give you a hug as I think this will be my last visit."

This takes Dr. Neeves by surprise, "Why, yes, of course."

Chloe carefully removes herself from the table and stands. She wants to be on an equal playing field with Dr. Neeves, not a patient on a table. She opens her arms and wraps them around Dr. Neeves and holds her tight for a moment. She could feel the equal strength and sincerity of Dr. Neeves's reciprocal hug. Chloe is the first to release, she then takes Dr. Neeves's hands. "Thanks for making a difference in people's lives, especially mine." She is smiling but her eyes start to flood with tears of sadness.

Chloe's selfless words seem to hit Dr. Neeves hard as she notices the doctor make a fist and bring it to her mouth.

"Thank you, Chloe, it has been my pleasure. You're a remarkable young lady and words cannot describe how proud I am of you and the grace in which you have handled everything. Mrs. Wirrick, you have an incredibly amazing young lady here." And with that, she looks at Chloe, giving her a smile with every ounce of empathy she has. She turns and walks out the door, pausing to look at Chloe one last time.

CHAPTER 61

"Hey, guys, do you want to know which college I picked?" Chloe asks Henry and me as we are waiting for Corbin's class to start.

"Have you been keeping this from us?" Henry asks in a scolding manner with his eyebrow furrowed.

"Serious betrayal, Chloe," I add.

"Oh, chill guys, I just sent my acceptance out this morning and didn't see you guys until now." Then Chloe stands up and unbuttons her coat to reveal her shirt with HARVARD splashed across the front. "Harvard will be so lucky to have me," Chloe scoffs then breaks her sassiness with a scrunched-up nose and giggles. "I'm going to be a 'Harvardian' or 'Vardian' for short."

"Congrats, Chloe! We knew it! Henry and I bet each other you'd go Harvard. Not much of a bet, but we both thought for sure you'd go there. Boston, *wow*! You are going to have to buy some cold weather clothes."

"The good news is they have a harbor there. Maybe I can come up there and sail you around?" Henry says excitedly.

"Yes, I'd love that so much. And I think I can handle the cold."

Clearly proud, Chloe keeps her jacket open and takes her seat again.

As Corbin walks through the door, Henry yells out, "Yo, Corbin, we have a Harvardian in the house!"

With his quick rapport, Corbin yells, "Yo right back. Can I guess who it is? Maybe…Chloe?" He spins with his right arm outward, with his finger pointed, and lands on Chloe.

Chloe manages to push herself up from her chair and stand with the help of her cane. "That would be correct, Mr. Corbin." Quite proudly, she opens both sides of her jacket and exposes her shirt for all the class to see.

Clapping is heard along with a few whistles acknowledging Chloe's announcement.

Corbin places his bag on his desk as he says, "Quite an accomplishment, Chloe, and congratulations are in order. But not to leave anyone out, my question for the day will not be my usual thought-provoking question, rather I would like to know where and what all of you are going to do with yourselves once you get out of this high school hell. Let's start with Mindy over there and we will go around the room. Stand up, Mindy, and tell us the scoop."

Mindy was headed to the University of Texas School of Communications program. William, who always had the coolest makeup on and painted fingernails, was off to trade school at the Vocational Academy of Makeup and Prosthetics in Orlando to learn special effects makeup.

Honestly, Corbin's class has been my redeeming feature this semester. He's made the class a safe place. There has been so much stress, especially with Briggs gone. I can come here and not worry about things and feel supported. Anyway, because we have all completed our big projects, the last few weeks have been a breeze, and the remaining weeks of his class will be a complete blowoff.

However, he has warned us that our attendance counts toward our grade, but honestly, I'd come regardless.

Last week he had a close friend of his, who is a well-known director from Sony, come and talk with our class. He told us how he worked up from being an errand runner at Sony when he first graduated from college, to being an executive. "Persistence and the belief in yourself will get you everywhere," he had said. I had managed to ask a few questions, and it turns out he knew my dad back in the day. Small world for sure.

It makes me wonder what my dad would be doing now or what film he'd be producing if he were still alive. I wish I would have been able to work alongside him on a big film project. That would have been a dream come true. I know he would have been a tremendous help to me in my college film classes too. There are so many things I will not get to experience with my dad, and it hurts. The same is true with Briggs. So many dreams were destroyed losing two of the most important men in my life. A pain starts to swell in my gut, and I need to push it away. *Happy thoughts*, I tell myself. *Happy thoughts*. And then walks in Mrs. Wall.

She now has white hair with a black stripe on her middle part. It must be her Cruella de Vil era. I'm looking for Dalmatians following behind her, but they are nowhere to be found. *Darn!*

"Sorry to interrupt, Mr. Corbin, but can you send Chloe, Henry, and Evy to see me during the last ten minutes of class? Oh, hi guys! I see you," she says as she waves to us. "Hi, everyone. Stop by and visit me sometimes. I get a little lonely in that office and summer is almost here, so last chance to see me. Okay, buh-bye!" she says as she scurries off as quickly as she entered.

CHAPTER 62

I t's fifteen minutes before the end of day and Corbin excuses us
to go to Mrs. Wall's office. As we are walking down the hallway,
I look around and realize we may not ever come back to this place
once we graduate. "Are you guys going to miss this school?" I ask.

"Never," Henry is the first to respond. "Maybe a little bit. You
know, come to think of it, we did have a lot of fun here together."

"We did! And I'm going to take away a lot of good memories
here myself," Chloe chimes in. "After all, this is where I met you
guys. I just wish we would have gotten to know each other when I
first moved here. Bygones, but you two have sure made the end of
my high school years the best and I can't thank you enough for that."

"You are sweet to say that. And I wish I would have gotten to
know you sooner too. Who knew we'd all be such good friends?"

As we continue walking, I see Briggs's old locker that has re-
mained empty to this day, and I stop. Both Chloe and Henry follow
suit as they know why I'm stopped. I place my hand on his locker
and twirl the lock. "I'm going to miss this locker. It brings back
so many memories of Briggs and this was our meeting place." My
forehead now rests against the locker. "UGH! You should be here,

Briggs!" I let out and pound my hand on the metal door.

"You tell him," Henry says. "Yeah, man, you should be here."

Chloe comes from behind me, moves her cane to her left hand, and places her right hand on my shoulder. "We all miss him, don't we?"

"Always, every minute, every day, always," I say as I squeeze my Happy Pin on my shirt. I need to remind myself to be happy. That's twice today.

We arrive at Mrs. Wall's office, and when she sees us, she immediately stands at her desk and excitedly waves us in.

Green chair is waiting for me. Gentleman Henry offers both green chairs to Chloe and me to sit in as he stands and takes Chloe's cane from her, placing it behind her chair.

"Guys, guys, guys! Or shall I say guy and girls? Anyhoo, I wanted to give you some exciting news," Cruella is clapping her hands with joy.

"You're killing us, what is it?" I ask earnestly, egging her on. All three of us have a silly smile on our faces.

"I wanted to tell you guys that your program is making some waves. We've had so many students come through my door for counseling. I've even made several outside referrals for matters above and beyond my expertise."

Chloe's excitement shows as she steadies herself and leans toward Mrs. Wall's desk, propping her elbows on it. "Mrs. Wall? So, you're saying that our program is really working? Because if so, I couldn't be happier to know this. Come to think of it, I've noticed more Happy Face Pins being worn around school."

"That's exactly what I'm saying. You three have made a difference in the lives of some of your fellow students' mental health. I've been busier in the past month than I have in the last semester. And…

all the exposure your project received has other schools calling here wanting to implement the same thing at their schools. They want a Happy Face Project."

"Right on!" Henry says energized to the max.

I'm taking this all in and feel a bit reflective as I think of what it is she's saying. I think to myself, *Where there is good, there is bad. Where there is negative, there is positive. The world is equalizing itself.* I start to recall the words said by the pastor, "May we be a source to others that are suffering and be able to show them our love and support." We did that, we are doing that, for you Briggs and for those that suffer. We are doing it.

Mrs. Wall's voice interrupts my inattentiveness, "Chloe, I see your Harvard shirt. Boy, they are lucky to have you."

"Yes, Ma'am, I guess they are," she says proudly.

"Well, congrats to all three of you superstars. I know that good things await you guys in your next chapters. Now, don't you forget about little ol' Mrs. Wall back here in Morro Bay," she says as she exaggeratedly points to herself.

"Not possible. I mean how many high schoolers have such a cool counselor? I'm giving you an A+ on that new color," I say, knowing how to put an even bigger grin on her face.

"Thanks for always noticing," she blushes.

CHAPTER 63

It's been a lazy Sunday and Mom, and I are having dinner at home catching up when I get a Snap from Chloe. It's a picture of what I guess is her Valedictorian speech. The picture is zoomed in with her eyes wide open at the top looking down on a piece of paper.

Second Snap she sends says: *Are you available to film my speech this week?*

I reply with a picture of Mom and me. *Yes Chum-what works for you?*

Tomorrow or Tuesday?

I say: *Tuesday-my house? 6pm?*

That works. You're the best. I'll send Henry the deets. I need critiquing. Ha.

Doubtful Miss Perfect

Blah, blah, blah and thank you

Then she sends an up close big kissy face. And I send one back.

"Who are you chatting with?" Mom asks curiously. "Henry or Chloe?"

"Chloe. She wants Henry and me to film her Valedictorian speech. And did I tell you she's going to Harvard?"

Mom looks excited to hear the news. "Fantastic! I'm just so proud of you and your friends. I still can't believe you are so grown up now and getting ready to leave me. Where has the time gone? I remember people warning me that your kids grow up in a blink of an eye, and it's true. I just always think of you as my baby, and not this beautiful, wonderful, woman that you have become." She pauses and looks at me for a long second. "I mean look at you. How did I get so lucky? I'm going to miss you. It was hard enough with Jules gone, and now you." Tears well up in her eyes.

"Oh Mom," I lean across the table and offer her my hand. I see before me not only my mom, but my best friend who has been my rock and my biggest supporter. "We've been through a lot together, haven't we?"

She nods, "We have, and we still have a lot of good times ahead of us."

My curiosity is getting the best of me and I'm wondering what life will be like for my mom when I'm gone. "Do you think you'll ever date? I mean, you've been alone for a long time. And I repeat, you're going to be all alone."

I think she's blushing as she says, "Inquiring minds want to know, huh? You don't need to worry about me. You and Jules have always filled me with so much purpose."

"Exactly, but now we will both be gone. Don't you think Dad would want you to find someone?"

"Yes, of course he would want me to be happy, and I can promise you I am just that...happy," she says with a pat on my leg. "Now, don't you be worrying about me, you've got bigger things like graduation and college to be worried about."

TBH, I'm counting down the days until graduation! I'm so done with high school. Speaking of, I need to get a dress ASAP as Henry,

Chloe, and I are going to do our graduation pictures together. Henry wants to do his sporting a captain's hat on his boat, imagine that?

"Looks like you have it all under control. But don't forget to enjoy the days you have left at school. This is a special time in life. There may be a day you look back and wish you were back in high school again."

I doubt that, but nonetheless, I hear what she's saying, noted. As I twirl my ring on my finger from Briggs, I tell my mom about our conversation last week with Mrs. Wall. She seems excited for us.

She tells me, "Even with all the pain you are carrying, you're turning a tragic situation into something that will help others. You're paying it forward and that's what It's all about. I couldn't be prouder. And I know Dad would be too," she says.

CHAPTER 64

I t's Tuesday night and I'm sitting on my bed getting some much-needed studying done while I wait for my chums to come over. I hear the doorbell and run downstairs. Henry is the first to arrive and I invite him in. The doorbell rings again, and when I go to open the door, I am surprised to see that Chloe has her mom with her. "Hi, guys, Mrs. Wirrick, good to see you." Chloe has her cane, and it's now decorated with rhinestones—another new one for Chloe. She has a little bit of makeup on and a cute royal blue sundress with a lightweight white sweater over it.

Mrs. Wirrick speaks up, "Good to see you, Evy and Henry." She gives me an outstretched hug still holding onto Chloe, then she gives a wave to Henry in the background.

"Do you want to come in and stay?" I ask her.

"Oh, you are too sweet. I think I'd make Chloe nervous. Here's Chloe's bag if you don't mind taking it," she says, handing it to me.

Chloe raises her eyebrows and chimes in. "My mother has heard my speech one too many times," she says, turning to her mom.

"I'll have my phone on if you need anything," Mrs. Wirrick says, looking directly at Chloe.

"Thanks, Mom. Love you."

"Love you, too," her mom says, smiling back.

"Bye, Mrs. Wirrick," Henry shouts out. "Can't believe I beat you here, Chloe. You must be slipping."

Chloe's eyes get big. "I'm getting called out? Okay, no excuse but I had to wait on my mom. She wanted to drive me here."

"Is it because of your leg?" I ask, as I have been noticing her constant reliance on the cane.

"Yeah, as you can see with my little bedazzled cane here, I'm still needing it," she smiles, tapping the cane.

Henry walks up and hugs Chloe. "Shazam-looking cane, girl. You…are…getting…fancy…on…us…now. My little rebel is now a sparkly rebel. I'm digging it," he says grinning, as he checks her out.

Henry notices Chloe is needing more help, so he takes Chloe's hand and leads her into the back office room, where I have everything set up to film. I can see the fragility in each step she takes, and it concerns me.

I ask her, "What does your doctor say about your leg? Is it going to get better?"

"This old leg? She thinks it will probably continue to cause me problems but says there's hope. Hence, I shall shuffle along and rock my cane until my body says otherwise," Chloe says in a positive manner.

Chloe sits down and reads over her speech while Henry and I get everything turned on and situated. Video camera and lights are ready to go. I am so glad I got everything ready before they came over: the markings, the backdrop, etc. I love when I'm in producer mode, it gets my juices flowing.

Henry decides to bring a chair to the markings where Chloe was going to stand. "Do you think you'd rather stand or sit? I'm thinking sit."

Chloe has a puzzled look on her face trying to figure out her thoughts, then says, "You're right. Sitting might be better for me tonight. It's been one of those days." She reaches into her pocket and pulls out two thumb drives. "Ev, could you make me a thumb drive and keep one for yourself too please? I want to be able to go over it and critique myself."

Henry sits in the chair he just placed so I can get my camera angle adjusted. "Thanks, Henry, perfect." I spend the next few seconds adjusting my lens. "Okay, Chloe, we are ready for you."

Henry goes to the couch to help Chloe up and carefully walks her to the chair and helps her sit. If Chloe is having any problems, I'd never know by the way she saunters to the chair ever so gracefully. She sits, adjusts her dress and white sweater, then tucks her hair behind her ears. She starts to fumble around looking for something.

"Do you need something?" I ask her.

"Yes, please. Henry, can you grab my bag that's over there?" she says pointing in the direction of where it sat.

Henry picks up the bag and brings it to Chloe holding it as if it is a fragile item and carefully places it on her lap. From the bag, Chloe pulls out what appears to be her royal blue graduation gown, rhinestoned cap and stole. And so it is, Chloe is officially in her rhinestone era. Harvard is written on the cap with maroon-colored rhinestones outlined by white rhinestones. It is quite the statement piece. I'm standing here a little puzzled as I watch her put her gown on, followed by the stole, then she carefully places her cap upon her head. She reaches back into her bag and pulls out some bobby pins and secures her hat to her head. Henry and I are looking at each other clearly both thinking the same thing, *Isn't this just a practice round speech?* He shrugs his shoulders at me.

Exasperated, Chloe speaks up, "Okay I'm ready."

"Um, Chloe?" I suggest, "Isn't this just supposed to be like a rehearsal?"

"It most definitely is," she replies.

Henry speaks up, "Then why are you getting all graduation-y looking on us? But I mean you do look fabulous, and that cap is the bomb! You sparkle, girl!"

Chloe touches the top of her cap, "Is it too much? I mean the sparkles?"

"Not at all, your cap is amazing. Job well done. Just wondering about why…all the gown and stuff?"

"Right," she says, nodding her head. "I want to fully be in the moment you know. Just take it all in. I think it's helpful."

Chloe with her perfectly straight posture, sits direct and delivers her speech with a bang, sailing through it flawlessly, with poise, passion, and a powerful message that makes both Henry and me give her a standing ovation when she finishes. I feel goose bumps and can't help but tear up, as does Henry. *Like hell she needed practice.*

"Well, what do you guys think?" she says, nonchalantly, acting as if she didn't just blow us away.

"That's a wrap! Amazeballs!" I exclaim.

Henry claps his hands, "Here's to our future Mrs. Decked-Out-Rhinestone Superstar. Incredible."

That's our Chloe—amazing at everything and always surprising us.

CHAPTER 65

My school week has been long and busy which kind of gets me frazzled. I haven't seen Briggs's parents in a little while so I decide I should make a quick detour and stop by and see them. I don't want to go empty handed, so I stop at our local grocery store to pick up some flowers for the Sullivans and grab a Ramune. I'm skipping the Hot Cheetos today though. I don't need orange cheesy fingers while I'm typing.

The flower section is surprisingly quite nice here. I can't help but get lost in the displays and look at all the different types of flowers and smell their fragrance. I'm having a hard time making a choice until I spot the tall yellow sunflowers. They instantly remind me of Briggs. Tall, bold and strong. I remember Briggs telling me about them when he brought me to see the butterflies. "Butterflies, especially Monarchs, are attracted to the sunflower's nectar. And sunflower plants display a quality called heliotropism, which means the young blossoms and buds will face east in the morning and follow the sun as the earth moves during the day." We even talked about doing a time lapse video in a sunflower field so we could capture them twisting with the sun.

I grab two plastic-wrapped bunches, one for the Sullivans, and one to bring home to my mom. It will be a nice surprise for her. The lady at the counter wraps both bundles separately each with brown paper and a raffia ribbon. The sunflowers look as cheerful as they make me feel.

I won't stay for long I tell myself, but I just want to check in with them. I arrive at the Sullivan's house completely unannounced. Their car is in the driveway, so I know they are home. I didn't notice it at first, but to my surprise, there is a For Sale sign in their yard. Oh gosh, they can't be moving away, can they? My stomach gets a sinking feeling. That wonderful feeling I was feeling just a few minutes ago, well, it has subsided. I step out of the car and head to the door.

When I knock on the door, I can hear Mrs. Sullivan say, "Just a minute." I wait patiently, still baffled by the For Sale sign.

She opens the door a little startled and yells out my name, "Evy! So good to see you. What a nice surprise. Come in, come in." She ushers me in, wrapping her arms around me with a gentle squeeze. I manage to keep the flowers from getting smashed. Then she turns her head and calls out to the back of the house, "Sam, Evy is here."

"These are for you," I say, handing the flowers to Mrs. Sullivan. I can see her face light up, which is making me feel all warm and fuzzy inside in the best way.

Mr. Sullivan approaches us. He is in his work clothes, tall and handsome with sharp features and a square jawline like Briggs. Instantly I see him differently than just Mr. Sullivan. I don't know why I haven't seen the resemblance before, but I notice that he is like an older version of Briggs. I am frozen and forced to catch my breath as I feel chills spiral throughout my body. I never thought I would see Briggs as an adult, and that he would be forever eighteen in my eyes, but this very moment gives me a vision of what Briggs would be if we could have grown older together.

He gives me a hug snapping me out of my thoughts as he says, "What a nice surprise to see you! And how lovely of you these bring sunflowers. If any flower was ever to be a smile, it would be a sunflower. You know Briggs was fascinated by sunflowers."

I take a double look at him, examining him closely, looking for Briggs' features in him again. "I did know that. As a matter of fact, they immediately caught my attention." My thoughts return to Briggs. "Heliotropic," I say matter-of-factly knowing that Briggs would be proud of me for remembering.

"Correct. Come sit down," he says as he leads me to the couch where I have sat many times. Where I've also kissed Briggs, hugged Briggs, and fallen in love with Briggs in this house. And now they are moving.

Mrs. Sullivan returns to the living room with the flowers in a tall, opaque, glass vase. She has cut the stems and arranged them perfectly, placing the vase on the coffee table. "Aren't these gorgeous?" she asks. "I can't tell you how happy we are to have you stop by." She grabs my hand and places hers over mine. "Sam, do you want to tell her about the house?"

Mr. Sullivan acknowledges her then looks at me. "Sure. Evy, I'm sure you saw the For Sale sign? Well, we were going to give you a call to tell you, but now that you are here, we will tell you now."

I look down on my chest and see that I have unconsciously started rubbing Briggs's Happy Face Pin. It has become my saving grace. *Keep me strong, Briggs.*

Mr. Sullivan clears his throat as he looks at me with a pensive face. "After careful consideration, Anna and I have decided to sell the house. We received an offer last night. As much joy as this house has brought us over the years, it now brings us pain. I can't even bear," he pauses and wipes a tear at the corner of his left eye, "parking in the garage or Anna going upstairs. We always had plans to maybe downsize once Briggs went off to college, and considering things, the time is probably now. We aren't going anywhere. We will be staying here in Morro Bay. And you are always welcome in our home."

I nod my head knowingly, understanding where he's coming from. I take a gulp and hesitate for a minute as the throbbing is setting in. "I…I do know how hard it must be for you both. I hurt every day with little reminders." Involuntarily, I inhale deep to catch my breath. My head lowers, and my body is crushing as I wipe away the tears.

Mrs. Sullivan responds immediately and moves to sit next to me and places her hand on my leg. "I'm sorry, we didn't want to make you cry."

I can hear the aching in her voice. "No, no, you didn't," I say, trying to make eye contact with a half-forced smile to convince them I'm okay. I bite my lip trying to think of the words I'm feeling. "I'm just an emotional wreck sometimes. I feel lost without him, you know. But I'm happy to hear you guys are staying in town."

She wraps her arms around me, her perfume smells of vanilla and sandalwood, and she lovingly pulls me into her chest as she says, "Come here, Evy." She holds me, rocking me gently for a moment stroking my hair before speaking again. "It's been tough on all of us in many ways. Please know we will always be here for you, Evy. We love you."

I tell them I love them, too. I try taking deep breaths to collect myself. As I'm calming down, I realize that once they move, I won't be able to see Briggs's room. *Panic. Shit, and now I have this over-whelming feeling that I need to see his room.* I inwardly debate about asking and feel quite awkward, but I know I need to for my own sake.

I find strength and slowly pull away. *Here goes.* "Would it be okay if I go see Briggs's room? I mean if not, no worries. I just…"

Mr. Sullivan is nodding his head. "Yes, of course. Please." He stands up and points his arm toward the stairs.

I stand up and Mrs. Sullivan squeezes my hand. "Go dear, it's okay."

My lips are pressed, and I muster up a small smile to give them acknowledgment. "Thank you," I say as I head up the stairs. My feet feel awkwardly burdensome as I begin my climb one foot at a time. I can feel them watching me and as I reach the top of the stairs, I turn to them to say, "I'll just be a moment."

"Just take your time, dear," Mrs. Sullivan says, holding her hands wrung at her heart.

I reach his door and take a deep breath. My left hand automatically goes to my chest to grasp my pin and hold it tight as I place my right hand on the doorknob. The ring Briggs gave me catches my attention as I turn the handle on the knob. The words on the ring speak to me in a whisper as I open the door: "U R My Everything". Chills run through my body as my eyes navigate Briggs's room. His bed, his prized Yeezy yellow shoes, his desk with our picture on it. Immediately, I am reminded that my "everything" is gone. I'm suspended in a moment of time where the entirety of Briggs's life stays standing still, perhaps even my heart.

CHAPTER 66

It had been a gloomy day yesterday, so we postponed our senior pictures until today. Henry insists we need good late afternoon lighting and so far, the day has been promising with not a cloud in the sky. I'm all dressed up in a pale-yellow sundress that is strapless and fitted to my waist with a fuller skirt. No lie, I kind of feel good about myself all dressed up. When I looked in the mirror this morning, I liked what I saw. Usually I'm like, blah, blah, blah, but today, I was slaying! I think I'm at the beginning of my glow-up. *Ha-ha!* It's no mistake that I chose yellow for Briggs, yellow for sunflowers, yellow for our Happy Face Project.

Henry wanted to coordinate in light colors for a pastel retro theme and we agreed he could take charge and assign us our colors, although he's opting to wear white, as he likes the idea of being neutral between the two of us girls. And he added that captains wear white, which he is, so how could I not agree with his plans? Chloe was thrilled with Henry's idea for her to wear lavender, a color choice that would be new for her. And then there's the blue from the ocean as the backdrop. So, there you have our pastel themed senior picture idea.

Henry and Chloe are there waiting for me as I arrive at the docks. I have my camera and stand with me. I wave as I walk toward them. I stop to take off my high heels as I find myself walking a bit gawkily in them. I can handle the dress- up thing, but heels, no thanks. I don't think I will ever be good at them. I prefer flip flops. I'm feeling quite excited and skip toward everyone carrying my heels, all the while being careful not to mess up my hair. "*Woohoo! It's time for senior pictures!*" I shout out as I approach.

"*Woohoo,*" I hear shouting back at me.

As I approach them, I notice Henry has light blue shoes on with his white pants and top. "Nice touch on the shoes, buddy," I shout out. At this point, Henry's arms are stretched out and open as I run into them for a big hug.

I turn my attention to Chloe who is seated on what looks to be some sort of cane that turns into a seat. Another new thing. She stays seated as I lean down to hug her. "Hey, Chlo."

"Hi, gorgeous," she says sincerely. "You look incredible in that dress."

"Doesn't she?" Henry adds. "I taught her well. I mean, I only surround myself with the prettiest of girls. I've got my lavender lily girl and my yellow sunflower. I'm one lucky guy!"

Chloe looks equally beautiful. Henry is right, she is a little lily. "Let's see that dress of yours, Chloe. Lavender is your color for sure."

She lets out a laugh, "I'd twirl for you, but my gimpy leg is really giving me trouble." Chloe does a little bow instead.

"Love it," I say.

"All these pretty colors, it's like Easter in May," Henry says beaming with pride. "And speaking of flowers, one sec." Henry brings over two flower bouquets, in pastel colors, of course. They are both the same, made with pink peonies, light green hydrangeas, and white baby breath sprigs scattered throughout. They are as exquisite as Henry's refined taste. "I thought they'd make for a cool prop for you girls." He hands each of us a bouquet, then reaches into his back pocket and pulls out a couple of pairs of sunglasses.

I take the sunglasses and inspect them. They have a cat-eyed retro shape. I put them on. "Love them both so much; good job, Henry," I say. I use my camera to snap some shots of the flowers and a few selfies of myself.

Chloe starts to talk but retracts for a moment. She closes her eyes, swallows hard, takes a deep breath then starts to speak with her voice slightly cracked. "Thank you, Henry. You've put a lot of thought into these gorgeous flowers and this day. This is a day for us to remember."

While she is talking, I can't help but notice a similarity between Chloe and the flowers. I'm intrigued and begin to take pictures of her. I start going through some of the shots and zoom in on one of them where I captured a distinct picture of Chloe looking down at her flowers. There is something poignant about this suspended moment that catches my eye. I see the strength they both exude, contrasted with the fragility they both possess. I take a moment to reflect on the juxtaposition.

"Are you gals ready for pictures?" Henry calls out.

I take a few candid photos of him also. He notices me clicking away and sticks his tongue out, then puts his thumbs in his ears and wriggles his hands and fingers like a clown.

"Yes, clown, we are ready. Chloe, you're up first," I say.

I shoot some shots of Chloe, while Henry directs her on her poses. She appears confident, insisting on not having her cane but, to me, she seems a bit unsteady. To be honest, she doesn't look that well. We are about done, when suddenly as if everything was in slow motion, I watch Chloe fall to the ground in a collapse. "Chloe?" I call out in a shriek. *Dammit. I was worried that would happen.*

Henry rushes to her side. I carefully set the camera down and rush over, plopping myself on the ground next to her. Henry looks at me with grave concern while stroking her hair. Her body is on her side laying in a fetal position. "Are you okay, monkey?" he says to her.

Chloe stirs then rolls on to her back. Obviously, she looks a bit bewildered and is looking around before she responds with, "Oh, hi guys, what's up?" A devious smile slithers across her face.

Henry is flabbergasted, "What's up? Seriously? I just about shit my pants watching you fall." He inhales deeply in a dramatic way.

"Oh, my God! *Eew!*" I shake my head at Henry and turn back to Chloe. "You're okay, right?" I ask her. I can feel a sense of relief overcome my body as I see Chloe stirring and propping herself up on her elbows.

Chloe carefully sits herself up with the help of Henry. "Yes, all good down here. I was just thinking maybe we should get some pictures while I'm lying down here on the ground. You know, like from the scene in *American Beauty*? We can spread some flowers around me. Very artsy, right?" She is sitting up now and running her fingers through her hair, getting the grass out.

"Wrong. Wrong. Wrong. Don't you dare do anymore moving around. I want to make sure you're not hurt," Henry pleads.

Chloe moves her legs, arms, feet, hands, and head around to show she is unharmed. "See? All good. Now help me up, and let's get the rest of the pictures done before we lose our light."

I'm amazed that she is unscathed after that fall. I have a feeling she wouldn't let us know even if she was hurt. Henry and I both help her up to a standing position. Once she is stable, Henry goes and grabs her seat and sparkly cane.

Despite her pleading with us, we make the executive decision to take our group shots and then send Chloe home to rest. She begrudgingly agrees to the plan and calls her dad asking him to come get her in twenty minutes. Henry and I lock eyes in a worried look while she's talking with her dad. He makes a gesture with his hands crossed over his heart and inhales deeply, rolling his eyes to the back of his head. He is a bit freaked out, as am I, about Chloe. This is not how I thought our evening would turn out, but no big deal. Henry and I were going to take each other's pictures anyway, so she won't be needed after we get some group shots. Retro pastel-themed senior pictures are still a success. All that matters is that Chloe is okay. Our concern right now is that Chloe gets home. Poor Chloe, I don't think things are going that great for her.

Henry and Chloe get into position so I can set up the shot. I dial to the self-timer on my camera and focus in on the two of them. "Move over a little to the left," I instruct them. "A little more, left, left, okay, stay right there." I push the button and run to Henry's side. The light on the camera starts flashing. We are all in place. "Smile guys! We are about to be graduating seniors."

I turn in toward them both, capturing this moment mentally and with my eyes acting as a camera, wanting time to freeze for a moment where everything is perfect. Our smiles say it all; we are thankful for our friendship and this time together. As usual, my thoughts then turn to Briggs. If there were phones in heaven, I think Briggs would facetime us right now to say hi and join in. *I miss you. Please call me, I miss you badly.*

CHAPTER 67

Over the past couple of weeks, Chloe's fatigue levels, balance, and mental status have been rapidly dwindling, not to mention the increase in wrenching pain attacking her with no warning. Her symptoms come and go, ebbing like the waves of an ocean, rushing in, then gently retreating. It is predicted, but not welcomed.

Last week in Calculus class, when Mrs. Phillips called on her for an answer, her brain froze right in the middle of explaining how she got the answer. Her words felt trapped inside her, she couldn't move or think about anything. Mrs. Phillips kept calling out to her, but she was totally unaware of where she was or what she was doing. It scared the crap out of her. Then suddenly, she snapped out of it. She thought about the scariness of losing her mind, then recalled the fall she had while she was doing her senior pictures. There were other incidents too. The combination of it all is pushing her close to the edge. "I can't have it be like this," she quietly says in a whisper to herself.

She is sitting up in her bed feeling so exhausted, reflecting on what has been happening to her, while examining her leg, and then her stomach. From her bed, she can see all the medication bottles lined up in her bathroom, shakes her head, and sighs deeply. She is too tired to get up. Her thoughts are disrupted when she hears a knock on the door. It is her mom.

"Chloe? It's time for dinner. I ordered your favorite veggie pizza from Surfside," she calls out through the door. Chloe can no longer take the stairs by herself. It is becoming too dangerous. Hence, she is escorted upstairs and downstairs every time she goes to her room. Her Mom waits for Chloe to answer.

"Okay, mom, you can open the door." *Yum,* Chloe thinks. She loves their crust. Usually, she was a pepperoni pizza girl, but meat had really started to bother her stomach when she ate lately, and she had made a point to mention to her mom that any future dinners probably needed to be more on the vegetarian side.

Her mom was not going to take any chances and helps Chloe stand up from the bed and holds her around the waist as they navigate to the hallway and down the stairs carefully. Once they reach the bottom, Chloe takes over. She wants to do as much on her own as possible while she can.

When Ben sees Chloe, he runs toward her with utter excitement. "Chloe!" he yells out. He runs to her side and takes her hand. "I'll help you," he says as he walks her to the table and pulls out the chair for her.

Chloe thanks her brother and adjusts herself on the seat. "Thanks for getting the pizza tonight," she says, directing her words at both her mom and dad.

"Easy to do when we know how much we all love Surfside," her dad says. He directs the spatula into the big pie and breaks off a piece of pizza that he places on a paper plate and slides toward Chloe. "Only the finest dishes tonight," he chortles.

"Thanks," Chloe says. As much as Chloe delights in pizza, the minute she inhales the smell of it, a rather unpleasant wave of nausea strikes her, causing her to gag. She grabs her napkin and brings it to her mouth; afraid she may puke. She's about to gag again, so she closes her eyes and keeps the napkin over her mouth and pinches her nose to avoid inhaling the scent again.

Her mother instantly notices Chloe's discomfort, "Is the smell bothering you? Do you need something else?"

It takes Chloe a minute to regain her composure before speaking. "All good. Just had a moment." She places her napkin back down in her lap. She picks up the slice of pizza, grinning, opens her mouth wide and bites into it to show everyone she's fine. But she's not, and doesn't want to worry her family, so she chews the first bite several times before swallowing. *I'll get through it,* she tells herself and presses on to the next bite. She manages to eat one whole piece, while silently suffering from the nausea. Had only she taken her medicine beforehand, she might have been able to enjoy her meal.

Her dad was talking about Ben's new interest in stars, when Chloe's pain erupts like a volcano in her stomach. "Tell Chloe your favorite new constellation, Ben."

"Volans!" Ben exclaims.

Chloe inhales deeply, and musters some strength to speak, "The flying fish?"

"Yeah, you know about Volans?" Ben is intrigued by his big sister's knowledge.

Chloe nods her head yes, as it is too painful to speak now. She takes slow deep breaths trying to work through her pain.

"Wouldn't it be cool to fly like Volans, Chloe?"

Chloe has already started drifting into flight with her meditation trying to rise above the pain. "Flying frees you, Ben. I dream of flying all the time." And with the little bit of energy she has, she closes her eyes, extending her arms out, and begins gracefully flapping them in the air.

"Fly, Chloe, fly," Ben says, clapping his hands, enamored by his sister.

In Chloe's mind, she is already floating through the sky. "I am," she replies. "I am."

CHAPTER 68

 send a Snap to Chloe and Henry. *Hey, guys, finally downloaded the pics and they are amazeballs.* I had just finished looking over all the pictures and putting them in a zip file. I couldn't wait to share them. Shockingly, I like almost all of them, including some of me.

Send now. Henry fires back almost immediately.

I screen shot one of my favorite pictures of him and Snap it back to him along with the words *"hot stuff."* He just doesn't take a bad picture.

Holy Cow! I'm handsome.

Not fair to us straight girls. Check your email.

Then I send another picture of the three of us via Snap. I'll admit the pastel theme was a winner. I send Chloe the zip file also, in anticipation of hearing from her. I find my favorite picture of her and Snap it to her.

I receive another Snap from Henry. *Digging these pics. And you, my princess, are stunning. Wow! Loving all of us.*

Let me know your favorite of the group shot. I send back.

I start going through the pictures again, narrowing down the ones I like. I stop at a picture of the three of us that catches my attention. The sun had been setting low, turning the sky into sheets of soft pink, blue and purple, which of course just happen to fall in line with our pastel theme. With our help, this is one of the few pictures that Chloe was able to stand up without a cane. She insisted that there "would not be a cane in any of her pictures." She looked radiant with an innocence about her and her smile was one of pure delight. Behind Chloe's head, there was a parting of the sky that radiated in a yellow color creating some sort of tunnel coming from the heavens and funneling straight to Chloe illuminating her like an ethereal angel. The effect wasn't from the sun, as we had been facing the sun in these shots. Maybe something reflective? It baffles me. I send it to Henry.

Here's my favorite, thoughts on the special effects?

Chloe is the chosen one. Did you edit? Henry's message asked.

No, original pic. Fucking cool, huh? I studied the picture more. *Mad skills.*

I feel something flutter in my heart. *Could it be? Briggs? Am I crazy?* Two people can look at the same photo and see totally different images, so maybe I'm seeing something and maybe I'm not. I needed Henry to ground me, so I shoot him back a message.

Maybe Briggs was looking down on us or trying to come see us? Am I cray-cray to think this?

Aw, baby girl. Of course it was him.

I want it to be him. I admit.

He's watching over us. Always. Everyday E.

I love you, Henry, thanks. I shoot back.

Love you even more. Forever. What did Chloe say?

Crickets. Haven't heard back from her yet. Sending her this pic now.

Okay. Got to go. Headed to boat with Dad.

Have fun. See you tomorrow.

I study the picture of the three of us more intensely and enlarge it on my screen. This picture gives me reassurance. Something tells me it must be a sign from Briggs. I sigh, feeling my heart tug, or maybe I'm feeling it tear. I sit quiet for a moment with my eyes closed, holding my pin. I let my memories of Briggs take over my thoughts. I can see his toothy grin with his brilliant blue eyes dancing. He is hugging me tightly and kissing my cheek. I never want to lose his memory, to do so would crush me. I quietly begin to sing words from "You Were Mine." All I know is, I was lucky Briggs was mine.

CHAPTER 69

Chloe awakens in her bed totally bewildered, with both her mother and father sitting in chairs next to her bed. She is not sure what is going on. Her vision is hazy as she looks down and sees that she is in her bed. She doesn't remember how she ended up here.

"Hi, my beauty," her dad says. He looks elated seeing her open her eyes.

Her eyes come in to focus better. "Mom? Dad? What's going on?" She is feeling discomfort in her arm as she lifts it and sees clear tape on her arm. "An IV?" she asks. "Oh gosh, what happened?" She is feeling so confused. The last thing she remembers is dinner with the family.

Mrs. Wirrick places her hand on Chloe's cheek gently stroking it. In a gentle, calm voice she replies, "My sweet girl, you've been out for a little while. But you're awake now and doing better. The IV was placed by the paramedics to hydrate you with fluids. They left the port just in case. We will get that IV port out in the morning."

Her mom did not want Chloe to know how truly scared they were that she would not wake up. Chloe had passed out at the dinner table, and they couldn't wake her. They had called 911 and they arrived at the house within fifteen minutes. The paramedics couldn't get Chloe to respond with more than a moan, despite a quick IV and smelling salts. In a panic Mr. Wirrick had called Dr. Neeves and left a message with her answering service. Within a few minutes his phone rang, and it was Dr. Neeves. Mr. Wirrick frantically told the doctor what he knew about his daughter's current condition, "Thank you, thank you for calling me back. I am so sorry to bother you, but it's Chloe. We were all sitting there at dinner together and then Chloe just slumped over. The paramedics are here."

Dr. Neeves insisted on speaking with them immediately. He obliged and handed his phone to one of the medics. He paced back and forth waiting for the phone to be handed back to him. Mrs. Wirrick never left Chloe's side while the paramedics were assessing her. He watched the terror in his wife's eyes as she held onto their beautiful daughter. His mind raced with desperate thoughts. *Where had all the years gone? Weren't they just holding Chloe in their arms rocking her as a baby? How was this…this crap happening to her now? Please save my baby,* he pleaded silently as he watched Chloe's body lay so still.

"Here you go," the paramedic tapped Mr. Wirrick on the shoulder catching him by surprise.

Mr. Wirrick nodded his head in understanding and placed the phone to his ear. "Dr. Neeves?"

Dr. Neeves spoke up, "Yes, hello, Mr. Wirrick. I've spoken with the medic and gave them Chloe's history. They are going to make sure she is hydrated and comfortable."

"So is she, will she…be…okay? I mean she's going to wake up?" his voice trembled; he was not sure he could handle bad news of any kind.

Dr. Neeves wanted to be very straightforward with him, it was part of the job she hated but knew it was so very important to set the expectations for the family and patient. "Mr. Wirrick, I believe that Chloe will soon be in a phase called 'terminal lucidity.' The patient can unexpectedly go in and out of consciousness like she did tonight, followed by bursts of energy or mental clarity. This cycle can last for months, weeks, or days. It is a telltale sign that the end is near. I'm so sorry."

"Okay, yeah, uh so," he couldn't speak the words and continued pacing. He paused, wiped the tears from his eyes, "So you are saying, we need to enjoy every minute with Chloe?"

Dr. Neeves took a long, slow breath, "Yes, Mr. Wirrick. Hold on tight to that amazing daughter of yours. Bring her to bed and let her rest. Her body needs it. I will call hospice to come check on her tomorrow. I'm here if your family needs me." And with a heavy heart, she ended the call.

CHAPTER 70

Chloe's fevered mind begins to race. By deduction, she realizes that she had passed out during dinner last night, as that was her last memory—talking with her brother. She starts to panic wondering how long she's been out. "What day is it?" she asks, hoping it was still Saturday evening.

"Sunday night, 8:00 p.m.," her mom says attentively.

Chloe starts to do the math in her head, "Then I've been out for over twenty-four hours? About twenty-six to be more precise."

"That would be about right," her dad says, mentally counting the hours.

"The good news is it only seems like an hour," Chloe says, letting out a quiet little giggle.

Both her mom and dad look at her surprised, not finding anything positive about this situation. They had both been so wrought with uneasiness and uncertainty in her gaining consciousness.

Chloe uses her arms to push herself up in bed. "Mom? Dad? I'm just making light of the subject. This is not a surprise. We all know what will happen. We know the outcome. I'll be honest, I've noticed a lot of changes in my daily abilities and the discomfort and pain are more present than not. Medicines don't even work."

She is interrupted by her mom. "Why haven't you told us all this?" There is anguish in her face.

"Because this whole process is difficult on all of us already. And you guys know, nothing is going to make a difference. I know what I'm up against and I've just tried to enjoy every day, and I truly have. Honestly, I've come to terms with everything. I knew this conversation was coming. And after this incident, I feel even stronger about things being on my terms. I refuse to let cancer get the best of me."

Her Dad speaks up, "We agree, but we want you to be as comfortable as possible. It's hard to see you hurting. Have we told you how incredibly courageous and strong you are? But you don't have to be. You are more than we could have ever asked for in a daughter. We are here for you. And more importantly, we love you more than you will ever know." He leans in and hugs Chloe tightly.

Her mom joins in, and the three of them hold each other, taking in the moment and being present. Suddenly, the door to her bedroom swings wide open, and Ben bursts in.

"Chloe!" he exclaims. "You're awake! I want a hug too." At once, he runs to Chloe's bed and joins in on the hug fest.

"Thanks for the love, but I guess it's time for me to get up and get out of this bed. Apparently, I've been in it too long," Chloe is saying when she hears a ding from a phone. "Oh, is that my phone?"

"I'll get it," Ben says eagerly, wanting to take care of his big sister. He goes to her bedside table and brings the phone to Chloe. "Here you go."

"Thanks, Buddy. You're the best little brother ever," Chloe tells Ben lovingly and kisses him on his head.

"Do you guys mind if I take a look at my phone for a second before getting up?"

"Not at all," Mr. Wirrick says.

"Thanks, I'll be just a minute." She looks at her screen with a surprised expression, "Quite a few missed messages. I'm so popular." There were about fifteen Snaps from Evy and Henry. She opens up Evy's first and is pleased to see a couple pictures pop up on her screen. Evy had sent her pictures from the photoshoot. "My graduation photos are in," she says out loud to no one in particular. Everyone gathers back near her. She examines the photo of herself first and smiles with approval. "Look!"

"What a gorgeous picture of you," her mom says. "The lavender dress was a good choice."

"You're so pretty," Ben says.

"What a beautiful woman you are inside and out," her dad interjects.

She moves on to the group picture and shares it too with everyone. "Me and my besties."

Ben looks intently at the photo and zeros in on the golden tunnel shooting down from the sky. "Is that a tunnel from Heaven?" he says innocently.

Chloe looks at the picture then looks at Ben smiling with complete sincerity. "Yes, Ben, it must be a sign from heaven." She then turns to look at her parents and nods with a gentle acknowledgement.

Her father is a little taken aback by Chloe's comment, so he stands, "What do you say we head downstairs and get Chloe something to eat?"

"Yes, and can I have ice cream?" Ben asks.

"Me too," says Chloe. "Ice cream for dinner. Why not?" She winks at her parents.

CHAPTER 71

I'm excited for today. I've been counting down to this week as it's our last week of school. My senior year is coming to an end. *Woohoo*, let me do a happy dance. Graduation is on Friday night and I cannot wait to graduate! No more high school after Wednesday afternoon. No more early rising, or high school bullshit.

I check my phone and see that I finally got a response from Chloe. Her message reads: *Thanks for the pics. Got the email too. So many good ones to choose from. Love the ones of us chums. Too cute. See you at school.*

Mom knocks on the door then quietly opens it. "Happy last week of school." She is carrying a plate of food and has a cup of coffee from Top Dog's Coffee for me.

I jump out of bed and run to give her a hug. "Aw, aren't you sweet? Thanks, Mom. Avocado toast and coffee—yum!" I place the food on my bedside table.

"Just wanted to wish you a great week. I can't believe my baby is graduating," Mom says, staring adoringly at me.

"I'm no longer a baby you know?" I tease her.

"Wrong, you will always be my baby. Even when I'm eighty and you're in your sixties, I will still see you as my baby."

"Isn't that a little creepy?" I ask. "I'm imagining you at eighty, cradling me like a baby when I'm sixty. Believe me, it's not a pretty sight." I can't help but laugh out loud.

"Good point. I'll make sure not to do that, smart ass," she giggles. "But remember, you'll never be too old to hug."

"That I can handle. Deal."

Then, out of the blue, Mom starts to hug me, but tricks me, and scoops me off the ground, cradling me like a baby. We both laugh like crazy. She kisses me on the head then sets me back down. "I'm going to tell you that the best part of you growing up is that I'm gaining a best friend. And with that, I've got to go to work now. Love you, Evy. Have a great day."

"You too, bestie." I take a sip of my coffee and watch an incredible woman who has given so much of herself to both Jules and me, walk out my door. I finish my breakfast, then brush my teeth and get dressed. My hair is going in a ponytail today as I don't have time to deal with it. Quickly, I make my bed, then search the room for the gift I'm bringing for Mrs. Wall. *Found it!* Off I go.

The plan is to meet Henry in the parking lot at school. Chloe sent a message that she was running late. Sitting here in my car waiting, I decide to listen to music. New drops were out on Spotify on Friday.

It's been a while since I have checked on his playlist, so I decide to do so. I type in "Quiet the Buzz" and it pops up, bringing a smile to my face. It's still up there in the rankings. He'd be so proud.

A loud noise startles me. I turn to look out my window, and there's Henry, with his mouth open and face pressed against the glass. My heart skips a beat as I let out a shriek. I bang my hand at the window, then roll it down yelling out, "Okay, Pennywise, you scared the shit out of me! I may have even peed my pants a little."

Henry is basically belly laughing and obviously finds my reaction so funny. "You should have seen your face—priceless," he chuckles.

I roll up my window and step out of the car. I poke him in the ribs, "Don't worry, I'll get you back."

Henry makes a *tsk* sound, then wraps his arm around my waist, "Doubtful. Sorry to scare you, but it was funny on my end. Your face..." He kisses me on my cheek. "So how is my princess doing today?"

"Quite excited to be done with high school. Can you believe we've been best friends since kindergarten?" I stop walking and turn to him, "We've been through so much together and here we are with you still by my side."

"I made a promise to you way back when, didn't I? I'll always be here for you; you know that right?" he says in a serious manner. "I may not get to see you every day when we head off to college, but you will hear from me every day."

"You better. Thanks for being my BAE," I say, clutching him. I can smell his scent of bergamot and marine, so amazing.

"A present for me?" he points at the gift.

"*Ha*, no. Not after that scare fest." I chuckle. "It's actually for Mrs. Wall."

"How thoughtful of you," he smirks.

I smile back. "She and I developed a little friendship, you know. It's just a photo I took of her that I thought she'd like. Speaking of, I need to drop it off at her office."

We continue walking into the school building. I admire our sign that is hanging in the hall as you enter through the doors: "The Happy Face Project" it reads. It makes me feel quite proud to see it. There are several other of our signs posted throughout the school. There are stands that hold our pins, making them available for anyone who needs one.

"Okay, see you shortly," Henry says and heads off in a different direction.

I make my way down the hall to Mrs. Wall's office and find the door open. I snap a picture of her as she is sitting at her desk. I have no idea what she's doing but I can hear her harmonious cackle. I wonder if it's about the new hair color she's sporting: rock lobster red. Pushing her door slightly open, I call out to her, "Mrs. Wall?"

"Evelyn Peters! Get in here," she says as she gets out from behind her desk and greets me with a firm couple pats on the back. "What a pleasure to see you. Have a seat. I'm just reading my daily joke of the day."

I get comfortable on my old friend "the green chair." "You've outdone yourself with red hair, Mrs. Wall. Nice color job," I say, admitting that the color is quite extraordinary, if you like that kind of thing, which I don't, but for her it works.

"You are always so keen to notice my hair, thank you. You probably know that red symbolizes love and courage? I am expressing my love to all you seniors and praying for courage when you go off into the world." She seems quite satisfied with her explanation.

"Meanings are everything, I like it." I say reflectively. All along I've known that there was more to her than just a color change. Perhaps that's why I've been such a frequent visitor to her office.

"So, you're graduating this week. How about that?" she says in a motherly kind of way.

She lifts her leg in the air and stretches it, puts it down, then lifts the other leg stretching it too. "Pardon me, I square danced this weekend, and now my legs are giving me a bit of discomfort from all those twists and turns on the dance floor with the Mr."

My eyes get big as I am caught off guard by yet another one of the many facets of Mrs. Wall.

"Sorry to hear they're sore." I transition to, "I can't believe my time here at Morro High School is coming to an end."

"*Aw ha*, but new beginnings are right around the corner for you and that's exciting," she says, swirling her pointer finger in a circular manner. "How's life been going for you? Are you holding up, okay?"

Lightly gripping the edges of the jungle chair and shifting my body weight, I try to find a more comfortable position as I take a second to think about my answer. "Over the past month, it has been so much easier to sit in this chair and talk with you. Time has allowed me to be better at processing all the changes and those to come. There are days I hold both grief and joy at one time. I guess you can say I'm kind of learning to swim in the ocean. Sometimes the water is easy and calm, and other times the waves crash so hard on me. But I keep swimming."

"That's right, you keep swimming and keep smiling with those sweet memories of Briggs," she pauses and presses her lips in a gentle smile. "And don't you dare forget that I'm here for you if you need me. You might be going somewhere, but I'm not," she says, pointing at her desk.

"Deal," I respond.

Mrs. Wall leans over the desk, "Also, I'm glad you are here, as I wanted to tell you that we have received some district funding to continue The Happy Face Project. It's been a huge hit not only here, but everywhere. Kudos to you, Henry, and Chloe for making such an impact on our students and school. We collectively decided that we will make this a priority in our budget every year."

"Fantastic news! Well, what I came to see you for today, was that I wanted to tell you, thank you for making time for me and listening. From the bottom of my heart, I want you to know how much I appreciate you. I'm not sure if I could have made it through this semester without you."

I reach to the side of my seat and pull up the gift bag. "Here you go. This is for you." I push the bag across the desk to her excited for her to open it.

"For me? Oh, my good golly, you didn't need to get me anything, but this girl does love presents. May I open it?" she asks, wild eyed with excitement.

"Of course."

I watch as she pulls the gift wrapped in a lavender tissue paper out of the bag and carefully unravels it.

"I love this! Hot diggity! I must say you captured my best angle," she exclaims. "This is me in my lavender phase. Thank you! Thank you! You truly have a gift, Evy." She proudly places the framed picture on her desk and looks at it with adoration. "So nice."

"You're welcome. I loved your lavender hair; it was my favorite."

"Lavender? Really? I'll keep that in mind," she says, touching the ends of her hair as the first period bell begins to ring.

"Well, that's my cue to go. I'm glad you like it."

We both stand up and Mrs. Wall comes around to my side.

"Hug time," she says, reaching her arms out, beckoning me to join in, and of course, I acquiesce. "What color do you think Briggs would have liked for me?"

"Yellow, definitely yellow," I say.

She whispers in my ear. "Yellow. That was one of my favorites. Okay, girl, stay strong and go out there and keep making a difference. I'll be cheering you on."

She has made me seen and for that I am grateful. "Will do," I say, as I untangle myself from her embrace. I gather my belongings and walk out the door. I might actually miss my visits with her.

"Talk soon."

CHAPTER 72

It's last period. Every day has seemed to go in slow motion. "I'm so over all this," I say to Henry as we head toward Corbin's room. When we arrive, there is a sign on the door: MEET UP AT THE FIELD. Corbin's room is at the end of the hall with a door that has direct access to the back of the school, making it easy to get to.

"Sweet!" Henry shouts. "Let's wait for Chloe."

"For sure," I say, looking around for her. "I haven't seen her all day. Have you?"

Henry thinks about it for a second, "As a matter of fact, no. And I didn't hear back from her about the pictures I sent until this morning."

"Me either. I think her medicines are taking a big toll on her. I'm getting worried about her." As soon as I finish my sentence, I think I see Chloe coming down the hall with her cane and her very noticeable limp. "There she is," I point in her direction.

Henry takes off and goes to her side, taking her backpack, then grasping her hand to help keep her steady. "Well, if it isn't Ms.

Sassafras. Finally, we get to see you," he says to her.

Chloe manages a little laugh, "Just making my grand entrance. Good to see you guys."

Immediately, I notice the bandage on Chloe's hand as Henry brings her toward me. I exhale deeply. I don't want to think negatively, but man, she just doesn't look that healthy. "Chloe!" I call out and greet her with open arms.

"Hey, Ev, I loved all the pictures. They turned out beautifully. I want to thank you again," she says to me.

"No thanks needed; it was teamwork. Glad you liked them. Good news, we are headed outside for Corbin's class."

"So fun, right?" Henry says, opening the back door for us. "This way." Henry's eyes immediately land on Chloe's hand. "Girl! What happened to your hand?" Chloe looks down at her hand a little embarrassed. "It looks worse than it is. I just bruise easily. One of my medications must be administered by IV. No big deal."

"If you say so, but it looks like it hurts," I tell Chloe cringing. I can't hide the look of torture on my face.

"Oh, girl, I've had worse things, believe me," she says laughing.

"Truth," Henry says as we make our way out to the field, carefully escorting Chloe to where we see our classmates gathering. The weather is perfect, the haze has burned off and it's sunny with a few clouds in the sky providing some intermittent shade.

"Hey, Corbin," Henry bellows out. "Great idea to be out here!"

Corbin nods his head smiling with acknowledgment. "Gather around," he says, waving his arms to come in closer. He has shorts on today, something I haven't seen before on him. His T-shirt is white with The Beatles plastered on the front of it. His curly hair is loose at his shoulders. I'll admit he's cool, especially for a teacher.

We find a place to plop down. Henry makes sure to help Chloe get seated, treating her like delicate China. I sit next to her, and Henry goes to the other side of her. Chloe leans back on her elbows and tosses her neck back, face up to the sky.

"The world is beautiful, isn't it?" she asks us. "The sky fascinates me." We both look at her, then lean back with our faces to the sky just like Chloe.

I'm about to speak when I hear a strumming of a guitar being played. We all sit up and look to see Corbin playing. I take out my phone. It takes me a minute to figure out the song, but once he starts to sing, I recognize the song right away. It's by John Lennon, hence his Beatles shirt. There is a hush in the crowd as we all stop what we are doing and lend our ears to Corbin's music. He softly begins to sing the song "Imagine."

The song comes to an end, everyone begins to clap. What a beautiful rendition. Almost every minute of it was captured on video by yours truly. Some of the students are standing. Henry gets up, but I stay seated next to Chloe, knowing it would be too difficult for her to stand up. Corbin bows his head in thankfulness. Some guy shouts out "Corbin, you're a rock star dude!" Corbin holds his hands up making a stop motion. Everyone quiets down to hear him; there's still a few whistles being heard. I look over at Henry. He raises his eyebrows in surprise.

"Thank you all. Very kind of you guys. Mostly, thanks for not booing me. That's my end of year surprise for you," Corbin laughs. "Hey, guys, seriously, thanks for joining me out here today. I'm happy to see that everyone is in attendance as per my request. I thought we could just enjoy ourselves out here today. With this being our last class day, I can't let the year end without asking a question of you."

A few moans are heard. I might be weird, but I look forward to his questions. He continues, "Now, now. Here's what I'm putting out there: I'm going to give you a second to think about the one word that you are going to put out in the world as you move forward in your new journey." He starts to move around, strumming the cords on his guitar and building excitement.

Chloe, Henry, and I all look at each other. "I think I have one," Henry says. "Ridiculousness?"

"You're such a dork. Be serious." I say as I look at Chloe who is fully invested in finding her word.

Corbin stops, turns and points his guitar to Stephanie who is also one of the school's best athletes. She won state in swimming this year.

"Oh, hi! Are you asking me?" She looks up at Corbin.

He nods back at her. "Stephanie, tell us your one word." He waits for her answer.

"Commitment," she says proudly.

"Love that," he says, strumming the chords of his guitar, then runs over to Bryan. Bryan's a big skateboarder. He has a sleeve of tattoos on both his arms.

"Dude, uh, okay. Motivated is my word," Bryan says, patting his skateboard.

Corbin then makes his way to our group with the guitar still playing. He points his guitar to Chloe. I tap her on the shoulder to get her attention.

Chloe seems a little startled, "Sorry about that. Your question?"

"Your one word," Corbin says patiently, strumming some chords.

Chloe adjusts her posture, "My word is…cherish, yeah, cherish. And I will always cherish each one of you." She looks around at everyone, giving them a genuinely sincere smile.

Meanwhile, Corbin continues his interrogation, of everyone's one word. My word is resilience. However, it's a word that somehow chose me.

He wraps up his talk-show-style class by going around the crowd and lands in the middle of everyone. "All right, guys, great word choices. I'm sure everyone is breathing with bated breath wondering what my word is, right?" He doesn't wait for an answer. "Authentic. I challenge each one of you to be authentic in anything you do. Be transparent, be intentional, and most importantly be… who…you…are. This is your life and your time to be who you were meant to be. You get to choose your path. Go forth in this world and show up." He plays a few chords, then stops. "What are you guys waiting for? Go, get out of here. It has been my pleasure being your teacher. Class is dismissed now. Happy graduation." He goes back to playing "Imagine."

Chloe speaks to both Henry and me, "What a perfectly amazing afternoon. I don't want it to end."

"It doesn't have to," Henry says and stands up. "Why don't we get out of here, get some ice cream, and maybe go to the boat?"

His words perk my interest. "I'm in. Chloe, are you feeling up for it?"

"Yeah. Let me quickly text my mom. She was planning to pick me up." She gets her phone out and sends her mom a text. "I'm good to go, guys," she says happily. "Let's get out of here."

Henry helps her up, and I collect all her belongings along with mine. We all want to thank Corbin, so we walk over to where he is and talk with him for a minute.

"I am proud of you three and we will see you guys at graduation on Friday," he says.

Chloe becomes very serious and looks at him for a moment before speaking, "Mr. Corbin, I need to tell you that I am lucky to have had you as a teacher. I want to thank you for being an extraordinary person. You have enlightened and enriched my life as a student. Thank you for making a difference. And I think I'm speaking for all of us." She looks at us for a confirmation. "May I thank you with a hug?"

Corbin is caught off guard by her kind words, and so am I. He places his hand over his heart. "Why thank you, Chloe, and yes you may," he says bashfully. "I've enjoyed having all of you. How about a group hug?"

We say our goodbyes and head out. Hands down, Corbin is the coolest teacher ever. I will miss him. Next stop Foster's Freeze for ice cream.

CHAPTER 73

Collectively, we, meaning Henry, Chloe, and I, decided to make today, Tuesday, "senior skip day", an advantage of being a senior. I must be at school tomorrow as I have a test in English. Luckily, I don't have to study, as it's a creative writing type of test, so it makes skipping today very plausible. Henry picks us up this morning at 9:00 a.m. Mom had packed me a little picnic for our day of antics. She's the best. Before you know it, we are at the docks and heading down to the pier. Henry decides to pick Chloe up and carry her into the boat, avoiding any accidents. I help him untie the ropes while he starts the engine. Knowing it's going to be a little chilly, I head into the cabin to find a couple blankets. The temperature is already dropping a little and I know both Chloe and I will be the first ones to get cold.

Slowly, the boat makes its way into the water with Henry as our attentive captain, navigating out into the open water. It's peaceful at this time of day. The seagulls pepper the sky flying overhead in groups gliding gracefully up above us chatting away. Chloe and I are sitting together on the starboard side, cuddled up in our blankets. The slosh and splash of the water makes my ears wake up. I'm giddy with contentment being here with my friends.

Henry looks over in our direction. "Isn't it a magnificent morning? I'm glad we decided to skip school and get out on the water."

"Any day we come out is a magnificent day. I'm going to miss this once we go off to college," I say feeling melancholy. I get my phone out and take some pictures.

Chloe deeply inhales the ocean air. "I love how the ocean makes me feel. It gives me a sense of peace," she says, tilting her head up toward the sky, gazing at her surroundings. The marine layer is still thick making for a pleasantly overcast morning.

"I'm lucky to have been born into a family that loves boating. I have my dad and grandfather to thank for that," he says looking back at us. "Did I tell you girls that my parents are taking me on a three-week sailing trip to the Caribbean this summer for my graduation trip? I can't wait!"

"Lucky!" I say feeling a little envious.

"What a great opportunity to spend some time with your family," Chloe chimes in. "You are going to cherish that memory forever. Ha! Did you see that I used my word from today? Cherish."

We both laugh with her. "You're my favorite, Poindexter," I tell her.

"And I want you both to know how much I 'cherish' this time with you," she giggles. "I'm blessed to have you two in my life," she says now wiping tears.

I see she's tearing up, so I put my arm around her, "Don't be sad, Chlo Chlo. We love you, and we're always going to be best friends and keep in touch. We've got the summer and school breaks. We can visit each other at college. I can't wait to see Harvard. It will be so fun."

Henry, still at the wheel, points to me, "What she said, my little monkey, only happiness here, it's not like you're ever going to be able to get rid of us."

Chloe laughs, trying to regain her composure, "Don't worry, guys, these are all tears of pure joy. But there is something I've been wanting to do…"

"And what is that?" Henry and I say in synch.

"I want to be like Rose from *Titanic* and be at the front of the ship with the wind in my hair. Can we?"

"Why yes we can, and that would be the bow," Henry corrects her. "Keeping it real."

"Yes, at the bow of the boat please," Chloe says.

Henry brings the boat to a slow speed, then turns off the engine. He helps me walk Chloe up to the "bow" as far forward as she can manage. I stand behind her making sure she is safe and secure. Once Chloe is set, Henry runs back to the wheel and turns the motor on, moving the ship onward.

"Titanic: Jack and Rose at the Bow. Scene 1. Take 1," I shout out.

"Close your eyes, Chloe," I say, grabbing my phone and putting the camera in video mode. "Action!"

"Do you trust me, Chloe Rose?" Henry yells out to us from the stern.

I have a death grip on Chloe as she yells out, "I trust you."

Henry carefully increases the speed, feeling the wind brush against his face.

He watches as Chloe extends her arms out in a T-shape, and I hold on to her hips, bracing her frail body against mine, still managing to get a great video angle.

"All right, open your eyes" he tells her.

"I'm flying!" Chloe cries out.

Yes, my dear friend, you are flying. So epic.

CHAPTER 74

Hurray! I just finished my last high school exam ever. Pretty sure I aced it. My high school era has ended. *Peace out!* I place my test on Mrs. Graham's desk boasting a big grin and skip, yes, literally skip, out of the class. Henry is waiting for me outside the classroom, wearing his sunglasses pushed down toward the end of his nose and leaning up against the wall like he's posing for a magazine cover.

"Greetings, high school graduate, congrats!" he says, full of excitement.

"Congrats right back at you," I put my palm in the air and high five Henry. "Shall we do one last stroll down senior hall?" I ask, even though we planned on doing this anyway.

Chloe was supposed to be with us, but she didn't make it to school today. It's our very last day at Morro High School, so obviously both Henry and I are concerned and wondering why we haven't seen or heard from her. Chloe had so much fun last night, and she even seemed to be quite spunky. It seems totally unlike her to miss her last day. She has had what seems like a lot of doctor appointments, so maybe she had another one today. Maybe I'm over analyzing things, but who misses out on the last day? Apparently not Henry or me.

"Why, yes. May I?" he says as he puts his arm out, bent at the elbow ready to escort me.

I lock my arm into his and we head to our lockers. We stop at Henry's first. He rummages through his backpack and pulls out a glossy headshot type photo of…make a guess here…himself. He finds the tape in his bag and tapes his photo to the inside door.

I'm watching Henry hang the photo, "What are you doing putting that ugly mug up there, Mr. Lucky Blue Smith?"

"Just keeping it real. Just wanted to let the next person using this locker to know how lucky they are to have the locker of the future famous Henry Wyeth Preston. This will be a collector's edition one day." He grabs the rest of his things out of his locker and places them in his bag. He stares at his picture proudly, blows it a kiss, and slams the locker closed.

I laugh, not surprised that Henry would do that. "Let me get a picture of you and your picture." I grab my phone, while Henry reopens his locker and snap a picture of Henry proudly leaning up to his locker door baring a sexy smile. "I need a sharp pin to pop that big head of yours."

He winks at me and flashes me a million-dollar smile. "Okay, let's head to mine and then to Briggs's. We will pass Chloe's on the way. It's a bummer she didn't make it today."

We are walking down the hall, when I see Amber from my class, who I talked with a couple weeks ago, who appears to be on the phone crying. The closer we get, the more distracted I get watching her. We pass by her with her cries still audible.

I stop and turn to Henry, "Can you give me a moment?"

"Sure, I'll be right here."

I turn around and walk back over to where Amber is. I tap her on the shoulder, which startles her. She turns her phone off. Her mascara is running down the corners of her eyes and face wet with tears. "Amber, what's going on?" I knew better than to ask her if she was okay. She is taking deep breaths trying not to cry.

She places her hand webbed over her face and closes her eyes, "Same old shit," she weeps.

Gently, I touch her arm. "Do you want to talk?"

"I've talked enough to enough people. It's just my fucking life," she says in an exhausted tone.

"I'm available, or I can walk you to Mrs. Wall's office?"

"Thanks, but I'm good," she says, even though her body language says otherwise.

I take my backpack off my shoulder and reach inside until I find my bag of pins. I hand her one. "I know I've given you one before, but sometimes you need two or three." I smile at her and get nothing back but sniffles. She doesn't take it. "I just want to remind you that there's a number on the back. People are there to listen and help you." I extend my hand out again with the pin in my fist.

Hesitantly, she reaches out and opens her palm, "I threw the last one away."

I place my hand in hers and firmly plant the pin in her palm. "No worries, plenty of these things to go around." I point to the one on my chest and wink at her. "Don't hesitate to call."

She doesn't say anything back to me, but that's okay. I give her a very abbreviated hug not wanting to encroach too much on her personal space anymore, then turn and walk toward Henry.

"What's that all about? I saw you give her a pin," Henry says, seeming a little baffled.

"Just girl stuff. Maybe I'll tell you later. Let's go."

Chloe's locker is just a few feet away. Still no word or sign of her. My locker is next. I open it up and grab the few things I have remaining: an old water bottle I need to throw away, and a few pictures I had on the inside. One of the pictures hanging up is with Henry, Briggs and me. We took it the first day of senior year, to pacify our parents who wanted a first day of school picture. We are holding up a sign that says our names, our first day of senior year, and how old we are. We looked goofy doing it, but it's funny how a picture like this can make your parents wildly happy. I shut my locker and say goodbye to it as Henry returns the favor and snaps a picture of me.

We land at Briggs's locker, and it feels so bittersweet. This spot brought me so much joy meeting him here at school between classes, hanging out with him, laughing, stealing kisses from him. Yet, it's brought me a lot of pain over the past few months knowing he will never be here again. I've tried to avoid being at this spot physically as it's just too painful. Sometimes, like today, I'm able to stop here and reflect on all the good memories of him. Today I am balancing the joy and grief once again as I stand here with Henry. I open his locker to find the bottle of Ramune I had placed there on purpose a while back. I'm happy to see it's still there. I wish it could stay for an eternity along with our memories, never letting anyone have access to his locker, only me. Henry takes a selfie picture of us at his locker. I run my hand over the inside of the locker, perhaps tracing where Briggs's hands had been, and say goodbye. Maybe one day I'll be back walking these halls, cherishing all the nostalgic memories Henry, Chloe, Briggs, and I made here.

CHAPTER 75

Mom took a few hours off from work at the end of her day today so that she could take me to an early dinner at Windows on the Water to celebrate my last day of school. With Friday night being graduation, it will be hard to get reservations, so she wanted to get a jump start. Jules can't come in until Friday for graduation due to her work schedule, so it's just Mom and I tonight. We both get dressed up. Mom is wearing a low-cut black sleeveless dress that ties at her waist and black heels. She has a strand of pearls on that my father had given her. She only wears them on special occasions, but I think she should wear them more often as they suit her well. She has an elegance about her tonight. I wore a light blue dress that is ruched in the middle. I like it, because it gives the illusion that I have more of a shape than I have. If I didn't have boobs, I'd look like a twelve-year-old prepubescent boy, because somehow my gene pool didn't allow for a butt or hips.

The restaurant is upscale, with panoramic windows across the back of the restaurant, allowing for a fantastic view of the bay while dining. In my opinion, it's one of the best restaurants with a view in Morro Bay.

We are at the end of our meal sharing the chocolate ganache dessert, when Mom says she has something for me. She reaches in her purse and pulls out a neatly wrapped package about the size of a book. She reaches across the table and hands it to me.

"Aw, thanks, Mom," I say as I tear at the corners of the pink floral wrapping paper and unwrap it. It is a tanned leather journal with a suede string tied around it. "It's a journal!"

"Go ahead and open it," she says to me, anxiously awaiting my reaction.

Carefully, I untie the strings and open the front cover, revealing a handwritten passage from my mom. I read in silence, biting my lip, "To my beautiful daughter Evelyn, I wanted to leave you with a piece of my heart as you go off to college. This journal is a collection of thoughts, memories, and dreams I've gathered just for you. As you step into this new exciting chapter of life, I pray these pages serve as a reminder of how much you are loved. I love you, Mom." I couldn't get through her words without tearing up. I take my napkin and dab at my eyes. "This is an incredible gift, Mom," I say tearily, holding the journal to my heart. I push back my chair and go over and hug her, whispering in her ear. "I can't wait to read it. I love you."

We get home around 7:00 p.m., and as soon as we walk in the door, I get a phone call. I look at my phone and it says Morro Bay High School. That's weird, especially because school is closed at this hour. I decide to answer it.

"Evylyn, I'm so sorry to bother you at this hour," my brain is trying to figure out who this is. Then it hits me when the voice on the line continues, it's Mrs. Wall. "We did it," she says in a weighty voice.

I needed to confirm it was her. "Mrs. Wall?" The red lobster?

(I left that part out.)

"Oh yes, yes, sorry, I forgot to tell you it's me," she says exasperated.

"We did what?" I say, totally confused.

In a serious voice Mrs. Wall continues. "Evelyn, oh my gosh, this is sad news and my heart breaks, but we were able to intervene in a suicide attempt. Tonight, through the school hotline. The Happy Face Pin, it worked, it helped, they called. We were able to help someone."

My heart sank for a second knowing that as great news as it was, I couldn't help but think about the terrible pain the person had to be going through to have to call for help. I had to take a moment.

"Evylyn? Are you there? We helped save someone."

"I'm here. And I'm so glad you called me. Is the person okay now?" I feel my body flush with heat.

In a somber tone I have never heard from her mouth she says, "I can't give you specific details, but they are in the hospital, and the doctor said the person should be okay, but they're still being monitored. He said as a rule, he would never have reached out to me, but he had recognized the Happy Face Pin the person had on their shirt when they received him/her. He had seen the news broadcast about your guys' Happy Face Project. He wanted to call me, as I'm the counselor, and let me know that he thought the pin's hotline number may have saved this kid's life. He wanted you kids to know. Can you believe that?"

I stood frozen. The pin. Briggs's pin. It made a difference. Was it Amber from earlier today? I grabbed at my pin and twisted it so that I could look at it. I brought it to my lips and gave it a gentle kiss. "Thank you, Briggs."

"Sorry, what did you say, Evy?" Mrs. Wall asks. "I think my

hearing is bad."

I'm a bit flabbergasted and tell myself to focus, "That I'm blown away. I'm so grateful that the person is okay."

"Me too, amen. It was the pin," she reiterates. "Do you realize your project may have saved their life? Consider yourself heroes."

"Thanks, Mrs. Wall. I think Briggs would be the proudest," I sigh.

"You're right, he would. He's probably giving you a standing ovation," she pauses. "Do you mind sharing this news with Henry and Chloe? I've got to go feed the family," she says.

"Will do, Mrs. Wall. And thanks for your call."

"My pleasure," she says, hanging up the phone.

After I hang up, I tell my mom the news. She is beyond pleased. "Didn't I tell you that you were on to something good?" she says.

Next call is Henry. He's devastated, but pumped about the news that the person is okay. I suggest we three-way call Chloe and give her the news. We still haven't heard from her, which still seems so strange. We dial her but there is no answer, and the phone goes to voicemail. We leave a message and shout out: "Chloe! Call us!"

Fifteen minutes go by, and Henry and I are still talking, but no word from Chloe. "Let's just go to her house and see what's up with her. Surely, she's there," Henry suggests.

"I'll come pick you up," I say.

CHAPTER 76

We knock on Chloe's front door full of excitement, ready to share the news. Her dad answers and seems to be caught off guard by our visit.

"Good evening, Henry and Evylyn. What a nice surprise to see you two," he wavers, and seems unsure if he should invite us in.

We are about to speak when from behind him, comes a voice, "Who is it, honey?" Mrs. Wirrick approaches with a dish rag in her hand. She is surprised to see us.

Henry speaks up, "Hi, Mr. and Mrs. Wirrick. We came to see Chloe. Is she home? We've got some great news to share with her."

I nod my head in agreement as Mr. and Mrs. Wirrick look at each other.

"Wendi?" Mr. Wirrick motions to his wife to take the lead.

"Please come in. Chloe's upstairs sleeping. She's uh, been a little under the weather. Nothing contagious, it's just her medications, they do quite a number on her," she reassures us. "Why don't you guys have a seat and let me go check on her."

"We'd hate to bother her if she's not feeling well. It's just that we've got this great news…and she hasn't been to school, and we've been trying to reach her," I say, feeling bad for coming here unannounced.

"Don't you two worry one bit. I'll run upstairs and let her know you are here," she says and turns toward the stairs.

—

She gently wakes Chloe, who is sleeping in a fetal position in her bed with a fluffy fur-like blanket covering her. Medicine bottles are neatly lined on her bedside table, along with her Stanley cup, a washcloth, and some rice crackers. She is quite groggy but manages to open her eyes.

"Hi, Mama," Chloe says in a scratchy voice, turning her head to look at her mom.

Her mom is pleased to see that Chloe is responsive as she has been going in and out of sleep over the past thirty-six hours. She places her hand across Chloe's forehead to check for fever. She is relieved that her skin temperature feels normal with a slight warmth like you have upon waking. "Hey, I hate to bother you, honey, but you have visitors."

"Visitors? Who's here?" she says, stirring, somewhat surprised. She stretches her legs out fully and pulls off the blanket. She feels a little achy, but nothing she can't handle.

"Henry and Evy are here waiting downstairs with your dad. They had some news they said. I told them your medicines were causing you to not feel so good and I'd check with you to see if you were up for visitors. I can send them away."

Chloe thinks about it for a second, "No, it's okay. They can come up for a little bit. But can you help me look more presentable first?

I don't exactly want them seeing me this way." She perks up at the thought of seeing her friends and manages to push herself up to a seated position.

Her Mom goes to her bathroom, turns on the faucet and grabs a washcloth, which she runs under the warm water. She squeezes out the excess water and carries it back to Chloe's bedside handing it to Chloe to clean her face with. She goes back to the bathroom and returns with Chloe's brush and gently combs Chloe's hair. Chloe feels more presentable. "Okay, you can bring them up."

The door to Chloe's room is open, and she can hear her friends call out to her.

Chloe is sitting up in her bed with a duvet over her. She looks pale but very put together as she always tries to be. "Come in, chums." She hopes she can pull this off, as she is starting to feel extremely tired again.

Henry and I walk in together and see our little monkey in her bed. She doesn't look too sick, but as we get closer and give her a hug, her skin reveals a pallid gray undertone, which changes my opinion.

"Hey, gorgeous, are you doing, okay? We've been worried about you," Henry says sitting down next to her on a chair with me perched on the side of her bed.

"Yeah, we haven't heard from you and got a little worried. We missed you today…on our last day of high school," which I'm sure she is quite aware of.

"Sorry I didn't get back to you guys. I've been sleeping a lot and haven't been on my phone. And I know, what a bummer. My doctor changed some of my medications and I've been having to get used to all the new side effects," she says, pointing to all the medications on her bedside table. "They're making me pretty exhausted."

I'm quite confused, as she's told us she is fine, but it sure doesn't seem that way. New medications? "Are the medicines at least helping you?"

Chloe fidgets with her sheets, "No need to worry about me, they are definitely working," she is trying to put on a reassuring smile. "Just gotta get through the side effects. I'll be in a good place soon. I promise." It's obvious she is trying to change the subject. "You have some news to share, my mom said?"

Henry, trying to lighten the mood, clears his throat. "Wait for it," he says in a dramatic tone. He stands up and starts to pace the room. "Evy? You're better at this, you tell her."

Henry looks in my direction, encouraging me to speak. So I begin, "Actually, this is very serious. I'll make it short. Mrs. Wall called me earlier and told me that a student at our high school tried to take their life."

I am interrupted by a big gasp from Chloe, "Oh God, no," she cries out. "Are they okay? Who is it?"

"We don't know who it is, but the doctor said the person should be fine. He called Mrs. Wall, because he had seen the news story on our Happy Face Project and the student had the Happy Face Pin on their shirt. He wanted to pass on that the pin probably saved their life as they had called the hotline number on the back."

Chloe looked astonished. "That's incredible." Mentally, she starts putting the pieces together and realizes what this means. "That means...our program...our pin...helped them. We saved one!"

With pride, Henry says, "We did. Who knew the three of us could make such a difference?"

"Well, we are quite the friend group," I say satisfactorily.

Chloe folds her hands together, placing them over her belly and takes a moment before speaking again. "There is a quote from Abraham Lincoln who said, 'Next to creating a life, the finest thing a man can do is save one.'"

We did just that, saved a life. I have to believe that Briggs played a part in all of this. I look down at my ever-present Happy Face Pin and feel a tingling throughout my body.

Henry notices Chloe nodding off, and nudges me. "Time for us to go," he says, which startles Chloe a little.

"Oh, sorry about that. I appreciate you guys, with all my heart, for coming by," she says.

"We had to let you know and we've missed you big time."

"Yeah, feel better so we can celebrate on Friday at graduation, okay? And use your phone," Henry adds.

Knowing she couldn't make any promises, Chloe replies, "I'm going to do my best. Now come give me a hug, you guys."

And so, we do, with her frail body squeezing us as tightly as she can. She gives both Henry and me a kiss on the cheek, then whispers, "I want you two to know how much I love you guys. You both mean so much to me." A tear trickles down her cheek.

Henry and I both reply, "Love you more, chum."

Henry nudges me that it's time to go. He looks at Chloe, "Love fest is officially over for now, see you at graduation, little monkey. And get well."

We thank her parents for having us and apologize again for coming over unannounced, then walk out the door. Now outside, I ask Henry, "Henry, do you think Chloe's going to be okay?"

Henry opens the car door for me. "I hope so, I really hope so."

—

As soon as Henry and Evy leave, Chloe's parents make their way to Chloe's room.

"Did you have a nice visit?" her mom asks. She is eyeing Chloe with concern. She knows her daughter specifically said no visitors, but she felt compelled to let them see her and thought it would be good for Chloe. "I'm sorry, I know you didn't want anybody to see you this way, but they arrived unannounced, and they seemed so eager to see you."

"It's okay, Mom. They brought the best gift anyone could give me," Chloe says reflecting on her visit.

"I'm confused. I thought they had great news? What did they give you?" her dad asks.

"They came to tell me that somebody's life from our school was saved today because of our Happy Face Project. It was the gift of life," Chloe says, detailing them on the news. "We've worked so hard on the project, and I had always hoped the pins would make a difference in at least one person's life. I know I can leave this earth now, knowing that there's hope for others."

Her mom leans in and gives Chloe a kiss on the cheek. Her dad does the same then holds her hand, looking directly into her eyes and says, "You are remarkable, and you're right. That is the best gift ever."

CHAPTER 77

GRADUATION DAY

Henry and I made plans to drive to graduation together, with me picking him up. Mom and Jules are going to come together later to meet us. We had sent several messages to Chloe, but it was crickets on her end.

We arrive at the school and follow the signs to the ceremony. We had to get here about two hours earlier than our family to get directions on lining up, etc., to receive our diplomas. I don't mind, as it's pretty much a big social hour right now seeing everyone in our grade. Summer will be busy for most, and I may not see some of these classmates for years to come.

To be honest, I'm getting antsy, as there is still no word from Chloe, and we are getting ready to start lining up for show time. She's the Valedictorian, and everyone is expecting her to give a speech today. I wish I had her parents' phone numbers to call them, or better yet, enough time to stop by her house again to check in on her.

Henry approaches me looking handsome and regal as ever. His hair is slicked back with a gentle wave to it, the ends of his hair falling into loose curls just above his shoulders. His skin is a golden tan from being out on the water so often. He has seersucker blue-and-white pants on, with white driving shoes, a white button down, and a light-yellow tie. Best of all, he's wearing his Happy Face Pin on his gown displaying it proudly, just like me. "Anything from Chloe yet?" he asks curiously.

I sigh, "No nothing. I'm hoping she shows up. Her Snap location is off," I say taking out my phone to look at her location. "It's not looking good."

CHAPTER 78

Last night Chloe's condition took a turn for the worse. The abdominal pain became unbearable and sadly, unmanageable even with her prescribed pain medications. As per Chloe's instructions, her mother had called the hospice nurse that had been assigned to her and asked her to come over. She arrived around 9:00 p.m. and hooked Chloe up to an IV line, administering her some medications, which gave her much needed relief, getting her through the night.

When Chloe wakes up this morning, it feels like a new day to her. Her pain is now only a 5 on a scale of 10, with last night feeling like a 30. First thing on her agenda, is to call Dr. Earl, which she does. She has a nice conversation with him and thanks him for his guidance.

She showers and needs her mother to help her blow dry her hair, as she is too fatigued to lift her arms. She puts on her lavender dress that she took her senior pictures in, as she feels quite beautiful in it. While they are getting her ready, her dad, with the help of Ben, cooks the family his famous pancakes and egg breakfast. Chloe manages to eat a good portion of her meal but cannot finish it. Ben, on the other hand, has piled the powdered sugar on top of his pancakes and plans to eat every bit. By the end of breakfast, there is more powdered sugar on his shirt, than there is in his belly. The sight of him has Chloe smiling.

When breakfast is over, everyone loads up in the car. Ben carries Chloe's graduation cap and exits the house, carrying it in his hands, excited for Chloe's graduation today. Her mother has packed a light picnic to bring with them, complete with four champagne glasses, and a bottle of Dom Perignon, and a non-alcoholic champagne for Ben to drink.

They arrive at the docks and soon find themselves on a 42-foot captained catamaran. For the next couple hours, they sail around Morro Bay, heading south to Pismo Beach, then looping their way north to the Cambria area. Chloe, sitting at the front of the boat with her family, is taking in every minute appreciating the beauty of the world encircling her. She is enjoying the coolness of the ocean air whispering about her skin. The seagulls glide in the sky and dip down splashing into the water looking for fish. Chloe, surrounded by her family, knows at this moment that she is loved with every ounce of their unconditional love. No matter how much pain she is in today, she refuses to allow it to ruin her day. This is exactly the day she had planned and envisioned.

About two hours into their journey, Mr. Wirrick has the captain stall the motor, slowing the boat down to a gentle pace. The graduation ceremony is about to begin. Chloe's dad is officiating the ceremony along with Ben at his side. Her mom is assigned to be the photographer.

Her father takes a spoon and a champagne glass, clinking the back of the spoon on the glass, making a celebratory gesture. "Hear, hear," he says, gathering everyone's attention. "It is with esteemed pleasure that we celebrate the most incredible young lady who has ever graced Morro Bay." His eyes pool with tears. "May I present to you, our Valedictorian, Chloe Grace Wirrick."

On cue, the captain sounds the boat's horn, and cheers come from her family, making Chloe beam with pride, wearing her graduation cap, tassel and all. She would have loved to be at her actual graduation but knew that being with her family was far more important. She tries to hold back the tears and smile. Ben runs over and hands Chloe her "diploma" that he had made for her. She hugs him dearly as her dad and mom look on with tears in their eyes. Her dad pops the cork of the champagne and pours some into the three glasses. Ben is disappointed that his bottle doesn't have a cork to pop. He hands out the glasses and makes a cheer: "Congratulations, Chloe. We are extremely proud of you and all of your accomplishments. You have faced every challenge with bravery and fierceness," he says with a crack in his voice. "You did good, kid."

Her mother becomes teary-eyed as she manages to form the words, "To Chloe, you are our everything, we love you." The four of them hold their glasses up, and toast their sweet Chloe.

After an amazing afternoon on the water, the Wirricks have returned home. Together as a family, they are sitting on the couch all together, snuggling up in the living room, looking at old pictures and sharing stories. There's a knock on the door, it's the pizza guy bringing their early dinner. They continue their family gathering at the dinner table, laughing and telling more stories while eating pizza. Once again, Chloe's lack of appetite keeps her from eating much. She does manage to lick the chocolate buttercream frosting from the cupcakes her mom had made. Chloe looks at the clock on the kitchen wall and sees that the time is 6:00 p.m., exactly the same time her graduation ceremony is starting.

CHAPTER 79

Principal Arndt is at the podium welcoming everyone. The graduation ceremonies of the Class of 2020 are officially underway. Both Henry and I are a little freaked out, because there is still no sign of Chloe. I search the stands, looking for her family, but it is difficult to see anyone as there's too many people here. I can't focus on Principal Arndt's speech. I check my phone and there's nothing. I nudge Henry and whisper, "I'm sad that Chloe's not with us."

Henry gives me a WTF kind of look, "Me too," he whispers back. "She didn't look so good the other night, and don't forget, she missed school Wednesday. Maybe she's still feeling sick?"

"But it's graduation," I say under my breath. Douglas, the guy sitting next to me, gives me an awkward nudge. I turn to look at him and he tells me to "*shush.*" Henry must have seen what just happened and starts to giggle.

I draw my attention to the stage, when I hear Mrs. Arndt introducing our Valedictorian. *Oh shit, it hits me that she's really not going to be here to give her speech.* I grab Henry's arm and startle him. "Her speech…"

"Chloe Wirrick? Chloe?" Mrs. Arndt calls out on her microphone. "Chloe, if you are here, please come up to the stage."

Quiet whispers are escalating as all the students and everyone in the crowd turn to look around for Chloe. I turn around and see that her seat is still empty.

Henry puts his hand on my lap. "The USB port. You have it right?"

"Yes, holy cow, it's in my car," I realize. *How did I not think of that?*

"Go get it. Now!" He pleads with me, giving me a gentle push on my back to get up, "Go!" He takes a stand, leading the way for me.

In a panic and without even thinking clearly, I shout out loudly, "Hold on. I need to go get something." I can hear a silence fall on the crowd with all eyes on me as I start to run out of my row. I can hear the escalating chatter as I sprint out of the stadium.

I'm finding it difficult to run in my high heels, so I briefly stop to pull off my shoes. My feet start to carry me faster and faster now. I haven't run in forever, but the adrenaline inside me is propelling me to go, thank God. I dash to my car and pull my keys from my pocket to unlock it. I open the door to the passenger's front seat. *Quickly I rummage through my backpack. My hand starts searching around all the junk I have in there, which reminds me that I desperately need to clean that out.* I find a small hard rectangular object and pull it out. *Yes!* That's it, the USB port Chloe gave me to have "just in case." I slam the door closed and run as fast as I can back into the stadium. People are clapping for me and the monitor is spotlighting me on the jumbo screen. Great, I am looking forward to my fifteen minutes of fame, but this is not the way I had planned it. My adrenaline is still pumping as I make my way to the stage and hand Mrs. Arndt the USB port. She looks confused.

Breathlessly, I tell Mrs. Arndt, "Chloe's sick. She's not here. This is Chloe's graduation speech. We recorded it."

Mrs. Arndt seems a little puzzled, and leans into her assistant, who has joined her on the stage,

"Can you get this plugged in to a port to show?"

Her assistant nods and takes the USB and heads to the back of the stage for help.

Mrs. Arndt raises her arm high in the air trying to get everyone's attention. "Attention, please, everyone. There will be a slight change in our program. Unfortunately, Ms. Peters just told me that Chloe is not here." She was interrupted by gasps and mutterings from the audience. "Luckily, we have plan B. Ms. Peters has handed me a recorded speech from Chloe, so we ask for your patience."

Shortly after she speaks, her assistant returns and tells her they are ready to go. The crowd claps waiting to see what happens next.

The video begins streaming on the big screen, quieting the crowds. Chloe's image pops up on the screen, with her sitting on the chair in my house, with a white background. In true Chloe fashion, she is sitting perfectly straight, shoulders back in her cap and gown. You can hear my voice making a countdown: "three, two, one, action!" *Damn it, I should have edited that out.*

CHAPTER 80

Chloe is sitting at the edge of her bed with her mother and father by her side. There is a beautiful bouquet of mixed flowers with hydrangeas, peonies, gerbera daisies and roses sprinkled with baby's breath. Earlier, she had the honor of reading Ben a book and putting him to bed. She had gifted him with her old velvety soft stuffed pig. She had named her Charlotte as she had been obsessed with *Charlotte's Web* when she was Ben's age and had secretly always wanted a pig. Ben loved Charlotte and would often ask Chloe if he could sleep with her, which he did, especially during the time Chloe spent in the hospital over the past couple years. She held Ben and Charlotte in her arms with the help of her dad. She told Ben how much she loved him and that he was the best brother anyone could have. And with that, she kissed him on the forehead and told him sweet dreams, holding back the tears. Afterwards, her dad helps her out of Ben's room, bringing her to her room, where her mother is waiting. Chloe is weeping softly, hurting, having to say goodbye to him.

The hospice nurse arrives shortly after Ben goes to sleep. Her Dad spends time talking with the nurse, going over Chloe's care, while her mom gets Chloe into her pajamas. Her dad returns to the room to be with Chloe and his wife. Chloe looks at the medication bottles on her bedside table and asks her dad to reach for the one with a blue peace sign scribbled on top of the cap. He does as she asks and pushes down on the bottle to loosen the cap.

"You're sure this is what you want to do?" he asks before placing it in her hands. He wanted more than anything for her to change her mind. He is struck with grief and wants to shout out to God and ask him "Why?" Why was his beautiful daughter going through this?

"Yes, this is the right bottle," she says, reading the label, "Pentobarbital, take one by mouth as directed." There are three tablets in there. She realizes she might need something in case of nausea and asks her dad, "Can you get the Zofran bottle? I just need one tablet from there."

Her dad pulls the covers back on Chloe's bed before helping her move her legs into the bed. He gently places her in the middle of the bed with her head propped up on the pile of pillows supporting her. Her Mom slips in on the far side of her bed. Once the two girls are settled, her dad reaches for his phone and puts it on airplane mode. He connects to the Bluetooth speaker and turns on some music.

"George Winston's piano music, right Dad?" Chloe says. George Winston's music she felt was evocative, always offering her peace and respite from any troubles in her busy world. She fell in love with his music during her chemo treatments. It helped to transcend her to a better place when all was not right for her. It seems fitting for tonight.

"Yes, as per your request," he says, and gets in on the side of the bed closest to the door. He shakily hands her a glass of water.

Her throat is dry, but she manages to take the four pills from her dad and places them in her hand. She swallows one by one and hands the glass back to her dad. She looks at her mom, then to her dad, and grabs their hands.

"Thank you both, for being the most amazing parents. Every day of my life I have felt loved and supported. My life has been amazing and there is nothing I would change, except for maybe a cure for cancer," she lets out a small laugh to lighten the mood. "I had the most marvelous day spending it with you guys and Ben. Thank you for supporting me and allowing me to do this my way. I know it can't be easy for you guys, but I am in a good place and have made peace with my condition long ago. I have no regrets." She can see the tears forming in her mother's eyes and that her father is using all his strength to hold his back.

Her mom nestles in closer to Chloe choking her tears back. "We love you, our beauty," she says, cradling Chloe and wishing she could turn back time.

CHAPTER 81

PLAYLIST #21: "YOU WILL BE FOUND" BY BEN PLATT, FROM DEAR EVAN HANSEN

'm settled in my seat and watch as our sweet Chloe lights up the jumbo screen.

"Dear graduates, esteemed faculty, friends, and families:

Today, as I sit before you, I'm honored to represent Morro Bay High School Class of 2020 as your Valedictorian. I am filled with a mix of emotions; gratitude, humility, and a profound sense of purpose. I am incredibly honored to share this moment with each one of you.

Graduation is not only an academic achievement but also a significant milestone in our lives. It is a culmination of years of hard work, growth, and perseverance. I am proud of each one of you who has overcome challenges, embraced opportunities, and shaped your own path to this very moment.

Life, as I've come to understand, is not just about the destination but about the journey; the people we meet, the lessons we learn, and the impact we can make along the way.

This year I had the privilege to align with my two best friends and implement 'The Happy Face Project.' What started as a required senior project, quickly became a passion to acknowledge mental health struggles and to do something about it. Sadly, we lost our dear friend and fellow classmate Briggs Sullivan this year. He was a light that shined so brightly to others, but inwardly he struggled and lost his life to mental health problems. We knew we had to bring awareness to this issue, so that this doesn't happen again. I can tell you, that the success of our program, is single handedly, my, our greatest accomplishment.

So many of us suffer in silence, but we want you to know that there is help. Most importantly, you need to know that…YOU… are…seen. I encourage you to stand up if you've ever felt worried about your future, stand up if you have ever felt sad, stand up if you've ever felt alone. Hold out your hand."

I look around and see that students and people in the crowd are starting to stir, and slowly, some are standing up and others are holding hands.

More people start to stand. Henry gets up from his chair, as do I, placing his hand in mine.

There is a purposeful pause, then Chloe's speech resumes. "Now look around. See that you are not alone. Remember this as you set forth in the world. Find those that need help to stand up to the pain they are experiencing. Our goal was 'to save one'. If you can do that with just a smile or a gesture, or even a Happy Face Pin, you've made a difference. Remember that each of you has the power to shape the future and make a difference in ways both big and small.

On this day, I urge you to embrace this milestone not only as an end but as a new beginning. Cherish the friendships you've formed, the knowledge you've gained, and the experiences that have shaped you. Take risks, pursue your passions relentlessly, and dare to dream big. Remember, the only limits that exist are the ones we impose on ourselves.

In the face of adversity, let resilience be your guiding light. When uncertainty looms, let your courage propel you forward. And when you encounter moments of doubt, let your inner strength remind you of your limitless potential.

Class of 2020, I know that this ceremony is not just the end of high school, but a celebration of new beginnings. As you embark on the next chapter of your journey, I challenge you to live authentically, love passionately, and leave a legacy of kindness and compassion. Thank you for allowing me to share this special day with you. May your hearts be filled with hope, your minds with wisdom, and your souls with an unwavering belief in the power of your dreams and your ability to make a difference in someone's life.

Congratulations, graduates! Go forth and make your mark on the world."

Her speech ends, and it's a hit! But wait, there is another little clip of Chloe still sitting on the chair. She speaks into the camera, "So what do you think?" Turns out, I had zoomed in on her face, perfectly capturing her smile and sparkling blue eyes. I think you're amazing, Chloe. And so does everyone else I see as I turn to see that the stadium is filled with people clapping and whistling for our sweet, absent Chloe.

CHAPTER 82

Fifteen minutes after Chloe takes her medication, she is feeling quite drowsy, which is a side effect she was told she would experience. She has a few minutes of experiencing extreme happiness and lucid conversation with her parents. During these minutes, they reminisce over cute stories about her childhood with her parents. They laugh about how one time in kindergarten Chloe insisted on being a ghost for Halloween. Her Mom had made her costume out of a white sheet and had made cut outs for the eyes. Chloe believed she was an actual ghost and refused to take her costume off, even sleeping in it. The next day she tried to wear it to school, but the principal had to call her parents and ask them to come pick up her costume as Halloween was over and costumes were no longer permitted at school. Somehow Chloe had convinced the principal that taking away her ghost costume would anger all the other ghosts, and she would at least need to be able to wear her costume as a cape around her shoulders to keep the other spirits happy.

"Some things don't change," her dad says. "Once you're committed to something Chloe, you give it one hundred percent." He knew in his heart that she had given one hundred percent to her fight against cancer. She couldn't win, but she could oversee how she dealt with it, and that's exactly what she did. She did it her way.

The side effects of the drugs are in full effect now, and Chloe is beginning to fall in and out of sentience. Her eyes are getting so heavy, and she is finding it difficult to stay awake. She drifts into a state of euphoria, feeling like she is a bird ready to take off. She can feel her arms raising and lowering, ready to take flight. In a moment of consciousness, she squeezes her parents' hands. They have not let go of her hands since getting into bed with Chloe.

"What is it my love?" her mom asks. Her heart is breaking, knowing that the moments with her little girl are slipping away quickly.

In a quiet whisper Chloe says, "Momma? Daddy? I love you. I'm ready to fly. It's…so…beautiful."

Her mom draws in a heavy breath, "We love you, Chloe. Fly, my angel, fly."

Her dad slumps, feeling defeated, but manages to find the words to be strong. "It's okay to go, Chloe. It's your time to soar."

In a moment of silence, a deep expiration of air comes from within Chloe. Her parents feel her grip on their hands soften. Their baby girl has left this earth.

Her Mom cries out, "My Chloe is gone."

CHAPTER 83

Names are being called to receive their diploma. Our row is up and standing by the side of the stage waiting for our turn to walk. Principal Arndt is standing in the middle of the stage with Vice Principal Jackson ready to shake our hand as we cross the stage and get our picture taken. I'm just about to be called, with Henry following right behind me.

"Cari Owen… Douglas Parks." My name is finally called to come to the stage, "Evelyn Peters." I can hear clapping.

I hurry up the steps to be greeted by Mrs. Red Lobster Wall who is passing out the temporary diplomas. She gives me a quick hug and tells me congratulations. I make my way to the center of the stage for the obligatory picture and handshake with Principal Arndt and Mr. Jackson. I never like this kind of awkward picture where you are forced to smile, but I give in with a big cheesy smile for the camera. I'm supposed to exit the stage, but Henry has convinced me to wait for him so we could "do a little something fun." "Henry Preston," the voice calls out.

Henry makes his way across the stage and greets me with his hand extended. As rehearsed, I grab his hand and he swirls me in toward him, then dips me backward. We can hear some giggles coming from the crowd. We exit the stage and are led back to our seats to wait out the remainder of the names being called.

"Briggs Sullivan" is called out with his picture gracing the big screen. Henry and I yell out, "Briggs! *Woohoo*," and we hear the crowd clapping. My heart feels an ache, but I keep it together.

Mr. Sullivan walks across the stage to accept Briggs's diploma and the cheering becomes louder. I am touched that he can accept it for Briggs. Briggs should have been here with us, but in some sense, I know he is here in spirit. More names are called, and we finally hear "Chloe Wirrick," and cheer her on with everyone else.

Despite missing both Briggs and Chloe, I am still able to savor this milestone. The moment we have been waiting for finally arrives.

Mrs. Arndt speaks again, "Class of 2020, congratulations to all of you. I ask that you move your tassel from the right side to the left. You have officially graduated."

Eagerly, I move my tassel to the left and let out a celebratory scream with Henry and the rest of the students. Our caps go sailing up into the air, then I find myself ducking trying to avoid a bonk on the head.

The stadium floor is becoming flooded with everyone coming down from the stands coupled with all of us students leaving our seats. Henry sees his parents and says he'll catch up with me later and takes off. Congratulations are being heard all around me. Then I hear my name being called. I look around and it's Jules running toward me with a bouquet of pink roses in her hand.

"Oh, my God. You're a graduate! Congrats, Evy!" she says with pure excitement in her voice, lifting me off the ground with a big hug, then lowers me down. We continue to jump up and down together with excitement. "Let's go see Mom, she was just here with me," she says, leading me to the back of the stadium.

As we make our way out of the crowd, I see something off to my right in the periphery of my eye and I'm forced to stop. Unexpectedly, I gasp.

"What is it?" Jules asks.

"Holy shit, that's Mom," I say pointing in the direction of my mother who is standing there holding hands with Mr. Corbin.

Jules's eyes widen in astonishment. "Did I just see him kiss her on the lips?"

Talk about being taken by complete surprise, I'm rendered speechless.

"Whoa, wasn't expecting that. Were you, Evy?"

"Mom and Mr. Corbin? Hell no. Awkward." *I make a gag noise.*

"I only lose her for a minute and that happens?" Jules laughs.

We watch Mr. Corbin walk away, before we head in the direction of my mom, as we didn't want to embarrass her or look embarrassed. I don't think she saw us. *Way to go, Mom! I didn't think you had it in you.*

CHAPTER 84

THREE MONTHS LATER

The summer has come and gone in a blink and it's hard to believe it's over. Summer didn't start off the way I had anticipated. Instead, it started off with the sad news of Chloe's passing.

The day after graduation, Chloe's parents asked Henry and me to come to the house. It felt strange to me that it wasn't Chloe reaching out, and it gave me a sinking feeling. I had been so worried about her, but I never imagined hearing the words: "Chloe passed away peacefully last night." Henry and I sat flabbergasted as they told us the details. Neither he nor I had expected to hear our Chloe died. I felt the air leave my body, and the emotion of grief creep back in. We held each other and wept for what seemed like an eternity.

Chloe had been diagnosed with cancer a few years ago, which we knew about. But what we didn't know was that her cancer had come back with a vengeance, Stage 4, terminal to be exact. Retrospectively, it made sense to me watching her over the past few months, seeing her limp get worse, her thin appearance, and the numerous doctor visits she had. We were told she didn't want to tell us, as she saw what the death of Briggs did to us both mentally. She didn't want to burden us with more pain or have people feel sorry for her.

Her parents reassured us that more than anything, Chloe was a fighter and wanted to live and beat cancer, but this unfortunately wasn't an option given her diagnosis. Instead, she chose to do things her way and relish the time she had left with the people she loved, without the constraints of treatment. The one thing she was adamant about, was that she refused to allow cancer to dictate how she would die. She went to great lengths seeking counseling and visits with her doctors before making her decision to die by assisted death. Her plan was to be of sound mind and body and choose when it was time for her to die rather than let cancer choose. She would carry on until her pain and symptoms became unbearable. And when it did, she would settle on a compassionate option to alleviate her suffering. Chloe endured the increasing pain, lack of mobility and strength along with the severe fatigue and carried on each day hoping for a sign. Hearing the news from Mrs. Wall that their project had made a difference and saved a life, gave Chloe the sign she was waiting for. It gave her the satisfaction that her work here on earth had meant something. Ultimately it was an act of selflessness, in true Chloe fashion. *Our little rebel; she did it her way.*

It's not for me to say, as I could never judge her decision and say if what she did was right or wrong. Instead, I'm inclined to accept that she had a right to die with dignity, which is exactly what she unapologetically did.

Chloe's parents had a celebration of life a week later for her. The Wirrick's backyard served as the location. The yard and home overflowed with what seemed like our entire class. The Sullivans, the Prestons, Mrs. Wall, and my mom, along with Mr. Corbin, were all there. It was still hard to swallow the loss of my sweet friend, but the ceremony was beautiful. Chloe had made her parents aware that she wanted something with a twist of fun, but most importantly a positive, uplifting event. There was a cotton candy machine, balloons, a candy bar, great music and, of course, Happy Face Pins for all who came.

A few weeks later I found myself on the Preston family's three-week holiday cruising the Caribbean. We had an incredible time sailing in the crystal blue waters of the Caribbean and island hopping. I had never been to that part of the world before, but I now know that someday I want to go back. Chloe's parents had given us a portion of her ashes to spread in the sea, which we did on our first night on the water and we said our goodbyes. Our days were lazy and spent soaking in the sun or swimming in the warm salty waters. We played music, danced silly, and took lots of pictures. We cooked breakfast and lunches on the boat and dined in beautiful oceanside restaurants at night. Henry and his father taught me the basics of sailing, which enabled me to become a handy first mate, if I do say so myself. But most of all, the trip brought me a much-needed healing of my soul.

Mom came clean on the fact that she had been seeing Mr. Corbin for the past couple months. She didn't expect it all to happen, and said the relationship took her by surprise too. She planned on telling Jules and me but wanted to make sure I got through high school without knowing that she was dating her teacher so as not to cause me any possible embarrassment. I was blindsided initially, but seeing my mom happy is priceless and well-deserved. It all makes sense why Mom had this glow-up right before my eyes.

Last week I stopped by the Sullivan's new condo on the water to say goodbye before I left for college. Their home is stunning with glass windows on the back of the house looking out to the water. They said they chose this home as Briggs would have loved sitting on the patio listening to music and hearing the waves. They let me know that the college fund had been set up for me as promised. My Mom and I had both tried to talk them out of it, but they insisted that it was important to see the money they had invested for Briggs's college be used for me. "Don't look a gift horse in the mouth," they had said. Most of all, they were excited to watch my journey and stay connected. They also let me know that they plan to do an annual donation to The Happy Face Project and help keep it going at school. Their kind gesture is the best gift, knowing that our program can continue to help other students.

This is my last day at home. I had packed last night so I could do a few things before leaving for school today. Other good news is that my day started off amazing, as I awoke to a magnificent dream. I was sitting at the docks watching the water and the boats. The air felt warm, with a quiet stillness in the air as if the world had slowed down just for that moment. My eyes were closed, listening to music, when someone tapped me on the shoulder. It was Briggs appearing out of nowhere. His blue eyes illuminated with joy as he looked at me smiling. He appeared so happy as if he had returned from a long journey. He said nothing but wrapped his arms around me and held me so securely. He radiated a warmth and a sense of calm as I leaned into him. He gently kissed my lips, and the moment felt timeless, as though we shared this sacred space beyond the constraints of reality. And then I woke up to my alarm. I half thought it was real and searched my room for him, but I was lying here in my bed alone. For once, I didn't cry. I felt calm and repose. If I had to analyze my dream, I would say Briggs was telling me it's okay to say goodbye, as he will always find me wherever I am. I feel that in my heart. He will always be with me. It feels good to be in a much better place than I was several months ago.

Now here I am loading up my car. Mom had to work a half day, but told me to get a head start, run my last-minute errands, and she would see me later this afternoon and bring down the rest of my stuff packed in her car. We have plans to go out to dinner with Jules tonight after we finish moving in and decorating my dorm room. As I'm loading the last bag into my car, Henry pulls up.

He steps out of the car with his skin glowing and bronzed and his sage green eyes glinting. He looks straight out of a *GQ* magazine with his white shorts and baby blue polo on. I'm in my cut-off shorts and a cropped tank, and flip-flops. *He always out-dresses me.*

"This is it, Princess," he says as he walks toward me, hands in the air, ready to hug me.

"Can you believe we're heading off to college?" I hug him back.

"Yep, ready for it. Weird to think we won't be at the same school for the first time since kindergarten." He looks as disappointed as I feel.

"Yeah, but we will see each other all the time and we promised to talk every day, right?" I say needing reassurance. "Swear on my life."

A sense of relief calms me. I know we have each other's back, and we always will. "Me too."

"Henry?" I pause, thinking about all the things I will miss. "It makes me sad not having Briggs or Chloe going off to college with us. I miss them both terribly."

Henry grabs my hand, "Ugh! I miss them too. How lucky were we to have both of them in our lives?"

"So lucky, but it still hurts. Hug me please before I start to cry." And so, he does. I pull back and look up at him. "Are you leaving now?"

"Yes, my princess, but I need to get gas, then head back home to meet my parents. They are going to follow me there. And you?"

Henry runs his fingers through his hair getting it out of his eyes.

"I'm done loading up and ready to go. I'm going to stop by and say my goodbye to Briggs on my way out though," I say thinking about the fact that I need to get a picture of the two of us heading off to college. "Let's get an 'off to college' picture." That perks me up.

We spend the next five minutes taking selfies and making goofy faces at the camera. "I'll send them to you," I tell him.

We hug goodbye, both with tears in our eyes. I know I'm going to see him probably within the next day or so, but it still feels so bittersweet. He has been by my side for years, always being my person. I truly cherish our friendship. And hey, I just used Chloe's word. Cherish.

CHAPTER 85

I make my way to Briggs's grave with a small bag in my hand. The day is beautiful, and the sun is shining with no clouds in the sky. As I arrive at his headstone, I see some debris scattered about. I bend over and brush it away before sitting. I sit cross-legged facing the marbled monument displaying Briggs's name and unpack my bag, taking out my Ramune soda and bag of Hot Cheetos. I sit in silence for a moment before speaking.

"Thanks for visiting me last night, Briggs." I pause to open the Ramune and push the ball down into the bottle causing a fizz to bubble up in the neck of the bottle. "I'm leaving for USC today, but I think you know that." I take a swig of my strawberry-flavored Ramune and gag a little. "I wish you had liked sparkling water instead. It would have been a lot easier to get down." I can feel the beginning of a sugar rush, but I do have to admit the taste is not that bad. "I think of you and miss you every day, you know. Day by day, I've gotten much stronger dealing with this awful thing they call grief." I pause to open my Cheetos bag and grab a handful of the messy cheese puffs and put them in my mouth and wash them down with another swig of my Ramune. "Then there was Chloe's death that broke my heart. It tore at me, as did yours. I've come to find out, it's the punches you don't see coming that really affect you. Our sweet friend was taken way too soon. I hope you welcomed her with open arms, but I have no doubt you did. I'm going to miss coming here to visit you, but I'll be back during breaks. I keep saying this, but it's hard to believe it's time for me to go out and see what college has to offer me. Or maybe it will be what I have to offer the college. *Haha.*

"Sometimes, I like to dream about where you would have ended up. Hmm, I can see you at Stanford, or maybe even at USC with me or at UCLA with Henry. Who knows, maybe you would have ended up on the east coast at NYU. But no matter where you would have ended up, in the long run, I always saw you and me together, forever. I loved you that much, and I will never stop loving you, Briggs. I have my ring on my finger and my Happy Face Pin right here with me every day to prove it." I twist the ring on my finger. With all this talking, my mouth is dry from the Cheetos, so I gulp down the remainder of my Ramune. "Most of all, what I came here for today is to make a promise to you, and by the way, you will need to hold me accountable, and that is to continue to bring awareness to mental health issues so that what happened to you, doesn't happen to others." I reach my hand to his headstone and trace his name with my fingers. "I'm going to continue to make you proud, Briggs Sullivan." I lean back and fish around in the pocket of my shorts and pull out an extra Happy Face Pin and place it at the base of his headstone.

I inhale, followed by a deep exhale, and grab my phone to see the time. I need to go, but I'm distracted by the wallpaper on my phone's opening page. It's been there for months, but today it looks different. It's a picture I took of Briggs when he wasn't looking. We were on the beach and the sun was setting. A new song came out that day that he had been waiting for. He hit play and started blaring it from his phone and began dancing around. In this photo, I captured a genuine smile on his face of pure elation. There was no denying that in this moment, he was happy. It's the smile I will never want to forget. It is the smile I will choose to remember him by. Seeing this photo makes me laugh. I'm puzzled though, as I feel something wet drip down my face and go to wipe it. I look at my hand and recognize that it's my tears. For the first time since Briggs's death, I am crying tears of joy.

EPILOGUE

Six Years Later

Remember that question: What do you do about something so senseless (like losing a loved one to suicide)? I asked myself that so many times and thought I'd never figure it out. But I did. It wasn't until our senior project that I found a partial answer. Chloe, Henry, and I implemented the Happy Face Project at our school. With the press we received, we set a trend for many schools across the country to implement their own Happy Face program. The Happy Face Pins were everywhere and still are. Over the years, Mrs. Wall has kept Henry and me up to date on the continued success of the program. Whenever I see that Mrs. Wall is calling me on my phone, I know I'm going to hear good news: another student's life is saved. My Mom told me that your purpose in life is to figure out what you're good at and your gift is to learn how to give it away. That's what I intend to keep doing.

I'm usually at home relaxing on a Friday night after a long work week. I make it my night to chill out, relax, and watch a good movie. The hustle and bustle of LA is exhilarating, but it's also exhausting. After graduation, I stayed in the Los Angeles area, and it feels like it's exactly where I need to be. Tonight, I made an exception to my Friday night rule of being boring and staying in, as it is a very special night: September 10th, National Suicide Awareness Day.

Wearing my robe and only undergarments underneath, a make-up artist by the name of Shannon is here finishing up my makeup and Erin the hairdresser is touching up my hair with a curling iron and spraying some hairspray that smells like tropical vibes. While they are fussing with me, Briggs's picture captures my attention. I reach out and touch the black frame with my hand that I wear my pinky ring from Briggs on. It's my favorite picture of him, the one of him smiling on my phone wallpaper, that I've had forever. I had it printed and framed and have kept it on my desk since I went off to college. Next to his picture, I keep the journal my mom gave me. All the things I treasure the most.

Erin in her Irish accent tells me, "Doll, you are done. Take a look."

Shannon does one last touch up on my face, then swirls me around to face Erin who's holding a mirror.

"Do you approve, love?" Erin asks.

I turn around and I'm blown away with how I look. "Who is this girl?" I say blushing.

"Why you're the hottest girl in Hollywood tonight," Shannon informs me. She is obviously proud of her work. "The touch of bronze makes you glow."

Her words couldn't be truer, I am glowing inside and out. "You girls did an amazing job, I'm transformed," I say, taking the mirror from Erin and examining the back of my hair. It is long and curled, with several bohemian-style braids coming from both sides of my front hairline that are brought around to the back of my head and connected into a messy bun. "Thank you both so much. I'm in love."

The girls gather their stuff as I go into my room to grab my dress. It is hanging in a clothes bag on my closet door. I unzip it to reveal my gown for the evening: a couture dress, full-length and strapless. Inspired by a Van Gogh sunflower painting, it is yellow complete with dark Swarovski crystals hand-sewn around the bodice. Carefully, I remove the dress and turn it around to loosen the corset and unzip the back. I drop my robe to the ground as Shannon and Erin come into the room to help me get dressed. They help me step into my dress while Shannon holds up the front and Erin is zipping up the back and adjusting the corset. I take a deep breath while the last modification is made.

"I feel like royalty," I say as I admire myself in my full-length mirror swishing my dress from left to right.

"You're stunning, love," Shannon says.

Erin nods her head, "Absolutely gorgeous. Have a fab night tonight, Evy. We'll let ourselves out."

They both hug me and then exit my room. "Thanks again, girls. You guys have blown me away." I say to them as they leave. I have one finishing touch left. I walk to my bedside table and open the drawer to find my velvet pouch, where I place it every night. I untie the strings and fish out my Happy Face Pin, holding it in my hand for a second and admiring it before placing it on my dress positioning it over my heart.

I hear a key turning, with a knock on my door. Henry enters

and calls out to me, "Evy? Your prince has arrived." Perfect timing.

I walk out to my living room where Henry is standing in a dark marine blue colored tux trimmed in black, with a pinstripe white shirt and yellow bow tie holding a magnificent bouquet of flowers. His Happy Face Pin is on his left jacket pocket displayed proudly.

"Aren't you the most beautiful princess I have ever seen," Henry grins as he walks toward me with the flowers and hugs me dearly.

"Thank you, my prince, they are beautiful," I whisper in his ear and hold him tight. I release him and step back, giving a little twirl. "So do you like it?"

"Très chic, Madame Evelyn. You're totally radiating the glam. What a lucky guy I am to have you on my arm tonight." He sets down the flowers on my dining table. "Shall we go?"

"Yes, sir," I say, grabbing my clutch.

We take the elevator to the bottom floor and exit the building to find a matte black stretch limousine awaiting us. "Nice ride," I say.

"Only the best for you," Henry says as he helps me into the limo. To my surprise, there are two bottles of Ramune chilling in a silver iced bucket with glasses waiting for us. The driver takes off as Henry takes the lids off the Ramune and pushes the ball down into the bottle, careful not to spill it on us, and pours us each a glass. He holds up his glass and makes a cheer, "Cheers to our special night. To Briggs! To Chloe! And especially to you, my incredibly talented best friend."

I raise my glass to clink his, "Let's not forget you. We did this together, chum. Cheers!" We go old school and wrap our arms around each other holding the glass of Ramune and drink from our glasses entwined.

—

About thirty minutes later, we arrive at our destination, the chauffeur opens the door to a mob of people and the press with bulbs flashing everywhere. Henry exits first, and I can hear the excitement surrounding us, with people calling out our names. He extends his hand toward me and gracefully helps to pull me out of the limousine. I stand flabbergasted by all the commotion. My name is being called in several directions. I smile for the cameras and take my first step on the red carpet I've dreamed of since being a little girl in my dad's arms, as Henry escorts me down the aisle.

"Show us your pin, Evy," a reporter shouts out.

I hear, "Is it true this movie is based on your high school life?" I give a slight smirk back.

"Smile for us, Henry," another voice is heard.

Henry guides me down the long red-carpet walk. My adrenaline is soaring as I can feel my heartbeat leaping out of my chest. We stop to take several photographs in the designated photo spot in front of the sponsor sign. I've never seen so many cameras flashing at once. I'm wishing I had mine to take a picture of all of them, but this time I find myself on the other side.

Ten minutes later, we are escorted to our seats. I can feel the eyes of the crowd watch us as we enter and make our way to the front center row. My heart skips a beat when I see my favorite people waiting for us. They all stand up to greet us. Henry and I are hugged and told congratulations by Mr. and Mrs. Wirrick, Ben, Mr. and Mrs. Sullivan, Mr. and Mrs. Preston, Mrs. Wall with Big Bird yellow hair, my sister Jules, and by my mom and Mr. Corbin, who is holding her hand. Mom kisses my cheek as I pass her.

Three seats remain empty as per my request. The first empty

seat is next to my mom's and has my father's name, Brock Peters, on it. The next seat is Chloe Wirrick's, and the third empty seat says Briggs Sullivan. I have a moment of sheer joy knowing that in some form these three people that I have loved so deeply are here celebrating with me tonight. After all, tonight is for each one of them. I sit down next to Briggs's seat and Henry sits to my right.

The lights in the theater begin to dim and there is a hush over the crowd. Henry takes a hold of my hand and gives it a squeeze. I place my other hand over my heart where my Happy Pin lies. My film projects onto the screen, and the music begins. The theater is dark, then a happy face starts bouncing across the screen, followed by the words in slow motion: "Happy Face Production presents: *TO SAVE ONE*. Written and directed by Evylyn Peters, with special thanks to Henry Preston. This film is dedicated to the loving memory of Briggs Sullivan. If you, or someone you know, struggles with mental health issues or needs someone to talk to, please text or call the SUICIDE HOTLINE at 988."

The movie begins, and at this moment, I know that this is exactly where I need to be, surrounded by my loved ones. There is hope in my heart tonight that perhaps my film and my personal journey can help raise awareness about suicide and mental health. I want to make a safe space for others and most importantly, make a meaningful difference in at least one person's life. My greatest wish is to let you know that you are not alone, and there is help out there. From my heart to yours, I ask you to take this Happy Face Pin.

RESOURCES:

ALL SERVICES LISTED BELOW ARE FREE

If you, or someone you know, is facing mental health struggles, emotional distress, alcohol or drug use concerns, or just need someone to talk to, please reach out to any of the following:

Suicide and Crisis Hotline Text or Call: 988
988lifeline.com

Suicide Prevention Resource Center:
SPRC.org or call (800) 273-TALK (8255)

The National Action Alliance for Suicide Prevention:
https://theactionalliance.org

 Text HOME to 741741

American Society for Suicide Prevention: https://afsp.org/

 SpeakingOfSuicide.com/resources